A Whisper of Witches
(A story of Oundle witchcraft)

Anna Fernyhough
© 2019

Woodcut from *"The Witches of Northamptonshire"*, 1612.

Two weeks before these women were seized, William Avery
(a wealthy Northamptonshire 'victim') alleged that he saw
Agnes Brown, Catherine Gardiner and Jane Lucas
(riding a sow's back) on their way to visit
an old woman regarded as a witch.
They were hanged.

...ooo000ooo...

Best wishes
Anna Fernyhough

A Whisper of Witches
First published in Great Britain in 2019
Upfront Publishing, Peterborough, England.
http://www.fast-publishing.net/bookshop

A CIP catalogue record for this book
is available from the British Library.

ISBN: 978-178456-648-7

This book is dedicated to my family and friends.
(You know who you are.)

In our short, transitory lives
it has been my pleasure
to have spent suitable spells with you.

...ooo000ooo...

Mary Phillips and Elinor Shaw found me while I was
conducting research for an earlier book. I had not
encountered them before, but since that moment the
two 'witches' ensnared my imagination and would not
let me go!
They led me on a curious chase to identify with
characters living in the late 1600s and early 1700s.
These two local ladies (be they fact or fiction) are
recorded as being the last convicted witches in England.
This is my story for them.

...ooo000ooo...

Thou shalt *not suffer a witch to live*.
– King James Version of the Bible; Exodus, Ch. 22; 18

...ooo000ooo...

There are worse things that are real in this world
than stories of elves, giants, witches and dragons.
– Tim Fernyhough (1953-2003)

...ooo000ooo...

I am! yet what I am none cares or knows,
My friends forsake me like a memory lost;
I am the self-consumer of my woes,
They rise and vanish in oblivious host,
Like shades in love and death's oblivion lost;
And yet I am! and live with shadows tost

Into the nothingness of scorn and noise,
Into the living sea of waking dreams,
Where there is neither sense of life nor joys,
But the vast shipwreck of my life's esteems;
And e'en the dearest—that I loved the best—
Are strange—nay, rather stranger than the rest.

I long for scenes where man has never trod;
A place where woman never smil'd or wept;
There to abide with my creator, God,
And sleep as I in childhood sweetly slept:
Untroubling and untroubled where I lie;
The grass below—above the vaulted sky.
– John Clare (1793-1864)

...ooo000ooo...

It appears to me impossible that I should cease to exist or
that this active, restless spirit, equally alive to joy and sorrow,
should only be organised dust.
– Mary Wollstonecraft Godwin (1759–1797)

...ooo000ooo...

Prologue
Old Isabel

Isabel Godfrey was an orphan. She liked to tell people that she was 'the oldest orphan in town'. Indeed, there were many younger! She had never truly known of her true name, her parents or their account. What she did discern came from other people and reflected their feelings.

She had begun her life as a foundling, taken in by kindly folk when she was naught but a crawling, mewling babe, to be cradled and rocked by the benevolent Mistress Faith Godfrey. She was left with naught but a scrap of cloth; a token left by a destitute mother, one of the many urban unfortunates, so she could return for her child - if ever she was in a position to reclaim her. This had not happened. Isabel had been raised with the Godfrey children. Cared for, but never, ever truly wanted or loved. She spent much of her time alone and although the Godfrey family were most kindly, Isabel knew she was considered by others to be a 'good will' rescue from an early demise.

Isabel now looked back from her dotage to her childhood. She knew that in actuality her life was one filled with single-handed toil and a great deal of solitude. She had one close protégé whom she had taught to recognise and use herbs in a variety of ways - and how to cook. This was her neighbour, friend and lodger, Mary. She was pretty, but not beautiful, slim of body with slender, nimble fingers and a gentle nature. Most who met the girl liked her.

Both, Isabel and Mary were independent- with each keen to 'keep themselves to themselves' at times.

She was under the age of ten when she came to live with Isabel – and several years had passed since then. The old woman taught Mary what she knew, although, usually Isabel spent much of her time alone. This by no means meant she had been unhappy. Her most common companion was her cat, Catchevole. Yet, even her dark feline friend largely saw her as a source of easily gained food and was a fair-weather lodger, spending at least half of his time next-door with young Mary.

Isabel was reserved and private, some may say secretive, so was regarded by many as time-worn, private and solitary, which she accepted as commonplace for her. Living in the divided cottage (which had long ago had a stone wall built to divide it into two) gave privacy and the two small rooms each worked for them both. Isabel lived in the larger part with her cat.

'Customarily,' she croaked, rubbing her gnarled hands against her emaciated rump while stretching her back as far upright as possible until she perceived her joints crack, 'one of the benefits of having a companionable cat is the lack of pests in the proximity. Except the fleas!'

She stated this to the air around her, while squinting through clouded eyes into Catchevole's glaring, gimlet, green lenses. She knew he had caught a skinny, grey mouse only that morning. It was poking about in her larder, trying to get into her bag of flour. She was apologetic to the mouse who lost his life, but glad that her grain supply was safe for a little longer. Indeed, incontinent mice had a nasty habit of not caring to wash their tiny feet before 'running' all over her house.

She waited a moment, as if to listen, before casting her dim eyes around her meagre home. Seeing it for the very first time today, it seemed dustier than it was yesterday. She knew that dust motes flew in the air, but she could no longer see them. She sometimes felt with her old finger tips or sensed dust that had settled on her table or on the window sill. There was always much to do and each day she had felt less and less inclined to clean, tidy or to set it to rights.

It had been a long time since mice had finally taken over her barn-like home. Catchevole definitely needed some help. Like his owner, he wasn't getting any younger either! Mice were numerous and the feline had seen many during the eight years of his life. Isabel had kept him as 'company' from a time when he was an insignificant bundle of fur. To him it seemed like a long spell since he knew his warm, cosy mother, plus several snuggling siblings who smelled of sweet milk and love. They had all long since been purchased for a few pence by those who wished to keep their rodent infestations under control.

It was a lucrative time for Isabel selling kittens, until Catchevole's mother had not come home from wherever she had roamed. Isabel thought that perhaps she had been taken by a fox. Food for all, including wildlife and people, was in short supply during the year. Catchevole was thus named as he often brought home gifts of voles and rodents from kitten-hood. Isabel smiled at her memories.

'You are truly a good cat,' she said with great affection. She could no longer bend easily to stroke his ears and rub his head. He knew this and thoughtfully jumped up onto the barrel so that she could reach to touch him. The motion of stroking put them both at their ease.

After a few moments, Isabel sniffed, coughed and spat onto the flagstone floor. She pulled her shawl tightly around her shoulders for greater warmth and shuffled over to the window.

This year was not much better than the last, she mused. Firstly there was a strong breeze that came in from the north-west. Then came the crows! A whole flock of them, wheeling and diving from the sky above, settling briefly and taking to the air again and again, like dancing black specks in the grey welkin sky.

Next, came the gentle snowflakes. Twirling softly at first. Beautiful and white. Winding and spiralling downward to the brown earth. Their temperate appearance almost imperceptible at first, then a gradual thickening. Their clumps became denser and over a period of just an hour, the immediate world came to be completely hushed, crisp and white.

Blankets of glistening, white, ice-cold thistledown covered the ground. Only this was not thistledown! Blowing sideways and clumping it covered the earth. It had looked immaculate.

Whenever rare passers-by bravely ventured to market for victuals, they left their transitory footprints, until the new, uninterrupted snowfall obscured them all.

The following morning the customary sounds of the day were somewhat dulled, as was the grey sky. The town was hushed. The overnight fall of new snow was pristine on the ground again. The parish church bell tolled, letting all within ear-shot know that the market was about to commence.

Isabel doubted whether there would be many people buying or selling today. When the bell ceased, the silence grew, perceptibly. She listened. All Isabel

spering hiss in her own ears. The
...that this was the magical sound of
...w communicating with her.

...fter the largest snowfall, Isabel had
...pulsive. She had walked to market
...ad ventured outside their houses in
...er.

...opped for a moment to purchase a
...ggs from Wilf, the tenant farmer's son,
...tarily sheltered in a doorway before
...home. She quickly passed pleasantries
...seller (who was packed and ready to go).
...are,' they had called to each other as they
...owards their hearths, 'Go safely in God.'

...Isabel turned, she realised that she could
...s was no fault of her eyes. She stood,
...r a time as her bearings grew even more
...he blindness of the grey fog and misty shapes
worried her, but did not scare her. Unlike others in the
town she was not easily afraid of the things she could not
see, yet, she had waited so long that she was almost a-
feared of what hid in the gloom to make her trip or fall.

A murky mist had risen after the snowfall on the
warmer ground. Isabel was chilled and frozen to the
spot, almost afraid to move, but knew that indeed, move
she must. With little idea of in which direction to walk,
she had already perceived that her return journey would
be harder than that to the market. She took a faltering
step. Then another. The longer she took to move, the
more afraid she became.

'It is my own silly thoughts keeping me here in
the cold,' she thought. 'What I need is a small flagon of

beer, with a smell of malt after a warm poker from the fire is warmed to mull my ale.'

Isabel recalled the tempting change in taste when the beer was heated. Her fears began to melt away. She moved on. She noted that the Inn-keeper, Nathaniel Sismey, had not bothered to turn out to light his lantern as yet. None appeared to be out, walking home at this time. Isabel found a wall and traced its frozen outline with her brittle fingers. Guided by the stones, she fortuitously realised her location.

'Thank you, merciful God,' she prayed in acknowledgement. 'I am old, addled and very stupid!'

Slowly, so slowly at first, her hand moved forward in front of her body, until she had her arm stretched out before her. Shapes of trees appeared and moved in her periphery. At times familiar in form, at others, elongated shapes that could have been people stretching out their slender arms to touch her, but indeed, they were only trees.

Isabel was blind to any true light, but she could hear and feel the way using her faith in the familiarity of the ground beneath her feet. From time to time faded outlines let her know that she was on the right track to the comfort of home. Never had it felt so far away.

Isabel made arduous and trepid progress. It was almost a surprise when she, once again, touched a thing that was solid. It was cold, rough and hard. She instantly knew it to be the stone wall of her cottage. She breathed out a long breath of warm air and felt it soar from her. She coughed as the icy chill stung her lungs.

Isabel followed the wall along with her icy fingers, until she located her front door. Cold digits found the frozen latch and she stumbled inside (along with a small blizzard). She entered and inhaled in the warmth as she felt the worst of the squall cease. The door slammed behind her as it caught in the wind, saving her the effort of closing it. Her chilled nose dripped on her sleeve.

'Aunt Isabel! Where in heaven's name have you been? What were you doing?' said a sharp voice that made her jump in surprise. It was her lodger, Mary Phillips, from the adjoining cottage.

Mary raised her hazel eyes to take in the bedraggled appearance of the shaking old woman. She quietly remarked, 'Where on earth have you been? Come, Isabel, dry yourself and sit by the fire. You are chilled to the bone!'

Mary fussed around her. She grabbed a knitted blanket from the settle and pulled it around her elderly friend. She shifted Catchevole from the comfortable chair by the fireside and led Isabel to the cushioned seat. The cat watched through slit eyes for a moment, before making his decision to move out of the way on the fireside rush-mat. Isabel coughed to dislodge the mucus from her lungs.

'Look after him for me,' she said softly, pointing at Catchevole. 'He's such a clever one, that he is.'

Mary strained to listen, before giving a tart reply. 'I'll look after you both. As I always do.'

Isabel smiled and patted Mary's hand. 'Thank you, dear. I know you will.'

Isabel bore the curvature of her years, made all the more apparent by her recent sojourn. She no longer stood erect and her body bore a stiff, crooked nature. Her fingers cracked as she rubbed the back of one hand with the warmer palm of the other. As she sat, she tried

11

to remove her bonnet and scarf. She required help to untie the ribbons of the soaked hat that had tightly tied under her chin. Mary assisted, but Isabel had grumbled, not wanting to admit that she needed any help.

'I'm not an invalid. I can do it myself,' she stated.

Mary continued helping, but moved away once the silk ribbons had been untied. She took each of the bedraggled garments from Isabel and shook the moisture from them. She took the sodden bonnet and hung it from the mantel hook to dry.

'Rest now,' Mary advised, gently taking her by the arm, while leading her to a pallet. She swaddled Isabel in so many knitted blankets that anyone looking in through the window would have seen only Mary within the room. With strong hands, the energetic woman pushed her long dark hair from her narrow face, then leaned forward to poke the red embers and re-feed the fire until it crackled brightly. It lit the room until cosy. She brought warm broth and fed the old woman from her bowl, as the inky Catchevole watched with his head to one side. Once the silent feline was sure the bowl was empty, he stretched, yawned and moved back onto the inglenook chair, where he settled in its warmth to watch the commencement of the night. The cat was naturally suited for the dark. He was black as pitch, but bore a small flash of white on his nose that made him distinctively different to other felines in the vicinity.

That night, Mary was too worried to sleep. She did not wish to retire next door to her own one-roomed cottage or bed, but stayed to tend to her friend. The following day, Isabel took to her bed with determined permanency. Two days later, she was dead.

...oooOOOooo...

12

Chapter 1
The Languid Life

Rumours spread easily along the dirt tracks and down the roughly cobbled lanes. Softly spoken words are oft' unfair and frequently fallacious, but sometimes carry a kernel of truth about them that makes listeners stop, squint into the sunlight and consider if there is a validity to what is being said. Some determined that whenever unpleasant words were spoken about a person, there was probably a valid for them.

After the death of Queen Mary, news came from London that her husband, King William, was suffering from 'a nasty chest cold from which he may not recover'. These whispered words fermented and created an uncertainty for the days to come. Common folk stopped talking about the late queen or sick king to note the demise of the elderly Isabel. To some, this was as interesting as that of the sick King's "imminent demise".

To an outsider the town appeared sedentary, but merely skimming the surface would reveal a buzzing hub of information and misinformation. For the literate, handbills were pinned to the doors of local churches and inns to ensure news was spread. These were also read out for the illiterate to hear. For many the most vital news was heard from the pulpit each Sunday in Church.

The clergymen were not exempt from gossip, but worse still were those they hired. Ministers of the faith were responsible for choosing and employing a small number of men to form a 'Watch', obliged to law-keep property in the town. Those selected were instructed to stay awake at night and were duly paid by the trustees of the parish.

'The truth of it is that our men are tired after working for long hours during the day, so sometimes fall asleep when they're on duty at night – especially if all is quiet,' Catherine Boss had said in support of her husband, William, after he had been caught napping on duty. By the time the Churchmen who employed him came to hear of this, Bill had 'caught a criminal and had closed his eyes for a moment to recoup from his efforts on behalf of the people'.

The retelling of news was commonplace to watchmen, albeit with their own embellishments. They stood to chat as a form of relief for their weary bodies and stale minds after a somnolent nightshift in the damp, riverside town. The eyes and ears of the watchmen were expected to remain alert despite many holding two jobs. Sundry townsfolk held the hired constables in high regard. They favoured Constable Bill Boss and his attractive and amiable wife, Catherine. The young couple had married only a short time since, so shared a small house with Bill's parents in a nearby village. As yet they had no offspring, but prayed that one day they would have a son. Cat was sociable and pretty with plenty of friends in the neighbourhood. Her husband was not particularly learned or diligent in his work, but was striking, well-built and strong. In the day they lived and worked in Glapthorne, but each night Bill would walk the mile-long journey to town to work as a watchman. He listened to colourful exchanges in the taverns and inns he attended with fellow constable, John Southwel, who was around the same age and equally brutish and harsh on those he considered to be law-breakers. They routinely joined company to slake their thirst before starting their night shifts. Individually they accompanied traders to ensure their takings were safe from would-be thieves and pickpockets, especially whenever their patrons walked home in the winter's early darkness. Each watchman carried a stout cudgel with which to prevent robbery or assault. Twilight women were apprehensive of ne'er-do-well vagabonds and robbers, but distrusted the watchmen in equal measure. Whether harlot or pious young maid, few were reassured by their presence. There were times when innocent Mary Phillips had hurried home as the men leered like hungry wolves.

In daylight hours the town changed in character. The expanse around each stall set out in the butcher's row and its adjoining lane were busy – and safe. The only concern was an occasional petty thief who awaited those who could be easily swindled or fooled.

Today all were curious to hear the news. Mary had ventured out too. After remaining in the house for many days, she felt it was time to re-join the world once more. As she walked down the lane her neighbours greeted her with kindness. As she reached the market an acquaintance passed on his condolences to her. She casually perused the butcher's stall, deciding between a choice sausage or tasty meat pie. The plump, sweaty vendor tipped his hat towards her and pulled his lips into a sad, tight smile.

'I've heard of Mistress Isabel's passing. My condolences, Miss Phillips,' Richard Glas nodded at Mary. He remarked on the sadness felt by all he knew.

'Thank you for your kind words, Dicken. You know, she is … was … was like an aunt to me.'

'Aye. She looked after you like her own.'

She lowered her gaze for a moment. ''Tis a hard time for me,' she spoke with newly wet lashes, not knowing if there were any correct words to say, before moving forward to peruse vegetables and garden fruits. Mary knew that to linger would open the way to further query and she wished to avoid tactless questioning. Good fortune gave her a way out. The shapely Lizzie Coles had appeared nearby with a pursed smile on her rosy lips. Mary waved at the girl as she admired her friend's pale, lightly freckled face.

'Please excuse me, Dicken,' she remarked as she turned from the man with a sad a smile. 'I must get on.'

Her friend, whom some regarded as 'laughing Lizzie', was also in the process of escaping the clumsy advances of an equally assertive merchant. Lizzie was equally happy to excuse herself from his probing attentions to take a breather and pass some time with Mary. Lizzie openly hugged her childhood friend and deemed that it was good to be seen by others comforting the girl. The young women were of a similar height, but this is where their similarities ended. Their forms were much different. As children they had played together. Both had admired the local lads and talked over their dreams and desires for the future. Where Lizzie was curvaceous and shapely, Mary was slender and wiry. It was common knowledge that Lizzie often spoke without thinking and displayed irritation and resentment, whereas Mary was considered quiet, thoughtful and kind. Lizzie quickly surmised that Mary had clearly not bothered eating much since Isabel had died. Despite the bulk of her warm cloak, she discerned Mary's ribs on each side of her narrow frame. Lizzie studied her face and saw pale skin and hollow cheeks. She tried to cheer the forlorn girl through steady banter. Together they chatted amicably as they walked hand in hand towards the market Butter-Cross. Here they set-up their dairy produce and other wares on the shallow steps beneath the canopy. They noted Mercy Elderkin had already begun setting out her things and wished her a good day.

Mercy was a friend of a similar age. She had few good teeth and an asymmetrical face. Other than chattering too much in times of awkwardness, she was generally a good soul. She had already comfortably seated herself on the covered steps below the stone cross. Mary greeted her with a welcome nod, then looked up for a moment at the monument. Lizzie set out her eggs and butter on the steps whilst, simultaneously, she took up friendly conversation with Mercy.

Mary was perturbed when the two began their banter by noting the passing of Isabel - then talked as if the slight-framed woman could not hear them. At times their voices hushed to a whisper - and she could not.

'None can guess how or when they will die. Only God knows His plan,' Mercy sighed as she rearranged the packets in her basket.

'Isabel has reached heaven ahead of us. God rest her soul,' Lizzie quietly remarked.

Mercy nodded and kept her eyes lowered. 'I know,' she sadly replied as she rummaged in her basket between her soft bag and knife case. 'The news of her passing has moved from mouth to ear around the town.'

'I went with Mary and Sarah Short to lay out the old dear in readiness for her funeral,' Lizzie said. 'What will we do now? Granny Isabel's God-given skills were prized by many.'

'Her funeral is next Tuesday, after the noon bell?' Mercy asked with a sorrowful expression.

'Yes, it is.' Lizzie's quiet voice disappeared into silence for a moment. She whispered, 'Such a sad time. Mary is most upset. If she laments for much longer she will make herself ill, just like Mother did when her friend, Alice Barnes died.'

Mercy nodded and fiddled with the clasp on her cloak as if to tighten it. Clearly uncomfortable, her reply came as a statement. 'She *was* elderly. I've heard she caught a chill after staying out late in the icy-cold.'

Mary turned to her peers. She could no longer avoid joining in, so lightly coughed to clear her tense throat, causing the two young women to gaze at her.

'That is very true, Mercy,' she finally interjected. 'Little could be done for her, but keep her warm and proffer food and affection.'

Lizzie looked with sympathy at her friend. 'Mary, you did all that you could.' Her voice was gravelled.

Mary nodded again. When she spoke again, her voice was unobtrusive, almost as if talking to herself. 'Her demise was an act of God that none on earth could alter.'

As Mary moved to serve another customer, Lizzie surreptitiously hissed to Mercy, 'I suppose you know that Old Isabel inherited her cottage from the family who took her in?' Mercy nodded as her friend continued, 'Mother says they all died from a plague around fifty years since.'

Mercy sighed heavily. She knew there had been times when Lizzie was two-faced and duplicitous. She guessed what Lizzie was about to indicate, but waited without remark. As no comment came, Lizzie continued. 'Isabel had no remaining kin. Mary has inherited everything from her.' She nodded her head in Mary's direction, opened her eyes wide and raised both eyebrows.

Mary overheard, but carried on serving her neighbour, Constance Bold, with the batch of eggs that she gently placed into the woman's basket before taking payment. Fully aware of the interchange between her friends, she prudently paid little notice to the painful subject.

'What luck!' declared Mistress Bold, who was clearly aware of the girls' statements and hushed voices. She glared at the younger women. 'We wish that we could all inherit goods and house and never pay rent again,' she posited through pursed lips, looking as sour as her voice. At this juncture, she had been clearly overheard by traders and other customers standing nearby who keenly joined in with their discussion.

'Isabel Godfrey lived a long and full life,' fellow tradeswoman, Gladys Cooper loudly remarked, heaving a laden sack from her hip. She sighed as she released her heavy burden on the stone steps of the cross. She glanced at the lightweight wares of her competitors and silently envied them. Cabbages grew easily and sold well, but for need of a barrow with a working front-wheel she found market days were fast becoming a trial for her. She sighed loudly once again and pushed at unruly hair with dirty hands and little effect.

'Aye, Old Isabel had many years behind her. She was of a commendable age, let's pray that we all live as long,' Mercy agreed, smiling at Gladys' efforts. 'Come. Sit with us, Gladys.' She shuffled along on the step to make room for her colleague.

'Granny Isabel has gone and we will all miss her until we are called,' ventured the shy, quiet voice of their fellow trader, Sarah Short. She had listened to their melancholic conversation alongside selling pickled eels to her regulars. The tall girl, who did not resemble her name in any way, rearranged her brightly coloured shawl around her thin shoulders and looked warily at the goodwife.

'Aye, for many reasons too. She were outspoke', but a wise woman,' Gladys stated as she sat. She had liked Isabel and, like many, had visited her regularly. 'Aye. She did no 'arm. Sin free, she was. She'll be in 'eaven now, for sure. I 'eard the church as it rung out the passin' bell – twice - to chase away evil spirits lurkin' about … so we are all safe.'

Those around about assented with nods and stares. Gladys' idea of a good death was one that happened in bed at home, surrounded by friends and family, with a visiting priest in attendance to administer her last rites for the final forgiveness of her earthly sins, '… not carrying a bloomin' bag of spuds!' she thought to herself. She moved to rearrange her copious skirts so her equally bulky bottom would not be so cold on the stone steps. 'Ere, Mary, do you want one of my sacks to sit on?' she kindly asked.

Mary smiled gently. 'Thank you. No, Gladys,' she replied as she shook her head, 'I'm fine here wrapped in my cloak.' She rearranged her cloak over her skirts.

To cheer Mary, Mercy noted, 'Mistress Isabel Godfrey will be welcomed in heaven, snug with the saints, angels and virtuous spirits, for she was a worthy woman.'

Each of the womenfolk were lost in their own reverie for several moments. Their thoughtful silences were broken by Constance, who was somewhat older than the others.

'Mercy, I agree with you. She helped my boy with her prayers and ointments when he was a small stripling.' Constance coughed into her skirts, then sniffed and continued, 'Who will attend us now? She knew so much.'

'Well, m' dear, she definitely knew much about my youngster's spots and fever. She made 'em disappear with her tinctures and poultices in just a couple o' weeks,' added her sister, Judith, who had overheard the discourse and came to stand by her side. As Constance wiped her eyes, their conversation grew and burbled like waters of a stream charting its own course.

'Connie, d' you recall 'er showing us how to make a poultice when we were young?' Judith asked her sister. Her sibling nodded back at her, then turned to look at Mercy's frozen-cold dairy products. The weather had made each pat of butter so solid they would require melting by a fire before they would be of use.

'I recall her way back when she was much younger,' interrupted old Emma Craythorne. The eager septuagenarian had waited for her opportunity to add her voice to the conversation. She squinted upward, as if seeking a divine calendar in the sky that could tell her how long it had been since that occasion. 'That was before her knuckles and joints were stiffened by the years. She did her best for folk.' She sniffed loudly, then wandered off before bothering to purchase any items.

The goodwives and girls watched her go.

'Nosy old cow,' Gladys remarked with a meaningful nod. Mary smiled, while silently granting that, for all her issues, her fleshy workfellow was fairly perceptive.

'Well. I'm getting cold sitting here. When is the baker coming with his tray?' pursued Mercy conveying her musings back to the present.

Each looked around. The baker could be seen on the corner of Lark Lane making a sale to a finely-dressed gentleman in an embroidered cloak and taking the man's coin. It would not be long before he made his way over to them.

Mary smiled to herself on hearing the women's recollections. It was good to hear them talk so fondly of her late friend.

'Some of the old crafts the Godfrey's knew have died. They won't be repeated,' ventured Constance to the group.

'I'm not so sure. The learnin' goes on from one to another - be it friend, neighbour or kin,' concluded Gladys with a steady, knowing nod towards the dejected girl, while her kindly smile showed yellow, uneven teeth.

Mary only listened, as she did not care to join in with the conversation. She heard much of the women's dialogue between serving her customers with knitted garments they perused and taking pennies in payment. Trade was good for the time of year and with the slight respite in the weather, people had felt a sudden need to get out and take the air today.

Mary extracted herself from the gaggle with the excuse of purchasing a loaf from the now available baker. The loaf was soft and its fresh scent hung in the air. Before Mary knew it, quite some time had passed and with the noon bell she watched the gossiping group disperse as readily as they had gathered. The tradeswomen collected their wares and profits before heading for home. As the sky darkened, Mary felt tired, but content. As she arrived home to her empty house, she thought, 'Most mean well. This is the nature of our town gossips.'

Their talk of Isabel continued for many days after the solemn funeral, which was wet, but well attended. The cold wind and icy squalls ceased abruptly after the church service, allowing just enough time for the Minister to say his concluding prayers over the small coffin as it was steadily lowered into the frozen earth. Bundled bystanders departed as quickly as seemed polite to go to warm themselves at their own firesides. Mary went home alone, rekindled her fire and cried in her own sadness. Catchevole came to sit inside to watch over her.

...oooO00Oooo...

The following freezing days led slowly into balmy months. Mary took stock of what she had learned of cures and poultices. She steadily found herself in charge of those who had once sought the healing attentions of old Isabel.

As companions for the last few years Mary had enjoyed Isabel's common, non-formal instruction that she freely gave. Mary had welcomed this. She knew much of what was required for resourceful healing and was well-suited to helping out. As confidence grew, Mary supported her friends and neighbours in the same ways her beloved mentor had.

Mary used Isabel's room, attached as it was to hers, as a still-room. As she grew accustomed to her grief, she made changes to the house. She began by knocking a doorway through the central wall. She fashioned a suitably accessible store and herb preparation room. Young Ambrose King came along to give her a hand, as directed by his mother, who owed Mary for a pair of knitted, olive-green hose. At first the wan youth seemed to begrudge being there, but soon laid his hand to the task. He was a handy lad with a hammer. More brawn than brain, Mary had heard. When setting to with a large hammer, Ambrose cried out as he strained an arm muscle. Mary prepared a liniment rub to aid his healing.

'Thank you greatly, Mistress Phillips,' he had said blushing, with a sideways smile and tug of his unkempt ginger forelock, 'your touch is like magic.'

Mary smiled back at him. 'Magic has nothing to do with it, but you are welcome all the same,' she laughed.

Shrewd women quickly established that it was best to keep quiet about their skills – particularly when they made a comfortable living from them.

Indeed, healers were often termed 'wise' by some - witches or charlatans by others. Even so, some who could well afford to pay for a doctor might first discretely call on a local healer for help.

Mary recalled Isabel talking of a time long gone, from her childhood during the civil war, when the townsfolk had sadly mourned the death of the self-appointed witch-finder, Matthew Hopkins. He callously hunted healers and weak women whom he accused of sorcery, then condemn to death. Goodwives were left alone with the loss of their husbands and sons from a civil war that laid waste to the countryside. Women acted as help-mates and companions, but all were at risk of accusation from Mister Hopkins.

'God bless that man,' called the pious, 'for he has saved us from evil witches.'

Those who remained less certain, kept quiet, for fear of stirring a brew of trouble for themselves. Even today, people remained aware of the fears, distress and misfortune that was caused.

Mary was fair-skilled in healing, but she believed she could never achieve the superior medicinal skills of 'Aunt' Isabel. Her mentor had learned from the gentle folk who had adopted her and cared for her. In return, Isabel had cared for them until their deaths. She had tended them through their illnesses and had repaid their love. Astute skills had kept Isabel employed throughout her life, while she thanked her stars that the cruel days of the self-appointed Mister Hopkins were long gone.

Isabel had fledged with an uncertainty of personal safety – with war, plague and persecution. Hopkins, the son of Puritan clergyman, meant he was raised in a strict and pious household. Isabel had said that being a good Christian kept her safe during her life and assured her a place in Heaven. She could not understand how a Christian man could find such hatred.

Mary had only heard stories of those days, yet agreed wholeheartedly with her late-mentor. As much as Mary enjoyed scary stories, she was unsure if Mister Hopkins was a good man or made an agreeable tale.

…ooo000ooo…

Chapter 2
Three Barnes

Samuel Barnes had overheard talk about Isabel. He and his family had truly liked the old lady and were grateful for her herbal remedies and company. They were grieved and saddened to see her go from this earth. Sam recalled her standing at the gate, passing the time of day with a slender-stemmed clay pipe perched between her narrow lips, while laughing and discussing the latest news with his father. She had always seemed ancient and had not noticeably aged since he was a child!

There was much talk of her passing. Yet, Samuel constantly avoided town gossips and tattlers. He saw evidence that loose chatter was often unsympathetic and unkind. His father, William, had warned with acute awareness to dodge loose talk. He believed it came from an innate pusillanimity that he did not care for.

Samuel tried not to laugh at jokes told to the detriment of others, yet he would laugh if the recipients of the jest found them funny. He knew that quips could be unkind from the wrong lips. Witticisms could turn to unkindness with abundant ease. In the absence of a victim, there was little chance of rebuttal - as they knew not what was being said. Sam half-believed that some snipes held truthful words, but many held nothing but plain venom. He could not help but overhear unkind chatter, but promptly chose to forget things heard. Sam shared little with others, nevertheless, he understood that this did not in any way save him or his family from ill-spirited, cantankerous gossips.

'Keep your nose clean and all will be well,' his father advised. The clean-shaven Samuel had not understood what his nose had to do with it, but as a responsible lad, he looked out for his neighbours and their livestock. He was skilful with his hands and could turn them to almost any job. He dug, tilled, hoed and raked, besides being a decent herdsman.

Early in the morning he had risen and watched as the multi-layered sky turned from a cool grey to rose-pink, then a vivid orange-phosphorescent glow on the horizon. Here was the day-break. All portended well on this fine May morning. He led the animals to the field from the byre and settled them. The livestock would be left on their own to graze for a while. As he combed and tied back his hair into a pony-tail using a length of dark blue ribbon, Samuel knew that his brother, Wilf, would already be started out on his way to the meadow, whereas he was employed elsewhere. Today he would be active alongside the other men in clearing stones and brush-wood from property owned by the Lord of the Manor, William, the Earl of Rochford. The task was to be overseen by William Pickering, who owned lands between Oundle and Benefield. His fields were either rented out to tenant farmers or used for his own crops. Samuel guessed that they would be busy planting wheat, barley, rye and oats, along with beans and peas, plus vetches for food and animal fodder.

As the morning light progressed Samuel could hear the shouts of the men as they met in the lane. At the start of the day they were always louder than they were at the end, when their shoulders and legs ached from cutting back bushes, moving rock and stone then tilling the earth.

Sounds carried easily on clear days such as this. A few carts lurched and rumbled over the cobbles and uneven stones that marked the road and filled the ruts. Sam greeted some of the drivers as they whipped their beasts to move past with their heavy loads.

Briefly, Samuel greeted Wilf before setting off to accompany the growing convoy of men headed towards the distant fields. The small herd he had left behind belonged to numerous local families. Expectations were high as Samuel joined the back of the group. They passed several milk maids with empty pails that were balanced in the crooks of their arms or suspended on yokes. Some of the older men made friendly greetings, while others, like Francis Fisher and his cronies, made quiet remarks or whistled as if to call a dog to heel. Unlike the smooth skinned Sam, Francis was blemished and ruddy. His face bore a red glow. It was not that of good health, more a red from a suffusion of life-blood as the young man was unused to healthy exercise, but enjoyed the sudden excitement of a chase and alcohol. In contrast, Sam's skin was tanned and he was lean. Samuel nudged his equally good-looking friend, Thomas Ashton, who grinned back at him like the village idiot. Both men were smitten by pretty Lizzie Coles – along with several others from the town. Of all the eligible girls of the town within their social sphere, Lizzie was the prettiest.

The cows and sweet Lizzie looked at the menfolk through their lashes with large bovine eyes - the latter with a saucy smile on her rosy lips. Whenever he was free, Samuel would offered help to carry the wooden milk pail to the dairy store, rather than watch her struggle under its weight. Yet, today there would be no chance of this.

Both young men had discussed at length how Lizzie's smooth skin possessed the colour of newly-churned cream and how her hair was as fair as sun-ripe hay in the summer. In bright sunshine it created a soft halo around her face that Samuel believed to be a most arresting and beautiful vista. She was bold and outspoken, but Sam, like many other menfolk, saw sparkles in the sunlight and glowing angels in the trees when she walked by. The breeze and light created images that danced with movement in the trees around them. The crepuscular rays of the sun lit the patterned sky. God sent beams and shadows from the clouds above just for him. Samuel was in his private heaven when she favoured him, but doubted if she could ever be truly interested in him.

During their short lives Thomas and Samuel had lusted after a dozen or more lasses. Often they vied for the same maiden. They had appreciated several, admired some and desired a few - and usually discussed their newest targets of fancy together. Samuel dreamed of the flaxen-haired, Mistress Lizzie Coles, who wore her tresses in soft curls. Yet, Sam perceived there were things his friend, Thomas, left unsaid, as he also blushed whenever she walked by.

Lizzie lived near to the Barnes' in a reasonably wealthy smallholding. Sam knew and respected her parents, Joseph and Ruth. Ruth had been a true friend to his mother, Alice. Both, Joseph and Ruth Coles were well-intentioned Christians, who cared greatly for their five children: Martha, Charles, Lizzie, Annie and young James, who had just learned how to walk. Lizzie, the most attractive of the brood, was a middle child. She and her siblings worked on their parents' farm. Annie was a couple of years younger, but Lizzie found her objectionable. She disliked the way Annie looked, clad and spoke. Annie had a slight lisp, made worse by her sibling's comments and unkind teasing. Annie wore Lizzie's passed-down clothing, but by the time she got to wear any items they were well past their best.

Lizzie paid great attention to her own appearance and several of her friends wished to emulate this in every way. She and her clique often strolled past the Barnes' home. They enjoyed paying young Samuel a visit to talk with him while he took a moment away from work in the field. They waved, smiled, flirted and swayed their hips, offered compliment and words to make him at ease in their company. Unfortunately, this made Sam feel ill at-ease. He had recently become aware that his behaviour changed when he spoke with them - or perhaps it was the other way around and that they had simply started to pay greater notice of him. He was flustered by their attentions, but guessed they could not be interested in him as he had little to offer. His family were not rich, yet he and the other two men in his household always worked hard.

Today he blushed as a sudden chorus of birdsong accompanied their meeting. To Sam it had felt as if the nearby flowers had taken on newer, stronger scents in Lizzie's commanding presence. His grey eyes were open and his heart beat faster as if he feared this moment. Although very much a private person, Samuel wished to tell everyone about his interest and shout out to any who would listen how Lizzie Coles favoured him. His only concern was how his friend Thomas would react.

As with most men of his acquaintance, Samuel yearned for moments with Lizzie Coles, times when she turned her unruffled gaze upon him, looking under her long lowered lashes at him, yet he wished that she was not always accompanied by her friends. It was as if they wanted to view him, like a prize bull at market.

Lizzie stepped forward ahead of her brood to greet him kindly. Her sapphire eyes twinkled.

'Sam,' she had begun, 'as you will never get around to asking, I suggest we will make a fine couple together at the town fair next week. It's a day off. Will you accompany me? There's a big horse fair too.'

Shyly, he stammered, 'Umm ... well, I may be required to work at the mill ... and the Millward's might still need me on the day of the fair, but I'll ask.' Suddenly he was anxious of joining her.

She asked, 'Are you not going, Samuel Barnes? The whole town will join in with the May festivities. I only ask as we can meet and go together?' She blinked at him, but the girl was never given an answer as an overseer called out to Sam to 'come along' and he was forced to hurry to catch up with the men to begin work.

It had been a simple enough question, but Sam fretted over it as he had strove in the fields. He mulled over his dilemma as he toiled. After a back-breaking day he walked home, just as Wilf was driving the herd to the byre. Although inclined, he felt it was inappropriate asking for guidance from his inexperienced little brother.

He thought of his meeting with Lizzie during supper and after an uncomfortable night, Samuel was glad to escape his thoughts for a short time while unloading corn for his friends at the watermill.

Here he heard that Lizzie had pushed her sister in the stream in a spate of hate and that she had found fun in laughing at his friend, James Millward. He mused that if these were true stories, he did not wish to be associated with such a volatile young woman – or take her to any fair unless she changed her ways.

Sam worked and offered his strength and service for a few coppers. More often than not, for goods and produce. If Sam earned money on the feast day during the fair it would be beneficial. Sam particularly enjoyed helping the miller, Henry Millward, whose family had lived and worked at Ashton mill for longer than anyone alive recalled. Henry welcomed help and banter to make the day pass faster. His sturdy son, James, was around Samuel's age. He was a polite and pleasant, pimply lad. He had a strong body, yet was addle-brained. He could follow simple instructions, yet often made errors. He was keen to accompany other lads of his age along well-worn paths into the woods to hunt for rabbits and wild-fowl. As agreeable as he was, James Millward was a hopeless poacher, as he could not remain quiet enough to catch even the thickest pheasant. Some taunted him, but Samuel found him affable.

The miller oft' needed help that was reliable. Henry liked that Sam was quick-witted, trustworthy and pleasant to work with. The fact that Sam did not mock his son was important to him. The genial miller regularly used his services. Sam enjoyed spending time at the mill as it steadily ground the wheat into flour. The miller was always busy, but fair and generous in giving a half-bag of corn-meal as a wage for each day of hauling and help.

'Thank you lad,' he said as he shook Sam's hand, 'I'll see you tomorrow, bright and early.'

Life was both hard and harmonious by the riverside. The wheat store, at the top of the building, required strong muscles to hoist heavy bags to its apex. The process was long, but the smell was delicious as the heat of the grindstones warmed the flour. Sam was always more than ready to accept his payment in flour. His family had been hard hit in the past years, particularly after the death of his mother. Almost any wage was of use to help to feed the Barnes' household.

The May Day fair came and went while Sam worked alongside the Millward family. Lizzie had pursued her quest, but found she was getting nowhere fast. Having missed her opportunity to spend a day with Sam, she simply decided to bide her time.

...oooOOOooo...

By early summer all who lived within the town and vicinity had begun to make advance preparation for the oncoming winter. There was no way to judge how severe or mild the coming seasons would be. These were in the hands of God and each year the concerned townsfolk repeatedly prayed on their knees for a wet spring, a sunny summer or a fruitful harvest - alongside the penetrating fears and needs for their own families.

When Samuel was an infant, he had been baptised, then shaped and moulded into a God-fearing boy by his parents. His father, William, had been ill at ease for many a year since Alice had passed - just five years since. This was the way of life: God giveth and taketh away. Alice died after birthing Samuel's youngest sibling, who quickly succumbed to the same fate as her mother. William grieved for his wife and her gruesome death. He also mourned the babes lost, who knew not that they had even lived. The loss of Alice though, who was his daily love and irreplaceable companion, hurt him the most. He often thought he saw her shade watching him from the dark corner by his bed or from the shadowy garden. William talked to her by her grave and in the apple orchard, but not in the house. He felt it was in some way unlucky. Of late, his friends had begun to suggest he should take a new wife, but William was not ready for that as yet.

It was late afternoon and the chores were done.

'Aye up, Sam.' William gave a loud shout from the door of the barn to attract the attention of his son. He raised a hand into the air with a finger pointing skyward. 'Look to it, son. It's near time to eat,' he said. 'If you will, pick a few peas and greens on your way back in,' William continued. He rarely said please or thank you, unless it was to the wealthier land-owning gentry and he always pronounced 'few' as 'foo'. He had happily retained a broad village accent from his youth.

Samuel did as he was bid. The cool grey clouds left a low haze, but just proud of the horizon there showed a glorious pale-blue stripe of sky created by God's paintbrush.

In their cloistered garden-plot, Sam looked around. He headed straight for a carefully laid line of fresh growing greens. He selected a fine cabbage that he cut from the ground with his knife. It needed careful stripping of its tough outer leaves. These revealed small holes the caterpillars had casually eaten for luncheon. He now moved along the rows. He picked a handful of pea pods from the vines strung on sticks. He chose a fat pod, carefully slicing along its length with his right thumb-nail to release the succulent jade peas into his mouth. The taste was sweet and although it was fairly late in the day, the air was still warm. He stood for a moment by the sticks and ties of the stone wall.

'Mmm...' he moaned, as he expressed his delight. Samuel closed his eyelids and let out a long breath. He thought, 'This is the life. The blessed sun warms my bones. If days to come follow as this it surely bodes well for the future.'

He kept his grey-blue eyes closed and took another deep breath that filled his lungs with honeyed air. His senses took in the sweetness and scents of the landscape. The touch of the warming orange sun as it dipped in the sky and the taste of the peas, alongside the smells of mown hay and new earth were a delight.

Samuel smiled and gave thanks that the earthy smells of cattle were far enough away to be missed. He stifled a laugh as he thought about it. His ears heard the bell tolling in the town and the buzz of the nearby insects as they sought sustenance. His senses were wide awake and full of pleasure. He took a further deep breath and released it with a controlled slowness.

A clutch of hedge sparrows roused him with their noisy chatter. Arguing in the safety of the bushes, jostling to find a secure perch in readiness for the drop in temperatures during the evening and oncoming night.

Samuel roused himself from his moment of serenity and headed back to the small worker's cottage. He noted that the onions and shallots had been lifted already and laid out to dry on the lean-to roof. He felt them and pushed some of them into his jerkin pocket.

Samuel carefully tied his pea pods (together with a large onion he thought may make todays stew tastier) into his kerchief. He dug up the last of the beetroot and walked back towards the cottage with his garden-plot plunder.

Wilf gambolled towards him. He had been named as a tribute to the sainted Wilfrid, who established the town church. The boy was only eight and had not developed the responsibility that progressed with maturity. He carried with him his simple rod and held aloft a fish.

'Look! See what I caught,' he gleamed, proudly.

'Well done, Wilf. That's a fine fish for our meal. Fish stew is so much better than pea and cabbage soup,' he said, holding out his fingers with the empty pods in them. Sam rumpled his brother's tawny hair as he smiled down at the freckled face of his sibling. Wilf laughed at the jest and waved the flaccid fish in Samuel's face. When Samuel tried to grab at it, Wilf tore into the house at great speed, laughing loudly. Samuel sprinted after him with a cabbage held tightly between his arm and body. Wilf was fast and arrived inside first.

In the house, William had already settled himself to lighting a fire and putting a pot of water to boil over it.

'Here, boy. Mind that door!' he called out, as the wood slammed against its frame. He quickly changed his disposition when he spotted the joyous face and tasty fish clasped in his young son's hands. He smiled back with tenderness. 'That looks a good 'un, lad. Well done,' he declared.

Sam loosely chopped the cabbage into chunks and began the task of creating a thin stew for the family meal. William threw the hunks into the seething pot, while ensuring it didn't spit back at him. Samuel noted there was only a little chopped wood remaining by the grate. As he moved forward, there was a rattle in the chimney and out sailed a walnut from the hearth. It flew out from the flames and landed on the floor.

'Well, I never!' exclaimed William. 'Those darn birds are back up on the roof again throwing nuts down our chimney. What a kindness. They've given us another gift.' He lifted the spherical nut and rolled it in his hands before adding it to those in a basket on the window-sill. 'Still, as gifts from God, they may come in handy when the times are hard,' he supposed in quiet words.

William listened quietly with his head tilted at his shoulder. For a moment he waited for any sounds from inhabitants of the arboreal heights, particularly the caw-caw of the jackdaws or rooks, but heard nothing other than the crackle and sharp hissing sounds of the fire in the hearth and the bubbling pot above it.

Sam smiled kindly at his father, then calmly walked outside into the early evening sun to chop a little more wood for the fire. He glanced at the roof, but had a bird once been there, it had since flown. Bees led him along the path as they zig-zagged from bloom to bloom. The continued calling of crows marked his walk, as they competed for prime position and supremacy in the highest braches of the trees in the copse.

Wilf helped by collecting the cleanly stored utensils from the chest and cupboards. He set three places around their table. Each bore a knife and a wooden trencher alongside two drinking-bowls for himself and his brother - and a flagon for their father. Wilf filled the pottery jug with cool water from a lidded barrel and placed a small bottle of ale next to it on the scarred table. He dusted down the old wooden stools and benches; made for their durability, not beauty. Each stretched along the sides of the timber bench. Wilf keenly licked his lips in famished anticipation of their meal.

Water carriers sold water in town, yet beer and ale was preferable. Water could not be trusted and was often tainted. Samuel and his family had a wooden-water-butt that collected rain water for their own usage.

William repeated the words of his long-time friend, John Palmer, when he said, 'Wine, brandy and whisky are consumed by those who can afford them - and gin by those who can't.' Strong liquor was not for the likes of the Barnes family.

Supper was their evening meal when all the work of the day had been completed. It usually consisted of a single course for them, but in richer households it oft' entailed numerous savoury and sweet dishes. Poorer folk used wooden plates, but Samuel had heard that rich families like the Pickering family of Titchmarsh and the Oundle Bramston's and Creed's used pewter cups and dishes. They were indeed wealthy. Sam had met their cousin, John Dryden, who spent much of his time in Oundle writing poetry and plays, in the local public houses. He was kindly and paid for a beer or two for Sam and his friends. Happy with his lot, fine tableware was no dream of Samuel's.

The Barnes' used rush-lights to light the dark evenings. The peel was removed from green rind and inner pith, leaving a strip of rind of rush. When the rush had dried, Wilf was usually allowed to help by dipping the strips in mutton-tallow before putting them aside to set. Their holder was made from a piece of forked metal that William had fashioned himself. The rush was jammed into a cleft and burned for just under an hour. It was a common source of lighting, as it was easy to make and the cost was cheap. Conserving his supplies, William would not touch fire to the lights until dusk.

In Samuel's adolescence he had stolen a look through the windows of the rich with his friends. They had been amazed at the use of candles, so many candles, thanks to chandler, Thomas Chambers, with which they further lit their already luxurious lives. He had watched the gentry eating with pronged knife-like utensils that were used in selecting succulent sliced meats without greasing their fingers. His mouth watered at the memory of this. Nevertheless, Sam considered he was happy with his life - and his humble knife.

'What is their need of a two-pointed tool for stabbing and eating when you have a knife already?' he had wondered. Here, their sufficient household table and solid seating was uncomplicated and not for rich comfort, yet it served them well.

Samuel watched on. He rubbed his hands against his thighs to clean them on his breeks after finishing stacking the newly-cut wood by the door. Meanwhile, William had decided that the cool fish would last to supplement the morrow's meal. He carefully placed it in the bucket of water that stood on the granite slab in the small, cold-store that had been built to the side of their house. Perhaps he should salt it? Whatever he decided, he would use it wisely.

The sky was dusky outside and the sun was near to setting. He looked around and breathed in the evening air.

'It's time to settle in,' he thought. He sighed. 'Come along, let us prepare for the night,' he said aloud to his sons. They smiled and nodded in response. They knew their routine. In the distance the bell of St. Peter's church tolled the hour.

William was near two score years of age, but had endured much in life's course. He mused on the lasting beauty of the church he attended. It had stood for hundreds of years, long before he was born - and long before the Reverend Edward Caldwell had come here to preach in the town with his pleasingly deep, mellifluous voice. The church was a solid, seemingly permanent feature of stone, needing naught but small repairs of late. Its bells could be heard clearly, calling nearby villages to markets and festivals, baptisms, marriages and funerals, gleaning times and services on worship days. Its lofty spire, having been erected seventy years afore, served as a sight of hope and a prominent landmark for weary travellers.

The resilient community had existed here for over a thousand years; turbulently tossed from Popish Catholicism to Puritan Protestant for over a century until, finally the country had settled. It was near inconceivable that the church was still standing after all memory of the builders had long vanished.

The Barnes' family often found themselves at the dinner table as the bell tolled.

Broken from his reverie, William breathed an audible sigh and instructed, "Tis time to sup. Get yourselves to the table, lads.' A steaming pot was placed on the wooden surface as William stood at the head of the table. With bowed heads they said their thanks to God in gratefulness for His provision. Once uttered, they hungrily ate as the dark of the night embraced their town.

After their repast, the dishes were wiped clean of residue and set back onto the chest. As they tidied, they each discussed what they had done and heard in the day. Shutters were closed and barred before prayers and a favoured Bible verse concluded their day. William and his sons slept on two straw mattresses. Knitted blankets and their cloaks kept them cosy. Each mattress lay on a frame strung with leather thongs and ropes that needed tightening each week. In the winter, the lads shared old coverlets of fur for greater warmth, whilst William added extra blankets to his box bed. Daily, their covers were shaken out, as they oft' concealed creepy-crawlies. Exhausted, each found their space and slept soundly.

...oooOOOooo...

Chapter 3
Winds of Change

Mary was never disturbed or a-feared of the dark and shadowy grave yard. She was not ashamed to tell others that irrational beliefs could cause fear. She knew of many superstitions, but unlike her neighbours, believed in very few of them. It was said that if a mouse should run across your path it warned of a death. Isabel had cautioned Mary, 'The spectre of a white mouse is portentous of imminent evil.'

'To ward off bad luck, a toad must be skewed with a sharp instrument and worn in a bag around the neck of an ill-fortuned individual,' Mary heard the prattle of old wives, but cared not to listen. She was sceptical and fretted for the toad.

'Ivy brings ill-luck,' Aunt Isabel had told her, but it was useful in reducing swelling and as an aesthetic. 'Beware of bad omens: a crow flying alone, having swallows or jackdaws fall down your chimney or hearing the chattering of magpies.' Mary had laughed. It seemed quite clear to her that anything falling down a chimney would be bad luck as it would sweep soot down into the house. 'Magpies require a greeting of 'Good-day' or a naming of them,' Isabel had advised. Henceforth, aware of this warning, Mary was careful to do as instructed whenever she met one in her path. Whether true or not, it did no harm to heed the old woman's advice. She now smiled at the memory of her mentor and her many age-old rituals.

'If an apple tree blossoms and bears fruit at the same time, it betokens a death in the tree owner's family. Remember this to help you as you tend to our neighbours,' Isabel had warned. 'Be kind to all and they will repay the kindness.' Mary had nodded. This indeed was a message worth noting.

Light on her feet, as she walked through the quiet graveyard she was aware of the seasonal changes, as she swiftly spotted echoes and similarities with past years. She took the familiar cobbled path beside the church, noting the tangle of ivy growing on the tumble-down wall and the briars that needed cutting back. 'I wonder how Aunt Isabel would have dealt with the curse of this ivy?' she mused.

It was late, but she wanted to avoid walking past the corner tavern on route home. The tavern was often rowdy at this hour. The silent long passages, back ways and dark alleys were much more worrying and scary at night. It was hard to guess if cut-purses or other petty criminals lurked amongst the shadows.

To cheer herself, she recalled that each summer, no matter how hot it became out-of-doors, the 'House of God' stayed cool inside - with its musty scents of candlewax, dust and flowers. Mary knew the building was often locked at this hour to prevent godless vagrants from rifling the poor-box.

The trees shook in the slight wind as she passed through the creaking, wooden gate. Moonlight lit her way. Mary smiled as she recalled clusters of chattering girls gathered like gaggles of geese on their way to pray inside the poorly lit church. Their silent piety easily evaporated the moment they departed from each service. Unfettered, they wasted no time as they passed by the smallholdings, farmsteads and homes of their neighbours. They stopped to chat with all they met. Oh, how they had giggled and strutted; awaiting admiration from the young men.

Mary ceased her musings. She was glad to arrive at her cottage in safety. She never truly enjoyed entering her empty home since Isabel had died. There seemed a void that she could not fill. Hanging her cloak on a hook by the door, she looked down to notice a large tear in the fabric on the hem of her skirts. It had most probably caught on the wild brambles that flanked the footpath to the graveyard. She determined that it could be fixed in the morning. All of Mary's clothes seemed poor in comparison to those of her friends. Of late, the fashionable women had copied clothing from far away – some said the continent - hats of silk had replaced straw and their ties were now made from ribbon. Some of the older goodwives remarked, 'Heaven alone knows why these young women would want such broad-brimmed hats!'

These stiff-crowned, straw hats were tied beneath the chin. In more clement weather girls would let them catch in the breeze to fly from their heads, briefly showing off their hair. This was considered by 'society' to be brazen. Married women wore caps beneath their bonnets to avoid such unseemly behaviour. Modest Mary copied their lead. She was not prone to sudden changes in style and saw transitory fashion as a fascination largely intended for the rich. Wealthy individuals could afford to dress at any whimsy.

Mary thought of her sophisticated friends and confidantes. Principal amongst these young women was the curvaceous Lizzie Coles. Mary saw that many of the farm hands were attracted to her beautiful friend. Her long, golden hair framed her face. It cascaded almost to

44

her narrow waist. This she touched, brushed and twirled, either absent-mindedly or to gain attention. She ensured she looked best over her cronies. In contrast to the tones of hair and skin, her eyes were often dark, alert and watchful. Her sharp eyes looked for any source of entertainment, whether good or bad. Suffice it to say 'sharp' like her tongue, should anyone cross her. Mercy had once remarked that 'Lizzie's mood can spin from laughter to spite in the turn of a cartwheel.'

The young Mistress Coles was well aware of her own appearance - and her smile was mercurial. When crossed its beaming presence fast disappeared, like the radiant sun before a storm. She saved her most exceptional smiles for eligible men and their parents - or for any of the elite whom she considered important. Mary believed that Lizzie coquettishly laughed and tossed her head, rather like a skittish pony, when aware that she was being observed. People considered unworthy or beneath her, gained her ire. Sometimes, she could not be coaxed to speak, even to wish people a 'good day', unless she deemed them to be useful to her. While Mary was on some level aware of this, she had long ago decided that it was better to see the good in people, as she had often been taught in church.

After a good night's sleep, Mary had risen and gone to market. There she sold Lizzie some new hosiery. Lizzie bartered for some stockings and Mary took payment in goods. These included eggs, hedgerow fruits and apples. Both were pleased with their part in the sale and passed pleasantries between them. It was late and cool on her walk home. Her return home was, once again, dark and cold. As she barred her cottage door she realised that she was weary from her day, yet happy with the pennies in her pocket and new food for her larder.

...ooo000ooo...

Shortly after dawn, Samuel rose to beckon the first rays of the warm summer sun. He saw that, of late, the weather had been kind to the town and its surrounds. Sam had risen and hurried on his way to the fields to assist with the late harvest. He met Mary. It was a chance meeting, but agreeable all the same. Both smiled easily as they met. Mary explained that she was on her way to market and showed him the goods in her baskets. As they paused to chat, Sam recognised exactly how at ease their long-standing friendship was. Their exchange ended with laughter as he gallantly stooped to retrieve a fallen shawl that, caught by a sudden gust, was propelled from her shoulders into the dirt. Their hands touched as Sam shook the delicate fabric and gently re-laid it around her slender neck. They had felt a surprise at the convivial warmth between them, but also some panic in their close proximity.

Mary and Sam had been friends for many years, with each barely noticing their steady metamorphosis into grown adults. Having never stopped to look closely at the other, it now appeared to Samuel that Mary was stunning to behold. She was alluring. Although Lizzie, the object of his desires, was indeed dazzling, there were times when her smile did not reach her eyes. Mary, on the other hand, was both comely and happy. Sam was startled, confused and smitten with new-found feelings. Where had these been hidden since their childhood?

'Do you remember when we were children?' he asked. 'We would chase and hold hands.'

She nodded and smiled as she recalled the memory he had summoned for her.

'I wonder, will you agree to hold my hand now, Mary?' he politely asked with a smile. He held out his own with palm upwards. Mary hesitated for a moment before softly placing her hand in his. It was a simple act, but images of anticipation had appeared in each of their minds.

Mary smiled at him, expelled a long breath and then laughed aloud. 'Sam, you are truly surprising,' she softly chuckled. 'You know how to make me laugh.'

Samuel loved seeing her giggle and laughed too. He leaned forwards and before she fully realised what he was doing, he had placed a short, breathy kiss on her lips. Mary was stunned and elated. They held hands and caressed. Samuel had not kissed Mary since catching her in chasing games when they were children. This was very different. Here was a moment that, once begun, he prayed would never end. Likewise, Mary was thrilled to the tips of her extremities. They broke awkwardly and stood in silence for a moment before they had stammered a goodbye. As they parted each was sure that they would meet again shortly.

No words were spoken, yet they converged each day at the same time by the stile in the lane. They would then walk by the river to avoid prying eyes. Whether by chance or design their encounters occurred with constancy. They agreed to rendezvous to walk together, laugh and talk.

On a blustery, changeable day in early autumn, a fond moment was terminated earlier than both had imagined or desired, as they heard a cough as a throat was cleared. Guiltily, they sprang apart. They moved a distance from each other as they turned to find which irritant had caused the brief cough.

'Sam Barnes, what *are* you doing?' demanded a recognisably strident female voice.

There stood Lizzie with a face as red as a beetroot bulb. Her high-pitched, jarring voice carried in the ill-wind. She had noted them from afar and had wandered nearer. Lizzie could not prevent herself from addressing and glaring at them with venom.

'Good morning, Mistress Lizzie,' Sam blushed and stammered. 'Looks like 'tis going to be a pleasant day. Umm … How are your family? Please convey my best regards to them.'

'It had begun as a pleasant day, until I happened to chance upon two reprobates.' Lizzie revealed her subtly hidden spite. Despite her pleasant exterior, kindness was not inherent her nature at that moment. Lizzie narrowed her forget-me-not hued eyes and hissed between her teeth. Samuel blinked in surprise, then moved deliberately to re-hold Mary's cool hand in his own.

'Lizzie. I am happy to say that Mary and I have found our true affections.'

Mary gasped in embarrassment. How bold was this quiet man she had known so long, but never truly known? Sam remained composed whilst Mary smiled uneasily. Her face reddened as he tucked her hand into the crook of his elbow.

'I am sorry if we startled you,' he vocalised, but in truth felt no regret for his actions. He took a step forward, pulling Mary with him, before Lizzie could say more.

Mistress Coles gave a glare, turned abruptly and walked away from the offending pair. Treading heavily across the field, then down the lane without paying further attention to Sam or Mary; her cherry-coloured lips clasped so tightly that her tongue could not utter a sound even if she wanted to. Her eyes told of the words she dare not speak. Mary and Sam were dumbfounded. They watched her quickly disappear along the stony road towards the houses of the town.

As she reached the periphery of the town, Lizzie scowled. She now discerned why Sam was so distracted of late and why he would not answer her requests to accompany her to the fete. Lizzie knew now that it was Mary who had taken his attentions away from her and realised what this meant for the future she had planned.

'That bitch! She has put her spell on Sam!' Annoyed, intolerant and angry, Lizzie stamped her foot in fury. Her moue conveyed her annoyance to others. Neighbours watched from their doorways as she marched past them.

She spoke aloud to herself, 'Sam has always been kind. Kind and weak. Yet, he has been a friend to both of us for years.' Tears of anger came to her eyes. 'How dare she bear designs on him? The cat! She cannot entertain thoughts such as this?' She glared, quickly passing people in the streets as she stomped homeward.

'They have made me tired!' Indeed, she was sleep deprived and angry. Her irritated spirit, not sustained within the confines of her mind, burst forth from her pursed lips. Lizzie was furious. 'This can't happen. How dare that woman tempt him so?' she screeched. 'Sam was to be mine!' Lizzie did not care who saw her raw reaction. 'He was going to marry me.

He's not promised to her.' She growled as tears came to her eyes. 'That whore of an enchantress! She is naught but a temptress. As for my Sam, he should be ploughing the fields, not ploughing her!'

She picked up a stick to thrash bushes, trees and any unlucky animal that crossed her path on the way home. Arriving at the open door of the farm house she entered. Stopping abruptly, Lizzie squinted around at the sudden gloom of the interior. For the merest of breaths she waited, then screamed a loud and terrible tirade. The smaller children came running inside to see what was amiss.

'I detest her. Her crude spell-casting, magical charms and potions are not going to steal my Sam away. No one will stand in my way, least of all, that witch of a woman!'

Her siblings crept out through the door again, without wishing to be noticed and punished. Lizzie's mother, Ruth had overheard her loud arrival and her continued rant. She rushed to desperately quell her daughter's impassioned rage, but Lizzie was not to be moderated. She stamped, swore, slammed and shouted. The tempest that was Lizzie needed to blow itself out.

After storming to her room, she quietened. Later, when she felt it was safe to approach her unruly daughter, Ruth despatched Lizzie to the market on an errand. As she walked along the windy lane, Lizzie was so deeply involved in her angry thoughts and murmurings that she did not perceive Mercy silently appearing behind her.

'Lizzie, how are you?' she asked. Mercy noted Lizzie's flushed demeanour and angry pout before she realised her mistake. Lizzie was startled out of her ill-humoured reverie and glared at Mercy with wide, unblinking, cool-blue eyes. Autumnal leaves flew from the trees as the wind thrashed them in its wake. Lizzie took its lead.

'I am sorry, pardon me. What did you say?'

'I said a "How do you do?" and I ... I ... I asked how you fare today?' Mercy stammered and flushed before Lizzie's glower.

'Do you *think* I seem well?' Lizzie dourly replied, before bringing her qualms to the surface. 'I am pondering on what I should do about Sam?'

Mercy looked at her blankly and did not notice as dried, brown leaves skittered around her slim ankles. 'What?' She gawped at Lizzie.

'Oh! Don't be so thick, Mercy! I'm talking about Sam Barnes. My Sam.' She gasped for breath in exasperation. 'He has taken an interest in Mary Phillips and I am sore troubled for him.' Then she added softly, '... and for me too, Mercy.' Her lips puckered and wobbled. After waiting an instant for her breath to return and temper to abate she continued, 'She is gifted and people like her, but she is not for him.'

'Oh, I had heard, but surely it will not last ... 'tis but a flash in the pan,' Mercy soothed. 'I don't believe that either of them is truly interested in the other in a permanent way.'

Lizzie glowered. She was not mollified by her friend. 'I will not be thwarted, you know.'

With artifice Mercy coughed and nodded. 'Lizzie, when I saw you talking to yourself I thought you knew not how loud you were,' assumed her friend. '... Folk were watching you.'

Lizzie sneered and raised her chin. She stabbed a finger at Mercy. 'What is this to you? I have to *stop* that Mary Phillips from romancing *my* Samuel.'

'I do not believe he is p-promised to anyone. Are you not his kin through your m-mother's cousin?'

'No!' she snapped with a glare at her companion.

Mercy changed her argument, looking around as if pleading for help from the elements. 'How do you propose to halt them?' She looked wide-eyed and seriously at her friend. 'Whatever your future plan is, I believe if Sam's made up his mind there's little that you can do about it, Lizzie.'

Lizzie scowled and reddened. She showed more than a little surprise and much annoyance that Mercy did not instantly take her side in this dilemma. She answered sourly, 'I will most surely think of something, you mark my words.' Her lips curled as she spoke.

Mercy silently worried that this malevolent, malicious Lizzie was one that she recognised, but did not wish to meet. With this she bade her friend a short fare well and hurried home to avoid the shower. Indeed, the season seemed to change with Lizzie's mood. The autumn had come with spatterings of rain and storm.

Within a short time, Samuel and Mary were seen walking, talking and laughing together. Their closest neighbours noted silent glances and observed a change in both. Each had known the other from infancy and were comforted together. Each had lost a mother, so their fellows nodded in assent as they saw them beam.

…ooo000000ooo…

The bitter winter passed quickly. It was followed by an early spring full of buds and rain. Heads turned to observe as Samuel carried Mary's basket or helped make small repairs to her house. Silent smiles from their fellows spoke more than words.

Over a warming ale in the inn, Samuel had recalled to his friend, 'Thomas, I'm happy.' He sipped his drink. 'Moments with Mary are magical. Even remembering the fine seeds that blew in the breeze, then caught in her hair, has made me smile.' Sam revelled at the memory. 'We make each other happy. When we're apart I long for her company. If I smile, so does Mary. When I'm walking with her by the river, why, even the long-stemmed grasses whispered to us as we go.'

Thomas gave a wide-eyed look as he grinned at Sam, not wanting to burst his strapping friend's iridescent bubble of adoration. Romance bloomed as the flowers and nature reflected their closeness. Samuel continued to gently romance Mary throughout the season. Yet, they were not always feted with kind words from those they knew best. Many were the times they caught a bitter jibe or taunt that had been passed on from Lizzie's acrimonious tongue.

Friendly folk with an opinion did not consider the new romance would last long, thanks to spiteful words dispensed by Mary's old friend, who worked with stealth to sour souls against the pair. Lizzie, a jealous lass, was well-supported by those who desired her favours. Mary, clearly outnumbered by those in Mistress Coles' confidence, found her reputation slowly sullied as their long friendship swiftly waned.

Lizzie worked resolutely in her attempts to be noticed and appreciated by any eligible man. She had fair looks, which she enhanced with powders and garments. Her parents near-despaired of her. She spent much of whatever she earned before it could be used to help their living standards. If the finer ladies of the town wore their bonnets adorned with cumulative decorations of feathers and lace, then Lizzie wanted this too.

A number of local women made bobbin-lace, so new decoration was readily available - at a price, as it took time to make a strip of lace, no matter how nimble the fingers were that made it.

In her efforts to be noticed, Lizzie coveted the headwear worn by wealthy women. Her basic straw hat was not costly, but if she found a vibrant feather in a hedge or on her pathway, she would add it as an embellishment. This was sometimes a triumph, yet frequently a fashion failure.

'Well!' Ann had exclaimed as Lizzie came into view. Lizzie stopped in her tracks. Only Mercy saw her face harden in spite. 'What have you done with your bonnet now?' called Ann. 'What's the special occasion? Are you going to a wedding?'

The girls, Sarah Short, Ann Dolby and Hetty Linton, giggled and nudged each other in anticipation, while only Mercy remained neutral.

'This is going to be good,' whispered Ann to Hetty. The latter rolled her eyes and smiled in return.

'What does wool, ribbon, feather and lace do to such a hat?' cackled Hetty. 'It's a good hat, but it seems a little over decorous.' She mopped her watering eyes with her sleeve. ''Tis too much!'

'It does rather … attract the eye, but …' Mercy struggled for words.

'What? Do you not admire it? 'Tis the height of fashion, you know,' Lizzie boldly snapped back at her to hide embarrassment. Lizzie did not seek friends for their opinions. Later, she may well remove the offensive ornate flourishes, but not in plain sight. If she were to catch her reflection in the still of the river or the livestock drinking-pool to the north of the church, she would reappraise her appearance, but not in front of her friends.

Lizzie had easily obtained the wool from her father's small herd. Her home spinning wheel and hand spindle easily created fine thread from wool or flax to be woven or knitted into clothing.

'Hats of felted woollen cloth are not long lasting,' she thought. Most farmers and labourers wore woollen hats with their leather jerkins, jackets and trousers. The clothing was usually patched and tattered, with much repair. The relatively new hat was her pride and joy.

Lizzie's friends wore passed-down items and were glad of them. She constantly mocked others for their clothing. Lizzie did not care to note that she had also worn pass-me-downs from time to time. She noted that although Mary's sole wardrobe of three thin green, mulberry and grey dresses were cleanly washed, her substantial deep-green cloak bore signs of wear. Each of Mary's garments had been repaired many times and seemed well used. Lizzie perceived that others had worn the girl's work dress before her. It bore different styles of stitching, with patches from its past; some better applied than others. Many witnessed times when Mary cursed with vehemence if she caught it on a bramble-thorn or branch when collecting bark and berries. Before long it would be purchased for a penny or less by the rag man, who would sell it on to be made into paper.

Lizzie's blue cloak was slightly newer. It had been given to her by Mistress Creed in an act of kindness some years ago. The lady had long since bought new attire to reflect her status and wardrobe. Unmarried Mary only had her earnings, whereas Lizzie was comfortable in knowing that her family pooled all their resources. She looked down at her former friend with distaste, sneering at her poverty whenever she got the chance.

...oooOOOooo...

Chapter 4
A Knell of Things to Come

Neighbours had shown the grubby and diminutive child, Elinor Shaw, 'That's the house you were born in, lass.'

She looked to a small, ramshackle dwelling in the tiny village. Cotterstock was naught, but a few houses alongside a discrete manor and the Church of St. Andrew. Elinor did not recall her close relatives with any clarity, but when asked she described by them as 'simple folk who made do'. They were lowly farm workers and her memory of them was vague. Their neighbours, who took little Elinor in after the demise of her parents recalled "an old woman named Mistress Isabel, who came to tend to their needs before each had died of the sweating fever".

In recollections they were dim, humble, insignificant labourers, who showed no great duty or responsibility towards her. As simple folk, they had little for themselves. Ill-fated with their lot in life, they knew not what to do about improving it. After they died, those in the nearby cottages had shared looking out for the child, but she grew wayward. The girl cared little for them or for repaying their fleeting attentions.

After learning to walk, Elinor had been largely left to her own devices. She occupied her formative years in observing of all manner of things, whilst scrambling through brambles and ditches. By her early teens, the girl knew each muddy lane and byway: roads used by horses, carts, flocks and individuals as they travelled by. Few thoroughfares in the area were suited to coach travel. These remained remarkably quiet at night, whilst the girl slept hidden in beaten down grasses and ferns in nearby woods and barns. On the outskirts of the town, watchmen took turns to check for scoundrels and vagrants. This girl knew to keep clear of their watch.

Elinor was ill-aware of her neglect or education. Her learning came from watching others - and by trial and error. By the time she neared fourteen years she was alone, with only herself to maintain, devoid of affection or assistance from any. It was now that the wild juvenile, Elinor Shaw first chose to move to town to see what she could glean at market. She was quick fingered and could be appealing - when she felt like it.

Elinor was, most-times, seen by the townsfolk as an inconsequential thief or young vagrant. She appeared mucky, bruised and "unseemly of tongue".

On a cold day, as a chill wind bit at her bones, she found herself walking to town as she had so many times before. She was tired and hungry as she looked around at the bustling market. She recognized few of the tradespeople as they set out their saleable items. She did not know or recognise Mistress Mary Phillips at her stall of herbs, finely-knitted hose and other apparel. Neither did she know that Mary's solitary loneliness would soon create an encounter between the two.

On this particularly bitter day Elinor was busy, fruitlessly begging for coin with which to feed herself. Mary, who was not greatly older, had first noticed the adolescent girl standing by the corner stall, frowning and thoughtfully chewing on her lower lip while eyeing-up potential targets. Servants brushed her away from their employers. The woman watched as an unkempt, ragged Elinor repeatedly accosted affluent folk for alms. Many had either hurriedly turned away or looked at her with discomfiture. A few, not wishing to appear uncharitable, had passed her one or two small coins and moved quickly on down the high street.

Elinor shivered as her flimsy grey shift-dress blew in the gusts of cooling wind. She had inadvertently shown more than her wants at the market today, as her worn skirts flew as if a maddened demon tugged at the hem, exposing her grubby, bare legs.

She spoke, 'God's hooks! I'm to fly away!' With arms spread wide she faced the wind to let it catch in her moth-eaten shawl. The item, more holes than pattern, flapped before she was able to wrap it around her shoulders once more. Holding the fabric to her body, she eyed the carter as he pushed past with a barrow of apples. He stared at her as if reading her mind, before hastily looking to his path.

'Have a good look! Got your eyes full?' she called after him with a simpering-smile. Then, realising that many were avoiding her, she giggled childishly. Indeed, she tried to pull her small shift-dress downward to near-expose her breasts, assured by past provocativeness for the price of a bun. The scrawny Elinor scared some potential patrons away with this gambit, but she gained a few others. She was content to haggle and bargain with her body for a suitable transaction for eggs or loaves. Elinor recognised she was fast learning proficiency in her 'manipulation' of young men in exchange for reasonable payment.

As shoppers looked at the lowly Elinor, they could not perceive of the girl beyond her external appearance and rough speech. Uneducated and blasé regarding appropriate behaviour or dress, she provoked scorn while displaying her defiance to the world.

Decorum was unimportant in her sphere - and never had been.

'Got a farthing, ma'am?' she called to a finely-clad lady, amidst a fawning entourage. The woman sneered down at her as she passed.

Elinor had not perceived being watched. Mary observed the exchange as she sat on the familiar steps, warmly wrapped, whilst serving customers. She beckoned the pie-man and carefully removed a penny from her purse to pay for her purchase. She stared intensely at the girl before slowly walking over to her.

'You look hungry,' she stated in her matter-of-fact way. Elinor gaped at her and tightly pinched her lips.

'Well? Are you?' Mary asked in a kindly voice whilst proffering a warm spiced tart. 'This is for you if you wish it.'

'Can't afford it,' the girl looked at the pastry, then at Mary as she was forced to lick her lips at its enticing aroma.

'I want nothing for it. I bought it for you. Look.'

She held the pastry flat on her extended hand. Elinor grabbed at it, studied it for a second and then stuffed its entirety into her mouth. She savoured the exquisite taste before remembering to show gratitude, muttering, 'Mank hew kinbly, missus.' Like a cat, she licked the crumbs from her own hand. She concluded her thanks by grasping either side of her mud-covered dress and bobbing a stooping curtsy. Mary almost laughed at the pantomime.

'You are most welcome, child,' she smiled gently at the mucky adolescent, so asked, 'Where do you live?'

'Co'erstock,' came the short reply, as the girl wiped her mouth and nose with the back of her hand.

After a second, she quietly added, 'I don't live anywhere anymore. I've left.'

'So, where was your home in Cotterstock? Are you alone in the world? Surely someone cares for you?' The waif stared, but did not reply. 'Do you have a place to go? It's going to be a chilly tonight,' Mary continued. 'Have you truly no home or family awaiting you?'

'No,' came the sullen reply.

Mary considered for a moment. Since her mentor had died, the cottage was all too silent. She longed for a companion such as Aunt Isabel, or merely another voice to fill the corners of her home when the darkness came.

'If you are in need a warm place for the night you can come back with me.' She watched the girl and smiled with concern. With her head to one side she continued, 'My name is Mary... Mary Phillips. I live just down there.' She half-turned, narrowed her eyes and indicated with her index-finger to along a brown, leafy lane that led towards the outskirts of the town.

Elinor followed her gaze to look in the direction, past a row of tumbledown houses. She noted that most of the cottages looked reasonably serviceable and would be warmer than sleeping in the woods. She nodded and stammered, 'I'm Elinor, but they call me Nelly and Nell.'

Wiping her mouth and licking her lips to recall the delicious taste of the pastry, she continued in a more confident vein. 'They say I was baptised with a name the same as a mistress of old King Charles. She was a b-b-beautiful actress. Poor ... just like me ...' She flashed a lightening smile again, then darkened as the storm. 'Do you think I am ... pretty?' she probed.

'Indeed I do,' came Mary's polite reply. She coughed drily. 'Nell, you can stay with me until you find elsewhere to live,' she offered. ''Tis cold here today - and will be much colder tonight.'

Any reluctance that remained within Elinor vanished as she quickly accepted. 'I'll come.' She hesitated once again and her face fell reflecting doubtful dismay. 'Is this a jest or can I truly go with you?' she asked with uncertainty. Mary smiled and nodded. 'Ooooh ... and sleep in a real bed?'

'Yes. Of course you can,' Mary replied with a chuckle. She placed an arm around the girl. 'Firstly, let's see how this arrangement suits us both.' Unrelentingly, she smiled at the youngster. 'Living as two should be about as cheap as one alone,' she suggested to herself as she pulled a rose-pink knitted shawl from her basket of sale goods. She placed it carefully around the shoulders of the girl.

Elinor smoothed her fingers over the madder-dyed wrap and pulled it closely around her. It was knitted of the softest wool and dyed in a most appealing colour.

Mary needed no thanks as the look on Nell's face had already done so. 'You can share my food, light and warmth.' She convincingly broke through Elinor's reserve. This formed the genesis of their friendship. Soft-hearted Mary had pitied the youngster, offered her help, food, and had sealed the deal by taking her home. Here, together they explored Nell's new home ... and cat.

'This is Catchevole. He can be a very lazy mouser, but is a fine companion,' Mary chuckled. 'Catchevole, this is Nell.' She paused and smiled, 'Don't be fooled when he looks at you as if hungry. He lies. He is much shrewder than you imagine; cleverer than most cats.'

Catchevole's green eyes opened to glare, as if he understood her words. 'Then he's a very convincing cat, I found it hard enough getting people to feed me!' Elinor laughed as she reluctantly patted him on his head.

'He prefers being rubbed,' Mary commented, showing her how to brush his fur along the length of his body and tickle his ears. As she continued to pat and stroke him, the midnight cat stretched forward towards her, as if giving her permission to continue. Elinor was charmed.

Mary offered food to both Elinor and Catchevole, then led them into Isabel's room in the cottage. It was arranged as her herb room, bearing a bench laid with partially-made preparations and tonics. Elinor stared wide-eyed in delight as she smelt and touched each of the plants and possessions. 'This is my workroom and drying room,' Mary explained. She watched Elinor intently. With smiling eyes she quietly considered, 'The girl holds promise. She shows interest, is quick-witted and, best of all, I think that I can teach her.'

Mary having assertively taken Elinor into her home, gave one proviso: 'If you want for anything, ask me. Don't just take things or I will consider you a crook and will cast you out on your ear.' The latter nodded, clearly a scrawny waif in need of any succour. Elinor would soon discover that Mary could not resist any person or animal in their time of need. Her support in times of hardship or distress had been regularly noted by her neighbours.

Elinor rapidly grew to like her for many reasons. Mary was bright, kind and strong. She was gentle, caring and good company, although some considered her gullible. She had moderated Nell's sharp, crude ways as best she could. Nell had made friends with Mary's friends. Her life had turned for the better.

As days and weeks passed the two women steadily grew to be close friends. Elinor, dearly in need of a permanent family and a life in a regular home, flourished like a dry plant tended with water and sunshine. She attained a warming glow to her skin. Her pimpled, sallow complexion was smoothly burnished and her hair clean and brushed. She had fast turned out to be helpful and considerate, besides truly protective towards Mary.

Since moving in she was decidedly free from dirt and had learned how care for the house. She discovered where things dwelt, helped in the garden, fed their free-ranging chickens and put them to roost in the rafters of the shed for the night. She coaxed Catchevole to her, but perceived that some days he wished to remain aloof. Mary laughed as she oft' saw Elinor move one step towards the feline as he, in return, took one away as if taking part in an innovative dance. They steadily developed a simple friendship.

Mary quickly learned that Elinor felt a great need to tease and jest. One day, she tucked a small white feather into her hat and had tried to copy the way in which she had seen Lizzie walk, with her shawl slung low from her shoulders. She pondered with her hand on her cheek, made doe eyes at an invisible man, swayed her hips and used a high, sing-song voice to replicate Lizzie's. Elinor was fast becoming a fine mimic. Mary laughed aloud at the guileless, comical antics.

For her part, Lizzie was not impressed when she became aware of Elinor's lampoon. Sourly, she spat at the ground as Elinor walked by. Lizzie had then flounced away. Her shoes said 'farewell' as they clicked on the gritty ground. Mary had observed their interactions and had at first chastised Elinor, then taken her side.

'She has no sense of amusement,' Elinor protested. 'Whatever is wrong with that woman? Where is her delight?' She sighed before continuing, 'It's very easy for her to sit on her arse and say I've done everything wrong, but it would be kinder to point out what I've done right in my life.'

Mary agreed. She supported Elinor.

The childhood friendship of Mary and Lizzie had slowly fractured, seemingly beyond repair. She did not call on Mary at her house anymore. Likewise, Mary felt uncomfortable visiting the Coles' household. She was not invited in and was kept at the door when dispensing her wares. Henceforth, Lizzie insisted on calling Mary 'That Phillips woman' - or worse. As Mary realised Lizzie's abhorrence of her, she ceased calling her erstwhile friend 'Lizzie' and began to use 'Mistress Coles'. She could no longer call Lizzie by her familiar diminutive. As time passed the gap between friendship and hatred blurred.

'God looks after His people, woman. You are *not* one of these!' Lizzie sneered at Mary as they met in the street. She was fully aware there were people listening.

Mary was shocked. 'How can you say such things of me, Lizzie? Were we once not friends?'

'You're of lower stock and your friend is just a common whore ... and a thief.'

Mary grimaced. 'Oh my, Mistress Coles. So, are you so closely in communication with God to judge us? I suggest that you tell the vicar and help him with his sermons,' she called with an acerbic edge growing in her voice. She continued, 'While there, I suggest you seek higher counselling for yourself.'

As Mary rebuked Lizzie, the latter turned on her heel and strode away. Mary laughed sourly at the injustice of the meanly imparted sentiments. She sought peace and wished to turn back to a time when their friendship was good. She took a deep lungful of air and breathed in the wind. Mary tried to smile as she raised her face to the sky. She indicated to her friends at the market, 'Lizzie is like the sun that shines. Whenever she is happy there is warmth. The sun quickly disappears when she is not. This is this true, is it not Nell?' she held with asperity. Elinor studied her before replying.

'Lizzie says that we are lowly, but I would prefer to be on the ground alongside you, than to be on her level.'

Mary tucked her hand through Elinor's hooked elbow. She gently pulled her away and they walked in the opposite direction.

Ted Jackson passed by bearing a tray of warm loaves. The smell was tempting. Both watched him go.

'Penny f' a loaf?' he asked. Mary stopped. She released her grip on Nell for a moment to feel in her small drawstring purse. She had purchased two buns, but when she turned to look around, she saw that Nell was no longer by her side. Deep in thought, Elinor did not halt her journey for a bun. Mary took the bread from Ted.

'Thank you.' She smiled at him. The bread smelled so good and warmed her body as she held it against her rib cage. She continued her walk home, entered the house, placed the bread on the table, then stood by the window looking out. She slipped off her shoes and felt the cold flagstone floor under her feet.

Where was Elinor? Where had she got to? Mary had thought Elinor would continue her steady walk towards their home. She had expected her friend to arrive first. She knew that Elinor was brooding over her run-in with Lizzie. She also knew Lizzie would recover from her fit of pique and return to the market within a few days.

As the light dimmed, Mary watched the thumb-latch on the door for its familiar click and movement she sighed. She could not bolt the door until Elinor returned.

The bread could rest on the table until the affront had abated. Mary calmly thought, 'By then she will most surely be hungry.'

...oooO00Oooo...

Seasons steadily passed as Elinor settled into her new home. There were quiet concerns that Mary held about her lodger, yet both were largely content to share what they earned. Elinor had quickly made friends – and some enemies - on arrival, but overall she was settled and happy living her life with Mary, her newfound confidante with free bed and board.

Almost nine months had passed since her arrival in the town and now, as she sat waiting by the stile, Elinor wondered how long it would be before the arrival of her new sweetheart, Ambrose. After an hour she was bored with the view, no matter how lovely she had considered it to be only a short time before. After a couple of hours she paced up and down in the long grass by the path, wearing a trail in her wake. She expected Ambrose to arrive at any moment. Minutes felt like a much longer time. She grew tired and frustrated with his absence. As she turned to leave, she heard a deep-voiced chortle followed by a stifled cough. It was Ambrose. He had been standing watching her from the shadowy copse for some time.

'I wondered how long you would wait for me,' he grinned. Elinor punched him in the arm. He laughed.

'Ow!' he mocked. Elinor found he was annoying, but knew that he considered himself funny. He knew that it would not be long before she gave in to his charms and completely forgot her anger.

He had already silently measured, 'If she has waited for this long she will be impatient for my attentions.' Ambrose laughed and Elinor laughed too.

'What a wicked jest,' she said, as she stumbled into his open embrace. His arms closed around her waist and shoulders. He nuzzled and nipped at her neck. She returned his adoration in every way.

At the cottage Mary lit a lamp in the window. It was twilight and the sky darkening.

'Where has she got to?' she wondered. The lamp flickered and danced a gavotte until Mary blew it out and trimmed the wick. She relit it, then took up her knitting. She knew this pattern by memory and could count its stitches in near darkness. As her bone needles clicked together, much resembling fighting wands, apprehension grew.

'Tis late. Where is she? What has befallen her? Why does she do this? She knows I worry.'

Mary knew that by the time Elinor arrived home she must retain her temper to not chastise her friend for being late. They would argue, not from anger, but from worry. It would come bursting forth from her mouth and appear as ire.

She put away her work and sat on the hard stool by the sill and looked out at the black sky. Stars twinkled in the firmament. She wished to close the wooden shutter to keep in the warmth, but wished for Elinor to see a friendly light awaiting her arrival.

Aching, Mary wiggled her slim hips to sit more comfortably as she waited. Catchevole slept soundly on the settle seemingly unaware of her concerns. He had never been judged for the lateness of his night-time excursions.

Quite some time later, Mary brushed down her skirts and shook her shawl as she heard the familiar steps of Elinor walking along the lane. She presumed that Elinor may have visited Sam, the two having become mutual friends in recent months. For Mary's sake, the Barnes family had extended their favour to encompass Elinor also. She may have been invited inside to join their household for a little sustenance?

Mary coughed as Elinor came through the door. Elinor looked at her quizzically. Mary smiled and nodded. 'Good evening to you,' she chirped.

Elinor stared at her with wide, dark eyes; pre-prepared with indignation. Surprised by her friend's benevolent tone, she responded, 'What, pray, has made you so joyous this evening?'

Mary moved to within an arm's length of her. Elinor swayed. From her proximity, Mary could smell a staleness on her friend's breath. Elinor had clearly been drinking liquors at the tavern. Mary noted the slightly unsteady gait and sullen appearance. This was a 'Nell' she chose to not to be acquainted with. Intoxicating drink was a craving demon for the once-wayward girl - when she could afford it!

'I worried. You're late – again. It's so dark out.'

'I shared a hogshead at the Crown with 'Brose. Ambrose King. So, what's it to do with you?'

She spat the words angrily at her friend, huffed loudly in exasperation, whilst her green-grey eyes bore a glassy glare. Mary waited for Nell to compose herself.

At length, Mary reasoned, 'Firstly, Nell, do not take your frustrations of the day out on me. Secondly, I only wished to know if you met with Ambrose King and to ask if there is more that I should know, as you live under my roof.' She breathed. 'Drinking ale and staying out to this hour, do you not expect me to be disquieted or not to ask?'

In reply, Elinor rebuked her, 'Well! Do I ask when you meet Sam? Or what you did when you met him?'

'I meet Sam when the sun's shining - and when we are well-balanced on our feet.'

Her voice rose in annoyance.

'Well!' Nell answered in frustration. 'What I do when I am out of your house is really none of your business, is it?' She could no longer bear questioning. 'I do as I please. If you don't like it, I'll take my stuff and leave.'

Mary recognised Elinor's chequered early life, but was concerned that Nell would do something stupid for lack of sobriety. At length, she attempted to mollify the younger girl. 'Let's not be hasty. I meant no threat or judgement. So, Nell, tell me more about your day ... and evening?' She waited. Elinor did not offer a response, but her lips moved in silent reply, then pursed. Her eyes denoted anger. She picked up a half-made blanket and proceeded to study it. It was clear that the ebony cat had been disturbed from his slumber on the settle by the raised voices of the women. He now sought attention and affection by hovering around their ankles.

'Come to me to talk when you are sober,' Mary continued with a deep sigh.

'Believe me now,' Elinor said irritably, 'I am not fuddled with drink.' She stalled. 'Well … you vex me.' She narrowed her eyes, turning to a position of advantage to avoid further questioning. 'You … and Sam. Vex me!' She recognised how close Mary and Sam were and wished to taunt her with this knowledge. 'You wish to ask about me about what I do when I am with 'Brose, but I guess Sam has canoodled and kissed you too. Perhaps you've possibly done more! Who are you to question me when we are cut from the same cloth?'

Mary heard the annoyance in her voice and blushed. 'You and your questions,' she began, then Nell buckled.

'Yes, if you want an answer,' she said softly. 'Yes, he did hold me in his arms and kiss me … and it was marvellous to be loved and held. I am of an age. The girls all have suitors and swains.'

Elinor carefully put down the incomplete patchwork blanket onto the nearby chair, taking care not to drop it. She tottered towards Mary as she took a penny from her pocket and held it up between her thumb and fingers. 'We agree that we have both been foolish. Let's celebrate then. I have a penny, so let us walk down to the Crown and buy a draught of ale.'

Elinor was clearly quite intoxicated. Mary desperately considered her options. If she was able to talk to her friend, she might cooperate. Mary considered

71

explaining her reticence to comply with the suggestion. 'I appreciate your offer, but you ought to save your money.'

She wondered from where the shiny penny Nell possessed had come. She further worried for her young and impressionable friend, but she would not agree to join her for refreshment. With this, Elinor sealed her lips, gently pushed Catchevole out of her way and marched from the house.

...ooo000ooo...

Chapter 5
Ills and Ales

At home, William served soup straight from the blackened pot that hung over the crackling fire. He divided it into their three bowls and carefully passed two of them to his most cherished young men, Samuel and Wilf Barnes. Each son painfully reminded him of his late wife. They called to mind his hurt, pride and love every single day. It was a sorrow and a pleasure that they looked like his fair and gentle, Mistress Alice Barnes.

William was forever haunted and saddened by the memory of those he had lost. Shortened life of under forty years was largely due to poverty, disease or hunger - or in the case of women, from the hardships of birthing: blood-loss, injury, infection and other associated impediments. Alice had died several years past, around Candlemas. It was just forty days after Yuletide, she had lingered from a painful infection after the birth of her child. The date of the three festivals marked the date of her demise. She was ceremonially placed in the earth after the candles had been blessed in the parish church, but before the first lark sang or cuckoo called. Her husband and two young boys had stood to watch as the sexton had shovelled soil back into the grave.

William still grieved. He had some learning passed on from his own long-dead parents. He could read his own name and was able sign it onto documents by remembering shapes in the scribbles. He read slowly, sounding out each word. Some he recognised on sight - and some he could not. He nightly counted his blessings as he recalled or 'read' passages from the Bible. Each night he blessed his children, then kissed them soundly before retiring to his shadow-filled corner, straw-filled mattress and wooden-pallet to succumb to exhausted sleep. Once there, slumber would not always follow with ease. Oft' were the times that William mused on the souls of his wife and children, lying in dark and cold earth in the graveyard at the quiet terminus of Bury Street.

'They are together with God,' he held, but wished they were still by his side. Time without them seemed an eternity, yet William felt they still watched over him, Sam and Wilf. He glanced towards the corner where the boys lay quietly. 'How Alice would have been proud of them now they are grown,' he thought sadly. 'Wilf and Sam are fine lads and the Lord has made me their protector until He calls me to His side,' he thought, as weariness began to take hold and the embers of the fire kept the chill from the one-room cottage.

Only a short while earlier, Samuel had whispered a hurried evening prayer as he sat on his mattress. He had prayed for the continued presence of his family and for the soul of his mother. He took care not lean against the wall beside his bed, as the stones were always cold. Having spoken quiet words for his family and friends (alive or not) he carefully climbed in beside the prone body of his quiet brother.

Wilf was already asleep, completely ensconced amongst the thin covers. On his side of the mattress, Samuel lay with his eyes still open. He mused on the day that had ended. Today he missed seeing Mary. He had not noticed her passing by his field, yet he had been mightily busy with his pitchfork in the hay all morning. He contemplated, 'She is so full of fun and laugher. Maybe she was too busy at the market to venture near. By now she will be sleeping. Her eggs and knitting will have been sold.' He further mused, 'On the morrow I will hopefully be able to talk with her.' With a smile on his face he slipped into a deep slumber.

...ooo000ooo...

After a nightly excursion that she did not wish to discuss with anyone, Elinor returned home peeved. She did not wish to argue about where she had been or whom she had been with. Silently, the girl settled down to sleep.

A few hours later, Elinor was of a reasonably cheerful demeanour and had woke with the birds. As she performed her ablutions, she considered and repented her actions of the previous evening. Mary appeared at the door, carrying in a basket of herbs from the garden. She had already chased the chickens from the kitchen and had put on a pot of water to boil for a dish of tea.

'I am sorry, Mary,' Elinor apologised. 'You were right. I was not fully sober and I was angry. When I returned to the inn it was quiet, with few people there, but for Constable Southwel and a couple of old men.'

'I'm sorry too,' Mary conceded. 'You came in so late, I was worried for you. Perhaps I was amiss and should have joined you for an ale.' Mary continued, 'It is only that I worry that we don't have much money, as trade is not so good at the moment.' She looked at her friend. 'We have little for spending and work is a hard taskmaster.'

Elinor bowed her head. 'Mary, I shouldn't 'ave gone back to the ale-house ... I used the money we were paid for the eggs. I'm sorry I've spent our earnings. It was a grave mistake and I've a head to prove it today. Can you ever forgive me?'

Mary frowned momentarily in thought, before she brightened and nodded at Elinor. She took a long hard look at the hung-over younger girl's solemn face. She emitted a snort, then a guttural belly-laugh that was so unlike her, it made Elinor laugh too. She joyously threw her arms around her companion and hugged her. 'You are a fine friend, sober or in your cups and no one can deny that.'

Elinor perked, 'Yes, believe me now. I am no longer fuddled with ale, so will truthfully answer your inquiries.' She paused. 'Ambrose and I are ... walking out together.' She breathed out, 'Ambrose kissed me and I kissed him in return.'

'Ambrose King! Well, well! Bold indeed!' Mary felt herself blush as she considered how to ask Elinor the many burning questions that sprang to mind, without seeming presumptuous. 'So, he's not as shy as I had first believed. Still waters run deep!' At length Mary quietly suggested, 'Nell, I do hope that you are being ... careful. You know what I mean. I offer no judgement, but we can ill-afford an extra mouth to feed.'

Elinor opened her eyes wide at the remark. 'Mary! I'm shocked! How could you think such a thing of me? Do you take me for a careless trollop?' After a moment of reconsideration she added, 'I always take a paper of powders in warm ale after any man has been with me. I am beyond any endangerment, believe me. I am at no risk. Indeed, I am most practical. I've never got to be with child as yet.' She compressed her lips and stared. 'Ambrose loves me so much that he buys me beer and gives me money to spend.'

Mary looked at her seriously and in a firm voice stated, 'Nell, I think that thou art truly mistaken.' The girl was not best pleased with such an affront, but Mary continued, 'Nell, make no mistake, payment for your attentions is *not* love. Getting you tipsy and throwing you coin is *clearly* called something else!'

Elinor was annoyed as she sensed her friend was right. Her retaliation was formed of words that were not considered kindly. By way of reprisal, she proceeded to knock, thud and thump around the house. Tensions between them were not going to easily dwindle. They each exhibited stubbornly negative moods. Mary was angry with herself for raising the subject again. Not one was eager to back down or apologise. Neither woman spoke for most of the day. Each privately seethed in their standpoint towards the other. Mary sighed. She understood that it was going to be a very long day!

After some time, Elinor decided that it was time to go out. A burning fervour had been ignited in her and it was not going to be easily quelled. She felt an explosion was brewing within her and she needed to get outside and away from the house before it could happen.

...oooO00Oooo...

The carrier's carts trundled along the stony, rutted roads in a clattering convoy of noise. Alongside the random range of foodstuffs and wares destined for market, they brought passengers. Men uncoupled their wains where they desired, then tethered and watered their tired horses by drawing water from any nearby well.

Once done, the traders patronised local inns for a beverage and hearty meal. They had come to know which places offered the best food for the best prices. Many inns made their wealth by using cheaper cuts of meat or vegetables for their pies. Some establishments watered down their ales to make it stretch for increased sales. The wealthy took their pick of hostelries on arrival at their destination. The first through the doors were the first served with the pick of rooms. Those appearing late were obliged to share accommodations with folk they did not know. Many of the poorer travellers and hawkers who made their journeys by foot shared the cramped, airless fug of rooms that could be deeply injurious and affect their health. Dandies and fops also placed their health at risk by attending the coffee houses and inns. Many ventured forth to display their wealth and fashions, but poor ventilation, tallow candles and smoking firesides seemed to spread coughs, infections and illness. Other complaints issued from barely-wiped cooking utensils that were washed in stream and river-water, then dried on a dirty rag.

Once ill, those worst affected were sent to the Pest House. A place of plague, the pestilence houses each kept a 'fever shed' to house unfortunates afflicted with contagious diseases. They were much used in the past fifty years, accommodating individuals affected with dropsy, cholera, the pox, typhus, 'timpeny' of the lungs, bloat, coughing or merely wasting away from consumption. Almost every family knew a resident at the pest house at one time or another. Elinor knew that Mary commonly visited to dispense her remedies at each door. Mary recognised that the smells emanating from inside were not for those with a weak stomach. After delivering her tonics, she was happy to escape the noxious odours and feel of sickly demise the places held.

The fresh air of the low hill near her home was also blessed by views over the fields to the river. Gazing down from this distance, trees clearly demarked the edges of the serpentine waterway. The backs of roaming sheep appeared as dumplings floating in a green stew, until workers came to cut the long grasses they were largely hidden in. From the top of the hill the river mists seemed mysterious. From the bottom, the wild birds took sudden flight from the reeds when surprised by walkers or hunters.

On a mild day, it was a pleasant walk downhill to the river to swim, walk or fish. The river bore access to the grey tavern and boat anchorage, where supplies were brought in. Heavy cart-horses handled the hard work in the fields nearby. They were calm and easy to manage, while feeding on crops, they produced manure, which further fertilised the fields. These large beasts ploughed straight furrows and pulled carts bearing the harvest. It was a hard life, but for some it was preferable to the urban squalor of the town. Beggars traversed the streets seeking alms afore being moved on to the next village and town by the men of the Watch. There was a time when the young Elinor Shaw had feared that she would fall foul of the local law keepers. Her dread had diminished since meeting Mary. Mary had changed her stars.

Elinor, feeling vexed, had stomped from her home. She had left to seek more genial company. As Sam was always kindly to her she sought him out, hurrying past wealthier houses on the way to the common where she hoped to catch him.

Today he was nowhere to be found, having taken the cows further down the river to graze. No doubt he was busy with his duties. Soon it would be the time for the entire working population of labourers in the town to 'muck in' to help with the harvest, yet currently each worker was busy with their own employ.

Elinor slowed her pace and walked back again along North End road. She knew that at home there would be sweeping, washing and knitting to be done. She had already fed the hens and let them out into the back yard to peck in the dust. As she strolled by the alms houses she speculated on future days, in her dotage, when she might live someday. It had been about a decade since the kindly Parson Nicholas Latham founded his alms houses. His 'hospital' fulfilled his generosity and hospitably in providing a home for a few elderly ladies of the town.

The sounds of the boisterous play of children assailed Elinor's ears. The clamour emanated from the adjacent boys' school in the distinctive premises along the main street. The parson had also created this place of learning in his benevolence. She smiled as she passed and her mood lightened as she relaxed in realisation of this. Elinor had come to know many people since she had moved in with Mary and now greeted them as she passed. She deliberated on each of them. Here were the fell-mongers, who hung their sheared wool on posts along the road-side to dry in the sunshine. They required wool and dealt in hides, particularly sheep-skins from nearby farms. Some of the sheep came from smallholdings, such as that kept by the Joseph Coles and his family. Nathaniel Ball dealt in hides. His job was to separate the wool from the pelts in preparation for leather making. His tan yard stood at the bottom of Mill Lane to the south. He washed each pelt in the mill stream at the foot of his orchard-garden. He passed his wares on to the tanner who then cured the hides. As

Elinor looked at the townspeople she became lost in her thoughts. Moving away from the shrieks of the children, the only sound to be heard was that of her worn shoes upon the roughly hewn street. The girl had relied on the cobblers and shoe-makers to fix her shoes whenever she couldn't do it for herself. Her now shabby footwear had been constructed from part of a cured hide.

At last she arrived home. As she entered she was greeted by Catchevole rubbing against her legs and hoping for affection, if not food. He stood to serve notice that the house was empty. Elinor sighed. She had thought to find Mary engaged in the never-ending domesticity of running her small home. Suddenly, she felt aggrieved at the cold and deserted nature of the place. She had left the house in a fit of pique, slamming the door behind her. She had sought to punish Mary for her hurtful, but well-founded words, by her absence and now *she* was alone!

Catchevole jumped onto the window sill to watch her for a pause, before taking himself off to the fields to find his own food.

Some hours earlier, before Elinor's return, Mary, having found herself alone in the cottage, had decided to dissipate some of her uncommon ire by going out to collect herbs for her medicines. The speckle-breasted, sweet-voiced throstle sang in the apple tree as she left the house. She stepped out happily with her basket on her hip. She loved the singing birds and the sounds of anxious scuttling creatures as they disappeared into the grasses, logs and trees before being seen. The surrounding woodland yielded plenty of herbs and wild plants free for her use. The ridge and furrow fields were spread over the open land; toiled-on by tenants and managed by manorial courts. Spirited skylarks flew, singing then silent as they dipped and dived.

Myriads of brightly coloured butterflies flew from the grasses as the cattle sauntered over to the ditch to drink. Each cow was kept indoors overnight, but taken out along the open fields of the back ways in the morning to graze. They made the return journey in the evening for their safety. These slow, bovine beasts were generally milked twice each day by the dairy maids. Sometimes this was done where they stood, but in inclement weather milking was performed in various barns where it remained warm due to the body heat of the gentle creatures.

Mary hummed a tune to herself. She was not sure if it was one she had heard or if she had made it by herself. Mary stopped and smiled when she realised it was the tune of the rather unrefined song: The Milk Maids' Request. She walked on quietly; relaxed and contented in this peaceful place. If she sang or hummed it was as if the birds stopped their own singing to listen. The town was surrounded by woodland. When out hunting for mushrooms and fruits in the brambles, Mary often conversed with any she met. They almost always passed on good greetings. Today there were few people in the woods, so undistracted, Mary had completed her task much faster than usual. As she walked back into the town she looked at the houses and workshops.

Today, Joel Matthews, the hemp-dresser was not to be seen. He had taken over this business from his father, who was now too old to effectively perform his tasks. No doubt Joel was around the back soaking the stems of the hemp plants, extracting fibres from their woody outer layer with which to make ropes and coarse cloth. He was known to be an irritable man who frequently grumbled in his labours. The preparation of stems was most difficult, yet, Mary mused that Joel definitely earned a fair profit for his labours. His partner, Silas, a rope-maker and journeyman used fibres the hemp-dresser had no use for. He vied for the materials used by his colleague. Silas used jute, flax and hemp, along with other vegetable fibres as they were cheap to grow and easy to harvest. His coarse fabrics of burlap were woven into sacking. Some now hung from the rafters of his workshop.

'Good morn to you, Mistress Phillips,' he called out to her from the inn doorway, where he stood talking with Nathaniel, the cheerful proprietor of the local inn. Mary smiled and waved as a gesture of their acquaintance as she walked forth. The chandler was at his work as she passed. He was busy bartering with a customer, haggling for cheaper household items such as oil, soap, varnish and groceries.

Nearby, the town slaters and builders were busy making repairs. The thatcher and his men were working with their knives, straw and reeds, two-storeys above the road-side on roof-tops and gables. Mary determined that they were repairing the juxtaposed cottages not a stones-throw from the church. Two masons aided the work, making the houses robust for winter. Many homes were improved as the results of their labours.

Mary detoured from her perambulations to stop in the church vestibule. Here she said a short prayer for the souls of her parents and for her mentor, 'Aunt' Isabel, whom she remembered daily with a renewed sense of loss. They would often meet here together in times past to pray with the townswomen on days of rest or festivity.

She recalled Isabel saying, 'We live in modern times. At least the services are held in English once again and those who wish to follow other faiths can follow their wishes without persecution. If you want to follow the Popish faith you can with no fear. It wasn't like that in my day, oh no, it wasn't.' Isabel would then fall into reminiscences and Mary, sad to say, would often cease listening - as she had heard it many times before. Now, Mary regretted not having Isabel's comforting tones steadily accompanying her on her delivery route. With this in mind, she forlornly resumed her journey.

The sweaty smithy, Enoch Smith, who had followed his family convention as a duty, was hard at work in his yard. He was busily making neatly fitted shoes for horses that were tied nearby, awaiting repair of their iron work. Mary heard the sudden hiss of the steam as he plunged a newly-formed shoe into a cooling water bucket. His apprentice stood to watch, while taking a moment of ease from pumping the bellows that heated the fire. Mary continued along the road whilst smiling and waving to those she knew along its length. She lifted her skirts to avoid the wet puddles that formed in the ruts between the dirt and worn rocks.

Joe, the saddler, sat in the sunshine while busily mending a torn saddle-bag. Mary's shadow broke his concentration. He smiled up at the girl from his perch. 'Good morning to you Mistress Mary. Have you aught for me today?' he asked. Mary felt in her bag. She pulled out a wrapped bundle and placed it on the stone ledge beside him. 'Thank you greatly, lass, what do I owe thee?' he asked with a smile.

'Tuppence ha'penny, Joe,' she replied returning his smile. 'Please, don't stop your work. You can pay me any time later.'

'No lass, I'll pay thee now.' The thinning, older man stopped his labours and pulled a fine sheep-skin purse from his hip and loosened its thong. He counted out payment and handed it to Mary with his leathery fingers.

'I thank ye greatly, Mistress,' he said with a bow of his head. 'You are the best help for my aching bones. Your salve is my salvation.'

They both chuckled at his wit. Mary placed her hand on his shoulder and with a gentle gesture, she said, 'I must take my leave of you, Joe. Be well. I must not tarry for I have other deliveries to make.' She carefully tucked the tarnished coins into the pocket of her skirts.

'Ah, yes, deliveries of many kinds,' he said with a mischievous glint in his eye. 'Are you doing a delivery for Mistress Taylor today?' He grinned, knowing full-well that the lady in question was not due for at least a month.

'No, Joe, you well know that will be later,' she snorted with a pleasant giggle that reflected her amusement. 'Although, Master Taylor would most certainly be happier if it *were* today,' she observed.

'I most surely believe he would be. I heard he's experiencing all the aches and pains of his wife!'

At this both laughed in an understanding collaboration.

'Fare ye well then. May God keep you, lass,' Joe replied, returning his gaze to carefully cutting the leather strap-work upon his lap.

Mary nodded and smiled as she said farewell and walked on. On passing the Swann Inn, the smell of roasting coffee beans assailed her nose. It was a sweet and intoxicating smell that made her mouth water. It was fairly clear that brewers, coffee-houses and inn-holders made the best quick profits in the town. They purchased their brews from traders and were acknowledged social and recreational centres for many folk. They provided food and drink for regular guests, while offering accommodation to weary travellers. Their patrons included merchants, court officials and pilgrims. Many ales were locally produced, but spirits such as brandy and gin were brought from France and the Netherlands.

In ale-houses, betting and baiting tournaments were full of rowdy men. Events were held in courtyards of larger inns and on the common. Such noisy events were not the only entertainments to draw curious crowds. Whenever a travelling fair visited with its tantalising attraction of a tooth-less, claw-less, ragged bear, adults and children scrambled to watch, as it was led around and displayed by a rope-leash attached to a sturdy ring through the nose. Mary pitied the beasts, kept in dejected and shabby states and made cowed by default. They had no wish to circle-dance on tottering hind legs. They did not lack for beatings and Mary mutely grieved for them.

She passed by the inn courtyards where actors and singers, dancers and players were drawn to tell their stories. Here, the mummers wore adapted frock-coats with wide cuffs of varying styles, bought for the purpose of the play, before being sold-on again. They often bore sewn, internal pockets in their linings, in which to store and safeguard their hard-earned fee. They truly deserved their pay, particularly if the audience had not applauded. Many were the times when players were hard hit by words and flying objects, yet carried on as best they could. Inquisitive and determined, Mary knew what occurred in her town. She'd enjoyed merrymaking with her friends on many festive occasions. She passed by the fishwife who cheaply bought and sold the bounteous fish and eels taken from the river. She called out to sell her wares as Mary passed.

Here stood the corn-mill overlooking a green and pleasant view downward to the tree-lined river. It was set upright on the foot-worn track to Glapthorne. As Mary walked she heard the slatted sails creak in the wind as they turned. The miller came outside to say 'hello' as he wiped his flour-covered hands on his smock. He was busy grinding and selling sacks of grain. This was purchased by grain-merchants or the local baker to be sold in smaller quantities and made into bread. As Mary walked she passed a cart carrying local produce to the grocers'. Plodding along behind was the horse-dealer. He came to town from nearby villages, buying and selling equine animals, he was known as the 'jockey'. All she met on her journey had made a good living from the growing town.

In open pastures beside the flowing river, sheep, goats and cattle rambled together, seeking out the most succulent grasses. They grazed, unaware that their placid lifestyle was completely in the hands of those who owned them. The town boasted clever glovers who sought the softest of membranes from the skinners, then devotedly crafted fine hand-wear. Not to mention the butcher, Billy Heath, who would regularly take his pound of flesh from the unsuspecting herd.

With the changing weather the tradesmen were all sure to be busy. Each lived near, worked near and knew each other by name. Many knew Mary and had, at times, bought knitted woollens and ointments from her. As she passed their places of work they each happily called out to wish her well on that temperate day.

...ooo000ooo...

Chapter 6
Strong Women and Strange Stories

As Mary and Elinor lived closely closeted, they grew together in many ways. Over a period of time they found they were of like-minds and would often say identical words at the same instance or laugh impulsively together. As one, they collected wind-blown apples to make into sweet pies. They laughed as they picked juicy summer plums and licked the red juices from their fingers. The yellow quinces did not grow large in their small garden, but sheltered over by the wall they grew strong. They were not wasted for the women created jellies with a fragrance that easily lured one to eat.

Juicy fruits and ripe berries were autumn fare. As were busy vegetable plots with their yields of carrots, cabbages, marrows, beans and peas. These grew alongside onion bulbs, sweet tomatoes and crunchy lettuce. An abundant herbaceous border was tended by both women. They would often kneel together to hoe or cut tender shoots, before taking them indoors to hang from the rafters to dry. Here were the sweet smells of rosemary, thyme, sage, dill and parsley. Cleansing mint grew back every year, with each season producing a larger crop.

From their sumptuous autumn garden they observed children scurrying in the bramble bushes, lured barefoot to pick choice blackberries. They would eat some, take some home for their parents and leave those that were too high from the ground for the birds.

Mary laughed as Elinor crossed the lane to help the youngsters. She returned with blackberry stains on her lips and sage-green dress.

'You are worse than the children,' Mary playfully scolded as she checked Elinor's dress for new rips. Mary smiled to herself thinking of the many carefree, harmless hours when the two sat as one by the hearth fire, enjoying its light and warmth, thinking aloud with laughter and talk.

Oft' were enjoyable evenings when they entertained neighbours who came bearing gifts or payments for services. These families were always welcomed with a warming herbal broth, a dish infusion or a decoction of herbs and spices seeped in steaming water, to stave off the forces of winter darkness. Friends also visited to partake in their fireside company. Mary shared her favours and courtesies as she poured boiling water from the heavy kettle on its hook. It was forever simmering above the open fire to welcome guests.

At times when alone by the crackle and spit of the evening fireside, the two traded marvellous stories to keep themselves occupied and entertained through the long dark nights of winter.

Some of their tales told of the Great North Road - that led to faraway places. Some stories incorporated genuine reports of highwaymen and their associated terrors. The highway to Stamford and 'the north' was well-known to be busy during daylight hours with horsemen, team-drawn coaches, barrows, hawkers and walkers, which by dusk had disappeared to safe overnight havens. Smaller, undulating roads led through villages to the south. These equally carried hidden dread for unwary travellers caught out alone after dark. Stories of those escaping peril were so real that they caught the breath of listeners.

In daylight, many tales Mary told for children while seated by the river or in the garden came from folklore. Fairy-tales containing mystery or dreadfulness came forth as she reinvented goblins and imps to make them squirm. Mary told fantastical tales to elude a mundane moment. In stories she could be a beautiful princess or a nurturing mother - whatever she wished.

On one such favourable day, Mary had come home with her basket empty and coin in her purse. She concluded her daily house work in her distilling-room, carrying a brimming pail of water into the house. She placed it in the corner with a bump. She sighed with exasperation as water slopped over the rim and onto the floor. Mary gathered a rag to wipe the worst of the spill from the flagstones. Her attempts were cursory, as it would likely dry overnight.

'Come,' demanded Elinor. 'Finish now! I have made you a bowl of soup. Come, sit with me and tell me a new tale. You have done enough work today.'

As was their custom on dark evenings after the fire was lit to warm them, bewitching tales were told. Elinor had already hastened to light the kindling and crackling logs long before. Mary moved to put away the salves and ointments from the table to sit in her chair.

Elinor was impatient for the storytelling to begin.

Mary thought for a moment, then proceeded to retell a trickster tale. 'Verily, this tale is not long. It involves no fire or brimstone, but a flirty girl in red cloak and a very unpleasant beast – a wolf,' she began. Mary told it in her own way, as the bards do. 'Behold! This story combines trust, deception and lies,' she began.

The stories of rags to riches or eventual tragedy always made Elinor's hairs bristle from their roots. She subconsciously scratched at her scalp, as if affected by a 'barber's itch'. The stories carried warnings, but neither perceived exactly how important the warnings could be.

Elinor shuddered at the idea of the wolf fending for itself - and equally for an innocent girl who had lost her way in the darkened woodland. Elinor rubbed her palms on her arms in anticipation. She enjoyed each tale so much that she often begged Mary for more the moment one was ended. She complained, 'That story was very good, but it was far too short. Now tell me a longer one.'

That evening, Elinor had asked, 'Hag-stone pebbles have holes in them, horseshoes are lucky and knives crossed on the table or floor are unlucky. I have efficacious preventatives, but ...' she paused for effect, '... I also have a lock of Sam's hair.'

Mary, suspecting an ulterior motive blanched, shocked as she asked, 'Have you taken this lock for your own use?'

'No!' exclaimed her friend with a giggle, 'most certainly not.' Elinor blushed with the very mention of this. 'I want a lock of Ambrose's hair, but I was at William's farm and Sam was trimming his hair. I thought you would want it. Perhaps I should look out for some straws to make something ill on the morrow as you do not thank me?'

'Thank you, Nell. You are kind. Yes, please give it to me.' Mary was unsure if she wanted the love charm as it was not freely given. The fire crackled in the grate and convivial silence held them as Elinor brought the hair from her pocket, then poured them each a dish of tea.

It was as Mary sat beside the embers of their evening fire, absent-mindedly brushing Catchevole's matted, dark fur with a teasel head, when she decided upon a new scary story.

Once the cat was purring on her lap, she began telling an old tale of a blacksmith and the Devil. Her story began, 'I learned of a smith – very probably one of Enoch's forefathers. The lad's father had great respect for the Devil, but fell ill and died. The young smith needed help without his father around, so decided it would be acceptable to take on the Devil as an apprentice at his foundry.' Mary noted that Nell had settled in comfort to listen. She went on, 'After many days the lad came to trust his skilled new apprentice, so was glad to leave him to work as he saw that he did not need to watch over him all of the time.' Mary sighed in contentment as the curled Catchevole slept in her lap, as she took a sip of her fast-cooling infusion.

'One day the young smith slept a-bed late and failed to come to work, for he was mighty tired. On that day, a withered old lady visited the forge attended by her servant bearing a knife that needed fixing. The Devil quickly fixed her metalwork, then asked if she wished to return to her youth. The woman asked a price – and, as she was wealthy, knew she could pay the coin and milk that was asked for.'

Mary took a sip of tea before continuing with her story. 'She gave the devil-smith coins and sent her servant to buy milk. When the servant had left, the Devil seized the old lady with the pinchers and threw her into the raging forge where he burned her to ashes.'

Elinor gasped, but Mary continued in a low conspiratorial voice, 'Yet, this is not the end of the story.' She continued in a near-whisper, 'Naught but the lady's bones were left when the servant came back with the pail of milk, but the Devil emptied her scorched bones into the bucket. Lo and behold, within minutes out from the milk bucket climbed the lady, young, alive and very beautiful.'

The tale had truly gripped Elinor's imagination, but she did not speak to spoil the story. She sat forward in her chair as if to hear unspoken words. Mary smirked with contentment as she continued.

'The wife was delighted. She rushed home with her servant to tell her aged husband, who also wanted to be youthful again. By the time her gentleman husband arrived at the forge, the demon had gone and the young smith was back at work again. The smith was very confused when he heard the old man's request to be made youthful again. So, he consulted the servant on what had occurred during his earlier absence. The servant told everything he could remember. Soon, the prudent young smith agreed to do what he could for the old gentleman. By and by, he copied each of the actions the servant could recall, but only succeeded in burning the old man to death.'

'Oh!' gasped Elinor. She had an idea that things were about to go further amiss.

'Meanwhile,' Mary sighed and continued, 'his wife waited patiently for her spouse to return to her rejuvenated, but her servant ran home as fast as his legs would carry him to blather. He rapidly told the lady what had happened to her husband. She called for the constables to go to the forge, arrest the young smithy and hang him at the gallows.'

'What? The smith was arrested?' Elinor asked. 'But, surely he had intended no harm, he only did as he had been asked, for it was the Devil in disguise who had started all of this.'

Mary nodded in reply and continued telling her story. 'As the smith was about to be hung, the demon-smith returned. He convinced the young smith that he could undo his errors. He would resurrect the gentleman if the lad would promise to honour him, the Devil, to the end of his days. The smith quickly agreed to this pact.'

'Who would not in his circumstances?' asked the husky, wide-eyed Elinor.

'When this was done the husband returned to life, rejuvenated. The gentleman convinced the Watch that naught was amiss and the young smith was set free from gaol. Afterwards, the smith looked everywhere for the devilish workman, but he had completely vanished.'

Mary watched Elinor's face. Nell clearly believed this was the story's end, despite its imperfect conclusion. Nell looked as if she were about to begin asking questions so Mary quickly went on, 'Yet, this is not the end of my tale.' Both smiled broadly and Elinor giggled. She resettled herself in her seat as Mary continued, 'The Devil returned to the forge to see how things were going. The demon came to ask the smith for his soul, which is what he had wanted all along. The young man hurriedly promised his soul in payment for a pact that gave the smith supernatural powers of his own. The Devil wanted his soul and the smith wanted learning. He mainly wished to know how to weld and un-weld any two substances together.'

'That would be very useful for any smith, Mary,' Nell commented. She nodded wisely.

'The Devil obliged by sharing his knowledge, but when it was time to give over his soul, the young smithy had gained all of the craft he needed. He used his new-found powers to cunningly weld the demon to a very weighty anvil in an attempt to allow him to renege on the bargain.'

This denouement for the smith was a satisfactory conclusion so, once again, Elinor thought the story was ended. As was now habit, Mary paused, then continued.

'The wicked fiend had been trapped by the shrewd use of his own powers. The tables had been turned by the clever young smith. The smithy kept the magical powers and bought back his own soul in return for setting the Devil free to do his work elsewhere. The Devil can nevermore trust a blacksmith and will stay clear of them forever more. Enoch is safe – as are all the metal-workers in England ... and the whole world.'

Elinor gasped and opened her eyes widely in excitement. She grinned from ear to ear. 'Thank you for telling this story.' She jumped up, wrapped her arms around Mary and tightly cuddled her friend. 'Well, I never!' Elinor exclaimed. 'What a clever man. Do you think that a normal person can truly outwit the Devil, Mary?'

Mary smiled at her innocence. She gently remarked, 'I think not, Nell. It's just a story. Never believe all that you hear.'

'Well, let's hope no one hears us and thinks we're are laughing at the Devil!'

The women chuckled as their awakened cat watched them through gem-like, slit eyes. By the warmth of the fire, he had listened to the calm tones of Mary's voice, whilst equally enjoying the feel of her fingers as they untangled the snags in his dark coat. Mary contemplated, 'Better the devil you can see than the one behind your back.'

Meanwhile, Elinor had remained completely enrapt. She relished sitting in the warmth as the evenings drew in. Nell enjoyed many new feelings of safety and confidence on hearing Mary's stories. Before she had first met Mary these enjoyable sensations and comforts were unproven and unimaginable.

The following evening Elinor's attention was an easy captive. Enjoyably hearing the scary story of a girl who slept by the cinders of the hearth to keep warm and of her greedily jealous step-sisters, who madly sawed off bits of their own feet in order to fit them into a tiny squirrel-skin slipper, which had never been or would be theirs. Nell had considered that perhaps she was a little like the girl in this tale, as she warmed her feet by the hearth. Yet this story ended badly, with her adoptive-mother forced into hot-iron shoes and condemned to dance to death at the wedding celebrations of her step-daughter. To Elinor, this story bore particular significance for her. She reflected that she had never truly been understood by her parents. She had been a desolate child, yet her story had taken a favourable turn. She dreamed that her veiled life would emerge like a butterfly from a chrysalis, with an equally happy ending for her too. Spellbound in the fantasy world of wonders, Elinor listened as Mary told of the lovely Rapunzel who was named from the purple cabbage flowers. Mary explained, 'She was kept in a high tower from her childhood. Kept there until her hair grew very long. So long that she could hang it out of the window to touch the ground!'

'Hold!' Elinor laughed as she held up her hand to interrupt. She had suddenly been reminded what Mary had said to her earlier. 'I have long hair and you like the purple cabbage flower … so like the onion flowers that're your favourites.' She prompted, 'Is this story about us?'

Ever practical Mary, had indeed mentioned that her favourites included onion flowers. 'The story is not about us, but the flower is indeed my favourite. Your memory's sharp, Nell.'

Elinor ignored her. 'The onion that grew beneath the mother's window fits in with your choice too.'

'Nell!' Mary had declared with a snort. 'Ha! That is so like you!' She recalled bending to pluck a tiny flower several weeks ago and handing it to Elinor. In return, Elinor laughed and exclaimed in mock horror, 'Onion! Oh, Mary, you make my eyes water! Your favourite flower of choice just had to be for cooking, dyeing or herbal remedy usage, did it not? I should have known that your choice would be of a condiment used to add flavour to food and not because it was of beauty!'

Laughing together, they drank their tisane and Elinor apologised for distracting Mary. The two women considered the sad ending of the tale together, for in life what came also went.

Elinor continually mused on the stories, legends and myths she was told. 'Perhaps they warn us of futures to come,' she pondered. 'I now await my own heroic prince to rescue me. Perhaps my prince is Ambrose?' she sighed in a soft voice, just before she drifted into a happy, dream-free sleep.

…ooo000ooo…

Stories spoken in hushed voices around the town often rang true with no murmur of jest. Tales of river traffic important for trade, stories of a grisly 'black death' and the spread of bubonic plague not fifty years gone that hard-hit the underprivileged poor that tied the town together as a grief-stricken entity. In just six months over two-hundred had died in the town. The hill by Gotham bridge, along the road to Stoke Doyle, was used as a grave-site. Townsfolk still crossed themselves in the old way should they have need to pass by its boundaries. The farm and town women alike noted the dead in hushed tones. Mary knew none were immune to the devastating effects of plague, those who still drew breath carried the terror with them.

One evening, Mary regaled to her young counterpart the story of a wealthy, but untrusting man with a blue beard. Another favourite tale of theirs. This story had a sad ending as the man was a murderer of his wives. Each time Mary told this story, she added a new embellishment for good measure, just as her adopted aunt, Isabel, had done before her. She knew full-well that murder was extant in the district in many forms, but it was often a stranger to the law when it was well-hid. Occasionally people vanished, went missing, 'left' to move to new places. Sometimes they left after a trial – despatched by the hangman. Townsfolk heard and saw their bitter conclusions. Mary heard the talk in the streets of how trials were conducted. She tried to grasp how a world that oft' felt dark, could be revitalised with bright, optimistic love.

When Mary mentioned that she had a 'wonderful, murderous story to retell tonight,' Elinor had chortled in response, then countered that according to the people at the market the Reverend Edward Caldwell had declared 'dark stories are our new peril'. Both knew full-well that household story-telling would not die easily. The tales that were real were the ones most avoided – those of Matthew Hopkins and his murderous witch-hunts. These were just a tad too close for some, containing a tangible wickedness and were not just stories told to frighten children.

Reverend Edward Caldwell had quoted from the recent news. From the pulpit, he told of John Locke, the philosopher, who warned of the severity of 'spirit and goblin' stories that were frightening children and causing nightmares. As the wind blew, those from wealthy families had agreed with him that stories of the supernatural were the provenance of the poor and serving-classes. Locke was inclined to separate elite children from their social inferiors. Fear, like talk could cause boils, canker or infection. All spread along the streets, with some more predisposed than others.

On the windy autumnal days when Mary had visited young Gertrude Wade, she was in such pain that Mary needed to soak a clean cloth in hot water with which to bathe her boils. She had then proceeded to squeeze and drain the yellow, stinking discharge from each engorged pustule until they ran with fresh blood. Little Gertie had eased after a time, but had been disturbed by the sight of her own ooze. The child had been left pock-marked and scarred, but the ailment passed. Mary believed that the bodily ills, wars and aspects of daily life could be much more horrifying than any stories she told and heard.

Mary recalled dark plays she had seen performed in the courtyards of the local inns. Surprisingly, the stories from the mind of Mister William Shakespeare were full of murder, ghosts and fairies. Along with 'the Bard', Christopher Marlowe's demonic 'Doctor Faustus' had been carefully omitted from the list of stories that could not be told, as they were sponsored and adored by royalty.   For those who could read, stories were purchased for a penny in flimsy chapbooks, thus named as they were 'cheap'. All the same, Elinor adored hearing these stories - further embellished by her friend, recalled from memory alone. Neither woman noted or cared if they were overheard in their telling of them.

'There are worse things in life than spine-tingling stories filled with make-believe fairy-folk and sprites!' she loudly declared. 'They are fireside tales told in the dark before retiring to bed.'

For Nell, each was a momentary escape from interminable daily chores and a starved stomach.

...oooOOOooo...

Chapter 7
Compassions and Charms

Mary was woken by a cough that was not her own. Indeed, Elinor had given a sudden, uncharacteristic bark that roused them both. Lying on her back, Mary first watched the ceiling, then after gathering her wits, she looked around her. It was already daylight. The pale morning light filtered in through the cracked shutters and patterned the cold frame with frost. She could see her breath and was not keen to move from the warm blankets to relight the fire, which had turned to ashes in the night.

'Are you alright, Nell?' she whispered, hoping not to unduly disturb her friend.

'No,' Elinor's voice croaked. 'I feel terrible.'

Mary stretched her legs in preparation to make a move from the warmth of her pallet. She took a deep breath. 'Shall I light the fire and boil some water for a tisane?'

'No. I'll be fine in a moment or two,' Elinor raspingly replied, just before her body was racked by another coughing bout. 'I'll just rest here if I can. Just for a short time.'

Mary waited. She sniffed and wiped her nose with her hand. She had a cold and icy snout. It was perhaps for the best that she rose to light the fire. Overnight the temperatures had radically dropped. Winter was visiting!

Finally, after a little time, she decided to arise. This task took longer than she anticipated. She first found as many warm garments as possible to place over her shift. Yet, wrapped in her cloak she could still feel the chill. She splashed a few drops of cold water onto her cheeks from the bucket to wake herself and wipe the sleep from her eyes. She rubbed her hands through her hair, tottered to the basket, then bent to break kindling for the fire. Her iced fingers wrapped around the brittle dry moss, twigs and logs stored in her indoor basket, that was kept just inside of the door. She felt a draught of air as it pushed under the door to blow at her bare feet.

Mary scraped the basket over the flagstone floor, nearer to the fireplace as if to draw from its future warmth. She chose not venture out to collect larger, solid pieces of wood from the pile outside. She knew that there would be a white, slippery frost adorning the world beyond. Although it would be beautiful, she was not about to let the bitterness of the cold inside their abode. After an hour, perhaps a little more, the dried-berry tea was boiling. Mary took warm blankets from the marriage chest to wrap Nell in. Elinor was clearly not in good health. Her eyes hurt and her head ached. She felt the outline of her skull with her hand. There was a pressure in her skin and at the back of her neck. Her muscles had tightened overnight and she ached with tension. Mary worried for her. Her attempts to warm the small room were partly successful and the tea had calmed her cough to some extent. She looked at Elinor as she sat by her.

'My friend, shall I help you to move to sit in the warmth beside the fireside?' she asked.

'No, thank you kindly, Mary. I will stay where I am. I am not sure if I can move easily.' She coughed more if she talked, so Mary advised her to remain still and not to speak too much. As Nell was in more of a disposition for sleep, rather than talk, she let Mary tend to her and give her poppy-seed tea to calm her and lull her into an inert slumber.

For the remainder of the week Mary tended to her needs. She prepared, brought and carried her food, the piss-pot, soothing cloths and warming blankets. Elinor began to ask what she had done to deserve her malady. Slowly she began to chat with clarity and when she began to ask for food, Mary smiled happily as she knew that the worst of the illness had passed. She finally laughed alongside Elinor when she said, ''Tis unfair, for when I hold a sour head after drinking with Ambrose, at least I know why my punishment has been dealt to me.'

In time Elinor was able to move around the room. Her limbs were weak, but finally she was ready to take up her knitting again and help with small chores around the house. Mary fussed around her like a mother hen and quickly saw her ministrations were not wasted. As time progressed, Mary left her to go to tend to others who desired her attention. Elinor had not been the only soul affected by a cough, which had appeared from nowhere then spread through the town, from person to person, with the greatest of ease.

Entrepreneurial Mary earned coinage through her own efforts and initiative. She differed from others with her fastidious appearance and attempted cleanliness. She had learned to remain detached, when others enjoyed attention, her manner was easy with nervous women who insecurely chattered to fill gaps in conversations. Mary was content to listen.

Some patients recovered while others did not. This was the way of it. Mary was full aware of the tenuous nature of life. She prayed for recovery and was greatly rewarded as she had observed Elinor growing stronger.

Mary soaked some dried peas from her store to make a rich pea soup, with garlic and onions for a flavoursome taste. Elinor sipped her broth while Mary, who was tired from her work, ate with gusto. The two were happy to share their food with any who cared to visit – and with those she visited, who were sick or infirm.

'I can support myself and others,' she thought, 'whereas the poor have nowhere to fall.'

...ooo00000ooo...

Francis Fisher was not wedded, neither was he courting, but lodged with other tenants in a small house off East Back Way. Like his associate Samuel, Francis was best suited to manual labour, although unlike the Barnes' family Francis possessed no assets of his own. Samuel did not have much to do with the man when he spotted him drinking in the inn, but saw him from afar while working in the fields. Most often, ruddy-faced Francis worked as a cow-herd on the common land by the edges of the river. He was not an attractive youth, nor was he particularly bright. Working outside had left him rosy, but not overly handsome.

Overall, Francis was miserable, unless given delight in laughing at the misfortunes of others. He oft' sought to intimidate and harm those whom he perceived as being vulnerable. The young man did not take his casual work seriously and often his charges were found straying or in the river. He was oft' seen accompanied by his lackey, Edmund Cannington, who was a simple fellow. Trouble seemed to follow in his wake, which had lost him work and gained him an ill-reputation. Francis recognised Edmund as a fool and led him a merry dance!

For the moment, Francis Fisher was well-known for his frequency in being hauled before the local court. Usually this was to consider his disputes. He was chastised for sleeping in the barn, rather than watching the cows in his charge. Likewise, he was regularly detained for imbibing ales and losing his temper. He had no compunction about taking things that belonged to others and many chose to avoid him, as he was known to strike out rather than debate any of his difficulties. He was accused of 'blethering and prattling' and put under bond to be 'of good behaviour toward all persons'.

On one particular June afternoon, just after the time for sheep to be washed and sheared, Francis was lazing on a hillock watching the herd as it meandered around at the water's edge. The sun was high in the sky and wisps of cloud decorated its blue canvas.

Francis watched as young Elinor walked over the bridge. He had spotted her from afar and witnessed her progress. 'She's grown into a comely lass,' he observed to himself. He had not the benefit of Edmund's company at the moment so, at somewhat of a loose end, he desired Elinor as his sport for the day.

As Elinor drew near he rose from his stilled recline. Elinor looked towards the sudden movement. It was now that she noticed Francis rising from the knoll. He hurriedly moved to her with a smile on his face and stretched his hands towards her. Elinor flinched.

Accosting Elinor, he firmly gripped her by both elbows so that she was constricted. Francis smirked. He was wiry and strong, yet something was wrong with this girl – she pulled away from his advances.

'Come on, lass,' he had said with a leer. 'You know what I want and you want me.' He laughed in her face, while struggling to keep her in his grasp. 'You know you want me. I'm quite a catch and all of the other girls want me.'

At first Elinor had laughed nervously. 'Want you?' she repeated. She was amazed at his over-confident arrogance. 'What? What? Want a man with more pimples than intelligence!' she reposted, whilst pushing him away as best she could.

Francis did not like her words. He increased his strong grasp on her arms until it hurt.

'Ow! You're hurting me!' she yelped.

He did not let go when she pushed and twisted against his grip. He held her arms behind her, then caught her hair in his fingers. As she struggled, she realised his growing urgency. Francis grabbed out at her, hooked his ankle around hers and tripped her. He threw her to the ground, still wrestling as she struggled to free herself. She yelled as he tore at her soft close-fitted, cotton bodice with his spare hand. As this was laced to the front its thong-holes were easily torn, revealing her soft under-shift beneath. Nell fought fearlessly, tearing a scrap of soft cloth with a button from his coat, before raking his face with her finger-nails. She struggled in vain until his assault on her was carnally concluded. She felt his fetid breath panting, rapid on her skin.

Finally, Francis released his powerful grip for but a moment and she, taking advantage of her chance, hopped up onto her feet and ran as fast as she could. As she ran, she felt tears of anger and terror course down her cheeks, whilst she held her tattered clothing to her breasts.

Francis cussed and called insults after her as she clutched her chemise and skirts in her hands and fast fled for home. Francis laughed loudly so that she could hear, but in truth was annoyed that he bled while she escaped. He tenderly felt his own gouged face with his fingers as he stared after her, but did not try to follow.

Elinor glared, wild-eyed as she ran, but said nothing. Her mind was as wild as her demeanour. She had already begun to consider how to repay Francis' foiled attack with malice. Francis looked at his reflection in the shallow edge of the river where animals regularly drank. He could not hide his scratches, but he could tell another tale!

Later, in the inn with a pint in his hands, he reworked his story as he told his friends, '... and you know, Elinor Shaw tried to lure me into laying with her! Just look what she did to me when I told her, "Woman, there are better-looking cows in this field than you". She has marked me,' he whined. 'Tis one thing to be an old maid, but before long she'll be a sorry old thornback.' They were all aware that if a woman remained unwed as an 'old maid' for a length of time, she was thereafter unkindly referred to as a thornback.

His concocted, wild story regarding Elinor's desperate advances towards him, gave most who heard the story the notion that Elinor was impudent and immoral.

'She seeks a good-looking and fine husband that one, and if she can't get him any other way she will cheat him into a union.' His friends half-believed his story. Edmund had laughed long and loud, then retold Francis' story many times with great hilarity.

Elinor was furious when she heard the gossip. She considered telling Bill Boss and his wife, Catherine, but came to the conclusion that they would not help her, despite his job as a constable of the town watch.

'Nell, that man defiled *you*. You are his victim,' Mary grieved, yet she agreed to remain silent when Elinor had declared, 'There's little point in reporting it, for whichever side they take, I will ultimately be to blame.'

Mary had helped her bedraggled friend bathe her wounds after she had stumbled through the door. She cleansed and crooned over her. Elinor took powders to ensure she would not be with child and had moved between rants of anger and tears of sorrow. Catchevole also came to comfort her. He sought her side and sat by her as she lamented.

Mary mended the spoiled clothing as best she could, then went to the market, leaving the girl at home.

At market on the following day, she purchased a second-hand dress from the stubble-faced, rag-merchant, Laurence Landen. He gave her a good price for the clothing.

When Mary returned, her friend was in better spirits and further buoyed by the salvaged apparel she could not wait to wear. The dress that was once a loose gown, now bore inset sleeves and skirts that had been stitched together from two dresses, so bore side panels of a different material and a boned bodice. Elinor was delighted with her friend's choice.

While Nell stayed at home, within a couple of days, Francis was seen attending to his work with the herd as was usual. He had consumed a belly-full of ale during the day, but did not return home that night to his lodgings. This was not unusual, for he often spent time in the inns and at a house for whores, so did not always return until morning.

When his friends went looking for him the following day, they discovered him floating face-down in the river. It was assumed Francis had tripped while 'in his cups' and that, as a weak swimmer, he had accidentally drowned.

Later, as Mary took time to reflect on recent events, she was confused and bothered. She recalled that on the eve before Francis' death she had gone out to fetch water. There, she had found a corn-dolly bearing a worn scrap of cambric with a button attached. It was lying face down in the water-butt in the yard. The sight, though not overtly contentious, had for some reason bothered Mary. It was an issue for consideration and uncertainty. She did not wish to ask Elinor if it was she who had placed it there, but it did seem quite likely. Meanwhile, Elinor had recovered from her scare, scratches and physical blight. She was of a good disposition. She did not talk of the incident again.

...ooo000ooo...

Chapter 8
Green Lands and Hard Spaces

Lent began forty-six days before Easter - on the Popish Wednesday for donning ashes as a sign of penitence. Billy Heath would sell no meat today as Lent began with fasting and prayer. As eating red meat was religiously forbidden, Mary stocked her house with bread, greens and fish; plus a little butter and milk, which were also allowed in moderation.

On this pleasant Lenten day, Mary showed no hurry as she ambled to the baker to buy a loaf of bread and to get other supplies in the North End street shops. Mary looked forward to Easter, with eggs waiting at home at the back of the cool-room awaiting the time when they could be sold or consumed. At the moment the only punter for their dairy products was Catchevole, who benefitted from the fasting season.

Mary stopped to talk with her friends near a large building undergoing considerable alteration.

'Before very long this is going to be one of the most splendid houses in the street,' she had remarked in conversation with Beth Afford, the woman's small daughter and her quiet, widowed mother-in-law.

The shy child pulled behind her mother's skirts as Beth nodded in reply. 'We think so too, but there are others being built that might just rival it.' She observed, 'Little Dora likes to hear the workmen whistling and singing. 'Tis such a joyful sound.'

Now the winter had passed, the main door had been left open by workmen, allowing passers-by to peep inside. The workers didn't seem to mind as they were proud to show off their craftsmanship. Mary was amazed by the sheer size of the house, with empty land and gardens alongside for any future work. The family who owned it held fine Christian manners and were considered decent people of 'breeding'. The family always greeted Mary by wishing her a pleasant day. They lived comfortably and bought her knitted goods at a fair price. They stood in solid contrast to most people Mary saw in her capacity as a healer, who were impoverished folk living as large families in shared cottages. Poorer souls included Beth and her family who considered themselves lucky to live in a one-room up, one-room down dwelling, with a curtain dividing the space inside. These people were not of the swooning class. They could ill-afford to be.

As Mary ceased her musings she looked kindly at the child and said, 'Come, visit me in two weeks, I'll find you some eggs in celebration of the Resurrection.'

Mary glanced at the child and beamed. Although the reticent child still hid behind her mother, Beth thanked Mary and assured her that they would visit.

As she bid farewell to Beth and her family, a labourer sidled towards her and declared to Mary, 'T' local folk love to watch t' continual churning of t' other folk, like butter in a tub.' He indicated to the Afford's with his eyes and the merest movement of his head. Mary agreed with his sentiment as she went on her way.

As she walked on, hawkers trading from the backs of beasts and carts eyed her, certain she was an easy target for their trade. They moved from door to door to conduct their business, crying out their wares for all to hear. Mary had occasionally bought things from them, more out of goodwill than need. She bought a ladle from the travelling tinker, then continued her stroll through the thriving market. Horses, barrows, carts, cattle and sheep traversed the streets around her. She spotted Nell talking with Sarah Short. Elinor also saw Mary. She waved, then crossed the dirt-road to meet her. She nodded to the unkempt rag-merchant, Laurence Landen, who was busy with his family collecting a wide range of scraps to recycle. His brood ran to acquire household cast-offs. Laurence and his clan took the items home to be repaired and cleaned, then sold them on to other merchants. Mary watched as the Landen's called at the back entrances of the larger houses and knocked at the front doors of cottages. Laurence scavenged, bought cheaply and made his earnings from trading and swapping. Mary oft' used his services. The man was a master of novel ideas for re-use no matter what he found. His young family crafted toys and utensils of wood and scrap, which were sold as new creations to the locals.

'Why, look. There goes Laurence. I see he has dresses. Is there anything we need?' Elinor remarked.

'No, not today, Nell,' Mary replied. 'All he seems to be flogging are well-worn hand-me-downs from the Coles' household. I recognize them and refuse to be seen in Lizzie's cast-offs. I think there is naught we need here.'

Mary observed the gangly, unkempt man standing at the corner, pausing to reassemble his bundle of clothing and clanging, roped-together pans.

'Quick!' Elinor grabbed Mary's arm and pulled her down an alley. 'Mercy is heading our way.'

'No, Nell,' Mary said in surprise, while returning to their original route, 'that would be unkind. We can say hello, but tell her we're very busy today.'

Mary and Elinor walked back into the busy street and within mere seconds were intercepted by Mercy Elderkin.

'Good day to you both. I saw you looking at Mister Landen. He's a canny one, that's no mistake,' babbled Mercy, appearing at their shoulder. Neither of the women wished to talk for long with Mercy as her tattle was well known. They quickly wished her good day and moved on.

'She could change a half-farthing into a sixpence with her tongue,' suggested a bitter Elinor as they walked away.

Samuel, who had concluded his sale of two lambs in the livestock market, had scrutinised the young women for the last few minutes. He observed the girls as they stopped to talk briefly with Mistress Elderkin then, with a wave, headed in the opposite direction.

Samuel desired to talk with Mary, but had paid jobs awaiting. Later, as he walked home with a fine payment in hand, he considered his recent relationship with his belle. It seemed his dalliance with Mary had waned of late as they were both busily employed. He did not profess to understand her. Full with the activities of her work, he held the impression she had recently cooled towards him. 'We are so busy at the moment, then fatigued after working late,' he ruminated. Nevertheless, he was still enchanted by her. Of late she had been busy in day and evening, so they had not met as frequently as they had before. She had spent less time with him since the funeral of Francis Fisher and he knew not why. Of late, her time seemed taken by her lodger, Nell.

As he crossed the road, Samuel nodded and touched his forehead to acknowledge the gentleman lawyer, Stephen Bramston, who was busy building an impressive house at the top of Lark Lane by the bustling market. The gentleman saluted him in return. Bramston had recently attained prime position as a butt of curiosity for the lower classes. As gentry, possessing both power and money, the chatterers speculated on whom he would next be trying in the Courtroom. This work had paid for his fine and imposing home. Matching the ebb and flow of the nearby river, gentle chatter abounded in the community.

Later, inside the Ship Inn there was much to be assumed in speculation by those gathered over a convivial pint. Sam had completed his work early, so joined his father for an ale. 'Father, I saw Mister Bramston today. He looked in fine fettle.'

'Aye. He's climbed high,' William Barnes nodded to his tall son, 'as his friend, Mister Resbry, has. He's a chaplain to royalty,' he continued, 'but still pays visits to his friends the Bramston's … and his own family here, whenever he can.' He smiled slyly at Sam. 'I hear that he visits to show respect to his elderly father,' William stated while eyeing his own son and taking a sip of ale. His friends agreed with William's comments, while young Sam drank his ale and listened. He did not take the bait his father offered, for as far as Sam was concerned his father was not elderly, merely mid-aged. He saw that the townsfolk accepted any new subject for gossip with alacrity. The Bramston's, Creed's and Whitwell's were acknowledged affluent people with influence. Like other financially well-off families they were generally included in any local gossip.

Sam considered the Whitwell family over his pint. He had always admired William Whitwell, who always wished him a 'good day' in polite acknowledgement. The gentleman and his wife had settled in the large, newly-built Burysted House on their marriage, twelve years since. Mister Whitwell practised as a solicitor, yet rumour was not to be quelled. Garrulous lips held that the gentleman was late in marrying at twenty-six years, when he suddenly married the spirited sixteen-year-old, Sophia Borfett. She clearly was doted on by her husband. They were frequently seen walking arm-in-arm around the town. They were now a contented family with a son and daughters around them. The children played in the water in Duck Lane, a pond filled with lively quacking water fowl.

Sam knew that only three years since, William Whitwell had purchased the Tabret inn and had donated silver-plate to the church inscribed with his family emblem, the Talbot dog. As a trustee of the charitable 'Feoffees', he was keenly showed that he donated alms to the poor. Samuel considered that the town was built on the benefice of Christian men such as him. He mused on the man busy restoring the once timber-framed hostelry. The Tabret guest-house was rebuilt in stone with fine windows and slender panes of glass and flattened animal-horn that kept the warmth in and unwelcome creatures out. The impression of the labourers drinking in the pub was that all the rich people of the town were intermarried or related in one way or another.

Taking a familiar route around the town, Mary went out early the following morning, delivering salves and remedies. By the churchyard wall she paused to enjoy the comical ducks as they dipped in and out of the water, leaving shining liquid sparkles resting on their water-resistant back feathers. She observed those on the sides of the pond, tucking their heads beneath their wings to sleep in the early sunshine. Mary had noted Catchevole watching from behind the shadowy yew tree, but he made no attempt to creep forward to chase or catch them. Mary was sure that if she did not feed him her leftovers, a plump duck would make a very fine meal!

Mary strolled by the church. She looked around the boundary at the small grammar school, the 'hospitable' alms-houses reserved for men, which stood beside the tall house of God near the silent burial-yard.

As Mary delivered her wares to the large house set to the side of the church, she noted the vicar's wife, Susan Caldwell. Susan needed several pairs of stockings for their children and wards. By sight most knew her husband, the schoolmaster-vicar, Edward. He controlled his young charges with a sharp word and a quick cane. Once her trade with Susan had been completed with the usual ceremony of politeness, she continued following the narrow pathway.

Mary had to zig-zag to avoid boys racing from the building, enjoying a moment of respite from their studies playing with a rag-ball in the yard to the front of the church. Being children, they did not always look before they leapt!

The Reverend Caldwell looked aged, at two score and two. He had conducted old Isabel's funeral service and laid her to rest in the churchyard cemetery. He had more recently placed the bloated Francis Fisher into the cold earth. Edward preached good sense from the pulpit, setting out a devout charitable way of life for his flock. Again, none were exempt from tattle, for, after Caldwell's first wife died, in less than a year he had suddenly took a new bride, Susan Spenser. The fine-looking Susan carried her own rumours – and finances. She had been a young wife to old Edward Bedell, who died in 1693 and whom Caldwell had also duly buried in the parish churchyard. Rumour spread. The comings and goings of the vicar and his new wife, presented an excellent pastime for the babbling classes.

Mary dwelt on these thoughts as she exited the church grounds onto Bury Lane. She wondered if Susan knew what was spoken about her. Crossing the rutted roadway of Bury Street to the Turk's Head, Mary noted the busy ale-house was receiving a fresh supply of barrels. A large dray stood in the street swapping new for old, full for empty, while the horse bent its head to drink from a trough. Shouts and calls echoed from within the ale house. She passed-by a gentleman she recognised. He nodded at her and smiled as she bobbed a hint of a curtsey and smiled in return. His wife was a good customer who purchased hose on numerous occasions. Well-acquainted with her town fellows, she benefitted from their understanding and friendship.

The town thrived with taverns and resting houses of excellent repute, while others after dark were likely to raise an eyebrow or two, with adjacent passageways that, dimly-lit, served useful to whores and slatterns in procuring and servicing patrons. After earning a penny or two the least sensible would immediately spend their price on a filling pie or a pint of watery ale, without having to go more than a few paces. Others returned home to their families to put their money in a safe place for later. Mary knew women from each of these inclinations and had attended several. Here sat a pock-marked beggar, whom everyone knew had the 'French disease', sent as a punishment from God for bodily sin. Gum from holy wood or mercury pastes were the only treatments, neither was effective and this man could not afford medication. Mary knew many avoided him, as he was smelly. His disease was incurable. It caused insanity, rotted flesh and, finally, death. Mary stooped to put a small coin in his bowl before moving on.

As Mary walked by the open windows of the Tabret, she appreciated the smell of hot pigeon-meat pie - along with good ale (that had not noticeably been watered down). Although the street accommodated other inns and public meeting houses, none seemed as prestigious as the Tabret. Not a Gunter's chain away, the Crown held vicious dog fights in its courtyard. It was said to be haunted by an escaped Cavalier fighter from the last war who hid within to avoid persecution by the Parliamentarian militia. Mary assumed the man had been caught and strung up by the coach entrance, but had never seen any spectres. She was fairly certain that those who did had been inside, so were ale-soaked and in their cups.

Mary walked carefully past the steaming steeds, with equally steaming dung, newly arrived in the stables from York, Stamford or London. To the front of the establishment, carriages and horses waited for passengers and bags to be unloaded by the liveried coachmen. The stiffened ladies and genteel men had alighted and entered the inn to partake in refreshment and rest. Mary looked through the Tabret windows at them as she passed. She was interested in their drink - a costly, cold herbal infusion, the 'Countryman's Tisane', a cordial drink that was recently put out for sale - for the inflated fee of four shillings per bottle. It was advertised by locals and broadsheets 'to treat several distempers'. News of its efficacy travelled afar and Mary had heard that it was now sold in London.

Mary took a short cut through the coach yard to the lane and stables at the rear. Here she visited Joe, a stable lad, who had a painful inflammation in his eye. She bathed it with clear water and asked the youth to continue with a herbal sluice she provided. She was fairly sure that the moment she left he would fail to recall her instructions and discontinue the treatment.

Mary turned to return home uphill, by way of the drumming-well back-lane behind the guest house. Here were empty coaches and several sweating horses that were in the process of being rubbed down and stabled after their journeys. Mary heard the echo of her footsteps in the lane and knew of the water-well that was said to emit a military drum-beat prior to any shocking national event. Some said it drummed when King Charles had lost his head and for the Civil War. Mary had never heard it, but knew people who claimed they had.

This vicinity hummed with activity whenever a coach arrived. For poorer children who were not engaged in formal learning, this was an exciting daily spectacle. They could earn themselves a small coin or a crust of bread by helping out or by charming transient clients with their antics, unless they were hastily brushed away by the coachman and his helpers. Clouds scudded across the sky. Time moved differently and exaggerated the impotence of life.

She heard the bell and guessed that the children of the rich had completed their lessons for the day, while the poor laboured on at work.

As the day progressed, twilight meant lighting of lamps and candles. Windows twinkled as the rumbling of carts and padding footsteps steadily decreased until they ceased.

…oooOOOooo…

After the symbolic washing of feet in church on Maundy Thursday, prayer and planting of parsley on Holy Friday and copious cooking on Saturday, heckling adults and children squealed in pleasure at the St. George and the Dragon mummers in the market place. Easter Sunday came and went with its usual devotional celebrations. Pussy willows were carried in processions and crosses plaited from pussy willow "palms". These decorations would be valued and kept indoors to guard the houses from evil throughout the year.

Full of bread, milk and hare pie, Mary arrived in Benefield after a tiring journey. She had been called in to treat the frail, Mistress Susannah Wise. Here Mary discovered that she was dealing with a mystery illness. The woman's near-deaf, drab friend, Mistress Evans, was bellicose and quickly disliked Mary as she bustled the belligerent busybody downstairs and out of the house.

Mistress Wise looked frail, but under forty years. Susannah was clearly unwell and experiencing hallucinations. She talked in delirium of kittens that she saw on the ceiling, floor, shelves and furniture - even in the trees outside, although Mary saw none. Mary sedated her and visited daily to treat her needs, which she put above her chores and other work she needed to do. In her state of delirium, Mistress Wise seemed most concerned that she would not be able to feed her phantom kittens - as her cow could not produce enough milk for them all. Mary was not even sure if she had a cow! Mary gave her poppy seed tea to enforce sleep.

On a few occasions, Elinor accompanied Mary to the household – sometimes just joining her to walk home after Nell had bartered her items in the village. She perceived the journey was quite lonely and took at least an hour to get to the tiny downhill village from the town on foot.

After a week the small woman rallied. Mary blamed the onset of illness on the woman's drinking of strong wine and eating bad bread, which Mistress Wise admitted to consuming just before she fell sick. She now seemed quite rational. She thanked both Mary and Elinor for aiding her recovery. As she was much recuperated and had the benefit of close friends, the curers ceased their visits.

Soon all was forgotten, except by the coldly indifferent Mistress Evans, who remained aloof and bore them something of a grudge. Quite some time later, as Mary sold her wares at the market, she chanced to speak with Mercy and Constance. They perennially knew all the news and gossip.

'Did you hear what's happened to Mistress Wise of Benefield? Did you not treat her ailment last month?' they asked.

Mercy noted their confusion and hissed in a low voice, 'Susannah Wise died suddenly last night. Her husband's come to town to consult Reverend Caldwell and is now in the inn sharing his sorrows with all who will listen.'

Mary was aghast at the news, as she'd assumed Susannah's malady had abated. She could only suppose that the woman had been at the mouldy bread and acrid wine again.

Within the week, Elinor, she and a small group of friends walked to Susannah's funeral. It was very well attended. Appearing from nowhere, the woman's husband, Robert Wise, came over the damp grass to talk with the women and offer his thanks for their ministrations.

In contrast, Mistress Evans did not speak to the women and remained hostile and contentious. Mary took no offense as she realised the angry woman was grieving for her friend. As they walked solemnly home from the village funeral, Elinor commented to Mary, 'What a stroppy harridan. I sincerely hope we never see that woman ever again.'

After the long walk home, they arrived at twilight. The bats, as was their custom on clement May evenings such as this, were active, swooping and soaring in the fading rays of the light, catching flies in mid-air. They were oft' seen flying over the vegetable patch at this time of day.

Mary looked around at her garden with a grave countenance. Nell noted her sadness.

'Look, Mary,' said her friend as her fast-finger pointed at the flitting shape, 'that's my favourite. I've named him Westing.'

Mary gave her a quizzical look and at length asked, 'Why such a strange name, Nell?'

Her friend chuckled, ''Cos he's awake now – but in the day when ev'wy won wakens - he's westing.'

Both laughed until tears of mirth ran down their cheeks. Any levity on this grim day was a blessed respite.

'Come Nell.' Mary sighed as she guided her friend towards their abode. 'That's exactly what we need to be doing – resting. We need to eat some bread and cheese for tomorrow will not be a shorter day than today.'

With this the women, arm-in-arm, accompanied by their hungry coal-coloured cat who suddenly appeared as if by magic from the nearby shrubbery, entered the house and settled for the night as the bats danced in the pastel moonlight.

...ooo000ooo...

Chapter 9
A Bad Egg

At the Coles' household, the old dog lay in the sunshine. The warm rays moved steadily over the dirt floor, marking the passing of the hours. As the sun made progress, so too did the canine, keeping itself warm while he could. All seemed calm as Lizzie passed by her sibling as she entered the garden. Without warning, she deftly gave the child a clip around his ear that left him hurt and crying.

'Why did she do that?' whispered their sister, Annie, staring after Lizzie as she entered the silent kitchen. 'I don't understand Lizzie at all.'

There were smells of fragrant cooking, but she paid no heed. Lizzie kicked out viciously at the old dog with her shoe as she passed.

'Good for nothing dog,' she sneered. The side of her lip lifted as she shouted scorn at the tired dog as her mother entered the kitchen. 'Get out, you flea ridden bitch.'

'Good-day, daughter,' called her mother brightly as she turned from the oven with a steaming pot in her sleeve-wrapped hands. Ruth cast a sideways eye at Lizzie as she crossed the flagstones to the stone oven.

Ruth did not bear the same temperament as her daughter. Joseph, her husband, had oft' speculated, 'We've given Lizzie everything we can afford to keep her sweet, yet she's like a changeling; completely different in nature from both of us'.

Lizzie glanced in her mother's direction, but the girl remained coldly silent. She glared at her parent as she stalked from the room. Her mother looked at her retreating back. Lizzie was the most challenging of her children. She shook her head and looked down at the trembling dog. It raised itself and walked shakily through the door into the garden.

'Oh dear.' Ruth breathed in deeply and out again with a fearful intensity. She closed her eyes in exasperation as she carefully placed the pot on the table. 'What is it now?' she whispered to the empty room.

...oooO00Oooo...

Late in the day around midsummer, Samuel set forth from work later than was usual. As he strolled through the long grass by the river he chortled at thoughts of his future with, God willing, a wife and children of his own. Whoever he chose, they would be welcomed by his father and brother to live with them. Sam would most certainly need to work hard to support a growing brood, he mused. Life was by no means simple but, with a loving family around him, it would be near perfection. Sam rubbed his aching muscles in his upper arms. The day had been balmy and warm. The cattle, long since milked by the dairy-maids, were stowed in the barn with fodder for the night. Sam headed home to find if his father had already set to cooking their evening meal and if so, what it was.

'A farewell to you, my nymphs,' called a disembodied voice with a feminine chuckle. Sam heard a reply from another. The sound emanated from beyond the copse and nettle-filled ditch. His surroundings hid him so effectively that he could not see the girl or to whom she spoke. 'I will see you on the morrow,' continued a girlish voice. He detected a rustling, then the sound of running feet moving away from the river.

'I so enjoy our quiet times,' came a richer, melodious voice. 'My shoulders are so sore from carrying the yoke today. This is absolute bliss.'

Samuel listened to the familiar young women gathered down the sloped bank by the river. They were as concealed behind the thick foliage as was he. Samuel knew he should walk on, but continued to eavesdrop. He retreated further into the copse for cover. A sudden gust of air stirred the leaves, but he could still hear clearly, as the voices carried in the wind.

'Come. Come!' called a spirited voice. 'Just look how it glitters in the light. See how clear it is.'

'Come on in. Relax for a time. We've worked the hot day through, so come, ease your aches and purify yourself. The water is so cool.'

'Hoi there. Here I come! Watch out little fishes,' called a girlish voice, followed by fast pattering feet and a loud splash, as if something heavy had been tossed into the river. Voices shrieked, then boisterous, high-pitched laughter filled the usually peaceful place.

Samuel listened to the happy sounds and the low-voiced conversation. He grinned to himself. He guessed that the girls were dipping toes, paddling and swimming in the shallows of the river. Careless in their motions much as the diving ducks do. At first, Sam was joyfully heedless, but now his spying had reached a point where he could not easily move away. His mind pictured each young woman naked - as he recognised and set a face to each familiar vocalisation. He listened, stealthily tipping his head to one side to hear each illicit word - amused at the thought that he was not seen by the laughing individuals.

'I'm so, so … sorry if I've been slipshod,' came a satirical call. Snorts, guffaws and giggles followed as Samuel recognised the falsely jovial tone with which the voice spoke. A fun-loving vibrato contradicted her germinal words as girlish laughter beat upon his ears. Sam smiled in undisclosed kinship with them, while subconsciously creeping nearer to peep. He wished that he could observe them swimming, undetected. Departed were the days when, as children, they were permitted to swim and play together by the riverside. With this recollection, Sam softly turned to creep from the undergrowth and continue the walk home. His breathing broadcast too loudly, but he knew his feet had made not a sound. His broken journey had not been seen or heard by the unsuspecting lasses.

As he passed the end of the coppice, Sam turned his head to check over his shoulder. He spontaneously winced in discomfiture as he witnessed three gleaming girls hauling themselves to the top of the grassy bank. They'd known each other since they were tiny, but this seemed quite different. The women appeared pale and beautiful in the late, dappled sunlight. Frolicking, bare, with water-darkened filaments of gold and auburn, their tresses hung unfettered. Sam stayed spellbound by their exposed locks - glued slick to aquatic, gleaming shoulders and backs.

As he retreated, Sam heard Hetty Linton squeal, 'If you splash me again, Nell, I'll climb out and take your clothes!'

'That won't bother me, I'll just stay in the river,' Elinor replied with giggle.

'It will if I run off with them - and you have to return home in the buff,' Hetty joked. 'That would give all the local lads a treat.'

Elinor had laughed loudly, raised her arms skyward, stood for a moment and dived down into the sparkling water. She was a mystical mermaid in Sam's mind. The girls continued laughing and chattering (now too distant for him to hear what they said).

The group were unaware of his attentions. For a fleeting moment Elinor sensed she was observed, so looked around. She spotted a silent Catchevole in the shadows at the top of the bank, so called softly with a burbling laugh, brushing notions of another observer from her thoughts. Elinor grinned as the cat blinked apple-green eyes in the shade, steadily shook his head as he sniffed the air, stood, stretched and then quietly vanished into the long grasses. Nell dipped down to slide softly back into the ripples.

Sam walked on. 'On another scorching day around this hour,' he thought to himself with a chortle, 'I most surely need to pass this way again.'

...oooO00Oooo...

Elinor's body was at ease. Her mind was at peace and her spirit relaxed. The sound of gentle splashing and refracted light from the fading sun glittered on brilliant ripples, creating a soothing and somnolent mood within her. As the watery liquor engulfed her, she let the immediate world around her sink low in her mind. She did not heed sound, yet her perception appeared heightened. Her mother had given her a name at birth and she was indeed a 'shining light' - a bright one. She bathed in the twilight waters, long after the others had said their goodbyes.

Shortly after the rowdy drove had dried and departed homeward, an amused Mary Phillips strolled up to the water's edge. Her basket was near empty - her day's work complete. She clambered down the green bank, swinging her bonnet by its shiny, mulberry-hued ribbons. Her hair hung unbound. Elinor swam silently. She supposed Mary was unaware of her. Mary, lost in thought, removed shoes from tired feet to dip them in the cooling shallows. She was rapidly roused from her reverie by a spray of water that pattered onto her skirts. Mary looked around, angered.

Stopped in her tracks, she eyed Elinor. Her ire swiftly thawed like ice by a fire. There was a close symbiosis between them. With a giggle and a smile, Mary carefully stripped off her clothing by the felled log, just as others had done before, then languidly slid into the water to join her friend.

'Where are the others?' she asked.

'They've gone. They were already here some time before I arrived and are wrinkled like hags!' They both laughed, before Mary remarked, 'Nell, it has been a busy day. What have you been doing?'

Elinor snorted and pulled a wide-eyed face. 'Looking for a good man!' she laughed.

'Nell! You plan to leave me then?' asked Mary as Elinor flopped onto her back in the water with a loud splash, 'You are as a sister to me.'

'You also look after me. This is my happiness.' She dripped water from her palm and gently ran her fingers down her friend's back. Elinor continued, 'You see how people like you. You're careful with your tongue and easy in your manner ... Usually.' She rolled in the water like an eel. 'There is no man who can care for me better than I. It has always been best that I look out for myself.'

Mary closed her eyes and thought about this for a moment. In her childhood, she was considered 'sweet', with a spoonful of shyness thrown in for good measure. Mary knew that her friend envied her, but also guessed that Nell could create a smile on the faces of those she met without too much effort if she wished it. Elinor did not always try. Some folk were cautious and excluded Elinor from their ministrations. She had started life in a small, rural village, well aware she could never be considered 'local' by those born to the town. For no apparent reason the townsfolk looked down on 'outsiders', no matter how long since they had arrived.

'Nell, you are a remarkable friend. I know that you will always remain faithfully by my side.' With this Mary let the silence reign.

Their gentle splashing could be heard by the small animals and birds in the vicinity. The diminishing noises continued for some time, fading until there was nothing left, except for the awakening night birds – and a few small, crazy sparrows challenging and arguing for their night-time nesting places within the tangled branches and briars.

Long after the women had dried themselves on their shawls and had walked home with shoes dangling from their hands, the air was filled with the sweet scents of orange-blossom. Peace descended upon the tranquil river and its environs - as it had each sunset for time unbound. Each and every night after twilight, day faded into the familiar quiet of darkness.

The following morning a new sun rose as an orange orb, then steadily changed to a gold-amber honey ball in a blue, cloudless sky. Seeing this, Elinor had left the house in a good humour. She ran through the meadow and lifted her skirts to jump the wide grass-filled ditch. Here she collected brightly coloured king-cups from amidst the long grasses. She looked closely at the green plants. Mary had well taught her how to detect hemlock from cow parsley by the smell. She left the field to trip, skip and dance her way down to the street. She did not care who saw or disapproved of her, with her skirts lifted to reveal her shapely, bare calves. With a wide smile spread on her face and gentle, brown eyes shining, she cordially greeted those she met.

Not looking ahead, she had omitted seeing three similarly-aged girls standing at the corner house watching her progress. Elinor stopped in her tracks to remove wild teasels and seeds caught in her skirts. She knew it would be a challenge, picking the tiny clasps and hooks of the plants out of every fibre of cloth with her slender fingers. The young women watched silently.

Elinor stood transfixed to admire a ladybird as it landed on an ivy-leaf wall. She looked aloft at a nearby tree. There, splendid in its white waistcoat and blue-black jacket plumage, sat a magpie. It had landed in the lowest branches of the beech tree and eyed Nell.

'Good morning to you, Mister Magpie,' she said as the unusually silent gaggle nudged and watched on.

...ooo000ooo...

Lizzie Coles' father collected his youngest son, Tom, and the boy's pal, Wilf Barnes, to help him check rabbit snares in the nearby woodlands. On their walk to

132

the woods each carried an empty sack thrown over their shoulder. Joseph had warned the lads to remain as quiet as possible, so as not to disturb the wildlife.

'Take good care boys,' warned Joseph. 'Don't go touchin' or steppin' on anything you're not sure of … and don't get caught in a snare for the string and wire can cut through the neck of a rabbit with ease.' He continued, 'If the snare has caught something, you can cut it lose. Call to me, soft like, and I can set a new one in its place.'

This warning was hardly out of the man's mouth before he heard a snap. Too late, Wilf had found himself snared. The sharp thwack reverberated around the clearing. The snare had been well-hidden and its noose had caught him unaware. His lower leg suffused with pain. Joseph was by his side almost immediately. He called out to his son to stand very still while he release Wilf from the trap. He did not want two injured boys on one trip.

'Shit!' mouthed Tom. Joseph acted quickly. He tore a loose strip from his shirt and wrapped it around Wilf's leg. The boy wore stout boots, which had saved his limb from being sliced into two parts. With blood dripping freely on the flattened grass, Joe tenderly released the lad from the trap. Both boys were trembling – one from shock and the other from fear. The man tied part of the sacking tightly around the lad's leg and sent Tom ahead to the road. He hefted Wilf onto his sinewy shoulders, then carried the wilting boy on his back to the cart-track.

As luck would have it, Laurence Landen was passing with his horse and cart. Tom and Laurence helped a very pale-faced Wilf onto the back of the cart, before joining him there for the lift home. Their first stop was at the house of the surgeon, but he was not at home.

On arrival at the Barnes' home, William rapidly sent young Tom to run to find Mary, who came as soon as she heard and as fast as she could. Breathless, she and Tom ran through the open door of the house. She carried her sewing bag with her and swiftly stitched the wound that ran all the way around his lower leg. The bleed slowed to a trickle, then the compress she used quenched the flow.

'Your leg will be fine, Wilf,' she reassured the boy, 'it was saved by your boot and the woody plants that caught in the snare, but it will be some time before you can walk properly on it.' Mary grimaced. 'You will need some medicated tea to soothe the pain. I will make some.' Mary hoped that the infection would not be too severe. She looked to William. 'If Wilf develops a fever, has any swelling or a green discharge from his wound you should call me straight away … at any time … even if it is in the middle of the night. Promise me you will.'

Gently, she finished by tying up the fine cord and removing her wire needle. She knew the wound looked red and painful. She hoped there would be no infection to make matters any worse. William, stunned into silence by the events of the past hour, nodded his assent.

When Mary looked at the assembled group she decided they would all require some tea. She re-boiled the kettle over the fire and served them infusions until the colour returned to their gaunt faces before taking her leave of them.

By the time Samuel returned from his work in the fields with new blisters on his hands, his father had much recovered, sitting by the side of his youngest son, who was comfortable and fast asleep.

Wilf made a steady recovery over the next few weeks. Samuel and William were delighted whenever Mary visited to check on the boy. Samuel re-kindled his unique bond with her over the gentle care of his brother. As the boy convalesced, his family rallied round. They knew the lad felt guilty at not being able to work or take his share of chores around the home.

Once back on his feet again, Sam cheered his sibling greatly as he accompanied him on short walks and fishing expeditions. Wilf was quiet and patient, so caught several fish. Sam was almost as quiet as he observed his captivated brother.

'How unalike we are,' he thought. Wilf looked very much like a younger version of his father - and Sam more resembled his fair mother. As children they had argued and bickered, but this happened less and less as they matured and came to terms with their differences.

Whilst Wilf fished, they both watched the waterfowl and passed the time of day with walkers who cut across the fields to reach Ashton and beyond. They would amble past the cross-roads and sit by the gnarled tree to rest a while. Occasionally Mary would stop to chat on her way to the see the growing Millward family at the mill. As she returned home with a lighter basket, they oft' offered her a gleaming fish to take for her evening meal. Willowy Wilf was glad that he had thought of a method to repay her in some small way, as she would take no money for his cure. Catchevole would also benefit from the leftovers from his tasty offering.

Samuel went to great trouble to ensure his encounters with Mary were innocent within the sight of others. Yet, she marked his small tokens of wild flowers, eggs and small talk, as signs of his interest. Mary constantly blushed when they met together in public and felt this clearly showed others her feelings for Sam.

'It's as obvious as a fire in the dark,' she thought.

Meanwhile, Elinor was growing to be a pretty lass, no longer the gaunt child she had been when Mary took her in. At times, Elinor used womanly intuition as to where Mary would be at any given time. She often guessed that Sam and Mary were together. Whenever they met each were at ease in an accustomed friendship; often meeting by pure chance and good fortune, not by design. On her part, Mary felt relaxed and comforted by Sam – and easily attracted to him.

As weeks passed, he was frequently informed by his palpitating heart that Mary was both, well-disposed and beautiful in his eyes. Firstly, they only talked and laughed together. Samuel had noted their matched enjoyment in the world about them. After a time they held hands in conducting their close conversations.

Later, in moments when they met privately, her skin was smooth to caress and gentle against his lips. Samuel recognised with amazed clarity a moment he believed he would never forget when he met Mary by the plank bridge - by earlier agreement. They joined in the flood-fields beside the river, where no prying eyes or clacking tongues could halt them. As far as they could tell, none knew of their romantic riverside trysts. The fields by the North Bridge were wet and boggy in the winter and early spring. Few walked there as the land was likely to flood in heavy rain. As they walked they discussed small things, then they looked to their future together. Samuel felt obliged to ask Mary to explain their plans for the future to Nell.

'After all, Elinor may have to live alone when we marry and you move in to live with my family.'

Mary was uncertain that she wanted to move. 'Elinor is as close as a sister, how can I leave her?'

'I will do all for you, Mary. You are my one sweet love, but we can't live with a lodger, as our household will already be crammed,' he had explained, '... but we can both visit.'

Mary returned home unsure how to broach this with Elinor, but after a time, came to believe that Nell would understand. Yet, the young woman never found the correct moment to raise the subject with her friend.

As the days passed Mary and Sam's courtship continued and they were often seen placidly ambling around the town together, arm-in-arm. Many were the times that Sam moved to stand next to Mary when the crowds gathered to hear the crier tell of current events. Handbills were posted in prime locations, but Mary and Sam preferred to listen, faceless as part of the throng, rather than look at the illustrated hand-bills. In the bustling crowd, Samuel, who believed he was undetected by others, would silently slip his hand into the crook of Mary's elbow or hold on to the tips of her cool fingers, hidden in the folds of his coat or the pockets of her skirts. Both had failed to notice Lizzie as she privately noted Samuel's attentive closeness to Mary. Those who did see her, had no inclination of her thoughts and failed to see the sourness in her soul.

Some days later as the sun shone high in the clouds, pretty Lizzie set off to market. Today she walked alone. Solitary in her reverie, she felt joyful that the weather had somewhat improved. Her elation showed in her steps and voice as she pleasantly greeted people she knew. Lizzie had already marked Mary, who had been busy from an early hour preparing for the day. She observed as Mary walked ahead, so likewise, Lizzie slowed her pace. She gained an amusement in not allowing herself to catch-up with her one-time friend.

The more Mary loitered by each stall to check on food-stuffs for sale or slowed to speak with people she knew, the more Lizzie did also. She watched from the corner of her eye as Mary eventually settled on the steps of the cross, chatting to those already setting out their saleable wares.

Lizzie awaited her moment, primed with venom and ready for confrontation. She walked smoothly, with a smile on her Jezebel lips, over to the cross to look at the wares arrayed and displayed. Today Lizzie had ruminated on her troubles. Being steadfast in her own inclinations and motive, she ensured cordiality and politeness to all that might bear witness. She casually looked at several of the displayed wares, then plucked some eggs from Mary's stall as if to examine them before making a purchase. Within seconds they had slipped from her fingers and smashed on the ground with their runny yolks spreading like a yellow puddle.

People stopped what they were doing to watch. Lizzie gasped in apparent surprise, but Mary was fully aware that this had been no accident.

'Oh, my! Goodness me! Why, your eggs were slippery in my hands! What a mistake! Did you not think of wiping them clean before bringing them to sell?' Lizzie demanded. In her spite she made no attempt to pay for the broken eggs, yet moved her skirts so they would not touch the slimy vestiges on the ground. She smiled with her closed mouth widened, all too sweetly, before moving away a pace without apology.

Mary knew that she would receive no compensation for her goods or indignation. She would go home with fewer pennies in her purse. She was surprised and saddened, but part of her was also displeased and angry. As Lizzie turned away, Mary could bear it no longer.

'Damnation, "Lizzie Coles!' she called out to the girl's retreating back. 'Why did you do that? Stop stirring up trouble.'

'May hell's curses be heaped on you! I'm not stirring, you are the troublemaker ... a hapless woman with the brain of a woolly knot!' Lizzie yelled back. She made sure all who needed to hear, heard. Mary saw this as a deliberate act on Lizzie's part, to make her life harder. For now, she had more immediate problems to attend to, as two stray dogs had appeared as if by magic to quickly lick at the viscous egg slime around her feet. As they hungrily fed they cleared the mess away.

On her homeward flight, Mary met with Elinor on the road. Elinor, who was on her way back to the cottage from selling hosiery to Widow Cooper, was shocked to see Mary out of spirits. Mary was angry as she told Elinor what had befallen her. Nell listened patiently in silence for a time, then decided to go one step further. Her brow remained creased with furrows of fury.

'I have an idea,' the young girl said.

'What is it, Nell?' Mary pursued.

'Just an idea ...' She would say no more.

On arrival at the cottage Elinor narrowed her green-grey eyes to look away into the distance. She pursed her lips in thought. She entered their house, sat, paced the room, then sat once again. Catchevole, who had entered with them, stayed well clear of her.

'Sit Nell,' Mary had said, 'You are making my head ache with your continued pacing and fidgeting.'

Elinor glanced in her direction and paused. Finally she lifted her hand and pointed aloft with her index finger. She quietly announced, 'I have an idea. I believe that I know how to stop this from happening ever again.' She rose to retrieve her basket of threads. 'No person is going to make you unhappy, no matter who it is.' She cleared her throat. 'I will make you a charm to prevent us from losing our income to chance ever again.'

'Do you think that you can make an effective charm?' Mary queried.

Elinor did not answer, instead she steadily tied a carefully interlaced, woollen plait. This she placed around Mary's slender wrist and uttered a quiet oath over her home-made bracelet. 'May she who seeks to throw away our living have her own arrangements destroyed here-after.' She spoke simply and angrily, knowing that she had done all that she could in the circumstances. She surmised that if the charm did not work, she would see to it that something stronger would.

Mary remained distressed by the waste of eggs and by Lizzie's apparent hatred of her. They had been friends! She recognised that for now they, more likely than not, would need to survive with a little less income from their market sales than they had hoped. She also knew that there may be some days ahead where they would go hungry as a result of their spat, as the market women would no doubt tell their friends of what had occurred. Elinor promised her help in any way that she could.

Two days later the women of the town gathered once again by the butter cross to sell their wares. Several shoppers admired the pretty new wristlet that Mary wore. Elinor explained that it was "a magical charm" and saw that this was perhaps a new trade for them. She could make and sell charms in the market to their profit. Over the coming days she made several more trinkets that sold very well.

Subsequently, Nell began by charming any passing traveller with her growing range of ointments good-luck charms and the mystical words that passed along with them. These seemed small-fare for her, but gained a good exchange. She contributed to Mary's larder stocks with her sales.

'I can enchant it for you if you wish?' she offered, as she passed a tied heart to a young customer. The customer considered her offer, then shook his head and paid for the piece.

'Easy, Nell,' warned her friend. Elinor paid little heed. 'Perhaps selling to strangers may not be best for us? Just sell the bracelet, they don't need enchanting.'

A tall traveller perusing wares looked askance as Elinor moved her smiling gaze from him to loudly curse as Lizzie passed by. Nell wished a pox on her for her past misdemeanours. Lizzie retaliated with discourteous words of her own. The row was also noted by the street dogs, who were bothered by the ruckus, so proceeded to move some distance away. The wide-eyed traveller moved a few paces away in kind. Out of sorts, Lizzie, set up her wares nearby was unable to sell anything on that day.

As time passed, Elinor realised that she made easy money selling her homemade charms at the market, especially as Lizzie would no longer venture near. Elinor noted that the charm she made for Mary was still seemingly working as Lizzie kept her distance.

Nell's new trade was easy work, relative to the efforts involved in knitting stockings or making small pieces of fragile lace. She put her hands onto Mary's shoulders and looked her in the eye. She was calm and easily convinced her friend that now all would be well.

In celebration, the two went out for an ale. There, Nell was shushed by Mary, as she had made light of the controlling powers of England - almost as much as she was scolded for her immodesty. Exiting a tavern, she shivered as the blustery wind tugged at the ribbons at the throat of her gown, wrapping them around her neck. Mary unwound them and glanced around at the watchmen standing in sentinel stillness. A jolt took her with a feeling of forewarning as intuition warned that someone watched. Mary turned and saw, lingering silently by a wall, a strange stripling of a child. She stood aloof, unaccompanied, as people passed without a glance. The girl's manner caused Mary's hairs to stand on end. She shivered, but not from the cold. The child stared back with vacant eyes. Mary looked away. When she glanced again, the ragged, pale girl had gone. Mary looked around intently, but the child was nowhere to be seen. None nearby had noted the rag-tag urchin. Uneasy, Mary returned home.

…ooo000ooo…

Chapter 10
A Harvest of Passions and Desires

The seasonal labours progressed without respite. The reaping and mowing had been, more or less, completed for the year, with the chaff for fodder, hay and grain safely stowed away before the turning-colours of the leaves in autumn. It would not be long before the wheel of time turned and children played quarrelsome games of conkers with shiny horse-chestnuts on thongs as the town and its nearby farms prepared for the coming winter. For now, mowing and scything skills earnt labourers 'a shilling-'n'-eight pence' each day, with ten pence more if the worker went on throughout the day without lunch. Young Wilfrid was delighted.

'I have a whole shilling and eight pence,' the lad smiled as he happily checked the coins in his hand. His father patted him on the head.

'Indeed you have, son,' William remarked, 'and you can keep a whole four of 'em for yourself.'

Wilf was well pleased with this deal. He saw that his hardy brother earned much more, yet every morning Samuel needed to rise with the sun, while Wilf could stay abed a little longer. Soon Sam would progress to more difficult jobs and Wilf would be the cow herder.

Today, Wilf had watched from their cot as Samuel poured cold water from the wash-jug into a dish to quench his thirst, then took a quick 'splash' wash in a little more, before hurriedly dressing and quietly leaving the house. He knew that, in a few weeks from now, the wash-water would stand frozen in the jug!

Their father had not stirred and neither son wished to awaken him. Today, Sam picked up a small crust of bread from the crock to eat on his way to the field. His stomach grumbled in agreement. If he was to meet anyone on his way he would defer this to consume as a midday repast. In the summer months, more times than not, he would leave the house without eating.

After Sam had left, Wilf swung his legs from the wooden frame of the bed. He looked at his injured leg and flexed it. He would always have a slight limp, but the limb had been saved by Joseph Coles' and Mary Phillips' quick reactions. Wilf was glad that Sam and Mary were sweethearts. He was not sure about Mary's irrational friend, but she held no impact on him. She would probably be in the fields today. For, after the annual harvest was gathered, all knew that a time of celebration followed - full with high-spirited gratitude.

The early morning gleaning bell called to all poor cottage-dwellers with no land of their own, as they were allowed to collect leftover harvest remnants from the edges of the fields. It would toll again at dusk to end their work. Those who were not fit enough to collect the surplus crops, over-ripened fruits and vegetables were often given welcome gifts by those who could.

By mid-autumn the weather had set in. Sam went slowly down the sinuous lane with a squelch and slop in seasonal sludge, collecting muddied cattle from the smallholdings. Careful not to slip, the fresh-faced man passed each house while tenants chased out their beasts to follow him. Each cow knew Sam. They were keen to reach the common-land to graze on tufty clumps of moreish wet grass. Samuel needed to chivvy them along. They preferred to wander whenever succulent grasses lured. Farmers often butchered their own stock in icy winter months. Meat lasted longer in the cold.

144

The beasts were slow and held their own mind to pause wherever they wished to munch in juicy pastures. Like the cattle, Sam was in no hurry. He knew the herd - and who owned each of them. Sam led their own cattle to pasture with those of his neighbours. When the time came he would help in the task of cow-'nobbing' to remove their horns to make herding safer and milking easier. Nothing of the fattening beasts was ever wasted. Cows provided milk, meat, skins, while the versatile horns were whittled by the horner's to make fine flasks, spoons, combs and buttons.

On Sam's arrival at the shared land that remained 'common' for all, he would spend warmer days herding the milk-cows. Sam guided them with a staff to prevent them from wandering too far. He frowned as he caught sight of the sleek, svelte Catchevole as the morning mists rose. There skittered the stealthy predator, as the lithe feline lurked in the overgrown bushes, catching mice, rats and voles - or trying to secure himself a small bird. Samuel stilled his walk, bent at the knee and held out his hand to this early morning companion. Catchevole came nearer. His shining eyes keen and alert. Perhaps Samuel had a titbit for him? Samuel spoke in a soft, quiet lilt, as he took out his pack and tore small crumbs of his bread for the cat, then stood slowly to continue on his way. Rarely was Sam allowed near enough to stroke the solitary tom or hear the blackened beast purr in pleasure, but knew that he could. He saw this cat and he held calm company.

The alert mammal bore soft dark fur that, every now and then, was matted from rooting around in a leafy copse or a climbing scratched tree to catch unlucky prey with piercing teeth and pin-like retractable claws. Oft' were the times that Samuel questioned if the cat possessed a power that allowed him to suddenly fly into the branches of any gnarled, shady tree. The small fiend was fast and skilled in the uppermost branches. Catchevole also knew his way home and how to navigate around the town safely. The adept watcher was also a practised listener. Sam hoped that Catchevole would not catch birds, although he knew that it was in his nature. The sudden deaths of a rodent or two did not disturb Sam, but tossing and catching small birds seemed a cruel game. Often the cat did not eat his prey, but teased and played with the creature until it died. On steadfast, firm feet, it was mere play without appetite or gruesome gifts for the two women who co-habited the cottage with him.

Sam's affection for the lush woodlands and fields was full-fledged in him from childhood. He now knew birds by their song and each tree, brook and safe crossing place. He recognised the gentle rise and fall of the mellow green-brown landscape. Even in cold days when blanketed in white, he loved the land he called home.

Each day, another of his loves would appear, singing her way along the lane, before she could be seen. Mary was habitually happy. Samuel longed for the moment she would walk by on her way to market with a gossiping drove of women or to tend to her charges. The younger girls of the dairy went together after the milking was done with the older, married women leading the way. His Mary was not one of these, so never loitered. The girls were tardy and in no hurry to reach the hubbub of market and later would gain further chores if they hurried home.

Walking slowly, full of spilling-conversations, they ambled by old Granny Craythorne, who went to market when she could. She was not fast, nor was she related to the girls, but everyone called her 'Granny' as a title befitting age and status in the small community. As she bimbled, Granny yakked on about her copious aches and continual pains. The growing multitude of which included those of her legs and hips. Few paid her heed, as the old woman loved explaining that she was 'awaiting the grim Reaper' - for more than the last decade.

With arms linked the girls sang whenever they thought no-one was listening. They were a genial, jolly lot most of the time. In the colder months, they shared shielding their produce from bitter winds, sudden gusts of rain or sleet that chilled and whipped their cloaks and skirts up around their knees. Like little birds, they would seek shelter in the lee-side of a building or take refuge in a barn as rain drummed noisily on the protective thick thatch, while they hung-together, giggling and shouting above the reverberating resonance of the squall.

Today, Sam noted, they had apparently left the old woman in their wake. As the younger women-folk went on their way to market unattended, he could hear them talking. From his repose by the barn, Samuel heard one ask, 'Did you hear about young Dick, the carpenter's apprentice?'

'What?' queried her friend. 'That his daily wage has gone up to two shillings? Yes, I heard that.'

'No,' came the annoyed rebuke with the huff of sharp outward breath, '... about his new darling.'

'His sweetheart? No.'

'Well, I heard that he's courting Meggie Willis,' she said, 'but that may not be absolutely true, as I've not yet seen them together, I just heard it from Ambrose.'

'I've certainly not heard that.' The other shrugged with an irritated air, '... and Ambrose is a bit of a wag.'

'Well, you have not kept up! That was ages ago. He's now walking out with Kitty Laxton and she followed after Freida Bassett and before that ... Well, you know.'

'We all know what Dick is like, but he's nothing special.'

'Mark my words, a day will come when Kitty will make a married man of young Dick - and she'll look after his money too,' the speaker replied. Sam knew without question the voice of Mercy Elderkin. She had an ear for news and gossip, did Mercy.

The girls tittered behind their hands at this piece of spurious, but valid news. They accepted any rumour alongside news at face value. Whether true or not, there was value to be had in blather and gossip. Their conversation continued with tittle-tattle and remarks that transitioned to be more libidinous as time passed. Often the girls would talk over each other in the hope of getting their words listened to.

'Have you seen Mistress Crick? She's made a beautiful new quilt,' Meg Webster declared.

Another quickly answered, 'Yes, 'tis indeed a sight to behold - and she put hours of toil in to it. I'd not dare to use it if it were mine for fear of spoilage ... I'd save it until I wed.'

'Aye, she will enjoy the benefits of her work when her husband returns from trading in France,' Mercy chuckled. Her frank statement made each of the girls laugh loudly. Now, their subject turned to more pertinent news.

'Did you know Kate has had another babe? It is a poor little mite. Her colour's not good and he sleeps for hours. Kate worries. She is ailing and knows not what to do.' The girl was cut short by a cacophony of added voices all vying to tell their opinion.

'I guess Mary is a-watching after her,' Meg posited. 'She's usually called to help at times like this.'

'Should the angels take the babe, Kate is still young enough to allow another,' Abigail, the tallest girl in the gaggle, quietly remarked. 'Plus, her husband's already proved himself to be virile!'

At this, the whole assemblage sniggered at the nerve of their brazen tale telling. Samuel noted that the girls were much more blatant without the guidance of old Mistress Craythorne. He pursed his lips in thought, then sped his step to catch them. As he approached he knew he had become the heart of their attentions. Their talk ceased and some preened. He wished each a good day and they, in return, asked after the health of his family.

He asked, 'Where's Granny Craythorne? I know she's usually here keeping you all in order?' He smiled at the group.

'She's turned back for home and Meg has gone with her.' Mercy paused as Samuel regarded her. 'Granny isn't so well today.'

'We have left her to recover,' Meg beamed with warmth. 'She had a bad turn only the other day.'

Samuel replied with sincerity in his voice, 'When you see her, tell her I wish her well.' Too many of the older people of the town had died of late.

'We will,' answered Mercy. Sarah and Abigail picked up on Sam's earnestness as Mercy explained, 'Did you not know? When Granny heard of her friend's death she too was taken ill. Now she's maudlin at times.'

After the slightest of pauses Sarah noted, 'It was her friend dying that did it.'

'I heard,' put in Abigail, '... the news gave Granny such a terrible shock that she took to bed for a time. The older she gets the more each passing touches her.'

'She is often sore affrighted by pains in her body.'

Sam idly wiped the back of his hand over his cheek to chase away a fly. The touch reminded him of how Granny would wipe his face when he was an infant. He pictured her ancient face, which had remained the same for as long as he could remember. In his mind's eye he saw her creased face and eyebrows as thick and hairy as a pair of twitching, charcoal moths. He held great affection for the old woman. Samuel would need to tell his father the news of Granny's woes, then William, would pay her a visit - with a small nosegay or gift of some sweetmeats to cheer the old woman's spirit and Sam could chop wood for her fire.

Granny was frequently checked-upon by her fellows and was undoubtedly in their care, as she had no relatives. Neighbours and friends would tend to her, bringing soup and other stuffs. Some would do her laundry, although she stolidly preferred to do this for herself, saying, 'I'm not dead yet, you know!' The elderly 'granny' had once chortled, 'No one is telling me what to do when I'm old.' She generally had a lot to say about the world as she understood it, despite her gender. She had lived long and was no longer bothered by speaking her mind. Enlightened by age, she did not defer to menfolk any further. Her age, well-beyond child-bearing, allowed for a certain bluntness. She had lived long and knew much. Despite an absence in formal study, she was neither pusillanimous nor craven. Many did not take her words seriously, as she was considered old and harmless.

Folk remarked, 'She recalls her infancy and early life with crystal clear memory, yet oft' does not see if today is Sunday or not!' That was true.

Sam recalled Granny Craythorne had reflected, 'Why, in my day, there wasn't much food to be had as the soldiers took it all. They called it a civil war, but there weren't much civil about it, you can mark my words.' She rattled on, 'Master Oliver Cromwell was military Lord Protector of a new Republic, ha! He ran the country until his death. He was followed by his son, Tumbledown Dick. My, oh my, he was a disaster - that he was.' Sam recalled her slapping her hands on her hips and pursing her lips in annoyance. Right or wrong, ailing or healthy, Granny always had an opinion to share with all who would listen.

After the girls had left to continue their chores, Sam noted that the sun had risen higher in a blue sky, with not a cloud in sight. He sat alone, enjoying the dust-motes floating in shafts of bright sunlight, moving like dancing fairies. He closed his eyelids, seeing them still in an orange-black aura. He felt the temperate warmth of the sun on his face. The day stretched before him.

On his way home in the eve, he saw butterflies in the lanes and fields communing with damselflies in the late light. Sam was aware of how beautiful they looked. Although still light, the moon awaited on the horizon. Echoes carried across the river to descend softly upon his ears. He paused to sit by his favourite tree for a moment. Smiling with pleasure, he recalled Mary had long since completed her engagement making pre-ordered stockings for the poor-house children. It was regular work, making and repairing children's hose - for which the overseers paid well. He assumed that now she would be free to see him more regularly. The lengthened shadows of the sun had not reached the gate as yet. He waited a while to regain his peace before strolling home.

Later the same week, the group of girls crossed paths with the lad once more. Sam noted there were even fewer women out than usual. Yet again, he was aware that Mary was not amongst their number.

'Where's Mistress Mary?' he asked carefully after biding his time.

The girls shared glances that Sam could not interpret. Lizzie stepped forward and placed her basket on the ground. She looked directly at Samuel and replied boldly, 'She will be along shortly. She is lax in her ways today.'

Elinor smirked at him. 'We came on ahead, that's all. Even I had to hasten to catch the group, as they'd set off early.' She viewed the girls with a stern eye. Nell appeared to be protecting herself by supporting both sides in the girlish spat between Lizzie and Mary. Samuel detected a one-upmanship between Lizzie and Elinor and a hesitancy in the manner in which the others spoke. Yet, these girls had always had moments when they bickered and squabbled over trivial matters that momentarily overrode their friendship. Perhaps this was the circumstance today?

With the exception of Elinor, they had all fledged together and knew each other intimately from childhood. Sometimes all too well. Samuel recalled old memories with a wistful smile. He wondered what the girls were holding in check. Their friendships and allegiances moved like the leaves – sometimes calm and still and sometimes whipped into a frenzy by a sudden breeze.

Samuel opened his mouth to speak, but Lizzie interjected, 'Beware of your heifer, Samuel Barnes.'

Samuel looked confused, until Elinor nodded towards a curious cow who had ambled over to watch them from the other side of the ditch.

The market bell tolled, so with a 'fare thee well' the simpering group moved on along the road towards town. Sam turned from the ditch as they turned on their heels and noiselessly ambled away.

...ooo000ooo...

That same day, Mary had risen early. Elinor, with few words, had looked out through the open window and had then rushed out with her baskets without eating, but Mary remained. She ate coarse bread with a smidgeon of home-churned butter to break her fast of the night, before pausing to collect her samples and wares. As her living was made from knitting hose, her merchandise was important to her. She collected the solitary brown stocking completed yesterday and matched it to its repaired fellow. She bundled them together and added them to her already brimming basketful. She tied her purse to her waist, beneath her apron. The sun shone outside, so she did not require her heavy cloak. Instead, she collected a light knitted shawl, which she placed around her shoulders before neatly tucking the ends into her bodice.

It had been quite some time since Mary had befriended Elinor Shaw, from the nearby village of Cotterstock. Mary had liked the girl immediately, despite the waif's already tarnished reputation for being dissolute of conduct, but two incomes were most certainly better than one. Mary was surprised that Nell had rushed away and guessed that, by now, the girl was at market.

Much later than was usual, Mary passed as Samuel herded his cows away from the river. The morning sun was shining and Mary appeared to be in a hurry. Nevertheless, she took time to give a fleeting smile and had raised a hand in salutation to Sam. At that moment Samuel was vexed in his attempt to push, prod and pull a particularly stubborn heifer from the ditch. He nodded at her, but with his hands full did not return her wave. Crossing paths with Elinor earlier, Sam had wondered where Mary was. Now, he wondered why she was in such a hurry. Where she was going? This he quickly forgot as the responsibilities of his day wore on.

In the time that Sam's interest in Mary had grown, he had also noted the aloofness betwixt her and her erstwhile clutch of friends. Both remained busy, yet they sought to meet whenever they could.

Over time, Lizzie's clique passed warnings to him. Their words were reduced to a daunting: 'Don't associate with Mistress Phillips or you will be linked with her alchemy' and 'Keep your friendship with us and not with her.'

'But ...' he had protested, 'I don't wish to take sides in your petty quarrels or unfair talk.'

'On your own head be it,' they had replied as a warning. Samuel could not see why they should feel it necessary to avoid an old associate. He was unconcerned and happy to take responsibility for his own actions - and possibly suffer for the result of it. He considered offering them a thick ear, but thought better of it.

As time had passed, Mary also noticed how she was distanced from other women of her age. Her relationship with them became sporadic. They oft' made fun of her clothing. Probably the reason for that her erstwhile friend, Lizzie. Supported by her family Lizzie wore well-styled clothing with a strong sense of elegance and opinion. Working women, like Mary, could not keep their linen as white and spotless as those who afforded servants. Mary wore a knee-length beige shift and like much of her clothing, bore a washed-out appearance. She used wool in her work, so many of her skirts and bodices were woollen. They could be easily darned and patched.

Sam was unaware of its origin, but talk had reached his ears concerning Mary and her tenant, Elinor. Loose tongues suggested that the latter sought the attentions of middle-aged men returning from partaking in an ale in the local tavern. She would do so with an occasional rogue remark and flashing her eyes (or slightly more) at passing men, with which to gain their attentions. They, being no gentlemen, agreed she was 'a charming and entertaining companion'. Gossips told that men purchased ale for her. Elinor's revenue was opposed to her reputation. Summary talk was that she was not so innocent in her ways of making money. Grog-blossomed inn patrons alleged that her meagre income was supplemented by 'entertaining' genial gentlemen. On their part this was pure conjecture, but it transpired that some neighbours would believe anything said of her.

...ooo000ooo...

Chapter 11
Toasted Grains and Hot Stones

William Barnes had watched as the late crops were devastated by frost, while prices steadily rose as winter set in. Discussion on the topic was rife. Many looked aloft as folk pointed heavenward, wondering when this insalubrious season would improve. Others spent time on their knees in apology for indefinite deeds, alongside asking God for more favourable weather conditions. The mulled ale in the draughty inn tasted good after the chilly walk from his home.

William and his companion had each ordered another ale, as neither wished to walk home until the sudden gale had abated. The aging man spoke to his friend, John Palmer, in the darkened inn as the rain beat against is shuddering windows, making the candle-lights shudder in its wheezes and gasps.

John noted, 'Neither rime nor roasting is particularly good for man or beast.'

Whilst the men were warmly stowed in the inn, a little down the road, Lizzie and Mercy sheltered from the sudden squall by a tumbledown wall. It gave them momentary respite. Here, they raised discussion on the wealthy Mister Creed, wondering what it would be like to travel far from the town and into a country where English was not spoken.

'They speak a foreign tongue in the places he's gone,' Lizzie huffed, matching her humour to the storm.

Mercy laughed, 'My, my, Lizzie. It is bad enough meeting my cousin from York, for I can hardly understand what she says – and she's English!'

Although Lizzie was not of Creed's status, she always had dreams of marrying a rich, handsome man. She'd heard of the love between a king and a humble orange-selling actress a mere couple of decades past. There had also been much talk of the dashing Richard Creed who had returned from combat in Flanders to spend a time with his well-to-do family in nearby Titchmarsh village. He frequently galloped the few miles into town to meet his cronies in the town. Many times Lizzie had watched him from afar. He'd looked noble, as he quickly dismounted and tied his brown steed to a post, gently stroking the animal's long nose whilst giving her a treat from his pocket. He'd even smiled at Lizzie once or twice as he walked by with his friends. It seemed no time at all before he was due to set off again to Europe in search of new exploits. Unfortunately, he seemed to show more interest in warfare than local women. Mercy squawked again as Lizzie mentioned this as the sky clouded. The wind changed direction and blew their skirts around their knees as an abrupt torrent of rain caught them unaware. They ran as fast as they could to shelter under a tree in the lane.

'Lizzie, we're close enough to run to Mary's for shelter,' a damp Mercy quaked in the spray as she spoke.

'No! Over their dead bodies, will I ever step foot in there again,' Lizzie had replied with some malice. 'They have wounded me and there is no forgetting what *she* has done.' She was adamant.

'My goodness! This weather is surely colder than a witch's wart,' Mercy placated. She could not fully understand Lizzie's ire. She suggested, 'Are you certain it would not be best to make friends with her and shelter in the warmth?' She pulled roughly on her shawl as she struggled to put down her basket, then rubbed her raw hands together. The rain was cold and her teeth chattered without control, as Lizzie narrowed her azure eyes to glare into the distance at Mary's cottage.

'It is not cold enough for me to resort to that, Mistress Elderkin,' she replied with finality.

Within the hour the storm had abated and the two, wet, mud-splattered women, soaked to the skin in their inefficient clothing, slopped miserably to their homes.

Meanwhile, in her snug home, Mary sat in the fireside chair and considered the score years of her age. She knew that she was seen as thin and worried, whereas Elinor, although an impatient girl, exuded a comely confidence and much-developed maturity for her age. Nell was funny and irrational in equal measure. Mary was disturbed by loose talk that spoke of her mentor, Isabel Godfrey, then of how her cottage had been passed on to Mary - along with her beliefs and practices, 'separate from faith'. Some said Isabel had 'held extraordinary gifts from God.' Mary was unsettled by the frequently repeated whispers, statements and dialogue.

Lizzie had heard the talk too. She carefully stored the information away for later. After her walk in the storm with Mercy, both were unwell for a time. Mercy blamed the tempest, but Lizzie, aberrantly, blamed Mary for her ills.

The spring marked a time that began prettily, with chilly frosts still decorating the land. Thereafter, the mild, warm days woke noisy bees and small creatures in their hedges and burrows. The sun defined each day with an extended daylight span that left Mary in a creative mood.

'In the summer, I collected some honey and thanked the bees with a song and a drop of their own produce,' Mary noted with a nod. 'Vinegar and honey syrup mixed is good for nausea and coughs,' she explained to Elinor. 'Be practical and always plan ahead for your winter remedies.'

Mary's friends and neighbours bought her tonics with confidence. Although, with the possibility of invoking Lizzie's outrage, Mercy had purchased a remedy that had speedily cured her chill. Luckily, in the wet season, Mary had stocked up on all the herbs she needed for the dank times.

Mary viewed the signs of nature and enjoined them. She spoke lightly to her neighbours, 'I expect next year will be the driest in decades.' Heads had shaken in disbelief. 'Plentiful times will be followed by a wicked wilting … and wicked people.' These statements upset those who heard, but Mary did not consider how grim the legacy of her bold advice could be.

It was a dry, late spring when Mary was sought-out by the thinning Matthew Gorham. He had walked from Glapthorne village to seek her. One look at him instantly bothered her. Overall, he was a good looking man, but his skin was pallid beneath ruddy cheeks from his strenuous walk. He bore sweat-damp, tousled hair. Those who knew him turned to watch, noting how anxious he appeared.

He knocked on Mary's cottage door with a loud rap. Wiping her hands clean of flour, she quickly answered it to find a flustered Matthew Gorham awaiting her. He knew Mary and Elinor by sight, and was roughly the same age as Mary. Matthew had needed to ask for directions on his way to their home, but recognised Mary the moment she opened her door and bade him enter.

He did not accede to her request, but begged her, 'Mistress Mary, please come now to my home with all immediacy. My family is in dire need of your help.' He gulped for air. Mary suspected he was near to tears.

'My home is down by the shallow place for watering in yonder village. My wife, Margaret, is tending to our youngest child, little Elizabeth, who is sore sick from fever and needs your attention. I know not what has made our sweet child poorly. Please, please come.' He coughed. 'I am willing to pay for such treatment, but I can ill-afford the town physic.' With a shortness of breath in his haste to explain his predicament, he continued, 'I can pay you a shilling if you come now. I do not wish to leave my wife a-waiting.'

Mary did not even consider the sum, knowing a doctor would charge much more, aware that her services were required and that Matthew was a careful smallholder, not a rich man. With this knowledge, Mary hurriedly packed her wicker basket with items she guessed she may need, grabbed her shawl, which she hurriedly threw around her shoulders and hastily followed him along the road. They turned westward from Leather-Bottle Inn, taking the rough-trod pathway up the steep hill-side by means of the narrow *Dweel-Wonc* (Dwelling Way) Lane, which was habitually used as a dumping place for old housewares.

Matthew and Mary paced out of the town by the common thoroughfare that passed the windmill, fields and cows grazing in open land to the nearby tiny hamlet. At times their steps followed an almost impractical course. The road was rutted from the tracks of the many carts that had passed that way. The time taken felt elongated by their desired haste to arrive. Walking fast, her skirts impeded her progress as they often tangled and twisted around her lower-legs. Mary knew that the journey should take no longer than it normally took to sweep her house. Her gown felt clammy around her knees as she hurried. She yearned for a passing cart travelling from town, so they could beg for a lift, but the road remained silent, except for the constant buzz of flying insects and the distant lowing of cattle as they hurried along.

Their ragged pace oft' resembled running. Matthew silently surged onward, while Mary filled her quiet by wondering how she could help. To clarify her thoughts Mary went through her method to determine causes and effects of pestilence. She hoped to reassure Matthew. She prayed that medicines in her basket would be of use. She had never met the child, but understood the fears held by her exhausted companion. Unspoken beliefs curled negatively around the notion that perhaps their arrival may be too late.

'She is in God's caring hands. He will decide if He wants her with Him,' she had quietly susurrated. After all, the girl had surely been baptised. 'God will decide what is best,' she asserted, catching her breath.

'Yes,' he replied, soberly. Sweating, he looked to Mary with little of the desired divine strength evident in his voice or eyes. Mary quickened her pace to keep up with the lithe, long-legged man. Both breathed hard from the pace set by Matthew. Neither wished to arrive too late. Mary craved for a waggon to pass and give them a lift, but none appeared.

She hoped to relieve the child, so spoke aloud, 'God willing, a tonic of honey-water and oats will give her strength.'

Matthew looked at her sideways. 'Will that help? She shakes so.' He held his mouth in a tightened pucker. 'We have prayed over her.'

He nodded steadily to show that he listened as Mary gave examples of what she may possibly do for his daughter, but she spoke more to herself than to him.

'We can bolster her with bags of toasted grains, hot stones or bottles filled with hot water. Warming cloths will give heat to her feet. A little soft food, if she can take it. Spoon-feed her if you must.' Mary panted, while her voice matched her step, '... perhaps warmed milk, barley, fried oats or chamomile?' She ceased talking to wipe the sweat from her brow, then began again, 'She shakes? Is she chilled or has she a fever? A draw-string bag of cereal can be heated in the hearth to warm her body. If her body's weak she'll need nourishment, medicine and our prayers, if you desire it.'

'Will you bleed her? She is only of four years,' Matthew asked with worry evident in his voice.

'No. If you call for a physic he will bleed her with his fleam. This will cost you ... and weaken her if she's sore-ill. I do not vouch for this,' she replied, '... nor will I use this method.'

Near exhausted from their haste, they arrived at the small house at the base of the hill. Immediately, Mary noted little Elizabeth Gorham was a weakened, sickly child of no more than four years. Mary instantly set to work by rolling her sleeves and feeling the child's forehead for signs of malaise. She nodded to herself as her hand instantly warmed at the touch, betraying clear signs of fever. Added to this, there was a strong smell of vomit that lingered around her person. The sweating child moaned quietly in her stupor.

Mary asked for water to be brought and Margaret ran to fetch it from the well. Mary took a cloth and bowl, then began bathing little Elizabeth's head and body. She remained unruffled as she further instructed Matthew, 'You will need to keep her cool, but close the door to avoid letting in further ill-spirits. I will provide you with a linctus. You should give Elizabeth a stomach tonic of lemon and salt of wormwood. It is a colourless liquid with a salty taste that she may find disagreeable, but it will give her sleep and should reduce her fever.'

Mary looked around at the dim-lit cottage. The Gorham's were not rich, but they appeared to have enough to sustain themselves. Food in the village was largely made up of homemade loaves, orchard fruits and vegetables, dairy goods and eggs. Anything further came from nearby market towns. Mary noted that there was a stock of eggs and root vegetables in the open larder. Salted fish helped the family survive, yet even a diet of the humblest ingredients kept people alive in times of hardship. Some men poached for rabbits and pheasants, but this remained risky on land belonging to the landed elite. Vermin hung from lines to show game-keepers were doing their job. Often a keeper could ignore their poaching – depending on the man. Pottage sustained a staple diet and ale was consumed in quantity. Mary determined that she would bring soup with her the next time she came. Yet, stoic Matthew Gorham and his family appeared to be managing against the odds.

Mary let herself outside into the plot behind the house. She set a pot of fresh well-water to boil over the fire, while she collected some fresh herbs for use. Mary prepared a concoction of willow-bark from her basket to sooth the child's head and joint pain, along with fresh garden sage. 'Better strengthen the brew to strengthen the child,' she thought.

Mary noted a cauldron of mush on the table. After a moment of thought, Mary said, 'Give her a little pottage if she wakes and seems hungry, but not too much.' The humble folk ate boiled foods cooked on a spit or in pots over the fire. Nothing was cooking at the moment. They were more concerned for the health of their child than the fullness of their stomachs.

After a time, noting the child's steadily calmed rest, Mary quietly added, 'If there is a change in her fever do not hesitate to come for me tonight. If you do not come, I will return tomorrow to check on your child.'

With these words, Mary wrapped her shawl around herself and quietly left. Matthew profusely thanked her and tried to press a coin into her hand. Her walk back to the town was mostly an uphill slog, but seemed to be quicker than the rushed journey down to the village. As she speeded her pace to be back before dark, Mary wondered about the nature of the child's illness. She pondered on this all the way to her cottage. She spoke not a word on her return as no-one appeared, but considered what could be done for the child.

'You never know if you are out of the woods when within the grasp of a fever,' she thought with a sigh. 'Let's see what the morrow brings.'

Mary had an overwhelming instinct that told her to avoid helping the family. A sixth-sense deep in her gut warned that all would not be right, but equally, she hoped to make the small child healthy again if she could.

As she arrived at her own door she realised she'd had no time to enjoy the usual sights of the evening light dappling the cottage fronts or of the swallows swooping gracefully in the mild evening air, catching flies.

Mary did not have a perfect remedy. She thought to herself, 'Time is a healer, God willing. I can guess at how to build her strength, make her slumber, then allow a spell for her to recover sufficiently. Perhaps a pine-needle infusion will strengthen her, with a tisane of herbs and fruits to improve its taste?'

'I have cut some annuals,' she said aloud and counted them off on her fingers, '... horehound, mint, penny-royal, sage, thyme, sweet marjoram,' she recited. 'The roots have time to sprout again before the winter.' She took a controlled breath. 'Horehound, mixed as a syrup will work, if it is an effort for her to breathe. Maybe something as simple as gripe water could aid her?' she wondered.

Mary's recipe required a homemade brandy and mature poppy leaves. She knew that her concoction should be left to steep for a few days before being strained and mixed with flavoursome liquors to make a palatable drink for her young patient. She feared she did not have time to make a new concoction, but on reflection, she realised that there was a small bottle in her pantry ready for purpose. Kicking herself, she thought, 'In time, I shall mix more for future patient needs.' Mary knew that three or four spoons of this mixture was sufficient for an adult. As for little Elizabeth, just one or two spoons with a little water should let her slumber. Sleep would greatly aid the child.

The following morning, Mary was up with the first birds and ready to attend to the sick invalid before the first maids had started milking at the dairy. Her non-stop visits to-and-fro continued for many days. Time passed.

Day after day Mary left early and returned home wearily late. Frustratingly, she saw little change in her patient. The linctus had partly worked. The small child slept fitfully in a clammy, wilting state, but she did not rejuvenate as Mary had hoped as the spell in time passed. Her fever persisted. Mary visited daily to try new remedies, while the family blessed her and prayed over their ailing infant. Witnessing his beloved daughter in a moribund state, Matthew became a haggard man driven by desperation. Mary began to note a hastening in the negative decline of the child, but kept hope these would pass.

By Friday, frail little Elizabeth Gorham slept, then failed to breathe, passing forever into the hands of God. Margaret was hysterical and Matthew morose, while Mary grieved with them. She prayed and mourned with the family. With no need to visit further, she did not desire any form of payment. Matthew and his wife were distraught. Margaret blamed Matthew for not calling a physic, then held Mary responsible for their petite daughter's untimely death.

She attended the gathering in the dark, candle-wax scented house that reeked of cascading death. She followed the serpent-like procession from the grieving Gorham's home to a shady place where all stood, head bowed, beside the tiny grave. Mary was forgotten, with not a word of kindness spoken to her. The Gorham family steadfastly looked downward, while their stone-faced neighbours beheld Mary by way of indirect glances. She stood apart from the group, ready to move after the final prayers had been said. Silently, the slim young woman slipped away to walk forlornly home. There she prayed for the soul of the child. Then, as Nell was out, was left to cry alone.

Within weeks of his daughter's funeral, Matthew, ventured out to walk to town to make payments. Here he bumped into old friends who gently coaxed him into the inn for a much needed ale. Margaret, tormented by mourning, ceased to attend to herself or leave home. Visited by well-meaning friends, her door was kept firmly shut should Mary venture near.

On the black-clad Matthew's excursion he'd cried to his fellows, 'My mind's sore-ill. 'Tis worse now. My animals ail. Today a magpie clacked at me with its wooden-rattle voice. 'Tis a portent of ill-luck and sorcery.' He'd repeated rhymes as a greeting to appease the bird, but felt uneasy. 'Do you know?' he emotionally remarked as he drank. 'I think that witch is now killing my horse and my oxen. Several have already died of the sweating sickness. My beasts are bewitched. If the woman doesn't lift her cruel curses my small herd is witch-jinxed … goners. Now they cannot work to pull a plough or give us milk.'

Those who surrounded him sympathised with his declarations. Later, they visited the smallholding to gaze at the dead beasts. One friend remarked, 'Matthew, we are so sorry, but they're only good for the crows now.'

Another advised, 'Your beasts should be burned to rid us of pestilence. Mayhaps the carter'll take them?'

Ambrose, who had a nose for trouble, suggested, 'The skinner may take 'em for their hides?' None replied.

'I don't know what I did to deserve this? I wish I'd never knocked on her door. How was I to know she's a witch?' Matthew lamented, holding his head in his hands. 'I take my hogs to market when they're grown fat at around twenty-six weeks, but have none to take now. What'll I do? I'm ruined.'

Vexed, a group of friends, entered the Gorham household to assuage his growing fears. Matthew spat phlegm into the open fire grate and heard it sizzle as he stared at his calloused hands. 'They've trouble brewing by cursing upon us and robbing us of our beloved child - and our livelihood.' His anger, like the fire in the hearth, flared. 'I've no idea what I do now, but there'll be a reckoning. They'll not avoid justice for this hurt.'

'They broke no law of the land,' his friend noted.

'Well, I believe they have! They've taken all that I have.' Matthew roared, as Margaret stared blankly into the fire from her chair. She neither moved nor attempted to join in the conversation. If the men had not been slightly in their cups they may have noticed that the woman had not even noted their arrival in her abode.

A grubby farmhand tenuously suggested, 'Perhaps you can talk with 'er. See if she'll lift the curse?'

'No,' snapped Matthew, all too quickly, 'I'll never, ever set foot near either of 'em darkened women or near their hovel of a home.' He breathed heavily. 'They're shameless. They've killed us. They're ill-luck to all who venture to 'em for help.'

Soon, it transpired that nearby hogs and sheep were dying too. They were all waste, with no strategy to render their carcasses for blood, feather, bone or fat for fear of spreading further infection. Even the experienced skinner viewed them with trepidation.

...oooOOOooo...

Chapter 12
Fatigue and Foretelling

Mary had been out all day trading hosiery and curatives followed by a cold, solitary walk back from Benefield. She wrinkled her nose and sneezed as she arrived back in the town. A traveller and his wife exiting the Ship Inn smiled kindly at her. They wished God's blessings on her to move the Devil from her shoulder, before halting to look in a shop window. Mary hurried home. As she paced, the frosty grass crackled under her feet. She sneezed out badness again, then open-mouthed coughed. Something evil had blown in a hostile wind. Portents of the coming brittle chill assuaged her senses. Soft, white ice-crystals landed on her upturned palms as she stood shivering near her door. She closed her eyes and opened her maw to the glowering sky, tasting cold sparkles on her tongue. She felt them melt on her warm eye-lids and lashes. They liquefied on contact with her warm skin and clothing, leaving her damp.

Mary turned her pale face skyward again and took in a deep, cold breath watching the misty vapour dissipate by magic. As she did so, she felt a gentle nudge against her ankle. Mary looked down to find nimble Catchevole rubbing and snuggling against her skirts to keep warm and dry, but achieving neither. His wet fur spiked on his back and appeared slick against his head. She smiled, bent down and stroked his wet head, then caringly and softly, gathered him up into her arms. He was light in her hands. The feline knew she meant him no harm, so let the girl lift him and enfold him into the layers of her dark-green cloak, to warm and dry him.

Steadily, she walked the last few steps on the path to her house with him bundled in her arms.

She lifted the latch with some difficulty as she held both cat and basket. Going inside she placed him down on the rushes on the stone floor. Then, quickly turning, she closed and re-latched the door behind her before the residual warmth of the house was able to slip deftly past her and dissipate. By the time she found a twisted paper-spill from the mantle-shelf and had lit the lamp, Catchevole was already purring on the rag rug by the dying embers of an earlier burning fire. Mary added a branch or two from the basket by the hearth to rekindle the glowing cinders. Fiery twigs spat out angrily with a sudden spark that caused the now settled cat to glare, hiss and move further away to the safety of the far edge of the matting. He knew not why the fire had taken a dislike to him, but would sit and watch for a while in its warmth. The damp branch was not going to burn quickly or quietly. It sizzled, smoked and spat at the hearth as if it bore a hatred of him. Catchevole merely moved a pace to avoid the death-throes of the branch, but not so far as to avoid its heat. Slowly, the branch crackled then, coaxed by the newly-awakened earlier embers, flared into renewed energy, making shadows dance over the walls of the house like wraiths and shades.

Bitter gusts made their way from end to end of the cottage. The poorly sealed windows and doors let in more than the cold. Small rodents appeared seeking refuge, yet Catchevole made short work of these as sudden exercise followed by a gift meal. He was by nature a crepuscular animal. He loved to linger in the twilight awaiting a speedy attack and swift snack. His mistress was more than happy to keep her surroundings clear of rodents with his help. Her efforts to de-mouse the house were mainly centred on planting mint in the garden, with some stored indoors to keep the mice away. Overcome with fatigue, Mary hastened to her bed, unlike the ebony tomcat who sat in the undulating glow of the flames until even his penumbra faded into the darkness.

Mary knew that the house was icy-cold in the early mornings. On waking she could see her own exhalations of air like puffs of dragon breath in the cold air. It was difficult to keep a fire burning in the inglenook all night long. This day felt the coldest so far. Mary was loathe to get out of bed, knowing that she would need to leave the comforting warmth of her woollen cocoon. Catchevole had waited until the fire died and Mary was asleep, then had slept on her bed, curled into the bend of her knees. If she awoke it disturbed him and he would be off to perch elsewhere. Come the morn it was as if Mary had only dreamed of his presence, yet the warm spot he had vacated was a clue to his quiescence there.

Mary dressed warmly before starting her tasks. Today, she would not go directly home after selling her wares at the spartan market, instead, she would go to the Crown to meet Mercy and Sarah. The women had arrived some time before her and were already 'whetting their whistles' as she was blown in a torrent through the door. They called and waved her over to the corner by the fire, before calling to the inn-keeper for another ale. Each, naturally, talked about their health, families and the weather.

'If it's going to get any colder the river will freeze over,' Sarah said. They revelled in the idea. What else was there to discuss when it was so chilly?

Wrapping the fabric around her slender frame, Mary slowly enveloped herself tightly in the warm folds of her cloak.

'What do you know of this frost and chill? Is it not something of concern?' Sarah asked of her.

Mary grimaced, 'It is surely cold, but this will not be the worst our land has seen ...' she hesitated for a moment, '... or will see,' she added. Mary continued, 'I measure that in the coming decade you will see a frozen landscape, hungry people, icy winds, black fogs and severe frosts.' Her contacts had looked askance at her prediction. 'We'll live in a land transformed,' Mary noted with a faraway visage upon her slim, serious face. None looked forward to going home by venturing outside in the cold maelstrom.

The girls giggled and looked for variation in the conversation, as Mercy whispered to Sarah, 'Why does Mary always decide to make our future hers?'

'There's a lingering quiet outside today. Mistress Phillips should choose her words with care,' Lizzie loudly joked from the far corner of the room. She sensed there were likely listeners for her in this inn. The girl was warmed by the fire and the mulled ale.

Mary deliberated over her opposition - between friends and eavesdroppers who chanced by.

'How dare she foretell our future?' voiced a large woman in the corner seat whom she had not recognised, echoing Lizzie's remarks.

'That young woman makes a prophecy,' another whispered ineffectively. 'Who does she commune with to know such? She should repent to mend her ways.' Indeed, her natural attitude and conversation had been twisted and had turned some nervous listeners against her. Others took little notice of her strange forecasts as Mary had done this for many years and saw it was mostly guesswork. Indeed, it was a trait Mary mirrored from Isabel's character.

'It's in Mary's nature,' Gladys suggested. 'She's sometimes a bit short in the head. Nowt will come of 'er talk. I know 'er and she speaks true.'

'Why declare such words?' asked a gangly youth. 'I heard neighbours and market-folk say they have seen her slip into apparent absences and vexing trances between serving her customers.'

'Oh, she does at times. We all do.' Gladys held.

'Maybe it comes from God?' the lad conjectured, '... or someone else - far more worrying?'

'I think she needs to eat some of her own dill plants for better sense,' a large woman suggested with a sniff as she wiped her dripping nose on her sleeve.

Mary could predict the future for friends, whether they liked it or not. It was rather like telling fables or stories. She enjoyed seeing which of her spoken seeds would bear fruit. She had predicted her old acquaintance, Ethel Ailsworth's employment in-service at the big house and later her happy marriage to a modestly suitable man. Friends seemed nonchalant about her 'excitable energies', but were aware that she most certainly held some uncanny skills in forecasting.

Lizzie wandered over and disdainfully pressed, 'C'mon Mistress Second-sight, who is the man that I shall marry - and when will it be?'

Mary carefully explained, 'My judgements are not like that. I can't see into your future, Lizzie.'

She was not inclined to be lured into frivolous untruths, even if that was what her friends wanted to hear. Some believed that her messages were to be taken seriously, whereas others were more suspect in their opinions. In the past, a few handed her a penny to predict their good luck, which was preferable for them to hear. Mary knew that none wished to hear of future sadness or ill-health. Here she was considered fey or gifted, insane or wicked - or an amalgamation of these essential requisites.

Two girls enjoying their beverages were not quick to relinquish their gossip.

'Mary tells your fortune,' one said to the other. 'She does for coin. Everything can be had for a price.'

'She oft says too much!'

'She made my old mother well again with her ointments and charms, so I cannot truly complain.'

'Again?'

'Yes, again. Each time, Mary gives comforts and poultices that make my mother's old joints ease. Furthermore, I trust her.'

'You may well trust her, but I do not,' interjected Lizzie who, listening in, finally decided to join the conversation. 'She is not trustworthy.'

'Oh, yes, *you* can trust her. She knows stuff. She even talks to the dead ...' a plainly dressed girl remarked, as nearby listeners gasped. Now, each gave voice, choice and opinion. Person to person no two sentiments or attitudes were precisely the same.

'It's wrong for a woman to be so well-informed,' a squinty, pock-marked man said. 'Above all, a common woman.' The chatterers shook their heads in disbelief as they moved to continue their individual banter.

Mary had had enough of being the heart of their discussion. She wrapped her now dry cloak about her shoulders and made for the door. The walk home was unpleasant, but not as unpleasant as the atmosphere of the tavern.

On her arrival home, Mary thought back to the unexpected morning when a younger Nell first came to her in the street to announce that she had nowhere to live. She potentially had a feeling – nothing more, but this was a turning point in both their lives. Mary had eventually agreed that Elinor's temporary stay could be permanent. Together, the two warmed the cottage more than one. Catchevole didn't seem to mind either, for when they arrived home after their day's labours, there he was, awaiting them. He now scampered to greet them both at the door and entered as they did. His sixth sense somehow would forewarn him of their imminent arrival, just before dark, when his stomach growled in ravening feline expectation. Luckily, most evenings, his stomach ended up purring in filled contentment rather than growling.

'Any home with three as company is a warm home indeed,' Mary had declared not soon after entering the cottage. This sentiment seemed to be agreed to by all.

Later that night, the two women cordially snuggled together for warmth, before the meagre bundle of kindling quickly burned to naught in the fire-grate, as they sat tightly wrapped in their grey-knitted blankets. Catchevole contentedly sat beside the fire with his eyes closed and his ears erect. He flicked his tail from side to side, proving to Mary that he was alert and not truly resting. He was listening to the sounds of the night outside.

When their neighbours chanced to visit on an evening like this, they were sure to find the two sitting opposite each other knitting stockings to sell. The pair would offer refreshment to their guests, no matter how little they had in the house. They were always kind and courteous. On some occasions they dispensed their home-made medicines to anyone who had need of them.

On days when they did not close the loose wooden shutters to block the wind, their voices would carry to their neighbours. The two were seen and heard talking with heads together, besides singing and dancing in abandoned merriment. They were also observed throwing sweet smelling herbs and twigs onto their roasting fire to make the room scented and pleasant; further ridding the space of the earthy, damp odours conveyed in the air from outside. Due to the recent talk, they were watched with growing interest.

News spread. Busybodies came to take a gander at their home with an auspicious eye, under the pretence of buying medicines or hosiery. Along with other visitors, Sam went to the cottage to collect ointments for his father. He found the two helpful and good company, never failing to make him laugh. Mary was the gentler, but impelled by ale or chivvying, both were emboldened with entertaining portrayals of folk he knew.

Spying eyes and telling tongues did not find their impersonations of fellow townsfolk quite so amusing.

...ooo000000ooo...

Chapter 13
Hardship and Survival

Seasons turned like a persistent creaking wheel. As an observing, serving man of faith, William Barnes prayed hard to witness his boys grow into steadfast young men. Although Samuel was beyond schooling, fresh-faced Wilf was not. The widower passed on wisdom and learning to both, no matter how limited he felt it was. Sam was busy from dawn to dusk and William's younger lad was required to work in the field at planting and harvest, which paid, so took primacy over reading and writing. These were tasks for chill evenings, when sitting by fireside in candlelight.

On a day that started cool and with little left in the Barnes' pantry, young Tom Coles knocked on the substantial timber door, then clicked the latch to peep inside to find his friend. Wilf looked around at his father, beamed and steadily shook his head. 'Here's Tom. Rabbits won't catch themselves, so I'd better be going.'

'Be careful, lads. We don't want any legs to fix this time,' his father warned with a troubled frown.

'Oh, father,' Wilf sighed. He grinned and waggled his hands above his head as ears as he hopped carefully through the door, followed by his friend.

William then addressed the empty room, 'Well, fish are not going to hop into the cook-pot either. There are always jobs to do here. What shall I do first?' He pulled himself upright and set forth to tidy. He dwelt upon his eldest son's absent-minded countenance. The older man knew that Samuel was no doubt pondering on how his swain, the healer, fared. He saw that Lizzie Coles was sweet on Sam - buy Sam had only eyes for Mary.

The Barnes family had always seemed rooted in the soil. In the meadow the morning was hot - and afternoon hotter. Sam's shirt stuck to his back, wet with sweat. On days such as this, the hours lingered and work was slow-going. No voices could be heard, just the steady hum of insects and the rhythmic swish of scythes. Whenever Sam paused to lift his eyes and wipe salty trickles from his brow, he gazed into the distance to see a low haze engulf the town. It was too hot for even the dogs to bark or move from the shade of barn, tree or wall. As the men finally made their way lackadaisically back to their dwellings, muscles cried out for rest. Their job would continue until the weather broke or the harvest was safely stacked and stored in the hay-barns before season's end. Everyone helped in cutting, drying, carrying and safely storing the crop. Women continued to gather armfuls of dried hay and carried them to an awaiting waggon and team. It was back-breaking work and even the smallest of children were sent to help, particularly as the weather seemed on the turn.

In the blink of an eye, the mottled leaves of the sleepy trees whispered with unforgotten dreams, as summer gusts blew around their boles. Full of rabbit stew, Sam bore a contentment. He was favourably restored as Mary passed by. It was hard to determine if his glowing complexion came from the benefit of seeing Mary or from the warmth of the sun. As she called her good-day greeting to Samuel, he noted that she looked tired and pale. As she spoke, Samuel saw she continually checked over her shoulder, glancing at the perimeter of the lane as if seeking someone she expected.

'Are you well, Mary? You look fatigued,' he remarked. 'Are you awaiting someone?'

'Oh, none in particular,' she replied. 'But … just … well …' she continued, biting her lip. 'It is nothing, Sam. Truly it is naught.' Her hands fidgeted with her shawl.

'I am certain that all is not as you say,' he replied quietly, taking her cool hand gently in his, as he looked into her dejected face. She appeared not to notice his caress, but leaned forward to furtively whisper, 'Over there,' she nodded. 'Who's that child? Do you know?'

Samuel turned and searched in the direction she indicated, but could not perceive any youngster. His eyes sought in the shadows, but there was nothing to be seen. Not wishing to worry her regarding an apparent phantom, he asked, 'Where?'

Mary pointed. 'There. Do you know her? The little one - by the hedge,' she said faintly, staring into the near-distance. She seemed so certain of the child, yet Sam believed a trick of the light had confused her, but he could not say as much as did not wish to hurt her feelings.

'I'm sorry, Mary, my eyes are tired. I cannot see the child. Only moving shadows in the blowing bushes and trees,' Samuel softly noted. Mary studied him, but by the time she looked again, the child had disappeared.

'She's gone!' She breathed deeply. 'I'm sure that there was a child … a girl, aged around four or five, wearing a worn blue dress. She is gone now.' Mary seemed saddened. 'I have seen her before,' she said in a troubled voice. 'She is very familiar.'

As she set forth on her way home, there was no glimmer of comfort in her eyes. Perhaps the prattling people hereabouts had wanted someone to blame for the local woes and were playing a trick on her. They had firmly fixed their focus on Mary following the death of little Elizabeth Gorham.

Sam had heard rumours that Mary saw things that other people did not, in flickers that moved and vanished. Later, when Sam was talking with Nell she confirmed this. He was told that Mary was not pleased with her gift, if such it was. She did not like to speak of her 'intense imaginings' for fear of distressing others.

'You have a vivid imagination,' Mary had been told, as people crossed themselves and moved away. She saw herself as a leaf blown in the wind. God would decide what would be her fate.

After the jarring apparition, Mary arrived home to discover Elinor stark naked. Mary could not decide which was the more disturbing.

'Oh, Nell! What will our neighbours say if they see you? Do you wish to gain us ill-repute?'

'It is none of their business what I do in our home!' Nell had somewhat tartly replied.

'Why under God's heaven have you taken your clothing off in daylight hours?'

Elinor replied, 'I've learned that if you truly want someone to fall in love with you, you should always bake food for them without garments - as cloth taints the recipe.' Finally adding, 'You rub the dough on every part of your body before placing it into the pan to cook. Absorb as much sweat into the pastry as is possible.'

'Really?' asked Mary with a bemused look. She was struggling in trying to remain polite. 'I am sure Aunt Isabel never did that!'

'Yes, every part,' Elinor insisted. 'Then, when your true love eats it he will be aware of your quintessence and you will become irresistible to him.' Her reaction to seeing Mary's bemused face was to laugh aloud. 'Believe me or not, the choice is yours.'

Mary was flummoxed, but not wishing to debate the belief, sighed and went about her business. There was little point in arguing with Nell when she was convinced of her exactitude.

The women chatted as they cooked over the open fire. Their dough was mixed, stretched and pounded on the wooden table, then placed onto a metal plate in the hearth-space to warm and rise, before being baked in the embers. A fireside oven had been built into the side of their chimney corner, allowing the sweet scents of baking bread to pervade the house. The comforting honeyed smells of cooking oat-cakes and spiced apple-cake often wafted around their house.

Elinor had made a rich porridge of oats to fill their bellies. She added a little salt to enrich its flavour. Mary, who had fewer cooking skills, loved the food that Elinor made, but in the future knew she may wonder exactly *what* it had been stewed in.

Elinor had learned how to make butter by skimming curds from fresh milk, then churning until it magically transformed. She had laughed loud and long, when Mary told her a story of how butter was first discovered by a man on horseback, taking home a container of milk. She had laughed, 'He thought it was witchcraft when he arrived home to find he had no milk - only butter!'

Food spoiled quickly. The women kept uneaten food in their meat-safe or in the cool pantry, cut from the northern wall, away from the heat. Flies were a problem in scorching weather. Should there be rotted food, it was promptly trimmed and fed to a neighbour's pigs. Usually leftovers were not 'left' - they were eaten.

Mary's dyed knitted products were oft' seen hanging on lines and racks outside the houses to dry in the sun. This unintended marketing brought new customers to their garden. Mary used natural dyes for her woollen skeins. Throughout the year the smells from cauldrons of boiling beets, red cabbage and onions used to make their dyes permeated the air.

The autumn coaxed Mary outside with its crisp, brown leaves then, after fields rested in white, the spring lured her out again with pastel-flowering bluebells amid delicate white Hawthorne blossoms, transforming nearby woodland into a sensory delight. She recollected picking the early primroses and long-stemmed white clover in her childhood; then giving the delicate blooms to 'Aunt' Isabel, who placed them in bright pottery jugs on the sill.

In contrast, Mary and Elinor had wrinkled their noses when the remains in their pots were noxious with rust-coloured roots, poisonous berries, bark, leaves, lichen and wood. The residue of these ingredients could not be safely ingested, but in poultices, were safe for purpose.

'People have said we went to the woods to forage and practice our craft,' Elinor remarked. 'They now think we're making poison potions to kill them all.'

'I don't care what they think,' answered her occupied friend as she potted poisonous deposits. 'Some townsfolk must have lives so boring that they have nothing better than to make up rumours about us.'

The decanted residue was to be hidden away in the rafters and corners by the pair to deter unwanted rodents from their pantry. Nell worried that Catchevole might be tempted to taste it, but Mary had correctly decried this. 'That cat is far too wary to ever eat poison!'

'I sincerely hope so.' Nell crossed her fingers. 'If it is unhealthy to humans,' she mused, 'it is most surely a useful rat poison and will leave a cat with less than nine lives.' Elinor wondered silently if she should save a draught for Lizzie, who could not bear to be near her. Instead, she picked a favourite topic: Mary and Samuel.

'You seem very close now. Does he say he loves you?' she enquired, teasingly.

'Yes,' Mary blushed almost as pink as her shawl.

'So,' announced sunny Elinor, 'You have charmed Sam. Tell me how make a charm that works - for me. I want it to make Ambrose love me. He is so handsome,' she had coyly noted. 'I can make false charms from cord and people believe they work, but I want you to make me a real one, Mary. You have the skills to do so.'

'I will if I find time,' her friend half-heartedly replied, eyeing a dew-bejewelled spider's web that hung, layered from the top of the window frame. 'Ambrose is a bit of a gadfly. Are you sure you wish to appeal to him?'

It was some time later before Nell's repeated attempts to gain a 'real' charm was fulfilled. Mary finally conceded - chiefly to make her 'shut up'.

Elinor, was in her element and very best pleased. Thereafter, her passion with Ambrose progressed.

...ooo000000ooo...

Chapter 14
Green-Eyed Monsters

The Coles family subsisted in a tithed, small farm dwelling. Lizzie had resided here for her entire existence, yet repeatedly dreamed of living in a distant city, somewhere where she could live in opulence - and marry a prince. If this was not to be, then she would just have to find a nice local man and wed him. With sights long set on the fine-looking, clean-shaven Samuel Barnes and, of late, his close friend, Thomas Ashton, Lizzie reassured herself that if one was not to be had, there was always the other.

As time passed she guessed that this may have to be the case, yet habitually appreciated rugged Samuel's fine physique, as he bent and stretched, repairing hurdles on his family farm and those of other livestock owners hereabouts. His muscular shoulders were firm and his smooth wrists strong, but gracile. She knew that he would often do work for free; as goodwill counted for good returns. Although born to hard-working stock, Lizzie had been cossetted from infancy and thoroughly behaved as such.

People orbited around this pretty, young woman - and she knew it. Although a little younger than Mary, Lizzie carried none of her sensitivity or warmth. The undercurrents of her hobnobbing and hints carried easily around the chattering classes of the town. There, her envious prattle often altered to be seen as 'truth' after various retellings. Like the dark ivy tightening its grip on subtle roses, attractively adorned and laced with an array of sparkling dewy cobwebs, the talk was forever trapped amidst a skein of shady, throttling vines.

'She could curdle milk, that one,' remarked Granny Dexter to her equally elderly friend with a knowing nod.

Matilda Humphrey, who was busy selling cheeses on the steps of the cross, turned back to her companion. 'Pretty enough when the mood is right, but then look at her eyes.' Matilda noted, 'She's fair of face, but her eyes are narrowed, yet not caused by sparkles of sunlight.'

'Aye,' Granny Craythorne agreed, 'In all my years of ailing, that girl and those eyes have followed a path to trouble.' The old woman eyed Lizzie's progress around the market, fingering merchandise with distain and not actually purchasing anything.

'Her nature's not humble,' said grim, gap-toothed Granny Dexter as she shook her head. 'Mmm, that young Miss is frivolous … and inconsiderate. Why, now, she doesn't care to share her moments with me, despite having me dandling her on my knees as a babe.' She puckered her lips and sucked her remaining teeth, whilst she slowly shook her head from side to side with great solemnity.

The old ones watched as Lizzie crossed the cobble-mud road. They could see she was gript in irritation. As she passed she did not trouble to look or listen to her environment, engrossed as she was in her own thoughts. The two timeworn women watched in stunned silence as Lizzie walked in front of the carter's waggon, finally hearing his shout at her, as he pulled back on the reins to slow the cart-horse's progress. With the click of cobblestone on metal, Lizzie turned. She almost fell and then, steadying herself, moved sharply to avoid an accident. She had near-missed being run over by

Collop's cart. John Collop's cart-horse, with the heavy wheel that followed, bowled passed her. It splashed her good yellow skirts in its wake and scared her. She blanched before yelling sharp words after the carter, who seeing no harm had been done, continued on his way. Lizzie pouted, humiliated and angry. To save her embarrassment, she quickly flounced through the milliner's shop doorway and sat heavily on her shapely rump on the chair inside. She had no care for the timeworn hags outside who resumed their discussion of her within hearing. Rearranging her skirts to look acceptable, she cast her eyes upward with haughty insipience at the surprised shopkeeper and loudly remarked, 'Bring me your coloured silk ribbons and show me the blue feathered hat in the window.'

Later, much recovered, as she stood in the street in new headwear, she spotted her prey. 'Come hither, Samuel … and you too, Thomas. What do you think of my new hat? Isn't it lovely? Come, talk with me and buy me an ale.' Her sapphire eyes flashed and eyelashes fluttered as she gave an affected laugh.

Samuel gave his apologies as he needed to finish the work he had begun earlier, but watched as the convivial, red-headed Thomas sat beside Lizzie, immediately captivated by her apparent charms. Samuel was amused by Thomas' unashamed gaze that rested momentarily on the girl's breasts. Sam said his farewells to both and headed towards the outskirts of town. He was generally of a chivalrous nature, but in this instance he remained wary.

Thomas, meanwhile, was besotted with the vision of loveliness beside him. It would not be long before he would be caught in the spun-web of Arachne's growing tapestry of intricate chat and flattery. By the time Thomas could realise his fault, he was strongly ensnared in the woman's tacky woven web.

He looked from her lovely face into his ale. The surface appeared calm, little knowing that beneath this, turmoil could easily ensue.

...ooo000ooo...

'Hell!' Elinor spat out frankly as a curse. She had been unfortunate in having been spotted in flagrante with a man she had met earlier, by a wealthy female customer. She had intended to be more discrete. The observer had looked away, but not before she had perceived what was happening in the alley.

Nell's day had begun when a well-clad newcomer to town had sidled up to her, bought her a drink and passed her complements. She was flattered. The man's interest in the girl led to a lust-driven proposal, with money offered. They had met in a back-alley and their transaction quickly concluded when they were stumbled upon. A little later, Elinor had walked down by the river with her still un-satiated companion in conversation, then was given a fresh 'green gown'. Needful desires were fulfilled in the long grass. It had been an easy swive for the woman - and the nearby river had been useful for a quick ablution. She knew that Mary would have been askance if she knew, but her time was accompanied by a fine payment that would comfortably keep her in food, yarn and new clothes from Laurence, the rag-man. Nell's new patron continued to seek her services for the remainder of the week.

'Thank you for your generous contribution,' Elinor had joked when the man had finally left town on a coach to York. She secretly wondered how Ambrose would react if he should learn of her financially rewarding trysts.

...ooo000ooo...

Meanwhile, unknown to Elinor, Mary had an assignation of her own. She had washed her clothing in the stream as she couldn't be bothered to collect the water to boil in the yard. The wash-tub and plunger were far too hefty for her knitted garments. She wanted to clean them hastily in the fast-running water and hang them in the branches to dry in the sunshine. She carefully squeezed them as dry as possible, without stretching them out of shape. She had been busy for hours and her back ached. As Mary wiped sweat from her brow, she considered how nobody had visited for days. She had kept busy and sales from her merchandise raised good money.

Samuel first spotted Mary with her hands in the free-flowing water, then had silently crept near to catch her unawares. She had tucked her skirts into her waistband and had waded into the shallows.

'Good day,' he had said softly in his orotund voice. Mary jumped, as she was greatly startled! She then blessed him with her broadest smile and he, in return, had felt a need to sweep her up and hold her in his arms. After few words they kissed, then worked quickly together to hang her laundry, before assembling the contents of her basket, retrieved from under the tree. He collected her bundled green cloak and lowered it to the ground to form a cover for the grass. Samuel was bewitched, even without the need for potions to make him receptive to the other.

188

'Spend this evening here with me, love,' Samuel had offered, then begged. 'I have no need to rush home - and neither do you.'

Mary considered, but eventually decided to turn down his offer. She considered herself a sagacious woman – now with an addled brain, swathed in love. Samuel was her sweetheart, whom she found strikingly handsome. She desired and admired him. As for Sam, he remained possessed by her prevailing charms. She was his love. He adored her.

Several hours later, Mary sauntered home with a newfound blush on her cheeks and with a fluttering heart in her chest beating excitedly. As she went, she lifted her skirts to skip along the path, transformed with devotion and affection. She looked up to see the stars were awake. She contentedly smiled. It was a bright night, with not a cloud to obscure a full waxen moon.

The shadowy cat's fur gleamed silver in the lunar beams as he sat on the newly flattened grass beside the river. A curious Catchevole had seen all that occurred. The moonlight rippled on the water. The occasional splash of a fish could be heard, as it rose to the surface and disappeared below into the dark once again.

...ooo000ooo...

It was a dismal day when a proclamation was announced in the windy market square. Skirts were blown aloft, along with bonnets and shawls, as the assembled townsfolk grouped to hear news that the King had died. It was not unexpected, but the listeners merged silently with heads bowed as they heard the announcement: 'Our King, William Henry, Prince of Orange, Stadt-holder and chief magistrate of the Dutch

189

Republic and King of England, Scotland and Ireland died on the eighth day of March this year of our Lord, 1702, before sighting the daylight of the morn.'

All knew that William's wife, Mary, had died only eight years afore. 'The King is dead ... Long live the Queen.' Listeners fretted, aware that the new queen, Anne, was aged thirty-seven and hearsay held that she bore ill-health. She was the late Queen's younger sister. The news was shared in quiet voices. People came asking, 'What's occurred?', 'Is it war?' or 'What's amiss?' Many seemed shocked by the news. Lizzie bowed her head, but watched to see how the crowd reacted. She was aware that she should show respect, despite bearing no loyalty to King or Prince unless, of course, she were to hook the eye of a prospective noble.

Despite the news, Elinor was of a cheerful disposition. She was impishly funny and caused Sam and Mary to laugh. Like Lizzie, when she heard of the monarch's death she held a neutral opinion. Workings of the rich and the crown were beyond her interests. The royal family would grieve, but Nell saw that her troubles were well beyond noble imaginings.

Elinor brushed hard with her broom to raise the dust from the door step then packed to deliver her charm bracelets. To her surprise, on her way home from selling talismans and stockings in Glapthorne, Ambrose had met with her and offered to carry her baskets. He grasped her around the waist and pulled her towards him. They discussed the latest news and the possibility Nell moving from the cottage so they could start life together. Nell laughed at his light-hearted suggestion. Later, Ambrose had undertaken chopping logs for her fire. By the weekend, they were seen collecting windfall apples together. This resulted in a fine pie for each of them. Nell had scented it as she had instructed her friend. Ambrose enjoyed his apple pie and came each day to the small cottage to visit his keen woman. Nell was blissful.

While Mary had been away aiding an ailing woman, Ambrose arrived in need of a physician. He gone to consult Elinor over his sore back. He was bid enter and peeled off his shirt. This served as a distraction for Elinor, yet she viewed his sore skin - while enjoying the sight of his firm torso.

'I understand your pain,' she said, as she lightly ran her fingers over his shoulder-blades. He quivered under her touch. 'These sores could be worse,' she observed. 'They won't kill you.' She laughed with a throaty giggle. 'Chafing has caused these blisters. Have you been set to heavy work?' She looked closely, 'Some are scabbed. They'll heal with this salve.'

She warmed the kettle, then soaked a soft cloth in warm salt-water to bathe his back. Ambrose winced as she applied the briny wash. 'This'll help you heal,' she said in a honeyed voice, as she applied a remedy of her own, which had nothing to do with blisters or medicine! After its initial sting, the saline quickly soothed. Ambrose left the house with a very satisfied smile on his face.

'Thanks be,' he prayed contentedly as he walked.

...ooo000ooo...

Chapter 15
Devilish Days

Moonlight lit the streets of the small town with no need for candles or lamps. The full moon was patterned with grey designs and wisps of cloud that briefly clothed the yellow-white orb and then moved on. The surface of the bright moon showed shadows and faces, wrought with mystical symbols and shapes that few mortals could decipher.

Robin Smith was young. He was a tall, slim, inexperienced lad - with far less brain than muscle. From the moment of his arrival from London on route to visit his aunt and uncle in Stamford, he had admired Lizzie - and she knew it. They had met when Robin bought cheese from her farm. He'd explained that he wanted it as a gift for his relatives. He had also told Lizzie, 'I am staying in Oundle for a couple of days to rest the horses and have them re-shod before travelling onward.' The attentions he paid to Lizzie presented her with the idea of a cruel jape.

For the joke, Lizzie used her considerable feminine wiles to convince her fledgling suitor, Robin, to visit Mary's cottage that evening. She knew that Robin was new to the town and knew few people. She gave him no time to consider his part in her plan. She explained that she wished for him to pretend to be the Devil. She provided a long cloak and a couple of cow-horns attached to a hat as his costume, then helped him to dress in the convincing disguise. She issued directions to the house and sent him to his task, with the promise of her affections should he do as she bid. For his part, he believed the trick to be a jolly jape as Lizzie chivvied him along in her scheme.

Come nightfall, he walked the uneven path to Mistress Phillips' cottage. He rapped at the door and Elinor invited him inside out of the cold wind. Mary, surprised to find that her friend had invited a stranger into their household, looked doubtful at his odd attire. As he crossed their threshold, both women were unnerved by his demonic visage, and shot glances towards his feet to check for cloven hooves.

'I am a traveller from another realm,' he explained in a youthfully-high voice. While Elinor smiled, Mary frowned. Yet, being of courteous natures they asked him his reason for such a late visit. Nell offered to take his hat and cloak. Both women laughed as horns and hat were removed as a single item.

The devilish young man spoke, 'I wish to buy an ointment for my behind. I think I have a tail coming through.' The women laughed with the man, even as he offered payment. They would not take his coin, but offered him a balm. He glanced from one to the other. 'This bum-balm will come in most handy,' he smiled, enjoying his performance. 'Your assistance to me will yield great reward for you in the future,' he assured them as Mary eyed her friend and gave the merest of shakes to her head.

Elinor, with a smirk, quietly suggested, 'Can we sell you some smelling salts to bring you to your senses?'

The man bowed low, re-clad himself in his mantle and horned hat, then replied, 'Thank you, no.'

With their token in his pocket and a flourish of his cloak, Robin took leave of them. As they closed the door behind him, Nell laughed at the countenance of the simpleton, while Mary worried for the young man's sanity. This was assuredly not an everyday occurrence in the town!

Robin hurried down the dark streets to the Ship Inn where Lizzie had agreed to wait for him. By the time he reached the inn, he had already cast off his disguise into a dense patch of shrubbery. He smiled broadly, expecting much in repayment from the comely Mistress Coles. Immediately, Lizzie spotted him as he rushed, red-faced through the entrance and down into the narrow beamed room.

Lizzie sat alone at a small table by the fireside.

'How did it go, Robin? Were they scared?' she rapidly asked, before he could gain his breath.

'Mightily at first, I'd wager,' he replied with a broad smile.

'Good. Did their neighbours see you enter?'

'Yes,' he replied, fumbling in his pocket. 'I saw some peeping from their windows as I traversed their path and knocked. Others looked out at me as I left, too. They would not take my coin.' He offered her the money.

'Robin, you can keep that,' she said, '... for the service you have done me.' He seemed puzzled by her words.

'I suggest you buy yourself a beer with it!' Lizzie advised as she got up to leave.

Robin's face fell. 'But ...' he started. 'Steady on, I thought you ...' He was beguiled by her, but too late realised to his shame that he had been enticed with naught but lies. Lizzie showed no love for him and now shunned him anew for having completed the deed. Shamefaced, Robin took himself back to the hostelry. Suddenly, somehow he had lost his taste for beer. The following day he left for Stamford. Vexed, he did not bother to return via the town on his way home to London.

...oooO00Oooo...

Many bawds found easy money in plucking homeless girls from the streets and training them for prostitution. They taught their nymphs how to communicate with wealthy men and dress to suit their customers' tastes. This is the life that Elinor had grown to know from her undesirable youth. She had begun early, having been on the street without help since her parents left her.

'Had Mary not saved her,' neighbours had remarked, 'Nell could surely be dead in a ditch by now.' Indeed, when times were hard, Elinor was suspected of supplementing her income with a few moments of casual, money-making coitus. She knew that Mary disapproved. Elinor put her reputation on the line, but thought nothing of it as long as her customers seemed clean. Often, she found that if her mark was fuddled with strong drink she could earn more than was traded for, without fulfilling her part of the deal. Having been ingrained, she was decidedly determined, motivated and keen not to starve.

Mary oft' felt concerned with Nell's behaviour, particularly after the beer-sluts and youths who frequented the inns learned of her penchant for dancing naked by the river in the summer months, free from all apparel. They spread the word. Voyeurs crept to the bushes by the river to espy her as she pirouetted and sang with abandon. Elinor was not ashamed whenever she spotted the sneaks. It was spoken that she would expose herself with flagrant exhibitionism for as little as a penny. Inebriated individuals of the hostelries laughed and coaxed her further. Only fear of Ambrose's retribution deterred such people.

Many good folk commented and began to keep their distance. In gaining and sustaining a debauched status for herself, she had become a celebrity, conscious of expected payment - a condition of her ill-reputed fame. Talk did not always displease her, as stories grew from acorn to oak tree.

'Go away. Leave us. You give the town a bad name,' her neighbours called. They beseeched Mary to get rid of her. 'Send her back to whence she came.'

Elinor would not leave. She could not leave. Where would she go? Women had little or no status other than being marriageable and childbearing. Many were entertainment for men.

Her repute worsened like an escalating storm arising from a clear day - beginning with nothing. The name calling grew so ruthless, that even children as young as four or five years called out to her, copying their parents as they jeered whenever she stepped outside her door. Children (who knew no better) and adults (who did) would point and yell, 'There goes a whore' and 'There's Nell the strumpet'. She swore vengeance as she gained infuriation at their insults.

Mary was shocked by the attitudes of those people she knew, yet told herself, 'The children are innocent. They learned from their elders, who should know better. I have known of them all for many years, so why do they treat us thus?' She considered, 'This is my house - my home. Nell will recover and they will come around to think better of us.'

'How did you come to inherit that house?' some asked Mary. 'Luck - or did you pay for it with your soul?'

Mary chose not to heed the cruel intent of their words. Unfortunately, the cat-calling worsened Elinor's demeanour. She expressed her displeasure by doing exactly what they had expected of her. Individuals showed revulsion and horror at her behaviour, whereas Elinor, being naturally of a choleric disposition 'was raised coarse', so swore retribution. It was in her nature.

Pretty bindweed in the garden grew upward toward the nurturing sunlight, slowly enfolding, until its cruel vines tightly gripped and wrapped around any nearby flowering plant - until it was choked.

...ooo000000ooo...

Lizzie snubbed 'the Phillips woman' and continued ill-chatter whenever the opportunity arose. Her looks and youth would hold her in fine stead. She would win back Sam, she thought, 'Just you wait and see, Mary Phillips. He shall not be yours.' With this she slammed the wooden shutter into place and put in the peg of the window, to close warmth inside and avoid the evil chills of the night to come inside.

...ooo000000ooo...

Chapter 16
Money, Mallow and Medicine

Before venturing forth, Elinor cautioned Mary against incurring Lizzie's verbal attrition and ire should they meet. 'Her words are deeply wearing and her manner is on the verge of outright bullying, beyond unkindness. Stay clear of her, Mary,' she warned.

Unfortunately, avoidance could not be circumvented, for in the market before the noon tolling bell, along came Mistress Lizzie in her familiar state of ill-temperament. Her arrogant strutting walk gave clue to her demeanour. She was clearly in no mood for chit-chat today. She was frustrated and annoyed with anyone who should cross her path. Even though Lizzie made no attempt to move towards them, Mercy and Sarah inconspicuously moved to the windward side of the market cross to avoid her sitting next to them.

All around the Shambles and butchers' row, the shoppers, stall-holders and the women sitting at the base of the butter-cross instantly saw that something was amiss when Lizzie animatedly accused the seamstress of trying to sell her a bent bodkin. The woman protested, but to no avail.

Lizzie required a new flat bodkin to thread ribbon through her corset eyelets, to make holes in her leather belt and use it as a needle. She employed the small hollow at the non-tapered end to pick wax out of her ears, then used it to smooth the filaments for easy threading. She already owned a wooden bodkin-case to hold her needles, but coveted a silver case she had seen in the home of the seamstress to the Bramston family. With little luck at the seamstress' dwelling she moved around the market to view the freshly cut flowers. These she knew she could ill-afford to purchase. They held a most delightful scent, which annoyed her even more.

She carefully tipped over a posy seller's basket with her foot and trampled on her blooms, then shortly rounded on the unfortunate girl who promptly burst into tears, as Lizzie stomped away from her. After meandering past several other sellers, she chanced to view Mary through slit sky-blue eyes and moved quietly up to her. She picked up a pair of woven stockings and appraised them.

'I gave you a shilling and you have only given four and one half pennies in exchange,' she shrieked in a shrill voice that carried along the road.

'Here, you can take your tatty stockings as they are badly made and I will take my money back.'

Lizzie tossed the pair of woven stockings on to the cobbles of the road. Mary quickly retrieved them, smoothed them clean of the leaves and then rolled them together to replace in her basket.

'There's naught wrong with those stockings,' she declared in truth, 'and there's naught wrong with my price. It's a fair price and good work has gone into the making of them.'

Lizzie raised her voice to draw the attention of others who could hear. She wanted them to be on her side in any argument. She continued, 'You were trying to short-change me. You have underestimated me. That will be your sorriest mistake.'

'What do you mean?' Mary replied shortly, 'You gave me no money.'

'Indeed I did and these good people will surely vouch for me.' Lizzie pointed around and responded to the glances of bystanders with her widest smile and as if in assent, gave a nod of her pretty head at the people nearest to her.

Mary rounded on her, but by now she knew that there was little point in arguing, as matters were bound to get worse. She knew that there was a reason behind Lizzie's awful behaviour towards her and she knew that it had nothing to do with whether or not her stockings were saleable. Lizzie stared straight at Mary with glowering eyes. She leaned forwards from her waist, towards Mary's guiltless face and spat.

'Get yourself away from here. Leave town, you wicked whore!' she hissed. 'You are no longer welcome.'

Mary stood astounded. After a moment she responded, 'Lizzie! You may look beautiful on the outside, but unfortunately you are not at all pretty within.' Mary's face showed her wretchedness, whilst tapping her straightened fore-finger against Lizzie's bodice stays. 'You have a grey heart and you are further turning it to black.'

Lizzie glared back at her. She flicked a stay strand of flaxen hair from her shoulder to re-join the others curling down her back. She smoothed down her new yellow bodice with its burgundy skirts. Her fingers played with the equally eye-catching red ribbon that she wore tied as a bow around her neck. She pulled near to Mary and sneered. Mary could feel Lizzie's hot, unpleasant breath upon her face. 'You are such a bitch!' Lizzie snarled. 'How can you insult me? You are the harlot and thief. You beguiled my Sam and I can't forgive you for that. You should be convicted for your other crimes – bewitching animals and people.'

Mary was unsure of what to say or whether to answer at all. She was stunned by the unexpected verbal blows and the idea of beginning a contest to find who could shout the loudest with the irate Lizzie. This was no way to conduct her business. Caterwauling in defiance was unacceptable, so she kept herself in check as Elinor had advised. Wishing to retain credibility as an artisan and healer meant there was naught she could do.

Lizzie faux-wiped her cornflower-blue eyes with her hand-kerchief as her lashes fluttered meaningfully. She looked down at the cobbles and then at her hands - and then back at her acquaintance, through her lashes. Lizzie well knew her efforts would work - she was a clever performer. Sarah Short crossed the road to stand with her as people began to watch with prying interest.

'Are you alright, Liz?' Sarah asked in her airy tone and evident concern.

Lizzie's plaintive, loud voice stated, 'That woman is a dreadful knitter and cheats in so many ways.'

The woman gained support as her acting skills were commendable. Lizzie's final blow came as a physical one. She had an advantage and took it, pushing her opponent to the ground with a solid punch. Thereafter she took Sarah by the arm, turned on her heel and walked away leaning on her comrade as if for support.

Mary steadily picked herself up from where she had landed. She had not been prepared for the clout when it came, so it knocked the air from of her lungs. She had landed her in the muddy gutter, bruised and embarrassed. Looking first to see who was watching, she then glanced down at her clothing in dismay. Wet leaves and mud stuck like glue to the lower edges of her soiled shawl and favourite mulberry-dyed dress. She tried in vain to brush off the worst of the grimy filth. Mary felt tears in her eyes, but would not sob openly in front of nosy onlookers. She wiped the sludge from her hands to no avail, as scathing voices carried a distance. The market folk and shoppers watched and listened to the exchange, but did not wish to become embroiled in any conflict. Mary stolidly packed her bag with her muddied knitted hose and woollen scarves. She trudged home. There would be no more trading for her today, possibly none tomorrow, as she came to realise the extent of the harm done.

Mary's walk to the cottage had been painful as she was sore-bruised, both, physically and mentally. Elinor was not anywhere to be seen. Mary guessed, 'She'll be chasing Ambrose somewhere – although that may be an unkindness; she may be visiting the sick.'

Her torso felt painfully tight and sore hands ached from gripping her basket. As she released her grasp, she realised just how tightly she had held on to the wicker handles. A deep, shuddering breath tore itself from her constricted throat. She swore, tiredly throwing herself onto her pallet and blankets, where she sobbed herself to sleep.

Catchevole crept through the open window. He lightly trod down from the sill to the chair-back and from there to the floor. He would spend his time curled next to his mistress for tonight. She was in dire needed of affection, warmth and comfort, no matter how little he could provide. In sleep, Mary's arm gently encircled his coiled resting form. He slowly opened jade eyes, but chose not to move. He felt the decline of Mary's consciousness, sensed her body droop as tensed muscles relaxed and awaited the steadied, effortless breaths of slumber. He purred contentedly for some time, then he too slept.

When Mary awakened she was cold and stiff. She discerned shapes and shadows in the low light. What had awakened her? Was that someone standing outside? She rolled onto her side to hear the latch click as a blast of cool air sped over the floor to meet her. The door closed. Mary held her breath as she heard the bolt being drawn across their wooden portal.

'Where are you? Whatever are you doing in this gloom? Are you alright?' came Elinor's most soft, inquisitive voice. 'Mary, what ails you? Why have you not lit the fire or the lanthorn?'

Mary stretched - and ached. She shrugged her shoulders and wiped the sleep from her eyes, as Nell looked down at her filth-covered friend. Mary rose slightly to find Elinor had begun covering her with the warmed cloak she had taken from her own back. She rose unsteadily, as Nell used the flint to light a candle on the table then bent to light the kindling in the grate.

'I am sorry, Nell,' she mumbled. Her voice was gruff and she sounded confused.

Elinor came to her again, wrapped her arms around Mary and gave her an indulgent hug. 'Oh, Mary! You are chilled. You feel iced to your bones.' She asked her a plethora of questions with concern, 'You look awful. Are you unwell? What is amiss? Why did you not light the candle or the fire while you awaited me?'

Mary roused herself enough to explain the relentless trials of her most unpleasant day.

'What am I to do?' she finally asked her friend.

At hearing of the intensification in Lizzie's loathing, Elinor first filled the air with fury, before successively trying to cheer her friend. As Mary watched Nell's face, she saw a sudden determined decision take root. Elinor marched sharply to the basket propped by the leg of the table. Here she grabbed a small handful of their, as yet, un-carded wool. She deftly twisted it in her fingers to create an elongated shape. To this she added more material, plus two pieces of wool tied around the frame that now resembled neck and waist. She worked quickly. The wool-tuft began to take on the form of a human character; as she added arms and legs made of wound wool. Soon the small felted figure came to resemble a person. Elinor's nimble fingers added two small bundles of wool as breasts and conclusively chortled as she held up the doll for Mary to appreciate. Nell decorously wrapped a snippet of ribbon around the dolly and added a red thread to the neck. Indeed, although rough, the shape had clearly taken on the appearance of Lizzie Coles.

'There we are,' Elinor announced. 'We can put her up here on the shelf above the fire, so that we can tell her every thought we ponder on her behalf.' She gave an impish grin. 'Perhaps a pin in the arse would help her? That would make her ache!' She chuckled heartily, before continuing. 'We can move her nearer to the flames to toast her a bit, like the fire and brimstone of damnation that should come to her ...'

She was unrelenting in tempting her friend to break her solemn expression. Although, at first, Mary could not find hilarity in her friend's humour, but soon found she could not remain remote or cheerless at Nell's feverish attempt to make her forget her troubles.

Little did the women observe that their fire-bright and candle-lit room was perfect for passers-by to see inside, as shutters had been forgotten in Nell's attempts to hearten Mary. Eyes watched as ears heard their words.

The following morning came accompanied by birdsong. Neighbours walked over to see what Mary would choose to pick from her garden. Some stood to collect savoury leaves in the adjacent lane and passed short moments in the day with her – more from curiosity than friendship. They witnessed Mary stiff movements as she collected herbs. They closely viewed what she did each time she left the house, whether picking lettuce, marjoram or mint. From her stocks of ready-picked herbs she carefully created tea for any who would visit. She added parsley for love, anise for good dreams and some chervil for friendship. As she drank her rosemary and raspberry lemonade, she wondered if she should use some angelica to guard against the magic of others, but deemed that this was not necessary.

...ooo000000ooo...

As the season drew to a close, Samuel had walked to the bottom of the hill to hurriedly re-patch the byre wall. He used dried cow-dung and straw to fill the weather-beaten holes. In the sunshine and drying breeze, it did not take long before it hardened to form a strong repair. When at liberty, he and his friends spent their hours meeting to fish or sink an ale in the rush-floored tavern, wherein it was dark and cosy by the fire. The group were a convivial bunch, they badgered and were loud of laughter. Samuel regularly smiled as he brought to mind their playful, teasing ways. He considered that of late his life was lived contentedly, with no new turbulences that God sent to challenge him. While Sam was satisfied with his lot, others were busy stirring a porridge pot of distasteful lies.

Most Sundays, just after listening to the sermon in church and taking his repast at home, it was his routine to relax. Samuel and his brother would often stroll down the hill to the river to meet with friends. Their walk was slow as Wilf still had difficulty after his injury, but this did not hamper his fishing skills. They would take pleasure in catching fish and eels that would nourish them throughout the week. When cooked properly, the eel meat was tasty, firm and fleshy.

'When uncooked, it is lethal. Perhaps this is why the Bible forbids the eating of anything without fins and scales?' Samuel mused. 'It won't be long before it is too cold to fish.'

In the afternoon, the young men, Wilf, Thomas and Sam, returning with fish strung from their lines, met with Mary and Elinor. The women were foraging for young nettles and berries in the thorny bushes by the mill. Mary had taken off her bonnet and her hair hung free. Bare footed with the wind tousling her dark chestnut locks, she looked beautiful. Samuel was besotted.

Nell, Thomas and Wilf took note that the couple wished to be alone and gave their goodbyes, before laughing and chattering on their way towards the farm. As they had walked away, they quietly discussed the pair amongst themselves.

'Sam is paying court to Mary. I believe it is with intent of an offer of marriage,' Wilf beamed.

Both Mary and Samuel lingered picking berries that stained their lips and fingers, fully aware they had been left in peace by their friends. Mary, happy to see that Samuel paid her great interest, showed him the fruits, flowers and leaves she had been gathering.

'Are you making a garland of mallow?' he asked.

'No, but I approve of these pretty purple flowers,' she remarked. 'The mallow plant has curing properties. Apothecaries use it for their medicines.'

'How does it taste?' he asked with growing curiosity. 'We don't use it, but if it can be eaten I'll collect some too.' He licked his lips thinking of his recent insufficient meagre meals. Mary smiled and nodded.

'I'll teach you how to use it.' She took a sprig and stroked it. 'It has a mild flavour,' she intoned. 'Mallow is thick, but cooks a bit like nettle.' Samuel watched as her slim fingers picked the leaves, selecting only the smallest.

He remarked, 'I like spicy nettle soup.'

Mary plucked a second purple-veined flower. She was so close to Sam that he was tempted to lean forward to kiss her rosy lips. She twirled the bloom. 'Furthermore,' Mary raised her eyebrows, 'mallow is a potent love medicine.' She laughed as she noted Sam's blush. She kissed the small flower, reached over and tucked the small bloom behind his ear.

'There,' she laughed as her hand gently brushed his face. 'A fetching flower for a fine-looking man,' she teased. Samuel laughed as he leaned to kiss her. An hour flew by before Sam reluctantly detached himself with a prolonged kiss, knowing his family would be awaiting his return.

...oooO0Oooo...

Chapter 17
A Clowder of Cats

Mary Phillips had enjoyed watching the antics of cats, as Aunt Isabel had before her. These determined creatures lived in the fields and scampered around the lean-to barn that stood nearby. She enjoyed their company and their play, but was often uncertain of if she should feed them all – as they seemed to breed quite freely. Mary was content to know that cats kept the rodent population down. Only her cat, Catchevole, lived alongside her inside the house. Other felines came and went as they pleased – on the outside.

On a particularly windy day, an old friend, Cicely Wagstaff, came on a visit the market and contacts in the town. She caused a stir as she arrived at Mary's cottage unannounced. Cicely was a plump, jovial woman, with a reddish complexion. For her years she was in good health and liked to laugh at the jokes of others – besides her own. This convivial, elderly matron was not invited, yet, always welcome.

Mary looked around at the house. 'Forgive the mess,' she said.

'You should beg forgiveness as this is truly a mess!' said Cicely with a cheeky grin, as she entered the small abode. Mary paid her words little heed. Cicely smiled. 'I ran into young Sam on my way here. He has a shirt that needs a-mending.' She winked at the younger woman. 'Be sure that you show him respect and fix his shirt well,' Cicely remarked.

'It is my house. I care not for your opinions,' Mary rebuked with a grin in return. Both were used to this form of banter.

Cicely continued, 'Then put the kettle on for a thirsty old woman. My goodness! Our dearest Isabel would have been appalled at the time you have taken to offer me a cup to quench my parched gullet.'

She glanced at the untidy bed-roll and badly-stuffed mattress in the corner. Cicely was aghast to see that there was a cat asleep on the pillow!

Mary knew the house was not as clean or tidy as it had once been under Aunt Isabel's scrutiny. It was sad to say, but Mary realised that the young woman who now shared the cottage with her was not very house-proud or the tidiest person she knew.

Cecily recounted bygone days, drank her cup and departed. A short time after she had left, there came another knock on her door. Mary glanced around the room. She had done her best during the day to sweep and shake the bed covers into some semblance of normality. She had taken up her broom and had swept as best she could. As expected, Mary knew her caller. He waited on the doorstep and reached down to stroke the soft fur of Catchevole's back. The cat allowed him to do so, which was a rare honour.

With a final glance around the tidy room, Mary opened the door with a smile. 'Good day to you, Samuel. What brings you here on this fine afternoon?'

'Father sent me to see if you could patch his shirt. He has caught it on the thorn bush and has made a tear in the cambric,' he replied as Catchevole took his opportunity to run back inside. Sam carried a bundle in his hands. Mary invited him inside and offered him a tea as he handed over the shirt to mend. Samuel refused the beverage with the understanding that he was busy, but could return for the shirt and tea later that the week.

'I can do this tonight, so I will expect you to call back tomorrow,' she had said, as she studied the extent of the damage to the material. 'If you cannot come to me, I can deliver it, but it will be after my usual sales and deliveries, so will be late in the day.'

'There is no rush,' he explained, but Mary was adamant that it could be done quickly. She knew that his father had no more than two shirts and would welcome its prompt return.

'Thank you greatly,' said Samuel as he turned to leave. 'I will return on the morrow.'

Mary was a fair seamstress. She could sew well when she put her mind and talents to the task.

As she worked on the shirt, she thought of Nell. Since she had moved in with Mary, the local children had changed from playing and collecting berries with them to walking behind, calling to them: 'vulgar baggage, sluts and whores!'

Mary guessed that Elinor had often taken a silver sixpence for a quick roll in the hay-rick. She knew when Elinor had more pennies in her purse than could be earned from the items sold at market. She worried that her own reputation was not as it once was.

...ooo000ooo...

As Elinor hurriedly walked home after a good day of sales at the market, she gazed down at her near-empty baskets and smiled to herself. This indeed had been a profitable day. Several coins jingled in the purse tied beneath her skirts. In her reverie, she almost collided with an old woman who had been standing still, watching her progress along the road to the kissing-gate.

'Oh! You startled me!' exclaimed Elinor with a shuddering breath. 'Did I hurt you, for I did not see you there?'

'Nor you worry, girl,' replied the woman with a crooked smile. 'I've bin a-watching you and your little sister as you walked along.'

Elinor felt a cooling shudder pass down her spine and she became aware that the small, fair hairs along her arms and neck stood erect. 'Mistress, you are surely mistaken?' she quavered. 'For I travel home alone today and I have no sister.'

'Nope,' came the old woman's reply as a declaration. 'I saw her as clear as I see you now a-standin' here.' She looked beyond Elinor along the road. 'You look alike in some respects, although her being younger makes a bit o' difference.'

She directed her gaze to Elinor. Nell felt disquieted, but the old woman continued, 'She ran alongside a-you and tried to grap at y' hand, but y' were far too busy rearranging y' bits in that there basket to pay her any heed.' The crone motioned with her knotted hand to the wicker basket held at Elinor's left hip and loudly clicked her teeth with her tongue, 'Tch, tch, I heard as she called you Nelly. Is that not your name?'

Elinor was irritated by the woman.

'Fret ye not,' the crone said, 'for she is a-watchin' out for when ye needs of her,' she called out, taking her leave and ambling away with not so much as a backward glance. 'If ye wish to speak with her, I can be of service.' The old woman held out a gnarled palm towards her.

Nell shook her head, 'I told you, I have no sister.' Not wanting to wait a moment more she turned and briskly walked away.

Once the old woman was in the far distance, Elinor continued to be unsettled by the encounter for many hours.

A little later, on her much relieved arrival at the snug and welcoming cottage, Elinor retold her events to Mary, who was busy tidying the wooden table of condiments and salves she had spent the last hour creating. Elinor explained that she had paid particular attention to the awkward meeting with the old woman on her way home.

'This sore vexes me, Mary,' she had said in a melancholy voice. 'She regarded me as slow-witted - and the child - she described little Annie from my old village of Cotterstock. Perhaps it was her or perhaps not. I have no explanation, but feel uncomfortable.' A shudder slid down her back and she shook herself like a cat ridding itself of rainwater. 'If it is Annie, I am content to leave well alone.'

'We can both guess at her game,' declared Mary, clapping her hands together loudly and then holding them out before her. She smiled over her linked fingertips. 'The old one sought to disquiet you. She was most skilled in that. Think! Most hereabouts have lost a loved one at a young age.' Mary continued, 'She probably wished to tell your fortune for the sum of the pennies in your purse or to reassure you that your kin is well and watching over you from heaven above.'

'That may be,' Elinor said, reflecting on the issue, while quietly insisting, 'but, she seemed to know me – or at least my name.'

'... and I am sure that the meddling old crone was not genuine,' cut in Mary. 'Anyone can find out anything they wish, if they ask around in this place.' She pointed a straightened index finger at Elinor and shook it towards her. 'Should you meet again, do not listen to her hogwash. She has sought to pass the time with you with her ploy.'

She reached her arm towards Elinor, but Nell was having none of it and moved to the other side of the table, well beyond her reach. She gazed at the partly-cleaned timber surface and breathed a long sigh of exasperation.

Mary justified her thoughts, 'There are many, many ways of cheating or knowing what to say to appeal to people. She saw naught, but her hearing was fine for the coins in your purse. What she said could mean something to almost all here with no names or details to bolster her claim.'

Elinor was askance. 'Oh, Mary, but what if she does know of the world beyond?' She sulked for a moment before busying herself with lighting the glim in the metal-work sconce hanging from their wall. The stone wall felt cold.

Mary rubbed the wooden chair top with her hands. She quietly replied, 'You only say such as you want to believe a truth in it, Nell.' She sighed. 'Believe what you wish, but clever charlatans can easily play on your emotions.'

Elinor pursed her lips and remained silent as Mary went about preparing their supper. Nell was angry with this opinion, yet had held her tongue. In Mary's house she was still a guest.

Elinor lit a candle. She saw the wick catch alight and the smell of tallow began to fill the air. She was aware that there was a great deal about life that she knew little about, but mused on how her life had been. Life could be a curse or a blessing.

Many women said that they felt unsafe going out after dark. Mary and Elinor would go out if they felt it necessary, such as when they were called out to attend a patient in dire need, but for the most part they stayed put at home. The cats yowled in the garden that night. Catchevole stayed out, no doubt revelling in the caterwauling clamour.

On rising early, the women dressed and broke their fast with a bowl of stewed fruits. Mary eyed Elinor appraisingly. 'Nell, have you suddenly become taller?' she queried amiably. It was not so long ago that Nell's skirts brushed the leaves as she walked. She had grown in the time she had been living with Mary and her skirts were nearing ankle length or shorter!

Nell looked down at herself, before saying, 'I believe my growth happened over time not overnight.'

She looked to her friend. Mary went to the tin box on the shelf, lifted it down and carried it carefully to the table. 'Do you have your purse?' she asked.

'I do,' said Elinor as she headed to collect the drawstring item from beneath her mattress.

Meanwhile, Mary removed some coins from her wooden box. 'Here, Nell take this to buy yourself a new wardrobe.'

'That is too much,' her younger friend remarked, looking at the money offered. 'I will not go to the dress shop for new.'

She stared at the coins. Making and mending was a way of life for Elinor and Mary. All levels of society required stockings, caps, darns, patches and repairs; so this was how they made their living. The women had to look closely to check stockings for broken stitches. The better the repair, the more money they could earn.

'I'll buy a serviceable, repurposed dress from Laurence Landen,' Elinor thought aloud as she counted her pennies on the surface of the wooden table, 'and I can afford one. The money I have, I will spend on me, not on the already rich shopkeepers. I'd rather put my money in the poor box.'

She knew that the penitent poor, who filled the rear of the parish church on Sundays, were clearly not well clad - or shod. It seemed that their situation could be worse than it had been a decade ago. Although Mary was rarely seen amongst the chastised congregation who bowed on bended knee (while their stern vicar remained rigidly upright by the lectern), she knew many who were. In the blink of an eye, faithful acolytes passed around silver plates for their meagre financial offerings. The priestly were not poor. The vicar of Saint Peter's, Edward Caldwell, seemed much more concerned with the spiritual security of his flock than for their corporeal struggles.

Most in the town prayed for extra work at this time, even Samuel. His friends had often been picked from the line to do a job or two, but when the harvest was over, work was scarce and labour less in demand. A foreman in Mister Bramston's employ took his pick from the healthy young men who came along seeking seasonal casual work. He carefully chose them to carry, tote and move supplies. If they worked well, he would employ them again. Some fell afoul of the law when drinking on their earnings. Mary had no doubt that Samuel's family always kept reasonably within the law. They were not wealthy, but were able to feed themselves and earn in hard times. Sam and Thomas Ashton were often picked to help as they were strong and reliable.

Poor families were sometimes called to stand before the magistrate when they could no longer pay their debts. They could ill-imagine being able to afford paying an expensive lawyer like Mister Bramston to quell their legal issues. Financially demanding times appeared on the horizon and many of the poor were being punished, unable to discourse with solicitors or buy themselves free - unlike their richer counterparts.

'Thank goodness we've never been called before the judge,' Nell had once joked. 'We'd never be able to pay our way out on our earnings.'

Within a matter of hours, Elinor looked out from their window as an unexpected chill blew through gaps, between brickwork and curtain, serving to keep out draughts. The day had turned blustery and Nell had never found a moment to seek out the Landen family for a dress. As the light flickered, she put down her knitting to rub at her tired eyes. Feeling weary, Elinor knew she should stop work for the night. She wondered how late it would be before Mary would return from tending Gardener Grey's inflamed legs. Her friend had been 'seeing to' the elderly man who had endured pain, with little apparent change, for some weeks. Painful hips and legs thwarted his movements. Several cures had been attempted thus far, but Grey's job depended on flexibility of limb, so his legs were a recurring problem that did not depart easily. Swollen, angry veins stood prominently crimson on his calves and thighs. Recalling this, Nell reflected that Mary may be some time yet. She firmly pulled the oil-cloth curtain over the window. She moved the dripping candle to the hearth and lit the ready-stacked pile of wood chippings and kindling. The fire caught and crackled, while Elinor sat on the nearby, low stool to rest and warm her hands and feet. Here, she briefly closed her eyes whilst awaiting her friend.

Back from Elton village and the Hall, Mary was rapidly quizzed by Nell on the progress of her patient. After recounting her protracted visit to John Proby's old gardener at the manor, she explained, 'I could not come straight home as I had to return mended stockings to their owners. The seven mile walk has seemed longer today with the sky threatening rain all the way back to Oundle and with the wind puffing in my face.'

'You have reminded me of the story of the traveller and the rivalry between the wind and the sun. Shall we tell that story after dark?'

Mary shook her head as she pushed the dark hair from her forehead, catching her fingers in the thickened tangles. She smoothed out the worst of its knots. 'Not tonight.' She sighed from exhaustion. 'I've walked home slowly from my visits and deliveries. I am weary today. Our efforts were, as always, high valued and most paid straight away. Patrons always appreciate a quick turnaround.'

'Good. Sit yourself and I will make you a cooling cordial,' Elinor pronounced. 'You look done in!'

'A cordial sounds lovely. Thank you. I shall sit and rest a while,' she yawned as she replied.

Sitting in the fireside chair, she closed her russet eyes. Elinor clattered around placing the bowls ready, pouring a little water from the bucket into the blackened kettle, before swinging the metal arm and chain back over the crackling fire for the water to heat.

As Mary reclined on the seat against the hard wooden panel on the wall, she sleepily thought on her work of previous days. She had traversed back and forth to Tansor, where she had visited Agatha Moore to help birth a difficult babe, who showed great inclination to remain twisted inside her parent. Mary had placed her hands on Mistress Moore's belly and with relief she eventually felt the babe move into place. After some effort the infant was born healthily and her family were thankful. Proud, but tired, Agatha soon had the new-born contentedly suckling. Despite her lack of formal education, Mary had ushered the jubilant family to another corner of the room to allow the new mother to nurse her new, healthy child. Agatha had deserved some quiet privacy after her exhausting efforts, yet others curiously crowded in the small room to observe and congratulate.

As Mary sat, she recalled that when she'd asked neighbours to leave, they'd looked at her queerly. At the time, Mary was too busy to pay particular attention to them, but on reflection, the memory had vexed her. She saw there were women present who took a keen interest, maybe born of jealousy of her skills. Mary could cleanly stitch a woman as carefully as she could seam a blanket! Aunt Isabel had taught her well.

Happy in relief after the bothersome birth, Mary had talked and hummed to herself as she worked. She had removed the soft bed of animal-hide from beneath Agatha, then had taken the cover outside, where she had thrown a bucket of water over it and left it to hang-dry in the wind. She had finally scrubbed her own hands, before repacking her bag. Seeing Agatha with her safely squalling little-one was a godsend and boon. Satisfied with the fruits of her labours, Mary had hummed like a happy honey-bee on her way home.

Returning from the reverie of her week, Mary moved from where she reclined against the hard wooden wall-panel. She had sat unmoved for some time and had stiffened as she sat.

'Ohh!' she moaned as her legs stretched and ached. 'Argh.'

'What did you say?' asked Elinor.

'I'm just thinking aloud,' she replied, vigorously rubbing on her calves. 'I ache so.'

Her friend laughed. 'Talking to yourself now, eh? They'll be saying you're demented next,' she noted with a twitch of her eyebrows, as she inclined her head towards the window. It was quiet times such as this that Mary wondered what the neighbours actually thought.

'It happens more often than people think,' Mary supposed. 'All people talk to themselves at some time or another. You talk to yourself too.'

'I do indeed. Come for supper, Mary. I was only joking.'

As they ate, bunches of fresh chives with their purple bobble heads stood upon to the cottage table as much a decoration as a foodstuff. Mary viewed the sage-green herbs that had been drying in her rafters since the days of summer. The scents of chervil, rosemary and mint permeated the room, flavouring their cooking, alongside her home-made unguents and 'protection-from-plague' potions. Mary had learnt her craft well. Appetising vegetables and pickles filled jars stood on her pantry shelves; some for her own use and others to sell – making her harvest plentiful.

Two days later, Mary visited the Moore family bearing gifts of a bold yellow blanket for the babe and a pot of pickles for Agatha. The family were well pleased with their new baby - and grateful for Mary's help with the troublesome birth.

It was as Mary held the baby gently in her arms that she learned of devious words spoken against her. Agatha had not seemed at all worried in repeating her neighbours' statements.

'Mistress Sharpe whispered to me when she'd come to be nosy. She said she'd heard you "talking a charm outside o' the door" to bewitch my innocent. She said, "Hold fast to your babe, Agatha" and had crossed her fingers behind her back as a sign.' Agatha scowled, 'I thought you'd want to know, but don't go worrying yourself, Mary. That woman's a strange one herself.'

Mary had shrugged gently as she kissed the soft head of the babe she held. 'Agatha, she's clearly not as sharp as her name denotes if she's touting such nonsense. I do not fear her.'

Mary did not heed Agatha's warning words, for she could no more change her ways than make straw into gold.

Suddenly, realising how late it was, Mary gave her excuses. She had hoped to see William and his sons before it got too late. She wished to gift more pickles waiting in her basket to the Barnes' for helping fix her roof before the rain came.

Talking with Agatha had let hours pass imperceptibly. She took the sleeping babe and carried it steadily to the heavy wooden cot. Agatha watched in fascination as Mary moved. She deftly let the child sleep as she placed her down.

'It is late,' Mary wondered aloud. 'An early moon is rising. I must take my leave and wish you a good night.'

She looked out through the door as Mistress Sharpe steadily pottered past. The sky outside looked darkened as Mary opened the door. Some folk were already lighting their candles which flickered on ledges. She hurriedly threw her dark-green cloak around her shoulders and pulled the hood over her unkempt flowing mane.

'I must fly,' she said metaphorically, as she fled out through the door.

...ooo000ooo...

Chapter 18
Remedies and Revenues

It was a fine, windy morning as Elinor danced outside the front of their home, sweeping away the multi-coloured debris of the night storm. Twirling leaves were caught up by her besom-broom as they convened to cluster by the door, as Mary returned from selling stockings at the bustling market square.

Nell noted that Mary's auburn hair appeared aflame with a nimbus of sunlight. With rapid sales and fair takings the latter felt particularly pleased. Mary approached her friend with a smile and a curtsey.

'Good morning, Nell, you arose late today,' she said with sarcasm. 'I'm glad to see that you now have some clothing on and are set to sweeping. You were sleeping when I left for market.' She put down her basket to appraise her friend. 'It looks as if some mischievous sprite has blown the leaves down from each of our trees overnight.' Nell did not answer, but stopped brushing. Mary continued, 'By the way, have you found the time to call on Laurence to buy your dress yet?'

Elinor sighed, then replied tartly, 'You are clearly enjoying your morning and seem in fine fettle today.' After a moment's consideration, Elinor chose to ignore questions regarding a new dress and flew with immediacy to her more pressing issue. 'I slept in, as I hardly slept after dusk. Night imps and demons came again to me in my dreams. I tossed and turned and they would not let me slumber. That is why I overslept this morning.'

'Oh no, Nell. Not again. I am sorry. What ailed you most this time?' Mary stayed aware that after many

222

particularly disturbed nights, Nell had bit by bit begun to tell of her fears. It had become the norm for the two to relay dreams from one to the other; yet Elinor remained vulnerable and worried. Mary listened aghast as Elinor explained her latest dream.

'I dreamed that tiny beasts came in through our windows with pin-sharp claws, nibbling teeth and rough tongues. I tried to escape them, but they would not let me go. They would not leave me in peace throughout the night. I saw the rays of a new-dawning sun glow in the east as they left. I hardly slept and am sore tired today.' She hesitated. 'They came to me and ...'

Before Elinor could complete her sentence, Mary had replied, 'The window was bolted, Nell! No one could get in from outside, unless they came down the chimney! Even Catchevole remained outside last night and could not get in. Nell, pray, when the little rascals visit again, send them to seek me out. I would greatly like to meet your new phantom companions and give them a piece of my mind!'

'But they were here, Mary! After they'd departed from my room I could hear them outside howling with the wind. Just look – all of our trees have been hag-ridden 'til all of their leaves have fallen off!' Elinor saw that Mary could not take her words seriously, but let them lie. The latter breathed heavily as she bent to retrieve her basket, then moved to the cottage, while Nell continued her task of vigorous sweeping to rid herself of an unpleasant mood.

Little did either woman realise that their conversation (and others previous to it) had been overheard, to be later debated and discussed by their inquisitive neighbours. The blathered words were easily misconstrued by subsequent chatterers; with the gist of their musings inaccurately misinterpreted, dismembered and then re-formed - leaving the unaware worrisome women perceived as wanton or weird.

From her garden, Mistress Maggie Seaton had overheard their discourse and had then told her husband. 'Firstly the Devil visited them, now his imps have come to do his bidding.'

Later, the solemn man was seen fervently hammering up a horseshoe above their door.

Ann Dolby also heard repeated words from Maggie. She, in her turn, told Hetty Linton. With stealth, other tales came to be initiated into the spreading spirals of words. Nell's "demon imps" bothered the God-fearing, who incessantly worried over all manner of shadows and spectres.

The Seaton's sore needed to gossip. Mistress Seaton told Cat Boss, who subsequently informed her husband, William, the local Constable of the Watch. Cat and Maggie had then hurried away to consult the vicar (an associate and close confidante of Cat's husband).

Mary was aware of her neighbours' apotropaic signs, fears and nebulous superstitions. Some held on to good-luck tokens and amulets. Others made gestures, silently crossing the heart in their chest, two fingers tapped on timber or simple sketched symbols on door-lintels to avoid evil from entering each abode. Mary had spotted these as small protective ciphers and wondered, 'Exactly what terrors are these signs intended to protect my fellows from?' She did not draw symbols on her house, support their superstitions or join in with each profanity. 'Are my neighbours plagued by the same ill-dreams as Nell?'

Mary drew her favourite blossom-coloured, shawl around her narrow shoulders. She stood in the garden watching the twilight descend with the wind gently ruffling her long hair, as it had done this so many times before. She felt safe and comforted in the sanctuary of her own garden. She spoke to the spider in the branches of the apple tree. Like a web, the woven stitches of their fates had begun to tighten.

...oooO00Oooo...

Catchevole glared at Elinor. He stood, stretched and trod out of their way with a sneering hiss as Mary instructed, 'Nell, here is a remedy for burns that you should know of. It requires new cats-foot, pork-fat, tallow, an onion, a couple of eggs, three scoops of hens' droppings and a smidgeon of horse-dung. This will make the best paste poultice for treating burns.'

'The foot of a cat?' her friend enquired, disgusted by the thought.

'No,' Mary laughed loudly as she replied. 'Cats-foot's a herb! It's not as awful as you imagine. It's a fragrant evergreen plant in the mint family. It is also called ale-hoofe or gill-go-by-ground.' She plucked a stem from where it lay on the table and held it out to Elinor. 'It has a mild, peppery flavour and is fine in food, but also works well on burns.'

They laughed together as Elinor quickly learned how to recreate Mary's many green-fingered potions and poultices. These were soothing and cooling and even if they were not functional, customers believed they were. They either improved over time – or died.

Catchevole moved back to watch the women. He was curiously independent; purring and vocalising contentment at being allowed to stay indoors to watch them work. Mary observed him and laughed, 'He believes food is forthcoming. We look as if we're cooking up something to share with him.'

He brushed against Mary's hands as she pummelled pungent herbs in her mortar. Affectionate and hopeful, the cat was secure in the knowledge that Mary would shortly take up his meaning. Elinor pushed him aside, then chortled aloud. She was not being unkind, just amused by his attention seeking antics.

'Nell, if you put this salve into a box to store for any time, it will dry out. Spittle will make it thin again. Anoint sores with it and I pledge they will heal.'

Nell sniffed the foul-smelling poultice salve and grimaced. 'Pleasant? I think not!' she complained. 'I prefer your tasty apple and honey cake. It is delicious and can coax any hungry person to eat.'

Mary knew that for those who could read kept medicinal lists and 'herbals' that detailed remedies. Mary did not need these. She had been making gauze dressings for many years. Her knowledge of letters and reading was poor, but she was secure in the formulas she retained by rote. Repugnant ingredients for cures were often written as 'receipts', alongside dull directions for preserving fruit or making of mouth-watering curds and wobbly jellies in the grander houses. Under Mary's direction, Elinor was steadily developing her own recipes by trial and error. Most of her receipts used ingredients that were easy to get. Eggs and red onions appeared in many of her recipes.

Mary opened an earthenware jar and poured a little powder into her mixture, while Elinor's hands moved deftly at her command. The pair gazed at the wide range of preparations on the wooden board.

'Take note. Some recipes are secret and they should always remain so.' Mary breathed deeply. She lowered her voice to not be overheard, although there was no other in the house. 'This is not so that others cannot repeat our physic, but when folk do not understand what it is we do, it adds a mystery to the treatment. Making cures offers a good income. If everyone could make a praiseworthy remedy we'd not be so well recompensed for our skills.' She continued, 'Nell, if you are summoned to attend a person - go - but be aware that situations may not be all that they seem.' Mary quietly warned, 'Folk can be hasty and shift culpability.' Nell nodded, but remained soundless as Mary spoke. 'Always remember, if someone dies, at least you've tried. It is not your fault. That's life … and God's will.'

Mary believed that any self-sufficient curer's primary wish should be to help others – seeking payment was a secondary reward. Nell saw this in reverse. What bothered her was the way in which help was always given - but so quickly forgotten.

Mary stopped her instruction and lit the candle. Catchevole looked up in time to see a shadow pass by the window, momentarily blocking the light. Nell saw this too and wondered if perhaps a passer-by had been pausing to listen. With feline agility the cat moved towards the opening, curious to see who was there. He lost interest when Mary, misreading his intention, brushed her hands on her skirt, reached out and found a tasty tidbit for him. She fed the suddenly vocal Catchevole her remaining pieces of stale cheese from the dish and gave him an affectionate rub. It would not be long before he began his nocturnal wanderings. He was glad of the darkness of the night and its associated rodents. His meal had been insignificant, but would be shortly supplemented with the local wildlife.

Mary made a thick porridge from the oats she kept in an earthenware jar on the shelf, whilst Nell cleared their debris from the table. The women ate quietly, then sat to warm themselves by the fire. None of their neighbours passed by or came to visit them - indeed they had not done so for many days now. The fire crackled and made shapes upon the stone wall and chimney-back. When lit by the firelight, Mary held a soft glow about her person that could almost be considered magical.

...oooOOOooo...

After daybreak, as Elinor left the house to collect water, she noted children rambling in the lane by their door. The children, running off, were further observed by a group of four young men who had followed Elinor from the road junction to the gap in the wonky stone wall. Nell was already aware of them, so put down her bucket and stopped to re-tie a shoe strap that had come loose, in order to let them pass.

The awkward quartet of youths did not pass, but loitered to gape at the slim ankle and shapely lower leg on display. Elinor was fully aware that they were watching her, but did not pause in her act. She tied the bow and checked it was tight. As they ogled and nudged, they whispered words about her. Their obvious behaviour suddenly incensed her. They giggled and pushed each other nearer, nudging and flippant, until they were a man's length from her.

Prompted to anger, she turned on them and barked, 'Can't you pimply lads see me well enough? What are you waiting for? Go home to be breast-fed, children! Or is it that you want a better look?' She sneered in annoyance. 'Come nearer for a clearer view and climb up my skirts! Perhaps you are in need of a quick-fumbled grope, but I'll bet you haven't a sixpence between you?'

The lads had the good grace to look abashed as she promptly flicked up her skirts and bent forward to reveal her sallow, bare bottom. Fully achieving her purpose, her act had shocked them into stunned silences. This action did not trouble Nell, but it had most certainly upset the group of surprised onlookers. Each astonished, shamed or embarrassed they had turned from her with glowing cheeks. The only pairs of cheeks without any reddened hue were Nell's. She readjusted her apparel. With skirts unfurled, she strode away down the dusty road without a second glance in their direction or any word. Her own annoyance was quickly forgot, but the young men went about in the town, repeatedly speaking of her brazen lewdness.

Talk of the coarse incident was oft' regurgitated. Men bragged to their cronies about what they would do (or had already done) with 'bawdy Nell'. The boys suggestively talked of her smooth body, but kept silent that it was they who had caused her irate irrational behaviour in the first place. In the ale houses one lad joked, 'The minute she hitched her skirts, I could have sworn that an evil wind blew our way!' The younger men brayed while their fathers were aghast.

Later, on Nell's cackled retelling of the event, Mary stood shocked. She worried on the incident throughout the evening. 'Oh, Nell, how could you? You'll give yourself a foul reputation, doing things like that! This is sure to rebound on us both.'

'You always worry too much, my dear Mary,' her friend counselled. 'There is so much more news from around and about for folk to discuss than my rump. Let them gossip and it will pass. They're still belly-aching about the little "gent in black velvet" who helped bring about the late King's death than to worry long about me.'

Mary was not so sure, but assumed Nell had spoken true, as within days she had learned in conversation that the Creed family had watched as their bold son, Richard, left to re-join his troop in France. The chatter reported that he had "writ a will". Some tattle-tales saw that the very act of writing his will had released some silent malediction. Mary, who knew many of the Creed's servants, disputed their words - as she believed in no such thing.

...ooo000ooo...

Sunday, the day of prayer and rest, was not an auspicious one. Nell caringly prepared a marchpane augmented with mandrake root, just enough (as her friend had noted) to enhance a man's libido. She carefully packed the sweet treat in a cloth, along with a cordial, in her basket. While all were at work, her aim was to walk to the King family's smallholding to pay a surprise visit on her beau - Ambrose. Hoping to find him there, working on the farm alone, she was certain that he would to enjoy her visit and any surprise benefits brought with it. In doing so, she had sourly discovered that his libido was perfectly fine without need of her marzipan cake - and that she was not his only suitor. Kitty Denton had already decided to pay a visit to Ambrose - with appealing dimpled sweetmeats of her own. Indeed, on catching the offending pair of lovers in an ungainly clasp, Elinor had angrily rounded on them.

Young Kitty Denton had immediately blanched and backed away from Ambrose as Elinor laid forth with an irate tongue and very direct speech.

'How could you cheat on me with this stripling of a girl? I can see she is a pretty dolt, but surely you do not need to bed us both?' she yelled. 'What is wrong with you? Was I not sufficient for you that you need this artless moll?' She glared angrily from one to the other.

Ambrose, in turn, remained equally sharp. 'Well, I have heard that you are not so innocent or pure either, Madam. I have good witness from patrons in the Swann that you are not untainted, Mistress Shaw. What do you have to say about that?' he spat back at her with fury and haste. His face reddened to match his hair as he wheezed in anger. He pushed a greasy, copper lock from his face with a newly un-clenched fist, then glared at her, dry of words.

Elinor quickly turned as she heard Kitty's soft cry. She scowled at her. 'Stop snivelling, you silly girl. You are indeed a dolt and a dullard!' She regarded the blubbing adolescent without sympathy.

Rubicund, Ambrose was furious, but his anger was not beyond that of Elinor's. They fought like cat and dog. One gave and the other gave back, trading slaps and words in almost equal proportions. Finally, Elinor turned keenly with her finger pointed as a threat to them both,

'You will be sorry for slighting me, Ambrose … and you too pretty Kitty.'

With this she spun and strode from the house without bothering to look back or close the door. She left it swaying in her wake. She heard it being quietly closed and the hushing of Kitty's cries as it did so. She assumed that Ambrose had fastened it to shut her out and to enable him to comfort his distraught and darling, semi-clad girl.

The gentle cows had moved away as they'd noted Elinor skipping towards the solitary farmhouse to see Ambrose. Now, on her enraged return, they lowed quietly and moved skittishly. The grazing bovines were not immune from the girl's sourness. Elinor eyed them with some trepidation as they seemed much larger close by than she had expected. To turn them away she clapped her hands, then held them wide. The cows were reluctant to move at first, but finally in a cluster, they ambled from their water trough, away downhill through the long grasses.

As she walked, Elinor, aware her hands were still shaking from the unpleasant encounter, placed them into the long pocket of her cloak. With surprise she made contact with something deep in the confines of the pocket that tickled her finger tips. There were leftover elements inside from her previous times foraging. She pulled forth a bundle of dried hemlock. In her anger, she threw the unwanted handful into a water trough as she was passing by. Unknown to her the plant with its seeds first floated, then sank. Still infuriated, she continued her journey home in the hope that Mary would be able to cheer her.

On her arrival, she discovered the small cottage was abandoned by humans and felines. She thoroughly washed her hands in gritted-animal fat, rosemary and orange-peel water before deciding what to do next.

'What a damnable wasted trip. I have need to unburden myself to a comforting ear. Where can you be now, Mary?' she muttered to herself. Realising the quietness of the house was bringing no solace, she left the cottage and walked to the centre of town.

'Good day to you, Mistress Nell,' called Silas Reedman, as he merrily raised a hand in salutation. He stood by his shop, but his smile turned to a frown as Elinor paced past without a glance his way, let alone an answer to his greeting. Determinedly, Nell strode to the White Lion for an ale - and no person was about to halt her. Silas had regarded her demeanour and seen her anger. He had noted how she rubbed her hands on her cloak and mumbled inaudibly to herself. 'This is not a day to tangle with Nell Shaw', he assumed, before returning his attentions to a length of burlap he was folding.

After an hour of solitude with an ale in the poorly lit inn, Elinor finally went home. She knew that in her absence Mary had returned too. On opening the door new scents assailed her nose. She entered to find that Mary was indeed back from delivering her wares and had begun warming some leftover meat and root-vegetables in a hearty-smelling stew. As Nell entered, her friend was singing to herself in the back room. Mary heard the door slam, so went to see who had come in. She perceived her friend's indignation, so helped remove Elinor's cloak from her shoulders. The girl's trembling fingers did not seem to function on the button and loop that fastened it. She observed on how Nell swayed and wondered if she had fallen. Her dark cloak seemed very grubby and held seeds trapped in its fibres, so Mary offered to wash it for her. Nell easily acquiesced and gave Mary her cloak to launder. This one small kindness cheered her. As the women ate dishes of steaming stew, Nell told of her walk to the farm – and of her return. The wind had left her sails, yet her tone remained bitter as she told Mary of Kitty and Ambrose's deceit.

Several days later, Nell felt much revived. Yet again, her renewed spirits were short-lived as news reached her ears that Farmer King had lost several of his herd. None could determine the cause, but talk was rife.

Mary was wary as she deliberated on the week gone. She fretted on what she surmised, but held her tongue. Safe in her own council, she reflected on her friend's hurt. She remained bothered that on that fateful evening as she had rinsed out Nell's filthy cloak, she had discovered small remnants of hemlock in the pocket lining. As she washed the seeds away and threw the incriminating toxic water into the nearby ditch to be absorbed into the brown earth, she wondered how the 'poison parsley' came to be there, as it was not fit for man nor beast.

...ooo000ooo...

Chapter 19
Courtship, Cures and Curses

Samuel awoke to the cool autumn sun as it glimmered and sparkled playfully though the cracked shutters. He rolled over on his pallet and rubbed at his eyes. It took little time before he'd clothed himself in a leather jerkin over his loose shirt, then hurried out. Normally he walked to each byre until he was, finally, guiding a full herd. Each beast usually awaited him outside their homes, but today the lane seemed unnaturally quiet. No cattle awaited him or came to his summons. Sam called out, 'Hoy! Hoy!'

He whistled as loudly as possible to beckon the beasts. Then had waited in the lane in confusion, until Hal and Todd Dobbs eventually appeared.

The Dobbs brothers looked equally dishevelled and flustered as Samuel asked how they fared. Todd Dobbs took Sam strongly by an arm and led him from the lane to the back of the barn. Here Sam grasped the enormity of the problem concerning the absent milk cows. Most appeared to be lying on their sides, unable to stand, breathing heavily – if at all. Their ears were low and a thick nasal discharge stuck around their noses.

Sam thought, 'They can't even be bothered to lick themselves clean.' Those not dead looked in the process of dying. 'Several of us have been affected. Folks along the lane with live stock animals are keeping theirs inside today, to ward off any evil that might befall them.'

The two men stood in silence as Todd walked to the edge of the open space and clambered through the ditch to the ridge beyond. Hal retched slightly as his brother pushed a prone beast with his boot.

'Bugger!' He cursed. Sam picked up on the fearful demeanour of his fellow. 'This sickness seems the same as the one that affected Farmer King's cows. What's caused this, Hal?'

'Not what, Sam. You mean *who*,' his friend cautiously replied. He walked over to pat one of the ailing beasts, then went on to explain, 'This is sour magic from evil spirits.' He steadily shook his head from side to side. As he rubbed his hand through his thinning hair, his eyes seemed to look only into the distance. 'Did you see them blackened crows sitting in the branches of the trees?' he asked.

'Oh, aye. They can be bad omens. I usually take them as a warning of ill-weather,' Sam advised his friend.

Hal nodded wisely. 'Well, I guess it's like when Farmer King's beasts died. Do you recall? Just after Ambrose discarded Nell.' He stopped to take a deep breath. 'I believe Nell Shaw has used her dark powers of hatred to hurt my cows now,' Hal said. 'I've heard talk in the town of the women – who know all sorts of magic and malice.' His friend spat. 'Nell, with the brash voice, she's a sibyl. She has summoned the crows. People who looked after her in Cotterstock said she was fay – and her workmate, Mary is ... well, bloomin' gullible. People cheat her right, left and centre and she don't notice naught.'

'No. What you say isn't true. I cannot believe this of Elinor - and Mary would not harm a cow - or a person. She's a healer. They are my friends,' declared Samuel.

Hal Dobbs almost shouted with bitterness, 'Do not call them that! How can they be your friends, lad? Look what they've done.'

Sam began to protest but, convinced in his own belief, Hal was no longer paying any attention to him. The man steadily shook his head as he viewed the carnage.

'Well, I differ in my opinion young man. Mistress Danford has lived long enough to know best and she said that the Philips woman can bewitch cats, beasts and people - and she should know. She knows all manner of things.' He cast his dejected eyes down to observe a loose stone that he kicked with his foot. 'My life's ruined. I can't afford to live. My cow cost me sixty shillin's at market. My brother can hardly talk about it.' Hal was mawkish. 'These dead 'uns may be used for leather and glue, but no sane person will want t' eat my meat for fear it's tainted.' He looked solemnly at Sam. 'If you want t' keep your job as a cattle herder, I suggest you drop those friends o' yours before they turn on *you*.'

With this, Hal turned and stomped away across the stubble of the field as Sam looked on with pity. He well knew that smallholders could be ruined by a bad year. He did not know how help the man, but knew from the past that if there was a dispute, Hal and Todd were most likely to settle the matter with their fists. Sam sat on a nearby stump to survey the scene of destruction. With his fair, stubbled chin held heavily in his hands he thought seriously of what had passed. After a time he returned home in low spirits to tell William of his morning. He arrived to find Mary visiting. After passing pleasantries they each discussed the age old issue of the weather. Wilf was happy to sit and listen to his father, while Sam wanted to know why the animals were dying.

'Well, lad. There's been scant rainfall and folk've remarked on the dryness of their land. It's been dry and is getting worse,' William began.

'But it's been a fine summer', she began.

'It saw smallholders complaining of drought.' Sam remarked.

'If it rained they complained, yet they also grumbled when the sun shone with no rain.' Mary smiled compassionately at the older man. 'Our streets stink and maggots have thrived. I see this has brought the sickness.'

Wilf nodded thoughtfully, but William was not so sure about this. 'Over a draught in the drover's inn, I stood amongst those who talked of warnings,' he said, taking a sip of milk. 'Talk in the taverns sympathised with farming families for their losses. They said our sins are the cause.'

Mary looked on with wide eyes as the three men discussed the many reasons for sickness and drought. She did not refute William's argument as she did not wish to anger her old friend or change their relationship by rebuking his beliefs.

...ooo000ooo...

As the season changed Sam and Mary met frequently by the water way. They avoided open land, said to be accursed, while farmers disposed of their dead animals via any who would take them.

Balmy late autumnal winds returned. They blew wisps of Mary's hair, exposed, as it escaped from her coif and blew over her face. An equally tousled, grinning Samuel gently removed the fine strands, one by one from her cheek with his calloused hands, as Mary patted the strands back into position her slim fingers. The wind played games with the couple, tugging at Mary's shawl until Sam placed his arm around her shoulders to hold it in place. Neither complained about the antics of the wind on this occasion.

'Just listen to the wind. On days such as this I feel God's breath on me, Sam,' remarked Mary as she closed her eyes in contentment, resting her head on his shoulder. 'Can you not hear His low voice in your ears?' She tilted her head and looked at him side-on with her nut brown eyes. 'I hear His waterfall of words.'

Sam looked to the woman, glowing with loving tenderness. 'The Lord gives His people the blessings of sun and rain. It's time to sanction our love – in front of our friends in the Church.' Undisturbed by the wind, he kissed her slender hand, then bent to pick a bright yellow kingcup tangled in the long grasses at their feet, which he handed to his love.

Mary's tinkling laugh rang softly in his ears.

'Let's be united forever, together under our Lord's roof. I have asked before, but when will you marry me, Mary? Why delay?' He spoke softly, whilst earnestly looking into her sparkling eyes. Capturing his gaze, she leaned slowly forward and tenderly kissed his lips. Neither hard nor gently, Sam wrapped his arm around her slender waist and pulled her toward him. For several minutes they remained enwrapped. 'Well?' he finally asked in his deep, low voice. She seemed hesitant. 'Can you say you're not content with me? Marry me, Mary.'

A sharp crack and rustling sounds brought them from their reverie and prevented Mary from giving an answer. They each turned to look to where the sound emanated. For a moment naught appeared, until

Catchevole, carrying a dead mouse from a successful hunt, launched himself from the waving fronds of the plentiful coppice. As if unaware of their presence, he padded past them, heading for the barn, where he would no doubt feast and rest.

The wind blew hard and the dry leaves of the thicket trees shivered and shook with a tremulous rattle. Mary trembled too. 'Are you chilled?' Samuel queried as he tucked an unruly length of Mary's hair back towards her nape. 'Let me walk you home, then light a fire to keep you warm.' He clasped Mary more tightly to him as he straightened her shawl once again.

They walked home along the twisting paths of the dimming wood. On arrival, Sam did not need to help start a fire at the cottage, as Nell had already arrived home and had done so. With this knowledge, he bid a fond farewell to each of the women and returned home. On his route, he listened to the song of the evening birds, particularly the resonance of the brown and cream-speckled nightjar with its strange repute for silent flight and fabled talent for thieving milk from goats! He chucked as he noted that Mary loved the friendly chirrup of each small brown reed warbler with their glad chittering. He knew he would press her for an answer on the morn – and every day, until she accepted his offer. Mary did also.

That night stray street dogs roamed at will. These were heard barking, chasing, fighting - and their din kept Mary awake.

The owl with its eerie call served to relax her – as did the comforting sounds of the high-pitched bark of playful foxes as they conducted their evening prowl in nearby woods. Mary recalled that, as a child, she would hold her breath to wait for her foxy friends to call again. She thought of the farmers who took in their fowl and livestock at night; locking them into barns, cages and houses to prevent loss. Eventually sleep overcame her. The nocturnal creatures continued hunting and playing, while Mary finally slept deeply.

She awoke late the following day, yet the house stayed dark. Mary heard stormy winds rattling shutters and posts along the row. From out, beyond their front door, there came a sudden crash. Then only the dark, growling wind could be heard as it whipped and thrashed in loud frenzy outside. Another abrupt sound suggested the squall had torn out a tree or destroyed part of an unstable wall in its ferocious onslaught. Mary knew she should check to find what damage had been wrought outside - once the storm had fully abated.

Awake too, Elinor rolled over onto her back to listen to the unbroken roar of the wind and occasional patter of rain. She had awoken to hear Mary turning on her pallet, so spoke softly, 'That was very loud – and close. What do you think it was?'

'I'm not certain, Nell. We can look later. It sounded like a tree taking a tumble.' Her answer was gentle. Her voice remained low. 'There's no rush from our warm beds into the cold air. There won't be a market today! Just hear the gusts.'

She was right. The wind bore no sympathy for the realm it destroyed. Rough weather had set in for a week. At the end of it there was much to talk about and plenty of cleaning up to do. The great storm had begun on the final Friday of November with a little quiet rain, then angrily, the shrieking fury of a gale-force wind gusted in from the south, flinging foliage in its wake.

Livid winds followed that veered west-south-west and finally northward, wreaking havoc and destroying everything within their path. Rain came again to wet the pounded earth. At first with tiny patters then with giant drops – as the hardened ground became a mud-puddle-pie, then a quagmire.

What Mary and Nell heard was widespread thunder and a storm that amazed onlookers as it ripped the sky and lit quaking trees in transitory flashes. There was a beauty in its madness and horror. Taking no recess, the rain came like a torrent, wiping each pebbled pathway clean; then running in well-matched courses of darkening liquid that raced with glee as each rivulet sought the fastest way to lower ground.

The women watched from their window as squalls tossed trees and leaves without care. For disconsolate hours the rain poured while the women remained captive, but safe in homespun warmth.

By mid-December news filtered from London, informing all that the storm had not just affected the insignificant town. As travellers circulated, their discourses clarified exactly how extensive the great storm had been. They told of hampered travels, of bricks, tiles and stones that were thrown hither and thither with such force that none dared venture forth from their homes for fear of being hit. After this foul tempest the countrywide cost of slate increased many-fold, while eleven miles north, the roofers in Collyweston smiled at their profit. Prices were compared as the town began its own repairs.

Within a matter of weeks, crystal icicles hung low from the eaves of frozen households in cascades of downward pointing digits. Drought was forgotten as cold, frosty days brought new fraught reports of devastation on the steaming breaths of strangers. This year, the cheer of seasonal drinking and dancing remained subdued, with plays and singing of psalms muted. Some reported that the Frost Fair on the Thames was a poor affair this year, with repairs to the capital being a priority. Green boughs and garlands of ivy and holly adorned church and houses as Advent began with an emphasis on the timeless discourse of winter darkness and candle light, evil and good. Holy days were celebrated as the clearing of debris continued around the district.

At least there was plenty of fire wood, damp as it was, to collect for burning in the wayside homes. By early 1704, hearsay from a haughty gent communicated that 'Queen Anne hath said that the extensive, devastating winter storm is a sheer calamity, so dreadful and astonishing that its like is not recalled by any person living in her kingdom.'

The gentleman did not linger long in the town as none wanted to hear of others ailing more than they. All were affected by the outcome of the weather but, as the fox-like Todd Dobbs sourly noted to his cronies in the inn, 'It's alright if you're the bloody queen. You don't have to fix your own bloody house if you're her – and she doesn't give a fart about us.'

An unnatural surge of tides had caused flooding as they gushed along the narrow rivers. News had it that twelve warships with a thousand men aboard were lost off the coast, while lighthouses were obliterated and ample numbers of vessels thought to be safely anchored were either destroyed or damaged. Many had drowned or died in wreckage, with hundreds more injured by plummeting airborne debris. Inland, land-owners complained of ruined farming acreage and woodlands with trees torn out by their roots. Families sought help to chop, stack and sell ruined timber in faggots of firewood. While houses and outbuildings required rebuilding, busy workmen were employed in repairs that brought unforeseen incomes from the storm; feeding families and offering nest-egg cash.

Although the town was not in the direct trajectory of the storm, there was still damage. Nell and Mary discussed the shambles left behind – and the people who had plundered the derelict ruins of buildings for any free buff-yellow limestone and wood.

Nearby Lyveden's 'new bield' ruin was sought for timber that was 'sawed out of the walls' as free material. This unfinished Oundle limestone shell stood off the ancient wooded track via Harley Way to Brigstock, on the periphery of Rockingham forest. A nearby cottage, in the process of being built, was using stone intended for the lodge. Workmen repairing the thatched roof had allowed Mary to shelter with them when she was caught out in a passing shower.

It was a lonely walk over hill and dene to Brigstock, so whene'er she passed she raised a hand to acknowledge the busy thatchers.

Working nearby, Samuel was torn between unpaid work at home and paid work around town. Whilst his father and brother busily repaired their house and barn, Sam lent a hand to others. Most spoke of the storm as a message sent as God's warning to change their ways. Sam heard over and over how the storm created nightmarish hardships "throughout the realm" - besides plenty locally.

Ted Jackson had emotionally remarked to Sam, 'We are ruined. God has thrown sea salt in our field! What a to-do!' Ted was unsure if land would be fertile enough for cereal growth to harvest and sell in the coming year. 'What will become of my crop?' he wondered aloud. 'We know the world was made in only seven days, but it's been devastated in almost as many.'

On Sunday morning, Reverend Edward Caldwell regarded the storm as he intoned in his morally sententious sermon. 'We remember the lives of those who have passed from us, for God has sent this heavenly sign as a warning to us. Bend your knee and repent of your sins.'

As vicar of the parish, Caldwell had sadly seen the demise of elderly parishioners, paying his pocket with funerals and mourning that brought about an increase in Sunday worshippers. He held, 'We have suffered alongside those who died as a consequence from our fall in faith.'

While some looked to God, others glanced at Elinor and Mary whom, rumour had it, had foretold the great storm. Illness accompanying standing, stagnant and dirty water brought Mary and Elinor new customers. Some sought them out to ask for tonics. One such was Matthew Abbot. From the outset of illness, Matthew's cattle were infected and sick, then his boy fell ill too. Mary visited Matthew and his son. Both looked thin, pale and bore a wicked cough. Matthew asked Mary to look at the lad and counsel him on what to do.

'What ill have we done to deserve this?' he wondered aloud.

Mary counselled, 'Matty, I believe there is an infection on your land - or a venom in your water that does you harm. Is there fresh dung nearby your home?' She had seen diseases that spread easily and prayed this was not one of them. She advised the man look after him own needs as his son needed him healthy. Matthew was not sure of Mary's diagnosis and knew not what to do. He further consulted the phlegmatic vicar, Edward Caldwell, for advice. In consequence, they prayed together.

Mary was exasperated when she heard of this. 'There's more to his problem than an act of God.'

None wished to hear her blasphemy. Neither the Reverend Caldwell nor the non-conformists in town had time for Mary. The Reverend Caldwell disapproved and saw any avowals attributed to the woman as blasphemy. As for Nell, neither man craved involvement with "the outspoken trollop".

Meanwhile, Matthew Abbott silently returned home. He had sat, then lay alongside his son on the edge of the bed to rest. Hs off-balance head quickly drifted into a deep, dark sleep. He woke with a start. It was already dark. He muttered to the silent child at his side, 'It is too late now to walk to meet Dicken at the inn – or to go to the church to pray. Tomorrow. I will wait until tomorrow.'

Matthew pulled a cover over the child and wrapped himself in a blanket. Feverishly, he slept again. On reawakening, his headache was worse. Matthew was certain that his head would shortly explode like a cask of dry gunpowder. He thought, 'I need a relief. Perhaps I should call for a medic for ... a tonic ... or to be bled?' He quaked as he further considered, 'That will come at a price. A price I can ill-afford.' He sweated and shook with fever; awake throughout parts of the night. He thought he'd heard his son calling, but was too tired to move or check. His cover and blanket were soaked, yet his mind did not warn him of this in his fragile, befuddled state.

'What was that?' he wondered.

Whatever it was, it called from a long way away. Was that someone calling?

'Go away,' he murmured. 'Leave me. Cease. I'm tired ... bone tired ... and my head aches. I'll check who calls me on the morn ... when I'm ... better.' He drifted in and out of sleep.

'Perhaps,' he thought, as pain pierced his brain before drifting yet again into delirious sleep, 'this is a test from above?'

He would come to know - all too soon.

The following morning Matthew, being no better, was missed in the drover's inn. He was called upon by concerned friends - and later by the priest. His friends had individually speculated on why the man was absent from their usual drinking place the previous evening. A couple had suggested the reason for that was his son's illness.

They knocked and entered his darkened door. The smell as they entered did not bode well. They tiptoed with trepidation towards the bed. Matthew stirred. He remained confused as his friends lit a lamp against the darkness and threw open the shutters to perceive more clearly. As Matthew was greatly confused, he did not comprehend that his son had died. His friends had not dared tell. They took it upon themselves to ensure he was attended to by a priest.

Faltering, Matthew attempted to talk with his friends. He spoke in stumbling words of Elinor and Mary – and of those long gone. This was a waking dream.

His friends did not wish to tarry for long, torn between friendship and fear of infection. They did not wish for to abandon their friend in his hour of need, yet their reluctance to linger in the presence of fever was overwhelming. They paid a physician and a sagacious woman for advice. The doctor took their money and the wizened woman gave Matthew a syrup that made him doze. He never returned to his customary cognizance as the barber-surgeon made notes and kept his own council.

Matthew's friends were shocked as they impotently watched their friend swiftly succumb to his own sickness. Within a matter of days his blotch-dappled body was found on the floor by the fire. At the inquest held in the Swann, friends affirmed that he had been unwell for days. They also swore, 'He'd been treated by the two women in the cottage at the end of the lane.'

...ooo0OO0ooo...

Once the many supplications for improved weather had been heard in the Church, the elements seemed to brighten.

Elinor had left the cottage in good spirits with the handle of her covered wicker-basket resting in the crook of her arm. She had been charged to deliver items for Mary to the nearby villages. She walked sedately to Ashton beneath grey, but dry, skies to deliver their wares. On her way back, she had visited the Millward infant. She spent longer than she planned at the mill; talking and dandling the small infant on her knees, whilst giving its parents a happy respite.

It was late when she finally set forth for home. Sudden mists swirled and layered the marshy ground by

248

the riverside. Nell had left that morning wearing less than she now needed. Outside, the hazy sun hid. As Nell walked, a cold chill crept into her bones. The sound of racing water warned her of freshwater, riverine elements nearby.

Meanwhile, Mary had looked out through her door many times whilst awaiting her friend - who had not come home. As it grew late, Mary decided that it would be wise to light a lantern, then set out to find her friend. She knew which route would most likely bring her home.

As Mary walked carefully along the well-worn way, avoiding stepping into holes or muddy puddles, her hair fought and twisted in the steadily growing blustery conditions. It blew into her tawny eyes, which she squinted to see through the gloom. Wind plastered her tangled tresses to her face. She let go of her cloak to push her locks aside with a spare hand as she walked. The wind threatened to tear the cloak from her shoulders. Suddenly the gale abated, as if satisfied it had already done its worst.

As she peered into the cold mist, Mary wished that she had thought to bring Elinor's cloak with her, as she had noted it on the hook by the door, but there was no sign of the sudden squall as she left. She chastised herself for being so unthinking.

As she neared the river, she was further bothered by the cold and rising mist then, precipitously, was much reassured to hear the pitter-pat of familiar footsteps in the gloom.

Elinor was overjoyed to see her friend. Both women sighed simultaneously in relief and both began to speak in the same moment. Mary placed her lantern on the ground as they hugged, relieved that they each was safe, before walking home as jubilantly noisy companions. Mary felt the chill of Nell's arms. She offered to give her warm cloak to Elinor, but as she refused, they shared. Pulling the fabric taut around their huddled shoulders, they stepped carefully homeward.

Later, in the warmth of her bed, aspects of the occasion bothered Mary. She fretted over the risks her young friend took, while observing that Nell did not bother with the most sensible decisions.

The following day Mary left the house early, as she had spent many evenings completing work for regular customers and had deliveries to make.

Quickly, she first traced her steps through the quiet town to a familiar grand house in the high street. On arrival, Mary walked down the side path to the well-used back door that led into a small vestibule, then into the familiar, warm kitchen. She hoped that cook would be there and would offer her refreshment for her trouble. She stepped up on to the newly cleaned doorstep and rapped loudly. After a time, a smartly-dressed, but dour maid, whom Mary did not recognise, answered her knock. The maid looked down her nose from the door to beyond Mary - out into the street - then uncomfortably at the caller.

'Good day. How can I help you?'

'I have come with the lady's hose. Your Mistress ordered them two weeks ago. George Addee, the footman, knows who I am. Is he not here?' She peered around beyond the maid into the darkened lobby. As she looked around the woman, Mary made to step inside, but the maid barred the door with her body.

Mary continued, 'I thought I was expected today? George's wife usually takes receipt of my goods for the lady. My hose are a good colour and a regular fit. I hope these are to your Mistress' liking.' Mary reached into the basket and lifted out her goods for the woman to take, yet the maid did not even bother to look at the merchandise. She stared indifferently into Mary's face.

'Mister Addee is busy seeing to his work, as is cook. I know who you are. Thank you, Mistress Phillips, but I've been requested to say the Master and his family no further require your services.'

Mary was stunned. 'What? May I ask why?' she asked as a frown creased her brow.

The maid had the good grace to look slightly abashed. 'I'm told my Mistress has found a new purveyor of knitwear. Thank you for your service. Goodbye.' She pursed her lips and blinked several times.

Mary placed her hand on the closing door. 'But … but, she knows me well … as I am reliable and she said I make the best hosiery in town.'

'I am sorry. Goodbye.' The maid moved a pace back from the door. Her face remained unmoved.

'I do not understand …,' Mary began as the door closed firmly in her face. Mary sighed loudly. She looked at the good in her basket, then down at her feet. 'I am truly a foolish nincompoop. What's happened here?' She had many questions, but no answers. 'What did I do wrong?' she wondered as she turned away from the house to quietly plod home, with not so much as a penny in her hand for all her hard work.

The remainder of that Tuesday passed uneventfully. Elinor arrived home slightly inebriated, but that night and beyond Mary found that losing trade and a drunken friend were the least of her worries.

For the next couple of nights thereafter Mary could not sleep. She was prevented from sleeping by the nocturnal, soft scutterings of an inquisitive mouse as it moved around the perimeter of walls, surfaces and tables. Mary had loudly spoken to it, 'Cease your roaming, rat. Go. Leave us in peace,' but to no avail. The mysterious mouse was not prepared to listen to any polite request.

On Friday night, as if by magic, there were no sounds to be heard. Mary slept soundly for the first time that week.

The next morn, as a dull sun rose in the sky, Mary awoke much refreshed and restored.

She stretched, rose and moved steadily around the house opening each shutter. As she sought food to break her nightly fast, she spied a nimble feline movement from the corner of her eye, so strolled over to the culprit. She bent to stroke a very self-satisfied Catchevole. If a cat could display pride or smile, he most surely did. She glanced around. There, on the surface of her clean table, as if laid for breakfast, were displayed inner workings of her nocturnal, tiny tormentor!

…oooOOOooo…

Chapter 20
As Rumour Has It

During the wet spring months, much chatter circulated in the defensive male-domain of the acrid, roast-bean scented coffee houses and smoke-filled inns. Patrons paid a penny for each steaming cupful, then comfortably seated, were content to talk over local issues and the infinitesimal evils of the world. Discussion was generally accompanied by a shaking of heads or the sound of arguments, acquiescence or resignation regarding the remembered past, present issues or guessed at future for the inhabitants of the town.

Each week Samuel's father, who had no taste for coffee, took time drink an ale or two alongside convivial friends. Here, they discoursed on politics and scandals. One perpetual source of news came from travellers who gave true and false congress as a gambling accompaniment to their bet and barter. They grumbled 'Cheese costs three and one ha'pence per pound now. Butter's a penny more!' and 'Wages 'ave stayed low as prices have risen,' with 'no financial help on the horizon to feed invalids or non-productive infants.'

'How clever of the landowners,' boasted a comfortable gent, whilst drinking brandy in the inn with his clay-pipe waving in his hand as he spoke, 'to keep lowly workers in their places while they help pay for us.'

William overheard and fretted over the labours of his humble associates. The few annual holidays they gained were meagre - and did little to alleviate the endless workload.

After fasting, for many reasons the high street was busy by Easter Sunday. This serious and sacred day led all righteous people and the celebrant faithful to a service in Saint Peter's Church that stood atop of the rise north of Osgyth's field. Fourteen nights later, on St. Walpurgis' Night, the same people left their houses in to celebrate the saint's eve that was filled with bonfires and joyful dancing. Mary and the Barnes' family sat convivially in the drover's inn considering merriments of hallowed evenings past, when spirits roamed free. William suggested that the night before Walpurgis' was as haunted as the night preceding the eve of All Saints' – especially after dark.

Mary laughed as she spoke. 'There is little that happens on these nights, other than my young friend dancing around the house like a nubile sprite - wearing nothing but her nether garments. There's little eerie about that.'

Sam could not help himself as he dissolved into laughter while imagining what their neighbours saw. He explained his views to Mary, through mirthful convulsions. Mary grinned back at him.

'They may well talk,' she said, 'but just you try stopping her when she's so blithe and carefree.'

Those who overheard were not so mirthful.

While Easter came quietly, then passed, Mary had hoped to see Beth Afford and her family, yet this year they did not visit for free eggs as was their usual rule. Market days and festival days, such as the first day of May, came as brief moments of joyful respite in a workaday life. Not a man, woman or child did not look forward to their days off.

Young lads, such as Wilf, proficiently chopped logs to earn an hourly penny-ha'penny. This helped supplement their family intake. 'Any with a young family needs up to forty pounds a year to keep 'emselves out of debt, before their children come old enough to be set to work,' William had declared.

The Bramston's, Walcott's and Creed's did not perceive what it was like to earn a labours' wage of a shilling a day (fifteen pounds each year), yet all deduced that harvest was most productive and profitable time of year. When the church bells rang out, people of all ages met in the fields to reap and stack. This was lucrative for flexible artisans like Mary, who would join with farmers and townsfolk to stack, dry and fetch each harvest safely in before any autumn rains appeared.

As she paced over the fields, Mary worried less over the amount she earned, than the amount she didn't. Recent income losses had meant less food in her dry-store, but she considered herself lucky in that, at least, she had her own home to live in.

…ooo000ooo…

On returning from the field bearing a sackcloth bag filled with rye grains, Elinor and Mary noted Sarah Short heading in the same direction. Mary called out to her and they joined to walk together across the field. On walking uphill in St. Osgyth's lane they encountered Meg Webster. Each gave greeting and passed the time of day.

'Shall we have an ale together before I sell these stockings?' Nell suggested as they passed the Anchor. This they did. All was well, until Sarah carelessly noted that she'd heard Nell was called a 'pitiful town tart who drank too much'. Nell slammed down her drink, slopping some of the amber liquid onto the dark wooden surface of the table. With arms akimbo, Nell swelled her chest, placed her hands upon her supple hips and coughed

255

loudly to alert Sarah to her anger. She shouted at the gossip in her own defence, while men in darkened corners listened and looked on. They were not averse to seeing two provocative molls having a scrap together.

'A hex on you, natterer. May the Devil take you, gossip-monger … That's if those lies of yours have not deemed you are already His?'

Onlookers gasped at her tirade. 'Did you hear her?' a neighbour unkindly remarked. 'She cursed us all.'

Sarah stoutly replied, 'It's only what I heard.'

This dry seed grew in later conversation, turning rumour to rampant forest fire. Hidden hints alleged, 'We've seen her at her door admitting the Devil.' The words were always "told in total confidence", of course.

Sarah, not one to be outdone, smarted with ire. 'I have reliable information that Lizzie observed Elinor entertaining the Devil … Late at night, Nell and her friend welcomed the Devil inside their door.'

'No. When?'

'I'm not sure, but can ask to find out.' Sarah was smug. 'I also heard in the last year they've met for immoral doings by the river – and conduct wickedness at home with the Devil. They have no scruples.'

Nell couldn't exactly decide when the quiet town changed, but changed it had. She had no taste for rotten rumours. Her maidenhood had long since been taken from her, yet she did not see herself as a whore - or in any way, one expressly used by any fallen angel.

After some consideration she decided to settle her score with the perpetrators of the unpleasant story. Returning home after completing her deliveries, Elinor quickly set to work in the silent kitchen. She unobtrusively mixed two brews that appeared the same.

She bottled them. Most contained a simple honey and elderflower tonic. Two bore elderflower, honey and a strong herbal purgative.

Smiling, she placed several flasks in her basket - and two into the pockets of her skirts. She sang as she walked the lane, heading for the inn most frequented by the Coles and Short families. She did not notice if the weather was inclement, as her destination and purpose led directly to the Swann.

On arrival, Nell bought herself a mulled beer and set up a conversation with Joseph Coles' friends. She offered these clients a "strong potion for verity and strength". Joseph arrived a little later with his daughter in tow. The drinkers chivvied them to try Nell's concoctions. Lizzie's father and his friends showed great interest, while Lizzie and Sarah sat glaring at the bountiful Nell from their smoke-filled corner. The clammy, drinking atmosphere of the inn was a perfect setting for Elinor to purvey her wares – as many had already imbibed enough to be tempted.

'Try some,' she sweetly offered, passing a honeyed flask to the men. 'Try for free. Taste and see how my elixir helps you. These tonics work well enough to soothe coughs and can reveal all that is truthful in a person to their friends.'

Many of the well-glazed men took a swig from a shared bottle and were pleasantly surprised at the pleasantness of the contents. Lizzie and Sarah showed little interest but, as was his nature, Joseph Coles was steadily coaxed to purchase a bottle for one half-penny. With simple sleight of hand Elinor put away his coin, felt in her pocket and swapped a small bottle she held for one in her pocket. She watched with bated breath as each of the men paid her. She knew that Lizzie was guaranteed to be tempted and bound to try some as she'd bragged to Sarah and Mercy that she was always truthful.

Elinor laughed loudly when, within two days, it came to Elinor's ears that Lizzie had flung her offending bottle of tonic into the privy, where she'd spent several wretched hours handling diarrhoea, vomiting and "a terrible gut cramp".

Nell's purgative plan had indeed worked, but it carried an undesirable effect contrary to her initial intention when offhand chatter turned to hateful outrage. Lizzie was not shy or slow in suggesting that 'Elinor has sold my papa a terrible poison that almost killed him'. Rumour spread and several families who knew Mary had abruptly ceased buying her remedies. This meant that she was forced to walk further afield to employ the skills Old Isabel had taught her: trading potions, birthing and healing.

Mary and Elinor were tired of the town babble and began to discuss leaving the place. They only delayed as people in the nearby villages still had need of their services. As the villagers held strong religious beliefs, Mary's help was not yet ascribed to 'curses and magic' when the treatment or cures worked. The only drawback of aiding people in the villages was each long walk to reach home before darkness fell. At night it was common for well-to-do travellers to hire a lanthorn and a porter if they traversed gloomy streets after dark. Mary perceived footmen and lantern-bearers as she returned home late. She was always glad to see those bearing a flickering lamp - as the lanes bore very murky corners and shady lanes.

Servants conducted their masters safely home in the dark with a lamp and sturdy baton that discouraged most 'filches' and prowlers. Without the advantages of this privilege, Mary often travelled alone - unprotected. She appreciated ambling behind any footman and felt all the safer for it.

Ladies, such as Mistress Elizabeth Pickering and her companions, easily identified by their alabaster skin tones, were accompanied by male servants, paid to look after them. Poor women were equally easy to identify with their work-roughened, tanned skin bought from labouring in the open-air. Market-trading, laundering and hanging out the washing of those who could afford it, exposed faces, arms and legs to the sun.

Mary was not bothered by wrinkled hands and a skin flushed with the kiss of summer sunshine. She bore a rosy glow and happy-creased lines radiated across the tops of her cheekbones to her ears. These were gained from smiling and squinting in the sunshine. Oft' called crow's feet, they resembled the feet of the many-toed crow. They were complementary to her unkempt hair and flecks of dirt that marked the edges of her nibbled nails. Her appearance reflected her work. She marvelled at how the landed gentry, with mostly indoor business to occupy them, bore white hands and spotless sallow faces.

Late summer news suddenly propelled the Creed family and their close friends to the grief of bereavement. Townsfolk mourned with them as news told of their thirty-three year old son, Richard, who had "died in France while bravely leading his troops in the battle at Blenheim". It took time for this news to filter through the town.

William heard in the inn, then repeated what he had heard at home. 'His twenty-four year old brother, John, found him dying on the battlefield and brought his body back to London.' Samuel told Mary, who sighed at the sadness of the event. Mary reflected on how, rich or poor, all were held accountable in God's control.

As days progressed, Mary well-recognised the smells of silage, sewage and refuse that grew worse in the heat. She guessed that the general public reacted to the 'summer stink' and succumbed easily to illness, particularly if they lived already in squalor. The townsfolk swept heaps of refuse and debris into the street to burn in small pyres. This cleansed the worst of it, but by no means cleared the problem. Mary no longer sang to herself as she soaked swatches of cloth in vinegar antiseptic for her patients. She kept some ready for use in earthenware jars in her vinegar box.

Matters did not improve when twelve year-old Charles Ireland fell ill in Southwick village. His father called on Mary in her cottage to beseech her to help his son. She was busy birthing the latest baby at the mill, so Elinor attended young master Ireland in her place. She saw that he was a sallow youth. He bore a sweating sickness and smelled of vomit. Reports crept through the village, when the sweating Charles, instead of quickly recovering, became worse.

'Young Charles has been bewitched,' some said.

Others recalled old Isabel (and a young Mary), who visited to treat the sickly lad in his childhood. When the lad died, it now seemed that the close-knit village had turned as a single entity to blame Elinor - and Mary - of his early demise.

'See what those women have done,' they said. 'One is always too busy and the other allowed venomous air to enter Charles' off-colour frame.'

Elinor had done her best. She had changed his linens and bathed his head, but the boy could not keep food down. The house and its surrounds smelled foul, with the nearby drinking water in the stream outside was polluted by those "taking a dump" nearby. Mats throughout the dank and stuffy house appeared active with fleas and lice that transferred from livestock kept in the same room. Doors were kept closed to keep 'bad' airs out. Indeed, Elinor itched all over as she walked back to the cottage each day. She was certain that she was carrying some of the little biters back home with her.

As chatterers clacked and customers ceased using their well-intentioned services for medication and other easements, the local inn-keeper offered loose talk that was re-hashed by diligent drinkers.

In Oundle, while talking with an acquaintance, Laurence Landen asked, 'Did you hear anything of the lad from Southwick?' He sipped his pint of ale and licked the froth from his stubble, before wiping his lips with a dirty hand.

'I've 'eard he died in agony,' Enoch Smith convincingly remarked.

'Indeed, I heard the two women gave a poison to make him suffer for laughing at them,' Raymond said in a quieted voice as if to avoid others from overhearing.

'I'm not sure he was well enough to laugh by the time they got to him.' Lawrence gaped at the fellow.

'Shame. He were a nice young 'un, Raymond,' the landlord spoke out. 'He was never very strong and had time sick than a-workin', but he were nice enough.'

'Nice and dead now though,' replied their severe friend, through pursed lips. He offered his empty horn cup to the landlord, who refilled it.

Lawrence promptly finished his pint and said his goodbyes. He did not wish to argue with Raymond. The man showed far too much interest in the affairs of others for his liking. Nevertheless, talk spread through the taverns of the town via thirsty traders. As lies spread, tales grew in equal proportion. It seemed that whenever a person or animal took ill or died, it was an opportunity to point an accusing finger at the two. Gossip progressed over the harvest months into late autumn. The women had heard some details of what was being said of them. This left Nell in a sour mood.

'Look. The leaves transformed their colours to fall from the trees,' said Mary, cheerfully, as they had rustled and crunched their way homeward.

'Yes, they have. Enchanted by the season's spell they've died. Nights come earlier and mornings later too. Perhaps our neighbours will say it's our fault - and blatherers'll blame us for it too,' Nell had answered drily.

...oooO0Oooo...

It was a chilly walk when Constable William Boss was summoned to a public house to attend a gin-soaked dispute. He knew there would likely be a free drink in it for him and his colleagues when they broke up the fight and arrested the perpetrators.

Boss knew that the cause was most probably ill-fated gamblers or dog owners, who'd downed too much ale and argued. Their packs of dogs were turned into a penned-ring on the open land at the back of the inn. Their sport was to harass much bigger animals by biting their legs and underbellies, whilst holding resolutely on to their muzzles. Pinning bulls was a manoeuvre of bulldogs and Boss knew that the bloody events attracted many loud-mouthed enthusiasts, winners and losers. Often the dog and owners went home bloodied and injured. Luckily for him, the problem at the inn was largely sorted before he arrived; yet there was indeed time for a quick drink or two as a bonus for turning up.

As Bill Boss and his friends quenched their thirst in the White Lion he caught up with the latest gossip. Thereafter, with his assistance, the accusing words he'd heard had reached the ears of higher authorities. It was only a matter of luck that none in the community was arrested before New Year.

Even Samuel was apprised of the talk from his peers, James Millward and Charles Coles, as they emerged from the autumnal woods with a brace of pheasants. Slow-witted, James openly talked of what he'd heard of the women, while Charles nodded in assent. Sam silently listened as they spoke. Both lads seemed fully convinced of witches causing harm in the town. James saw Mary and Nell's guilt by colluding with the Devil. Sam predicted Lizzie had a hand in influencing her elder brother's opinion.

'Be cautious, Sam', cautioned Charlie. 'Lured to harm, they were. I know you're friendly with them, but they're most harmful to any who speaks against 'em. Pa and Lizzie were both took bilious by their hand.'

Later the same week, Sam heard the opinion of brash horse-handler, John Collop. He, like others, was certainly convinced of their abilities to bewitch. Collop was overheard vociferously stating, 'Me Bible tells what's true. It says "Thou shalt not suffer a witch to live" an' I agree.' He argued on, ''Tis a valid defence to free our country of evil poisoners and witches.'

All Samuel could do was breathe a loud sigh and shake his head. 'My friends are *not* witches, they are simply women who are being picked on - and unfairly blamed for all sorts of mishap,' he replied through pursed lips. None listened. Sam knew friends who believed in their innocence would remain dumb – so as not to be "tarred with the same brush".

Indeed, even his father had advised, 'Son, hush. There's better safety in holding your tongue.'

As Sam make his excuses and departed the inn, leaving his drink half-consumed on a ledge, he spotted a poorly dressed beggar approaching along the muddy, misty road.

'Ho, there young master,' called the ragged man. 'I am early, but am a-*mompen*. Do you have a coin to spare for my empty purse?' The toothless fellow hopefully eyed Sam as he passed. Although mindful of scrounging schemers who took advantage of generous benefactors, momping at least allowed the poorest of souls to eat.

Samuel knew he had only a hunk of bread left in his pocket. He placed his hand into the pocket to retrieve the crust, when the wind made a decision of its own. It stealthily unwound his eye-matching blue scarf from his neck and waved its ends in Sam's face. Sam shrugged his warmly woven cloak and scarf back around his broad shoulders. He offered a tentative smile along with his crust to the emaciated man. The man thanked Sam with a mumble and a nod, then began to walk away. After a moment of thought Sam called out to the vagrant and ran after him to pass over his knitted scarf.

'This is a kind day indeed. I thank you, youngster. Thank you, thank you greatly.' With shaking hands, the tattered man wrapped the already warmed scarf around his neck and heartily shook Sam's hand with his own dirt-covered claw. He waved and called out several times in thanks before moving beyond Sam's hearing.

Along the road, the man passed by Mary's cottage. He had gained provisions there in the past, but with no sign of life within, he continued along the road without a further glance at the darkened house.

In her small corner, Mary was awake. She listened to the wind. She could not sleep. She had long since snubbed out her smoking rush-light in its sconce. Phantoms played on her inner-eyelids keeping her awake throughout the night; making her tired in the day. Her mind was full of fancies, frets and regrets.

Overnight, she mulled them over - and over, contrary to slumber. Troubled by the recent slump in her sales, Nell had suggested that they would soon need to join the poverty-stricken seeking handouts from the homes of the rich. Mary sighed and rolled over to face the rough stone wall. She wanted Sam to rescue her and wrap his safe arms around her. It was here that she decided on a most positive answer to his frequent question of marriage.

…oooO00Oooo…

Chapter 21
Hags and Herbalists

On awakening, Mary smiled, content in knowing that she and Sam were finally to wed. It had been a long engagement, but now she was ready to settle down as a good wife. On rising, she checked if there was a nibble of food left in the larder, then had swept floor free from dried leaves that had blown in overnight, from under the gaps in the rickety frame.

As she opened the door to sweep the foliage out to where it belonged, Catchevole slid inside, then left just as quickly, after determining there was little chance of sustenance. Mary's brow furrowed. Her hazel eyes closed in thought. Tormented, she took a stilted breath, placed her hand over her forehead and ran it down over her smooth face until it rested on her chin. For a time, she stared through the door, unseeing.

When Nell awoke, Mary assailed her with her woes. 'What do I do? There is a sick woman in Barnwell who's near death. I've been asked to attend. Do I go?'

Elinor stared at her now silent friend. She knew no simple, palliative charm would help.

'It's a dilemma, that's for sure - and if aught goes awry you'll be blamed. You know they tell tales of us?'

Mary nodded in agreement, but felt badly about her inflexible choice in the matter. She finally chose to send a message asking the matron to consult another healer. She knew her decision would annoy the woman's relatives, plus leave her vulnerable - and out of pocket.

'I am surely damned if I do and cursed if I do not,' she had skilfully assumed; with flawless conjecture.

The weather commenced its annual cooling chill as Mary attended a few who required her services. She stumbled, as she observed jackdaws pecking the remaining fruits of the apple trees, leaving them pockmarked on the wet grass beneath. She walked slowly with her laden basket from her cottage in the hollow. Ahead of her, on the path, she heard the quarrelling crows and had seen a red-breasted robin, so brave that he stood in her way as he cocked his head to appraise her. She smiled at the cheeky bird. 'You *are* a good spirit. You've come to eat our over-ripe berries and scatter their seeds. You're a pleasure to behold.'

As she spoke she noted others travelling in her direction, going to the busy winter fair in the town. Stall-holders traded alongside walking vendors selling hot foodstuffs and trinkets. Pickpockets were rife, but did they not deter gentry or artisan from sale or purchase. The day felt favourable. Mary trusted her usual customers would buy from her today. She managed to sell a pair of hose, a short grey snood and some eggs before she capitulated.

Mary took her half-full basket home, allowing the wind to blow around her ears and fill her mind with thoughts. She knew that soon it would be springtide - filled with levity and vivid violets bursting in bloom along the foot-worn tracks. She passed the mill. Today it stood silent; empty of its daily grind.

Mary took advantage of her walk to collect a small winter nosegay: dried grasses, black hellebores, dark green leaves and vibrant winter pansies that would look good in a jug on the sill on her arrival home. As she gathered some copper-red witch-hazel, with wiry flowers that grew along the sprawling branches, a hare sprang out of a tangled bush and ran, long-legged, along the track ahead of her. The fields appeared alive with animal life and winter flowers. She mused, 'It is hard to believe they'll soon disappear.'

Sam had begun his day early. Leaving home with a dim sun peeking over the horizon. He'd worked the chill-day through, knowing that the following day was a well-deserved rest day. He glanced up, startled and surprised by a hare, as it bounded from the thicket and ran fast along the well-worn path to the river on its long, nimble legs in the dappled, late afternoon light. Beyond, his eyes noted the welcome sight of a slight figure walking towards him with a transforming smile. Their hands touched as they greeted each other. Sam gently tilted Mary's chin with his hand, looked into her hazel eyes and kissed her softly, before walking homeward, arm in arm.

As they ambled, they passed two constables towing a rope-tied young man betwixt them. The dishevelled youth appeared thoroughly beaten and lagged a pace behind the sturdy men.

'A fine evenin' to you,' called Constable Southwel with a nod, making eye-contact with Sam. 'Look 'ere. The law's made Oundle safe today.' He motioned towards the youth, 'This lad's a thief. He stole apples from yon Master's orchard. We've done our duty 'n' enforced the law for all the good citizens.'

Southwel threw the remains of the core he had been gnawing into a nearby ditch. He wiped his mouth with the back of his wrist as the limping adolescent growled, 'Y'er master's a bloomin' lawyer an' I've little chance against him ... I was only scrumpin'.'

The lad was almost hauled off his feet by the watchman, who said his farewell to Sam and Mary as he hurried the young man along. Both man and thief could be heard cussing until they turned the bend in the track.

Mary watched silently as she considered, 'Do we have *so* much crime that we need so many lawyers hereabouts? I dread what'll happen to that lad. Maybe a whipping or worse? Judges are hand-picked from the wealthy, so they can pick nearly any penance for the lad.'

Mary felt the last rays of the winter sun on her face as her scarf and bonnet caught in a gust of wind. 'Did you grasp the constable didn't look at me? It's as if I was not here.'

Sam did not say a word. The final golden halo of the sun warmed the earth, creating an illusion of distant Biggin Manor ablaze. Sam smiled, 'If the hall's aflame, it won't much please his lordship, William Herbert.'

Mary laughed at his jest and snuggled towards him. She mused on the speed of marching seasons. 'These months have let Mother Nature stun the land. After autumn's yellow fields were scythed in the sunshine, she put on her cloak of gold, red and russet. Look. Copse, ditch, hedge and field are full of scurrying creatures and birds making ready for winter.' Mary smiled at her judgements. 'I think this week we'll see the silver-white mistress of winter as she visits again with her pure and sparkling cloak. She'll fold old crisp leaves into her embrace. By spring they'll be gone.'

Caught in an impulsive flurry, crispy leaves fluttered earthward like lost butterflies. Mary caught one in her hand. She laughed. The thicket and dense covering allowed small creatures to hide in its warm earth of fallen foliage throughout the winter. 'The damp'll set in and my home will need a fire for more than just cooking and laundering. I hope my cosy home-knitted hosiery sells - or I won't be able to fill my wedding-chest for the spring.' She silently crossed her fingers behind her back.

On passing the stunted tree that had, long ago, been hit by lightning, a tawny owl out a-hunting, spotted a movement from his alert eye - a minute mouse in the undergrowth. Startled, she watched as he took flight, soaring and swooping to catch his prey in sharp talons. His unhurried, dignified movements were easy, with no apparent effort, before he flew silently away into the woods. Mary thought, 'Lord help us. It will not be long before mists rise in silence in early mornings as cold meets warmth.'

Samuel and Mary passed the gate.

He'd watched as she flinched when the owl flew low over her head from the nearby tree. He knew his lass did not trust in omens. He had not noticed her silent prayer for good-fortune to safeguard them both.

...oooOOOooo...

After selling a few more items the following day, Mary and Elinor met on their routinely trod route. Chattering convivially, they trudged along. Their going was uneven and filthy. They often slipped and needed to avoid waste and slurry as they stepped along, while trying to avoid ruining their much-repaired shoes. Pass-me-down footwear gained cheaply from the peddler (originally thrown away in the refuse by a wealthy families before being fixed then resold) needed care. These were all they had. It was useful to note what the affluent in society threw away. Some were hardly used, prime to repair and reuse. As Mary liked to say, 'One man's waste is another man's gold.' Elinor was now familiar with her friend's frequent maxims and warnings.

Despite the misty grey day, they were in good spirits as they trudged through the winter-mire on the narrow track back to their cottage. They lifted their damp skirts to avoid the worst of it. Mary commented as she trudged, 'Even if there's not a fire in the hearth when we arrive, at least the worst of the wind will be held off by our stout walls. We'll soon warm up.'

'It won't take long to get a fire blazing to dry out our clothes. I can't wait to get out of 'em.'

'Better to shut the shutters this time, as you gave Nathaniel Ball quite a shock the other day!' Mary laughed as she recollected the astonished look on his face.

As they passed the well, Elinor's acute ears had caught some of what sour-faced Sarah Short and her neighbours discussed. Nell was surprised to hear that her discourse related to herself. She remained quiet until their door was closed behind them, then dutifully relayed the deplorable words to her housemate.

'Mary, they're saying we've harmed people with our remedies. I've not harmed a soul - 'cept for when I made Lizzie fart and puke ... which was not dangerous – and she deserved it. It was funny. They know we did no real harm,' she confided.

Mary could not consider why those whom she knew so well would speak badly of them, yet had begun to note sly, side-on looks as they passed. At the close of a bitter market day, a gaggle of girls had followed and called after them, as they hurried homeward. Eventually Mercy had caught them up. She was out of breath.

'Wait,' she called, 'why are you hurrying so? I've had to run!'

Mary enlightened her. 'We've been out for long enough. We need to go home.'

Out of breath, Mercy gasped. She spoke with seriousness, 'I heard bad talk, Mary. About you and Nell.'

'Really? Who do *you* know who spreads harsh words about me?' Mary asked, glaring at her.

'D' you know, the Reverend says there's evil afoot. He talks ... and says you're unnatural. That you're ...' her voice fell to a whisper that Mary could hardly hear, '... a witch, who's paid your soul for power of healing ... and death.' She panted loudly as Mary stopped walking. 'He's - They're calling you sorceresses - witches.'

'You heard ... *witch*?' she asked as they resumed their pace. 'Surely you are mistaken.'

Mercy stared owl-like at Mary, as if awaiting her response. Meg caught up with them, breathing deeply. Hot and bothered she quietly noted Mary's face. 'Did Mercy tell you? My old granny says anyone can summon the Devil by calling him, but ... Granny said not to say.' She laughed nervously and looked at them side-on.

'What? Did you do that?' Mercy whispered, as she looked from one to the other of the stunned women.

Elinor, stony-faced, rounded on them. She loudly observed, 'Thanks to the Rector and every humdrum chatterer in the town, it's probably already been decided we have wondrous powers.' She laughed with incredulity, while others watched her with concern. 'Lucky is the Wise Woman with the power to do well or ill. If you believe this is true, I suggest you stay clear of us.'

'But, Liz ..., well, umm ... some say you've gave payment ... for foul clout.' Mercy finally spat out with a pained look towards Mary. 'Did you?' she whispered, wide-eyed. Neither suspect spoke.

Never one to be outdone, Meg joined in again. 'Yes. Have you brought evil to us?' She twittered with a high-pitched laugh at her own nervous deliberation.

Mercy added, 'The Rector says only virtuous, well-respected citizens can be trusted. Those on the side of the Devil should be got rid of 'fore they to do ill.'

'Bugger the Rector!' Elinor stared directly at the reddening girl.

Mary spoke. 'You seem to know quite a lot about this, Mercy.' Mercy quietened.

After moments with naught but the sounds of their shuffling feet echoing in the road, Mercy continued in whispered solemnity, 'The Rector says evil people ...' she paused, 'Art you truly ... using witchery?'

On hearing this, the meddlesome Meg and her cronies crossed themselves. Elinor saw these warnings as fearful finger-pointing. She quipped, 'Perhaps that's where I got my devilishly lovely looks from?'

'Nell, do not jest so!' Meg Webster was mortified.

'Do we threaten you? Do you believe that by associating with us, your *friends*, you'll be tarnished?' Mary's voice rose as she eyed the group. Each glanced at the other with pursed lips. They shook their heads. ''Tis truly ridiculous. Whatever next?' Mary said loudly as they began to walk on. 'You're all far too quick to believe judgements based on hearsay for my liking.'

With this, each of the group were glad to go their own way. It took several mulled ales, before Elinor relaxed. As she drank she sank into the bench. She gradually became more and more loud and lewd.

'Don't worry. What do *we* care what *they* believe?' she held loudly. 'Let 'em say what they like.' She continued, 'Why listen? Who heeds dolts? Let the Devil take 'em an' their sinful tongues.'

Mary had need to coax Elinor out of the inn and away, before the landlord took their last coin or moved them on. Alert eyes and ears trailed them to the door – and beyond into the lane.

'Shh. Come, Nell. Hush. Let's go,' Mary enticed. 'It's supper time and twilight is here.'

She had earlier eked out a few coins to buy food for supper. She would make an offal stew, with the meat, carrots and a half cabbage that rested in her basket. As her food could provide many meals, Mary remained reasonably satisfied as the two plodded homeward.

The night wind came carrying new coldness that comes only with darkness. The women shivered as they heard a halting harmony of owls in the thicket. Mary placed her arm around Elinor, more for support than warmth. They were moments from their door when they became aware of a variation in the darkness.

There, beside their side garden wall, a shape took on form as they encountered a tattered beggar woman, who stepped forward into their path. Neither Nell nor Mary recognised her as living in the town. The old woman seemed haggard - and chilled in thin, worn clothing. Mary noted she was badly shod. Her walk was stooped as she slowly progressed nearer.

'Who's that, Mary?' whispered Elinor in a voice that flew from her mouth a little louder than she had intended. Mary did not answer.

They drew within a dray's length to observe her closely. The old woman appeared near-blind with yellow clouded eyes. She continued her approach, stopping a couple of yards from them. She spoke in a surprisingly resilient, cracked voice.

'Beware ye both. Take heed as yer days are now numbered. Be wary o' th' company ye keep. Note well all th' voices ye hear - or there will be no saving of ye.'

Mary looked askance, while Nell glared. Straightening to make herself taller, Nell held her basket to her breastbone. She did not like the impudent tone of the crone. 'Two can play that game,' she thought.

The scraggy, old woman had stopped talking to hack and spit phlegm into their garden. Mary swallowed hard. She calmly stated, 'Mistress, you require a tonic for that cough. I have some inside if you wish it.'

'Take a tonic? Not from ye, I won't,' the old woman curtly replied. As she puckered her wrinkly lips, Elinor noted stray hairs on her face, denoting her age.

'I ask your pardon, but there is naught amiss with my tonics,' Mary responded with indignation.

'I'll accept naught from ye,' the old woman wheezed in reiteration.

Mary thought she detected a rattle in her ribs. Elinor, who was not about to be ill-treated outside her home, joined in, 'So, wizened one, who're you to make comment? We've done you no harm.'

Mary enquired, '... and what do you think you know of us? We know naught of you.' Her usual polite tone slid away. She stood with hands on hips, conspicuous of the antediluvian woman, who breathed deeply and stared to the distance with a blank gaze.

'I know more of you than you do yourself,' she replied with a turn of her head, as if listening for sounds in the lane. She turned to take her leave, but halted. She stared blankly, tapped her cudgel-like walking-stick on the ground, before hesitating again. She half-turned to point at them with her stick. 'I know ye both too well. I have poor sight, but fair ears. Mark my words. I come not to harm ye, but to warn ye both or ye'll not make old bones, Mary Phillips. You, nor your friend, can see the future. Watch your workmate, as she has little sense.' With pursed lips, she regarded them with unseeing eyes.

Annoyed, Nell shouted out, 'Tell us more, old woman? For, if it concerns us, we should be told.'

'Shhh, Nell,' whispered Mary. 'Hush. Do not abuse her. Let her go on her way.' Nonetheless, something worried her about the unsympathetic nature of the opaque-eyed vagrant. The ale they'd imbibed now raced down to her guts and made her shiver. The icy wind at their backs did not help much either.

Elinor beheld her friend, before quietly adding, 'Don't fret, Mary. As you oft' say, let folk go as they please and they'll do the same for you.' She leaned forward to touch Mary's arm, then boldly called out to the retreating rear of the old woman, 'I'm assured you'll be keeping the worms busy long afore us. We're fresh and healthy, old one and you're ready to end up in the ditch at any time.'

Her words caused the hag to halt and turn.

'No, mistress, I know folk and I hear ye well. I'm old an' not long for life, yet ye're surely be gone afore me.'

'Fare ye well then, Mother,' Mary called sadly to her sluggishly retreating back. 'Go in safety.'

'Why call her Mother? She gave us no respect. She cursed us!' Elinor was struck with coldness, 'Any curse is on her,' she said. 'Did you not hear or see what she wore? Her mantle was thin ... she seemed sickly.'

As she watched the woman disappear into the gloom, Mary showed concern, just as she had for Elinor when first setting eyes upon her. 'She was old and cold. Most likely, with not a farthing in her purse. Mayhap she'd lift the curse if I'd paid a coin to go on her way.'

'This weather'll make her ache. She's aged,' Elinor measured bitterly. 'She'll be long gone before we are. We are naught much over two score and she is, most surely, over five. Just *look* at her!'

Mary silently considered their meeting, while Elinor made light of it. Hours later, on reflection, Mary was uncertain if her tie with Elinor was really practical. She bore new doubts as she speculated, 'Was the woman a fool or clever? Did she give a curse - or a warning?'

...oooO00Oooo...

Chapter 22
Trial by Tongues

Mary talked over her concerns with Samuel. He advised her, 'Do not to fret for these lanes carry many a mad woman. Let's agree to meet with the reverend, Edward Caldwell to discuss our nuptials. Why wait? Let us marry after New Year?'

Each day Mary saw how keenly Sam anticipated their marital happiness - and offspring. He'd saved much of his earnings and, in progressing with his plans, had already paid for their banns to be read in the church as, after any betrothal, it was expected that the couple would visit the Church to gain a marriage license. This legal document would permit them to marry. Sam could see the convenience of a winter wedding, as farming obligations were more yielding than during the summer. Mary desired all would be well, so agreed to meet with the reverend Caldwell as soon as they could.

It appeared to Mary that the reverend delayed. He was busy. Her guess was that Elinor's steadily tarnished reputation had some influence on the vicar's tardiness. She did not wish for Nell's behaviour to spoil her marriage. She knew how Elinor frequently supplemented her income with brief consultations in darkened inn-side alleys and hated the truth in the loose-tongued words she'd heard. Irritated by being "tarred with the same brush" by some, she knew Sam did not think badly of her. Yet, of late, she had watched as her strong-willed friend's immoral repute grew. It had led folk to follow Nell, calling out rude words. With no subtlety, they speculated on the women's carnal capabilities and placed recent deaths at their feet.

'They've started to believe their own words that are entwined around us like bindweed,' Mary warned.

Elinor had laughed reply. 'Yep, and tar sticks.'

Nell had taken to shaking her fist at the youngest of the hecklers, chasing them from the garden with her broom, while Catchevole ducked for cover.

'They ran down the lane and shrieked as if it was the Devil himself behind them!' She chuckled as she told Mary of several incidents. Both were aware that gossip and complaints to the authorities would likely stir big trouble. Neighbours had no time to paused to chat or while-away time in passing pleasantries.

'This weather keeps our neighbours indoors,' Mary stubbornly declared to her friend. 'It's most inclement.'

Within days, gloomy conditions had set in. A mizzling mist descended and going was hard. Mary had walked to a nearby village, but arrived to be told that her help was no longer required. As she walked dejectedly back to the cottage in the hollow, she stepped carefully, as could not see more than a few yards beyond her feet. The mist left a opaque halo about the shadowy grey orb of the spectral sun. The gloominess did not bode well. Mary had sensibly taken a lanthorn, predicting the weather would not hold, that she now held aloft to light her way. It did not greatly improve her vision. She trembled, as moisture hung fetid in the air and the eerie fields she passed smelled unpleasantly damp with decay.

Claggy, oozy mud quickly covered her shoes, but she did not attend to them as she wished to reach home as quickly as possible. She worried about meeting any stranger in this murk. Sounds were muffled by the mist, but for the crackle of twigs breaking softly beneath her damply clad feet. As she walked, trepidation grew. At times she had no idea of where she was.

'What if I should miss the bridge and fall into the fast flowing river? There's no-one to hear, see or help.'

No bird or animal made a sound. Almost afraid to breathe, she held the flickering lantern aloft. The flame burned unsteadily, wavering with her stilted movements. As she walked, she stumbled and in her fall twisted an ankle. She clutched at bushes to help right herself. Luckily her fear was mightier than her pain. She wished for lithe Catchevole to appear and lead her home, but guessed he would be comfortably snuggled somewhere warm on such a gloomy afternoon as this. The journey seemed much longer than usual.

She sighed as she noted home was near. She recognised the familiar voices of watchmen carrying eerily in the mizzle. The men could not be seen, but were clearly heard discussing some miscreant or reprobate - and what they would do with him when they caught up with him.

Eventually, she arrived home. Tired and trembling with an exhaustion that had consumed and stolen her spirit, she closed the door. The house felt empty. She sensed she was alone. It would take her a time to feel at ease. After some time, Nell stumbled though the door, seeming a little distressed and disorderly. She gave no explanation of where she had been - or what bothered her.

Long after dark the women were distubed by furious banging on their door. Mary rose from her warm fireside seat, carefully put down her work and intrepidly walked to the door.

'Hello,' she called out. 'Who is it?'

Elinor stood to watch, perhaps more aware than her friend of a need for safety. She glanced at the poker.

None replied. Mary looked at Nell and asked, 'Who can be here at this late hour needing my services?'

Mary opened the door. There was no-one outside. Elinor strode out with Isabel's stout walking-stick in hand. Quickly, she returned inside, firmly closed and bolted the door, then swore as a voice called out from the darkness, 'They'll be coming for y' soon, Nelly Shaw.' Disembodied voices laughed harshly.

'If she doesn't *come* for them first,' called another as guffaws filled the air.

Elinor in anger, summoned her pluck to unlatch the shutter, then look out to see who was there.

An indiscrete group of men lurked over the way, on the corner. She swore loudly at them before closing the shutter with a resounding slam. She cared little if they heard. She ensured the latch was firmly down before returning to sit by the glowing fire. Voices could still be heard, but the women ignored them.

Generally the pair trusted their neighbours, but tonight they bolted their door, then latched and barred each of the windows. Listening to every creak and whistle, it took many hours before the sounds in the street to allow them rest.

The following day, Elinor recognised faces in the street and at the market. She felt their eyes upon her and noted that they did not address her as they normally would. Aware, rather than definite, that there had been a change in the wind, today she'd made few transactions. She was irked as she overheard the butcher, Billy Heath, discussing her friend, Mary, with his confidantes and customers. He brazenly stared as he nodded towards

Nell. From the side of his mouth, as if caught by palsy, he gruffly remarked, 'You know 'er? She's trouble.'

'Who is she?' came the reply.

'You know. She's the one who's sold 'er soul for a whack in the lane. I wouldn't be surprised if the other woman hasn't too.' He nodded again as if in acquiescence, while those around followed his lead.

Elinor did not tarry to listen further. She bustled home to animatedly repeat all she'd heard. Wearily, Mary looked up from where she sat, resting her feet on the stool by the fire. She lowered her wooden needles and rubbed at her eyes.

Mary, prickly over the current town discourses, perceptively warned, 'Naught good hails from loose talk.'

'What can we do?'

Mary soberly replied, 'Nothing, Nell.'

'Don't worry so, Mary. People talk, but it's just that - talk. They'll forget it all in a day or so.'

Mary knew her apparent ease was a response to dread. She shivered involuntarily as she whispered, 'I feared as much. I saw how Mistress Bold and her sister stared me at yesterday. Now it's confirmed. I believe this rumour-mill was started by Lizzie and her wicked tongue. It's she who's spread reports of us and behaved poorly. She's not cared for me for some time as she's jealous of my Sam. What will she do when we marry?'

Elinor grimaced, 'May the Lord help you. Lizzie will be apoplectic!' Then, to lighten the mood, she chuckled, 'I hear the Coles' have a new reddish-coloured spaniel. Lucky it's a male - they would never survive two bitches in the family!'

...oooOOOooo...

282

The following Sunday passed. It was quietly uneventful. Mary avoided people. She did not pass the church, as it busy and she knew there would be folk in its yard. She knew her banns were to be read and wished to avoid further conjecture. Also, without Aunt Isabel, Mary had none to speak for her. Acknowledged courting allowed the young to meet unchaperoned, although parents and guardians controlled their capacity to marry before reaching the age of consent at twenty-one. Instead, Mary visited the mill, but it appeared the non-conformist Millward family were not at home. 'Perhaps they have gone to chapel?' she wondered.

She had walked by the river to relax, but shivered as she resettled her cloak comfortably on her shoulders for warmth as the chilled breeze playing in the trees. They rapidly danced to the tune of the wind, waving their far-flung branches in a sporadic frenzy. The rustling evergreens whispered with the last of their leaves as she passed; winter was here. She shuddered again. Something more than remote desolation disturbed her. Hunger assailed her as she trudged home to settle her claim on a chicken that no longer laid as it should! It'd had a good life, roaming freely in the garden and only confined its own safety at night. Now her time was up.

Meanwhile, Elinor had been seated comfortably in the ale-house watching and hearing convivial chatter. As she left the warmth of the building, she took a long breath of air as she noted the two constables standing shadowed by the barn. She recognized them as they pointed, nodded and moved silently towards in her. Although Elinor could not catch their words, she knew that they were speaking of her. She had no intention of stopping to talk with them. As Nell passed by the corner shop, a thickset man called out to her, 'Hey, slattern! Yer come-uppance is nigh. The Watch are comin' for yer tonight.' She didn't bother to answer. Unsettled, she hurried home to arrive breathless.

Mary was busily plucking a chicken that was suspended from a rope. It hung upside-down from a hook in the dark ceiling beam. A bucket of blood stood beneath the drained, spread-eagled corpse, whilst feathers littered the flagstone floor awaiting collection for pillow and mattress stuffing; longer feathers would be sold as spills or writing implements at market.

On tenterhooks, Elinor warned her, 'Mary, there are constables outside. I fear they bear us a grudge? It's an ill-feeling.' She wondered aloud, 'I've got the collywobbles now. They followed me - and a man called out to say they're coming for us. They've a serious, bad aura about them. What do we do?'

She panted, pulling at Mary's arm to make her listen and in doing so almost upsetting the pail.

Mary looked up at her, annoyed. Wiping her hands on her overskirt, she went to the door to look outside. Catchevole jumped up from where he rested and ran through the door as she opened it, from whence he disappeared silently into the night. Mary looked, then closed the door again. She shook her head.

'It's too dark out there to see now', she sighed. She had little time to ask more as voices of a gathering stopped beside their humble house. The sounds propagated. Before long, the rowdy group attained the mentality of an unruly throng. Voices, accompanied by barking of dogs, led to their doorway. Eventually, two paid law-keepers for the town arrived and hammered on the wood.

Their plan was to collect the two women to chill overnight in the lock-up, while lawyers decided over dinner what was to be done. The men hammered on the door, then called out to say that that they were watchmen.

'Open the door, Nell, for it's the Constables,' advised Mary. Elinor hesitated before doing as she was asked, then stepped aside to allow the two men to enter. The sallow moonlight flooded their flagstone floor, reaching as far as the blooded bucket. Mary noted the thriving throng assembled outside. They stood near enough to hear what was said. Ostensibly each man stood by to aid the Watch. If required they could be deputised on the spot.

The larger of the two men stared around and then at Mary. Unblinking, he ducked his head to enter through the doorway, brusquely stating, 'We are sent by the Law to arrest you, Mary Phillips,' he turned, 'and you too, Nelly Shaw.'

As the two men simultaneously stepped forward the women held their ground. Both recognised the men.

'Why, Mister Boss, may I ask why you are here at this hour? Who charged you to do this?'

'We are sent to take you,' stated the taller male.

'This is most unusual. What is it you say we have done?' asked Mary sweetly, as she glanced back to forewarn Elinor to hold her tongue.

'We have our orders,' specified John Southwel, the broader man. 'We are just doing our job.'

'How dare you?' Elinor exclaimed without batting an eyelid. 'Why have you come at this ungodly hour?'

Unfortunately, muffled as the men were against the cold, neither seemed particularly approachable. Southwell continued, 'I do not need to tell you, but you've been accused of causing a problem to the town. You need to come with us to stay in a cell overnight, but you'll need to answer questions on the morrow.' He sharply added, 'It's naught to do with us. We're just doin' as ordered.' He eyed the feathers and bucket. 'You need to come along with us now,' he remarked.

His colleague continued, 'The Reverend and Mayor 'ave 'eard from a good 'ousehold that you've bin makin' trouble. They made enquiries and 'ave reason to consider you carry some shadowy talents.'

He shifted his feet, eyed doubtfully by his fellow constable - as if he had said more than he should. Boss coughed to clear his throat. Perhaps he had indeed said more than his remittance, yet it was enough to start a loud tirade from both women.

William Boss and John Southwel were well-known as hired-help to keep the streets peaceful and safe, but many-times each were to be found located (enjoying a warm ale) in a local establishment. John lived and worked in the town alongside his colleague, Will from Glapthorne village. As jobs for constables and watchmen were not particularly well paid, but were considered prestigious volunteer positions, they often met 'over an ale' to discuss their work and each assisted the other whenever necessary. The men had no regard for gentility. As the women were arrested, they were roughly handled, grasped and bundled away through the irritated crowd with little idea of what was to come.

'Witch!' called a vulgar voice from the crowd.

Mary spoke quietly. 'I've harmed no-one and done nothing. Who would say such a thing of me?'

Elinor could not resist the temptation to shout out a stream of abuse to those passing nearby whenever she gained the opportunity. 'I know you - and what you want.' She lifted her skirts to her knees. 'Come on now. Take what you want and let us go,' she goaded with no response. The constables were not about to reply. The procession started to attract unwanted attention from others as they exited homes and inns to watch the moving appendage of the wormlike cluster.

'Who says this against us?' Nell persisted. 'All we've done is help people. They valued our help.'

Mary was amazed and aghast at the attention they were attracting, yet former sociable people hung back and did not speak out to her. 'I delivered your babies. Did I look like I could do magic then?' she demanded. Her hair splayed wildly and her arms wheeled outward as she called to a group of bystanders. She appealed to the constables, 'I protected you. I prevented ills. I didn't create them. Ask anyone.'

'What do you want?' asked Elinor, regaining some semblance of calm. 'You know me. I make stockings! I don't do magic or spells - or anything!' She heard grumbles and angry voices. Finally she contradicted herself, 'Alright, have it your way. I'm a witch if you think that I am, you cheats and liars!'

'Stop,' instructed her friend. She guessed, knowing her quick-tempered friend, this was not going to happen, but words spoken in haste could be repeated with ease. Bystanders turned away from her - as if afraid to speak to aid their neighbours.

It seemed that their eavesdropping neighbours wished to hear sinful denunciations after long-guarding their unfounded suspicions. Naught had been stated aloud before. Now men crossed themselves to protect themselves from immoral evil as the arresting constables gave licence to their thoughts. Few considered the women above malevolence. Talk was a persuasive ally in contrast to reliable credibility.

With no responses forthcoming, the two women were locked in the bridewell. No pleas helped as they languished in the cool cell overnight. There was little light inside, no food - no chance of sleep. Rodents squeaked and pattered in the darkest corners. Unsure of what would happen, the two women reached out to hold each other and wept at their discomfort.

For their part, the constables chose to make their stay as unpleasant as possible in order to speedily gain confessions for their crimes. Isolated from friends, Mary wondered, 'How can we tell our friends that we are languishing here? What's our error?'

The following day, Samuel, who had been informed of their arrest by a chirpy Charles Coles, was allowed into the small cell to talk with his friends. He had gently pacified them with a warning.

'Watch what you say. Be true and assured when asked questions. Be truthful - and steadfast.' He spoke, but in his core was not sure how his words could help.

The Rector visited to explain, 'You've been accused of *bewitching and tormenting in a diabolical manner*.' He would not say who had accused them. 'They say it's poison - that's your black art.'

'What! That is ridiculous. The black arts! Pah!' Elinor exclaimed after he had spoken. 'We don't practice any shady arts. We're healers. Ask anyone hereabouts.'

'I make remedies, but it doesn't make me a witch!' Mary explained. 'Why, Sir, I do believe that I made a raspberry-leaf tisane for your wife and poultices for several ladies in your congregation – and for your gentlemen with gout! I also recall your parents have been grateful recipients of my cures in the past.'

Much reserved, before the long table of lawyers and local tradesmen in the Swann, Mary cautiously eyed her friend. 'We do no wrong,' she stated calmly, just as Sam had advised, but was not heard for Elinor's rants.

'I'm no witch!' Elinor shouted, whilst holding her hands palms up before her. The more she said, the faster, more annoyed and shrill her voice became.

A court clerk sat in the corner and studiously made notes on their account. The women were allowed to speak for but a short time only before they were taken back to their cell. Now it was time for members of the community to make their statements. The lawyers seemed bemused, as Nell had to be dragged back to the cell, bawling, 'Nincompoops! You're out of your depth.'

...ooo000ooo...

From the moment the timeworn William Barnes had heard news of the arrests from John Palmer, it had bothered him greatly. At first he did not want wish to believe his ears. After considering problems derived from the women's arrest, he reserved utmost concern for his eldest son, who was allied by association with Mary. William truly liked Mary, but her younger friend was another matter. He wondered if mischief from Nell's witchcraft could in any way harm Sam.

'I've known Mary since she was a child. I cannot believe of evil in her. She healed our Wilf and he walks.'

'If the story's true,' his long-term friend, John, began, 'then we're all exposed and can be cursed by t'morrow if they wish it.'

William gripped an unshaven chin in thought, then rubbed at his forehead with a gritty palm. He groaned aloud, 'This is clearly not true. Mary's a good lass. I've not a bad word to say against her.' He folded his arms across his chest to denote he'd say no more.

His friend agreed. 'Aye. It's rare nowadays, but to have it happen is bad for the town.'

William sighed. He slowly bowed in agreement.

'Aye,' John responded. He nodded several times. Both allowed a lull in conversation as neither saw a way out of this situation. Unremitting, John suddenly continued, '... and your Sam is seriously a-courting Mary Phillips, is he not?' He pursed his lips and scrutinised his friend through squinted eyes. 'Make sure he don't get involved in all this and corrupt himself.'

'Yes,' William lowered his gaze and spoke softly. Browbeaten, he felt his full half-century of years as he replied, 'I'll need to tell him of this, before others get to him, for they will not be kindly.'

'So, are your family safe from the curses - or the tarnish that's carried with 'em?' asked his friend.

The men sat in silent thought. There was naught more to be said.

...oooOOOooo...

290

As the women woke in the cell in dim daylight, Mary observed the interactions of common folk and officials. She had blown a careful kiss to Sam from the window in thanks for all that he had tried to do. She was aware that he had gone to speak with Stephen Bramston to see what could be done to help.

When confined in the small, square cell, Mary had glumly asked, 'What do you think they want, Nell?'

Elinor quickly answered, 'I am not at all sure, but it is best if we show we're not shame-faced by them taking us.' She looked up to the ceiling. 'Tell no lies. We have naught to hide. Tell the truth and all'll be well.'

'You think this will go away? Some we know would trick us and tell lies. Others will trust any tales - as they have little in their heads with which to believe otherwise.'

'Mary, this awful gaffe will pass.'

'I don't know. How can you tell?' Mary probed.

'I can't. I know naught.' She sighed. 'Let's sleep on it. See what tomorrow brings,' she said. She turned her body away from Mary to wrap her woollen shawl more tightly around her shoulders. Neither was properly attired for the cold of that night - or their future trip to the county town in an open waggon. None of their neighbours had brought warm clothing from their house for comfort. Restrained, neither spoke; each dwelt on subjective worries.

Eyes and ears were hard to avoid, but she tried. Elinor was taken out, then returned to the cell grumbling and cursing. As Mary watched out from the small window, she perceived cold eyes upon her. There, in the shadows, stood a child. She recalled seeing her in the past. The sullen girl of five or six, in a worn mist-blue pinafore stared. The child beheld her with directness - and forlornly gave a solemn smile. Mary shivered. She had no idea of how much time had passed, but felt tired and unwell. Finally, exhausted, she slept on the dirt floor while mice nibbled through the cell's flea-ridden blanket. It now bore a rank smell.

Layer dressing against the cold and damp was not an option. Lice nipped and itched. Each day Nell saw her own warm breath escape wraithlike from her nose and mouth. She called out to people standing nearby each time she was taken from squalid cell to court – then back again, as grey rain poured down to wash the familiar street. Sheltering, folk stared back at her.

On her return, she woke Nell, who noted, 'It's a storm. Don't upset yourself with worry.'

Mary was not so certain. With profound concern regarding events, she felt their lives were about to take a turn for the worse.

...oooOOOooo...

After a continually chilled Christmas, the new year of 1705 was hailed by a blanched wintery time. Days began with flurries of crisp white snow, which vanished almost as quickly as it arrived. The town endured damp and dark, yet unseasonably mild days squeezed betwixt thick morning (and evening) fogs. Farmers knew that the weather could be close in February. The barren brown of the late-winter held a promise of spring that would be filled with snowdrops and primroses, yet this was not a season that Mary and Elinor could enjoy. The late festive season had seen them detained - as the community incessantly discussed doubtful testimonies. Consensus agreed, 'They've been caught out and should be tried for their ways.'

Mary lost track of the days. She had seen trials in the local court before. Nothing moved fast. The squire required folk to speak on behalf of the accused.

'Will anyone speak for me?' she wondered.

Pale daylight filtered below the short shade. A cock crowed in the inn yard some distance away. It took some minutes before Mary roused herself enough to accept her surroundings and grasp that she was not at home. She heard small birds twittering, welcoming the day in their early chorus.

Hours passed slowly. From time to time, precariously balanced at the end of their woven rope restraints, they watched from their barred window. There stood Beth Afford and her family, alongside Laurence Landen and his eldest. They were taking with a scowling Meg Webster, who periodically puckered her brow to look over the road at the building they remained detained in. Mary called out to appeal to them, but none heard. She remained invisible.

Gladys, Tom Barnes and Mercy walked by with their wares. Gladys, it seemed, had enlisted Tom to push her heavy goods to market in a small sack barrow. They had gone before Mary could call to them. Constance and her sister walked beside Anne, Hetty, Sarah and Kate on Sunday, on their way to church. She noted their embarrassment as she stared through the iron-banded frame, while others glanced in with pitying eyes.

Mary watched former friends tongue-tied with fear. She saw Agatha, her husband and their baby pass by.

'Lord, let me explain to them,' she prayed silently, 'for we've no quarrel with these folk.' She knew something fundamental had changed as she was treated like a criminal. As trials beyond the remit of the squire were sent 'up-County', a foreboding crept over her.

'We're powerless. What can we do,' she breathed quietly. 'Who'll help us?'

...ooo000ooo...

Chapter 23
Ideas and Indulgencies

'They say an ill wind blew dawn to dusk on the day Nell and Mary were placed in irons,' Mercy Elderkin alleged with wide eyes. 'They were furious – and so was the weather! They were taken to the court on the corner of Bury Street and are still there.'

She pointed towards the corner building as if seeing them. 'None can decide.' She looked at the town stocks-house and cage used for the punishment of offenders. Sarah Short and Ann Dolby nodded in agreement, but held their tongues, while Mercy pulled her brightly-patterned shawl around her shoulders against the wind. The latter whispered, 'I heard they'll be sent to the Assize Courts in Northampton.'

She repeated words heard from others as she looked supportively towards the lock-up where the two were detained. 'Perhaps I should visit them ... or do something?' she pondered

Since the women's arrest, some feared they may gain the same end as Will Hackett from Old Isabel's childhood. He'd spoken of his beliefs - and was hanged in Cheapside. Punishment was easily elicited from pawns without money or status: controlled in a game. Many who knew Mary and Nell had turned against them.

Associates, afraid for their own lives and kin, were fearful to speak out. For, if they showed support for the women, they could lay themselves open to being condemned too. With little formal regulation in the courts, lawyers saw workers as ill-informed and did not elucidate or help them. Like Mercy, Sam saw that gaining freedom would prove difficult.

The aged, rotund, Cicely Wagstaff promptly paid a visit to Mister Bramston and his wife to seek a speedy release for her young friend, but to no avail. After speaking with the mayor, who saw her as a busybody woman, she left with a flea in her ear. The old woman had then met with Maggie Seaton and the two had almost come to blows over their opinions.

Maggie was adamant, 'I see the Devil when he visited. There 'e stood, 'orns an' all - an' they let him in.' Cicely debunked her words as shameful, but Maggie shouted, 'My repute as a neighbour's good. I 'eard the women discussin' small fiends' sent to 'elp 'em. You a-callin' me a liar?'

Cicely was fairly was sure this was the case, but could do little. When her carriage came, she was loath to step aboard and ride home, but there she held no alternative.

In the market square by the cross, traders and customers discussed the home-grown trial. As they were passing, Ambrose and Samuel stood to listen.

'How can we help?' Samuel quietly asked Ambrose. The latter shook his head. 'A healer's an easy victim to accuse,' Sam persisted.

Ambrose sniffed loudly. 'Blame anybody linked to baffling illness or sudden death as none knows the true cause. On my part, I have fancy to believe the law.'

'So, how do I prove they're innocent?' Sam pressed.

'I'm not sure,' Ambrose said shortly. 'They *are* said to be witches. Who denies it?'

'I do. Do you believe everything you're told? How do you tell between curses or cures? Doctors and healers trust in God. Any man is not infallible.'

'Sam, everyone knows that in a town like ours, we need to curb unwanted activities. Good families like the Creed's and Walcott's won't want witches near their children, bringing ill to the town. It's a dilemma.'

Meg joined in, quietly advising, 'They consider us humble folk, beneath the likes of them. I'm in agreement with Ambrose. There's little we can do.'

'Indeed, there is not much we can do, Mistress Webster.' William nodded at her. 'Proof is inferred by folk who sometimes wish mischief.'

'Nell's deeds and behaviour are good reasons for anger.' Ambrose pursed his lips and looked seriously at Samuel, who sadly shook his head. 'You should see her when she's been crossed. I have been the butt of it.' He looked around, then promptly changed subject to that of the weather, but Samuel would not be deterred. 'You know what they are saying?'

Overhearing Sam, Edmund Cannington sourly sidled over to the group and rubbed his hands through his thinning hair. He would be called pale, but for the red, raw blemishes on his skin. Edmund scratched absent-mindedly at his pimpled face as he told, 'In a private meeting at the inn the magistrate discussed how the two lived. He said Nell's parents were not willing or able to give their daughter any manner of learnin', they had no control and she was left to shift for herself from the age of fourteen. It was then that she was first met her partner in wickedness, Mary Phillips.' He eyed Sam who glared back at him. 'They then discussed Mary. She's as local as us - born here. She worked hard until her coexistence with Elinor. They worked in a seeming honest way for some years, until the young'un was of marriageable age, thereafter the court-men described her as "rude *and* lude" …' He paused, "That's right ain't it? Nell Phillips *is* a hungry doxy and a harlot. She used her shameless libido with my friend, Francis, God rest his soul an' I'm sure she murdered him with her magic. There's been talk about her for ages. It's about time the law caught up with her.' Edmond scratched at his skin and stretched. A silent Henry Millward watched on.

William patted Sam on the shoulder before Sam could retaliate against Edmund's words. 'There's naught we can do at the moment, son. Let's see what comes of the trial.' He gently turned his son to leave.

'Francis was naught but a swaggering braggart,' Sam whispered to his father.

Henry, the miller, overheard and nodded, but did not wish to take sides.

The old man frowned, then suddenly remarked, 'I know. You won't remember as you weren't born then, but about fifty years ago two others pawned their souls in return for control of ill. I was just a lad then, but I remember well.' He coughed and looked askance at the group. 'Over the course of nine months, they'd killed fifteen children, eight men and six women by their enchantments and witchcraft.' He quietly concluded. 'Some say the women were suitably condemned. They were deliberately manipulated by court and people.'

Samuel took in a large breath and sighed. William rubbed his face with his hands, but kept his other hand firmly on Sam's back as he surveyed the group. Each was aware of Sam's torment.

Ambrose added, 'I was not born then either, but my old uncle said witches kill their prey by roasting an' pricking images of 'em made from scraps or straw.' He laughed with spite. 'Watch they have no straw in that lock-up or we'll all be done for!'

'Aye, I've heard that about *real* witches, but our friends caused no such ill.' Samuel breathed.

'Their neighbours say otherwise,' Ambrose remarked with a smirk, shaking his head in disagreement.

William made a 'tch' sound at Ambrose and steadily frowned at the disrespectful lad, while Samuel remained aghast as none tried to help prove Mary's innocence.

A recent upsurge in superstition came from poor evidence and erudition. Folk with little understanding of nature, distrusted all they had scant appreciation for; believing in the power of witchcraft for things otherwise unexplained. As he allowed his father to lead him away, Samuel wondered how to avoid anxiety over spirits that could 'melt into air' after great maelstroms conjured by magicians and witches. The more they talked of witches the more they suspected them behind every door.

...oooOOOooo...

Not far from the market place, in their cell, Mary whispered to Elinor, 'Nell, long ago, Aunt Isabel told me of Helen Jenkenson of Thrapston. She was arrested for bewitching a farmer and his cattle, but was released, much to the relief of Isabel. Yet, sometime later, Mistress Mulso accused her of causing her child's death and she was tried in court again. The second time, the court found new blemishes on her body. Isabel mourned the woman and swore that Mistress Mulso should come to know her own fears as she saw to it that Helen was killed. Do you think this will happen to us?'

Elinor listened, but did not comment. Her love of scary stories had waned of late, given their own predicament. She gazed out from the small barred window. Through it they could see all manner of folk as they passed by. Small groups gathered on the corner of Bury Street by the water pump to watch if the women were taken from their lock-up to the Swann inn to meet the magistrate. The trial was sensationally promoted as that of the "notorious Northamptonshire witches". Life and death were the workings of God's will. As God was blameless, a convincing explanation of unforeseen ill-fortune and death, bad harvests or loss of livestock were attributed to evil people coerced by the Devil. People could no longer remark, 'Nowt happens around here.'

Those who visited the prisoners said, 'Watch out. If people see you visit too often or you try to stand up for them, they'll will bring you down with them.'

Elinor's loose reputation (not her mystical deeds) led her to ruin. Gossip of her assignations was heard in the court. It decided that it was time to send the pair to Northampton for further trial as evil lawbreakers. Samuel realised with sorrow what this meant for his love.

...oooOOOooo...

When accused of selling their souls for evil powers, Mary and Elinor had laughed. Later, they cursed all who listened.

Samuel closed his eyes and drooped his head towards his heavy chest. He felt that he could not breathe. Rumours spread as people all held an opinion. In the inn over a pint, Sam told a solicitor, 'When Bill Allen fell from his ladder when fixing the barn roof, many had come along. Many stood around and viewed the spectacle of his pains and the agony of broken legs. Not helped or advised, but they'd watched on as a few had tried to help. Mary and Nell had helped.'

As a spectacle, no help was forthcoming. Samuel believed that the two held no rights. Furthermore, he believed that the public were inexplicably angry with the women and would not rest until they were removed from the town, albeit permanently.

The week after their arrest an impotent lawyer stood to address the small court. The prosecutor knew of the women as his wife oft' purchased hose from Mary. The man was a hopeless buffoon. Elinor stood as she listened to what seemed unreasonably complex claptrap.

'Elinor Shaw, you are accused of numerous crimes: mainly bewitching people and animals.'

'What?' she asked.

'Woman, you are accused of … bewitching … to death.' He glared at her outburst. 'With the aid of your companion, Mary Phillips, you tormented a woman, a boy and a small girl 'til they died. We have witnesses who will swear to this.' He waited for his words to sink in. 'Furthermore, your ongoing lewd behaviour has shocked many to the core.' The well-clad man then straightforwardly probed, 'Will you confess to being a witch?' He looked hard at her while she scowled angrily back at him.

Mary snorted in hasty reply, 'I make hose and cures. Perhaps there *are* things afoot in this world that we who live in it know nothing of. Do *you* profess to know all there is to know of the miracles in life? You find witchcraft in everyday things.' Her chest rose and fell with effort as she continued, 'Indeed, every woman is a witch in her own way. See how some beguile a man.'

She quickly realised her rash statements were a blunder that did not settle well with the judge. Many voices rebuked her, but the room swiftly hushed as the lawyer slammed down his hand on a large book to encourage silence. He shouted, 'Woman, you are accused of the witching of others.' With a grim face, he watched as the dust from the volume settled. 'You were seen forming spells and fashioning brews that caused ill.'

'*What*?' Elinor asked again to regain her thoughts. She felt sick to her stomach. 'When was this? Who spoke thus?' she demanded. Her breathing raced as flustered, she panicked with frantic thoughts captive in her head sank downward to stir in her chest. The court confused her with words and twisted all arguments.

'You are accused of a union with the Devil. You cannot deny this? Can you prove otherwise?'

'Who claims this?' she barked at her accuser.

Ignoring her, he continued without answering. 'You have been seen collaborating with the devil.' Nell scoffed as the man carefully read from his notes of times when she had been seen by her neighbours - as she spoke to herself (or someone unseen), whilst standing over a cauldron of boiling garments or steaming soup – when dancing unadorned in the garden. She tried to reason with him, but position and rank allowed him the upper hand. He looked at his notes and shuffled his papers.

'Muttering to oneself when overheard by a neighbour leaves anyone, witches or not, open to accusations,' she called. Nell tried to rationalise. 'Why, there are many reasons when people have need to talk aloud. Perhaps they are lonely? Perhaps, if a person is distressed they take ease in talking alone? It causes no ill. Talk provides an easy distraction: unaccompanied or with others.'

Her statement was ignored. None cared to acknowledge talking to themselves - even if they did so. This woman was clearly a witch!

A little later the same indictment of witchcraft was read out before Mary. Stunned, she first wept in shock at hearing the statement. She had initially appeared confident; boldly smiling at the assembly as they stared back at her, now she could not. A woman accused, she had no legal standing. The magistrate allowed all to speak out against her in court. A floodgate opened as each castigating voice craved a moment.

Virgil Eden was asked if he knew of the women. Mary was aware of him, but did not know him well. Yet, when asked, Virgil stated, 'My old neighbour, Daniel Bell, had an ulcer on his leg, an' they cured it wi' potions an' spells, but he paid them half o' what they asked for as it took so long to go. Then he had a boil on his neck an' it wouldn't go away. The witches 'ad cursed him an' put it there.' He'd seemed unabashed. 'There's no smoke wi'out fire, as my ma said,' he explained. Mary tried to clarify how the man did not know her. None listened.

Later, Maggie Seaton stood, with hands folded in front of her, clearing her throat to speak. She answered the questions from the jurors.

'Yes. I know Mary.' She could not look at Mary. Hesitantly, she described untruths. 'I heard they burned things in their fire to make people quicken and die.' She sombrely noted, '… like young Master Ireland! He was such a gentle lad. He did not deserve to die.' She pointed at the broken young woman, manacled in the courtroom.

Maggie had played her hand well. She shouted, 'That's her. She's the witch ... the witch who killed him.'

The small court murmured, aghast. Here, in a room of people Mary and Nell knew intimately, none dared speak a fair word on their behalf.

Mary looked down to stare at the hands in her lap. They were once steady, but now trembled without control as more evidence was pitted against them. Finally, came two statements produced by the constables who had arrested and held them.

'The prisoners were confined together, so it was easy for our constables to revisit several times in order for them to confess of their crimes. Not many people came to see the women while they were in the town lock-up, so it's pretty clear they are feared.'

'Not true,' shouted Nell. 'They said to us, "If you confess, the court can show mercy" and they wheedled and promised that there would be "a quick release" if we agreed to our faults.'

The men of the court laughed and jeered. The deceiving constables were thereafter feted and praised by the magistrates for "gaining confessions from the dreaded pair of witches". They had wrung words from the women by deceit, whist convincing declarations of hearsay were allowed as evidence.

The women began to despair. Despite deceits of a berating court, the women protested their innocence as much as they could. In rare moments when permitted to speak, they desperately tried to get the court to see sense and agreed to naught, but 'deaf ears' were the order of the day.

Neighbours watched on as the tall, erudite judge leaned forward on the wooden bench to note, 'Admit it,

I trust that you bewitched and tormented in a diabolical manner, Mistress Susannah Wise, the wife of Robert Wise of Benefield, till she died.' In turn, he stared open-eyed at each of the women before continuing the accusations. His face remained calm. 'You also killed, by wicked fascination, a small child named Elizabeth Gorham of Glapthorne. An innocent child of four. There is no denying she died by your hand. You are each judged of her death,' he stated as cat-calls and shouts came unchecked from the assembled spectators.

Before each accusation was read, the crowd had already made its summary opinion known. The charges continued, 'You are responsible for bewitching to death young Charles Ireland of Southwick, alongside slaying the horses, hogs and sheep – the property of Matthew Gorham, the father of the aforesaid boy.' With this the man stated, 'This trial will cease here...' as gasps were to be heard and a fleeting smile crossed Nell's face. The man continued, '... It has been agreed that sentencing will continue at the County Assizes.' At this, the gentlemen of the court concurred with nods and mutters. 'By mid-February, the accused women will be sent to our County town of Northampton. The women will wait in Oundle until the Spring Assizes begin. They will thereafter be heard and tried in the Lent Assizes.'

...oooO00Oooo...

Most lawyers of the town were busy with small-fare trials, as these paid well and were concluded quickly. Some gift payments could be lost. With no money the women could ill-afford a lawyer. Samuel recognised his income and status were lowly, with few savings to aid his predicament, he saw none who could help. His only support was prayer: to be with them in spirit.

Sam walked to St. Peter's, where he prayed for them to be found innocent - to be freed. He spent cold hours on bended knee on cool slabs; penitent, sore and with an aching soul. As Sam loved the Lord, he was surely seen as precious in return. 'Lord, save them. If not both, then Mary alone. Lord, grant me your favour.'

The vicar spoke quietly. He held little sympathy, but wished to keep Sam and his family within the flock. 'Don't despair, Lad. There's always hope if you place your trust in God. He protects the blameless,' he intoned, patting Sam on the shoulder. He hesitated, 'Unless, of course, they have indeed sinned.'

With hope dying, Sam joined his father at home. Imbibing, he asked, 'They're going to Northampton. What happens before a Quarter Session Judge?'

'They hold four hearings to try serious crimes. The last is afore Yuletide. Their court'll be first of the new year,' William answered, as he nodded slowly. 'There's naught we can do at this time of night - and worrying won't help your lass. To bed, lad.'

Meanwhile, nearby, Mary considered all means of liberation, but was inferior to judge and jury. Elinor's thoughts were much more basic. 'Perhaps I'll offer myself to a man who can arrange freedom?' The more she considered this, the less likely it seemed.

...ooo000ooo...

306

Chapter 24
A Waggon of Witches

Elinor and Mary had little time to prepare for their journey. The mere idea of transportation to the county gaol, accompanied by the hypocritical constables, frightened the women. Each knew they would no longer be surrounded by the faces of people they knew - and a few they trusted.

The cold morning was wintery. So icy that the women watched sprite-like breaths fly from their mouths in the cold air. In grey daylight they were bound, then taken outside to an awaiting waggon. Sam was awaiting them too. He had been outside stamping his feet and taking steps back and forth for some time. As the women appeared, he deftly stepped around their vehicle and handed his spare, dark-wool cloak to the shivering Mary. As their hands touched, hers were deathly cold. Sam then turned to speak severe words to their driver regarding the rough conduct and manhandling of the women as they climbed into the waiting waggon.

'Aye, you're right, son. I don't want them to be dead before they arrive or I'll be accountable, won't I?' acknowledged the driver with a sneer, as he gruffly noted Samuel's appearance. In return Sam gave him a serious look and rose to his full height. He was considerably taller and with a finer torso than the round-shouldered carter. The driver turned away and called out to the constables. With a crack of his whip, he moved the horses forward.

Sam moved back from the wheels. He watched as the sturdy cart rolled forward on the rutted mud and cobble road, taking Mary away from him. He'd watched with tingling eyes until they were out of sight. Several observed, but did not speak as they felt tainted by their denunciations.

It would be a long journey for all; with breaks to rest, feed and water the horses - and stops for food and comfort for the three men. Forty meandering miles to Northampton was about the limit for travel on a fair day. In this weather, all knew that it would probably take longer. The waggon would stick in ruts along the way and needed to shelter under trees if the elements worsened. The women overheard the men talking. The two horses were either to be changed for fresh ones around the halfway point or they had an overnight rest on the journey. This eased their minds. It was the unknown that worried them both. Days gave about ten hours of daylight at this time of year, less if the weather was inclement. Foul weather would greatly hamper them, with rain, gales and snow to slow their progress. This season was about the worst for any terrestrial trek.

Mary considered her predicament as she shared Sam's black cloak with Elinor. The tumbril lurched along. The broad-beamed constable jerked on his seat in the back. The other had chosen to sit up front, uncomfortably squashed alongside the driver.

Mary thought. She had plenty of time to do so. She recognised that she had to safeguard Samuel by not showing any favour to him in the sight of others. She had given a sad smile as he blew her a kiss on their departure. She could not wave, for her hands were restrained. She did not dare call to him, for any loose words may mean his arrest by mere association with her. As Mary sat awkwardly in the cart, she wondered what would become of them, now taken from the gaol. She knew

308

many of the goodwives had observed from nearby. Suddenly, her attention was caught by a sudden flash and a movement out of the corner of her eye. She looked. There was that wide-eyed child again, watching from the side of the road. Damnation! Where did she come from?

Mary's dark hair hung in lank lines, resembling slick rat-tails. She shuddered uncomfortably as a grey shadow passed overhead, while a dark patch obscured the dull daylight for a brief moment in the leaden grey sky. Birds wheeled in the wind. She heard the driver on the raised front seat imparting his knowledge of them.

'Rooks are unlucky. They eat carrion,' the driver called above the wind. 'Although they are pretty good in a pie!' The ominous birds cawed with similar sounds to any loose gate blowing in a storm. The birds flew onward until they were barely visible. Black specks in the dreary sky. The constable noted a familiar Bible story, 'The crow didn't bother returning to tell Noah there was land when the floods abated. The bird only thought of 'imself.'

'Bit like these two then', remarked his fellow.

Mary did not speak, but wondered, 'Perhaps this is an omen?' By the time she turned her head to gaze from her feathery distractions back to the girl, she too had flown.

The tumbril cart had conveyed them along the high street, past Lark Lane and along to the chapel end houses that stood amidst converging roads at the western extremity of town. The ridged road was somewhat flattened by the weight of carts relentlessly carried along its length, but this ride did not bode comfortable. It passed familiar cottages with smoky chimneys, where dismal-faced people stepped out to watch its slow progress.

Mary thought she heard someone cry out, 'Good riddance', but she may have been mistaken. As she looked southward, she saw Osgyth's field; the rough land that stretched far into the distance. It bordered the river to the south of the town with fields that dropped away downhill to the reflected sky-grey waters of the river with small, secret isles trapped therein. As they had passed, Mary recollected walking and swimming there with Nell and her friends as the unpaved route led onward to nearby villages. She smiled down at her cat-napping friend, bundled next to her on the floor of the cart.

Many cobbled, mud yards shared access to a water-well. At times their driver would call at a house to fill a bucket of water for his horses. By some houses there stood a post, hammered into the ground, bearing a metal mug atop. This travellers used this mug at water-butt or well to quench their thirsts.

Mary frowned in thought. It was far too cold to ask the driver to stop so that she could have a drink of water. Water remained white and frozen on this inauspicious day. When they stopped, in the brown and white, Mary noted tiny snowdrops that had pushed their way into the dim sunlight.

The roads led from village to hamlet - Stoke Doyle to Pilton, Achurch, Aldwincle, Lowick and Thrapston. Then onward via the tree-lined river to Denford and Ringstead. Mary hummed and made the hamlet names into a song. She taught it to Nell and they chanted together while the men watched on. Lane-like tracks meandered over barren fields. Many, only suitable for riders on horseback. A parish spire on the horizon, appeared, seen for several miles over the fertile, arable land, while ditch or bush that marked boundaries slowly diminished from their sight.

From Thrapston to Ringstead the road followed the river to Higham mill. From the small hamlet of Ringstead onward the two women had remained hidden in the warming cloak. They no longer recognised or cared about the places they passed through and lay-low in the cart in small villages, where curious people absented their warm houses to watch the fettered progress of the witches.

Conveyed ever-onward to Wellingborough they perceived the river in flood. They broke their passage beside a country inn where they each stretched their cramped legs and relieved their bursting bladders before continuing. The sturdy waggon lumbered forward with monotony, while its silent driver remained wrapped in his many warm layers of clothing against the biting wind. Alert eyes looked over the scarf around his neck and mouth. The constables chatted to each other from time to time, but the conversation dwindled the further they travelled south-west.

Desolate fields showed an occasional sheep or goat, but these were few and far between. Soon, all that could be heard was the creak of the wheels and the clop of the horses' hooves when they met with solid ground. The cold, ceaseless wind accompanied them. Mud dragged on the wheels and was really slowing them to a crawl. They were all relieved to reach the inn destined for their overnight stay. While the wind moaned overnight, the horses were cared for and fed. Mary considered that these stolid quadrupeds were likely better cared for than the people.

As an orb of cream-cheese hung low in the sky, it seemed all the nearer to the earth than it had the previous evening, yet tonight it looked as if a knife had sliced off a side chunk for themselves. Perhaps it was so creamy-fresh that it had run down and dripped onto the dark horizon below. A pale patch on the distant waters suggested this could be the case.

The Cannon Inn stood as the first dwelling on the Finedon road at the brink of the town. Nell had hoped the carter would stop, yet the waggon continued rolling onward toward a church that stood silhouetted against the darkening sky. The Hind rest-house overlooked the market. In front of the hostelry stood a stone cross. Steps, topped by a beehive-shaped rotunda with an octagonal roof, held a cramped chamber that served as an overnight prison for the women. Given a dry heel of bread with a beaker of water each, they were confined for the night. Grateful for a respite from the bumpy road and an uncomfortable seat on the base of the cart, exhausted they fell asleep, knowing that after this 'little peace' their journey would resume.

The Golden Lion stood at the foot of Sheep Street. It was a striking, stone building with an overhanging timber storey and thatched rooftop gables. This is where the horses and their waggon had spent the night. The constables took their repast and rest in the Hind, while their hired delivery service slumbered in the loft above the stables with other grooms.

The following day, the women discerned landmarks. Wellingborough's market square was laid out as a nexus of ancient roads, linking High Street, Silver Street and Sheep Street with London, Oxford and Cambridge. In daylight, the Hind and its visiting coaches appeared most striking. It bore the hallmarks of a wealthy inn. Stiff and aching from the previous day's journey, they were uploaded into the cart.

Mary overheard the stable-hands talking.

'I'll bet thee that the stout officer-fellow stayed on the upper floor, in Cromwell's room. It has a secret door behind a panel in the wall to the right of the fireplace and is an escape to the roof. Sir Christopher Hatton, Lord of the Manor of Wellingborough would stay there. It's a fine room.'

'Is it them scrawny witches they're a transportin'?' his pigeon-chested friend remarked.

'Aye, 'tis them'. They're goin' further on to Earls Barton today, then Nor'ampton.'

'Good luck to 'em, that's what I say. Many go that way, but few come back ag'in.'

On so saying, the oddly-shaped man vanished into the stable for a moment, then quietly reappeared with a skewed smile. He sidled over to quietly pass a sweet bun to Mary. He winked at her. 'Good luck, lass,' he said hoarsely. Mary thanked him quietly in response. She did not wish to get him into trouble for being kind. Mary tore the bun and passed half to Nell, who ate the soft morsel hungrily.

Eyes watched as the women were unceremoniously bundled into the cart to continue their journey. From the outset, they knew that this day would be harder and wetter with the ice-cold of a wintery February. Inclement conditions set each constable to grumbling whenever they were required to assist the carter. Indeed, today the constables were most certainly needed to help the sullen driver as he struggled to pull the waggon from claggy mud holes near watercourse crossings.

'This ain't my bloomin' job,' complained one grumpy man to the other, as his black cloaks flapped like a trapped birds caught in the strong gusts.

It was a light relief for Mary and Elinor when they were forced to disembark to watch as the heavy-set men struggled to shove and push the waggon from the sticky mire. By the time they reached the opposing side of each ford they were all wet, chilled and in no mood for polite conversation. Elinor quietly smiled to herself while watching the spectacle. In contemplation, she found it amusing to see the men suffer for a while.

'You have brought this on us,' said Boss, turning to look directly at Mary. His mouth was sour and his words bitter. 'You've summoned up the worst of the weather to make us ail, but it won't save your skins.'

The woman knew that it was not worth her while to make any comment, as the brute would undoubtedly disregard her to favour ill. Their journey continued without conversation as they passed countless farms, villages and towns. The journey lasted near two full days.

If they had believed the journey was hard before, today was worse. After passing Staple Mill the road was little more than a track with bumps, hidden holes and wet mud. Their path held unsightly views of a grey eel-like river, bordered by mud-ridden farmsteads. After Ecton and Billing, it gave way to a proliferation of smallholdings and an improved surface that was better served by traffic.

On reaching Abingdon, the county town began to feel closer - with an abundance of houses bearing coppiced woodlands between. As the essential roads were in constantly used, the thoroughfare had likewise improved.

In the growing gloom of the late afternoon, they had passed gibbets and gallows, clad with the hanging remains of offenders in various states of decomposition, creaking and swinging in the icy winds.

John Southwel leered, laughed as he pointed toward the gallows with a filthy thumb, then nodded at the women and drew a clenched fist, with right thumb extended, across his exposed throat. Mary and Elinor were chilled. They could not hear much of what the men said into the wind, but understood their crude gestures. The driver's only wish was to arrive, stable his horses and flee indoors for the night. He wiped his nose on his sleeve and turned away to proceed with their journey.

It was a late arrival at the municipality - already near dark. The postern stood between the East Gate and the Dern Gate, by St. Giles' Church yard and another called the Cow Gate that led from Cow Lane into Cow Meadow. Mary noted the gate their waggon had passed through. It seemed that its abutments were used as tenements for the poor. Blank faces looked out to watch their progress.

Once again people came forth from of houses and hovels to watch the celebrity prisoners. News had already reached them about the ill-starred women. They stared and called out curses or threats. Response remarks from the two were directed at bystanders. Their calls kept their minds away from the bitter reality of the cold. Ever-evolving crude calls from Elinor were plain for all to hear. Mary finally decided to join in. Yet was certain that anything they said or did would be reported - to their detriment.

'Let them report us,' she thought in anger. Although it was too dark to see properly, they could smell the cattle market where animals were confined to be sold. They were enclosed in pens in the nearby streets and were well-defined by the racket they made.

'Poor beasts for the slaughter,' whispered Mary. Nell, unsure if she'd meant the animals or themselves, didn't wish to question her friend on her words.

Lamps and candlelight seemed to shine as a welcome from windows, but on their arrival, they were taken and questioned before being reunited. Yet again they were locked together in a room with naught but their own clothing for warmth. Exhausted, the two huddled together on a bench for warmth. Each keeping the other as warm as they could. The woollen cloak that Sam had passed to Mary was of benefit to them both. In the darkness they silently thanked him for his kindness.

...ooo000000ooo...

After installation in the stark, rectangular county cell, their new gaoler paid a protracted visit to the small room. His unkempt appearance was grubby, with his physique bent and closely related to that of an old monkey Mary had seen in her youth at a travelling fair. His first, stooped approach was accompanied by the rattle of keys. He glanced at their fellow prisoner, a woman, who seemed unconscious in the corner. She did not move, but snored loudly from time to time. Her breath stank out, even from the far side of the room. Nell whispered that the dolt had probably been arrested for being drunk or lewd, judging from her apparel and stench.

The gaoler returned with two hunks of hardened bread and a couple of pockmarked apples that he placed in their hungry hands. The women rapidly devoured what they were given without words, while their gaoler leered at them as they ate.

'Ha! The rogue expects us to show gratitude,' thought Elinor with some meanness.

Early the following day he accompanied Mary to show her where to empty their slop bucket. He came again to remove the newly awoken slattern, who left with him, alongside much loud and vulgar cursing. The women waited, but she did not return. Later, the gaoler-keeper returned again.

'You have a visitor,' he said dryly, as he ushered in a man. He gave a closed smiled as the be-wigged and finely, brocade-clad gentleman wished a 'good day' to Nell and Mary. The fine gentleman did not banter words, as their oily gaoler hesitated in the doorway.

'I am the Rector of St. Giles'. I have come to enquire if you wish to pray for your souls with me.' The man instantly bent his head and began to intone the words of the Pater Noster, the Last Supper prayer, as the women watched on in silence.

'Our Father, which art in heaven, hallowed be Thy name. Thy kingdom come. Thy will be done in earth, as it is in heaven. Give us this day our daily bread and forgive us our trespasses, as we forgive them that trespass against us. And lead us not into temptation, but deliver *us* from *evil*. For thine is the kingdom, the power and the glory, for ever and ever. Amen.'

Averting her eyes from the man, Mary soundlessly repeated his 'Amen'. She knew the upright man had purposely emphasised certain words. She was fairly sure that he intended her to notice. He continued, 'Even our Lord was tempted. The Devil saith unto our Lord, "All these things will I give thee, if thou wilt fall down and worship me". Then saith Jesus unto him, "Get thee hence, Satan: for it is written, Thou shalt worship the Lord thy God, and Him only shalt thou serve." So I beseech you to fall to your knees beside me. Confess to the Lord of your wickedness and sin.'

Once concluded with familiar scriptural words he waited in silence then, without prior warning, asked, 'Do you know of a man, a farm man, named Ambrose King?'

Elinor smiled, nodded and said, 'Indeed, I do.'

The rector gave another disconcerting smile as he replied, 'I've heard Mister Ambrose King is dead.' He waited for a reaction, but the women were stunned to silence. He smiled again and narrowed his eyes. 'So, you acknowledge that you know of this man?' he asked. 'That will be of fair interest to the court.'

Elinor cried out in annoyance and anger, 'Perhaps you think we gave him a curse too?' She glared indignantly. 'I did not curse him, for I cared for him.'

The rector pursed his lips to ask if they wished to repent of their sins to him. 'So, you cursed others and not him?'

Both women were shocked at how he had turned their words. Nell promptly told him, 'Go back to Hell.' His unexpected news carried few details, but the rector clearly took pleasure in relaying this sadness.

'I beg of you, tell us more?' supplicated Mary. 'When and how did this happen?' she enquired on behalf of her friend. As a more pragmatic Mary tried to ascertain how Ambrose had died, Elinor stood angrily by the cold wall with fists and teeth clenched to prevent herself crying.

'I believe he was attacked,' he stated. 'For he was found slumped in a corner in Ship Lane, leading to the river. He was bloody and his head had been bashed.'

Elinor wailed loudly, 'No, no, no! This cannot be true.' She looked away and breathed loudly.

'Was he assaulted or robbed?' asked Mary with an emotional quiver evident in her voice.

'Probably,' replied the Rector. He added, with some malice, '... either that or someone wished to rid the town of his unwanted presence. Particularly as he has been closely linked to you.' He pretentiously preened his cuffs. Mary glanced at Elinor, then returned the Rector's steely gaze.

'Perhaps another of your associates will be next?' he blithely speculated. 'One ... Samuel Barnes?' With this statement ringing in their ears, he took his leave of them.

Mary was dumfounded. The Rector's parting words had seemed like a thinly veiled threat. Elinor seemed stupefied by the shocking news. The man appeared convincing, but Mary sat back and thought for a moment, then advised her friend, 'There is no way for us to check the truth of his sickening statements. Reports are sometimes fake.' She sniffed loudly, '... and I think he has reason to lie to us.'

'What? A man of faith?' quizzed Elinor.

'No. A man sent here tasked to manipulate.' She wondered how true his story was or did he merely wish to coax them to incriminate others? 'I worry where this will lead?'

'Stop fretting about the future. We can change little. As for dying: we'll both cease worrying over death once we're dead.'

...ooo000ooo...

The House of Correction stood behind the Sessions House. It had been used as a gaol for about a decade. Southward, across Angel Street, lay open countryside, but the women could not see it to be cheered by it. They were held in a below-ground chamber where Quaker women had suffered before them. These were said to 'quake and tremble in the way of the Lord', but this gaol had made them tremble for many other reasons - not least, the unpleasant turnkey. When abruptly roused by the intimidating man, they were indelicately led to a large panelled chamber where they gave an account to be recorded for posterity.

They nodded as a lawyer gave brief accounts of their births, lives and educations. They answered when asked and their words were transcribed. As neither could read properly, they would not know what they had signed their mark to. They were informed that women would sit to listen to their daily conversations and that formal trials would take place on Saturday, the seventh day in March. This bothered Mary as, like Isabel before her, she took the number seven to be an ill-portent.

...ooo000ooo...

William Rands was a magistrate and nonconformist preacher who had held the Consistory Court in Oundle for the past decade. He was known for his fairness, having treated his flock with a well-educated kindness. When called to attend the Northampton court he did so, after first having visited the women in the bridewell. He spoke briefly to say how the women lived and worked at home, but noted that he'd heard reports of 'lewd ways' from members of his congregation and that an 'unfriendly spirit had manifested' between Elinor and himself as she did not attend any church. This had simply not been accepted by the vicar or his flock. Rands said that when the women were to be questioned they would likely accuse others to make their case. This would be good for none. Conversely, he said, the Oundle towns-people had steadily turned against them for cursing, bewitching and causing death to animal and people. The court duly noted that, the destitute Elinor had 'moved to live with her local confidant, Mary Phillips'. Men of the court had already noted 'immoral lives as witches', whilst the vicar pointed out the 'Godliness of their unfortunate victims.'

Positive proofs were carefully omitted, but Mary and Elinor remained unaware. Overwhelmed by pomp and alien court formality, they were not at ease to speak plainly. Ensconced in Northampton with guards who were unfamiliar and cold, they were aware of their lowly status. None seemed supportive of their predicament. Even the rabble had largely pre-decided the outcome of the trial. The courtmen held the advantage of being well prepared. Witnesses came to say their piece - to tantalise and accuse. When Mary responded that she was a healer, the Law noted the deaths of the people she had treated.

'I was called on to heal. Surely you can see that if I had any magic I would use it to heal?' countered Mary.

'Well, if sold my soul to the devil, what do you think it would fetch, probably more than your wage?' Elinor mocked as she was fast removed from the court.

'Shh ... You'll doom us,' Mary hissed as they were pushed through the door. 'Guard your words, Nell.'

That night no food was forthcoming. As the light faded and sounds of people outside diminished, the tired women in the hollow chamber reflected on their plight. When Mary roused herself to use the night-bucket, she heard a woeful sound. Although fully dark, Elinor had heard her get up. Her voice made Mary jump in surprise.

'Fret not! Nothing can come of this mess. It will all blow over and be forgotten like a sudden storm.'

Sadly, she could not have been more mistaken - as it did not. Determined to state their case they worked hard at being truthful, but like water perpetually beating onto rock, their steadfast boulders were worn away and their confidence eroded. Below ground, there was no comfort to be had in their cell. They saw dim daylight through the small window that looked out to a narrow-strip yard where they were allowed to take some daytime air. Their chamber pot, a foul-smelling bucket, was infrequently emptied. It overflowed onto the floor and had already left a patch that could never be scrubbed clean in the corner.

'Is there not a candle?' she asked her warder.

'You pay your keep in this prison. If not, you go hungry - and live in the dark,' the hostile gaoler gave his gruff reply, then rubbed his hand over the greying stubble on his chin as if in thought.

Nell deduced his dishonour. He was a turnkey who was not prepared to help any, but himself. She guessed that his pay was meagre and that he supplemented it by payments collected from visitors who came to observe the condemned. The bent man was also responsible for persons kept in long-term imprisonment, awaiting further trial or release. Relatives recompensed him when allowed to visit with food.

There was no candle forthcoming and no cleanly covered pallet for ease or rest. A long-handled ladle rested in a half-bucket of water, which was stored not far from the piss-bucket. Mary managed to stretch her irons to move the buckets as far apart as she could. If she was going to be denied fresh drinking water, she was not about to leave the little they had next to a stinking slop-bucket!

The turnkey watched. 'I could remove your irons if you'll *behave* yourselves,' he offered with a smirk. He sniffed. 'Do you have any loose coins tucked in yer gown? Perhaps you have something to trade?'

Nell glared as the man twirled his keys around on the end of his finger. With no reaction from the women, he locked the metal gate. His footsteps echoed along the corridor as he went.

Elinor rapidly shook her head as if to purge herself of a tiresome fly. She rubbed both hands over her mucky face and glanced at her friend. Mary's finger-nails had been steadily bitten down to the quick and the skin around them chewed raw. She had carelessly gnawed upon them - hungry, distraught and detached. Unaware of doing so. As she looked down, she noted her once firm and rounded breasts had shrunk. She was fast becoming an unattractive shadow of her former self.

'That man has no sympathy.' Elinor quietly remarked with a sardonic grin, 'I'm returning to my early waif-state and do not care for it.'

Mary sat with her head in her hands as she wondered aloud, 'Who started this fearful hatred of us?' She silently considered that maybe Elinor had been at fault? Not as wary as Mary, Nell had been careless of the oscillation of wagging tongues.

The Assize's subterranean cells held only unhappiness. Mannish calls emitted from along the resonant corridor. The men here not so fortunate, for they had no access to outdoor air. Mary thought the cell for women was a blessing and curse, with rank smells alleviated by a door that could be opened in the daytime. It gave access on to a very narrow yard with, overhead, an iron grating that showed a strip of grey sky. It let out the stench, but let in the cold chill of winter. From without came voices of foot-travellers, as they strolled up-hill to view detainees. As passers-by walked on, the sound of their voices carried a normality that had all but ceased for Mary. Huddled with her back against the cold stones of the internal wall she wrapped Sam's old woollen cloak around her narrow shoulders. She breathed into its folds to further warm her chilled bones.

In daylight hours, people passed to ogle from street level. Some looked down through the overhead grating with reproach, insults and admonitions. Others just inquisitive - and curious to view a captured witch from close proximity.

…ooo000ooo…

Chapter 25
Caught by Court

The county held four annual Assize courts within the Sessions House. Built on George Row after the great fire of Northampton, it stood on the corner of Angel Street, conveniently near to the church of St. Giles' and the north-bound York Road. The building allowed easy passage for felons to places of execution and conveniently, guaranteed a selection of nearby lodgings in hostelries for men of the court.

The vast new three-storey provincial house was pale and stately; accommodating two courts with an open public space between. High entrances offered access, while columns reared imposingly from floor to ceiling. After their small home, this huge edifice possessed grandeur that held reverence and intimidation for Mary and Elinor. Often dumbstruck, few of their salient words were transcribed in the record nor, largely illiterate, did they know if these were noted correctly.

They were taken via back doors down shallow steps into their dark cell, so had no idea of the scale of the court until they were led along a dank, labyrinthine corridor an up steps into the centre of a large, bright room. Once here, they stared in awe at the panelled courtroom with long, raised wooden benches taking centre stage. Here, they stood as a severe judge entered to look down on offenders and onlookers alike.

Suspects were held in a dock in front of the court. The community viewed from the rear and sides of the room. Jurors and the wealthy sat to one side away from the riffraff and lower classes.

The general public did not stand by the rules. Long before details, defence or sentencing were decided, bystanders could not be stilled from giving loud opinions.

'Hang her.'

'Burn the witch.'

'Hang the hags for they are in league with demons,' they demanded.

Mary could ill-comprehend how in 'fair England' they could be condemned so easily, without a fair trial, on the basis of hateful lies. They strongly denied all claims of witchcraft, but people vocalised their opinions Mary remained convinced that the court scribes ignored her words and wrote those of others.

Over a hundred people packed themselves, crowded as they were, into the court room. When there was silence in the court, footsteps echoed from wooden floor boards. At other times, the assembled rabble stamped their feet to voice opinion.

Narrow steps led from a central dock, from whence the chained women were bundled downward into the cool passageway. This gave respite and calm after the heat of the many bodies of the room above. The women were taken to the right. Men called out from cells further along on the left.

Judges used an upper chamber that led into a pleasant garden. From the garden they could hear the calls of prisoners in the women's yard. The judges enjoyed respite as much as the women, for the courtroom was full of vocal people. Those supporting the defendants were encouraged to remain silent through coercion or in defence from threats.

At first, Elinor and Mary did not appreciate their waking dream, as they were accused of attempts and successful murders achieved with the help of demons. At first they had pleaded innocence, but the mood of the crowd and lack of sympathetic lawyers revealed a cast-iron certainty of no revoke – particularly with the superstitious testimonies spoken against them. Hopes diminished. They spoke to each other in whispers, while others watched closely.

The women hoped they might find an ally in their local lawyer, Stephen Bramston, but he steered clear of the trial. Although he knew of the women, he did not wish to take sides in a combat he considered already lost. Morally and physically the women were beaten and broken. He knew it would not be long before they individually confessed to any crimes they were accused of. He knew they would be found guilty.

Lizzie badgered her father, Joseph, to take her to Northampton for the trial. He remonstrated, but, as was usual, had finally given in to his daughter - knowing no peace until he did. Her mother had been most surprised to find Lizzie bearing a bunch of wild heather, aconites, snowdrops and pansies. The girl had hugged Ruth tightly as she presented her with the floral winter cluster. Ruth was taken aback but, despite her dumbfounded daze, she hugged back and asked no questions of her daughter.

Joseph and Lizzie packed their cases and travelled to Northampton in a covered waggon that took passengers and goods along ancient tracks and drovers' routes to the distant county town. Overnighting in inns, passengers, driver, drovers and horses were provided with accommodation, while the village smithy helped shoe the horses and repair broken carriage wheels and ironwork.

Their waggon had set off in the early morning and arrived midday the following day. Joseph had booked them in to a reasonably-priced ale-house within walking distance from the court. Here they could take their evening meal and some recuperative rest.

As they travelled south, Lizzie mulled over the days that had passed. Earlier, when she discussed her forthcoming trip with Mercy, the latter had seemed most vexed.

'Lizzie, I'm your friend and you ... would want me to tell you the truth ...' she had hesitated before continuing, 'I think it was you who first blamed and pointed a finger at Mary ... because Sam loved her. You went to Cat Boss - and she spoke to Bill. He always listens to his wife. Who would not? It was Bill who told his Lordship and the Church, so they instructed him to arrest her ... to arrest them. You caused this, Lizzie. Be it in your conscience to consult the vicar and pray for forgiveness.'

Lizzie recalled rounding on Mercy. 'Why do you insult me so, Mercy? How can you say such awful things of me? Am I not your friend?' Lizzie had demanded, inflamed. She had taken a deep breath, but secretly knew that Mercy spoke truthfully. 'Be gone if you'll say naught good of me.' Lizzie recalled that Mercy had then done exactly as she was instructed.

In the courtroom, the well-clad, but flustered Miss Coles noted flies that buzzed around the convicts, for they had not cleaned themselves for many days. She had begun to itch; whether from seeing the dirt or from flea bites, she was not sure. The women looked tired and unhealthy, with dirt-encrusted skin and un-brushed, matted and tangled hair. With dark circles around their eyes, who could trust such beleaguered looking so women?

Lizzie heard how the accused had been coerced into signing a confession that gave lurid details of how they entertained a "tall, dark man", who taught them to worship the Devil. Lizzie remained quiet on knowing that this was of her doing. She knew that if consulted, the young Robin Smith would recall his late night disguise and the hoax that was inspired by the pretty young wench. If they chanced to meet again she would need to offer money to him – or other inducements - to keep his mouth shut.

On proclamation of the visiting Devil, mayhem broke loose in the courthouse. Lizzie watched as the court erupted in a hubbub of noise. Men and women shouted, while others were overcome and needed to be escorted from the building. Lizzie remained self-righteous, but as the trial progressed she realised the results of her possessiveness. Listening to the judges' dominant dialogue, she pulled at her warm fur wrap. She glanced down, then recalled the small wart on her arm. What if she should be forced to give evidence? Could the appearance of such an innocent pimple be used against her? She guessed that Mary and Elinor had been checked for witches' marks. She glanced up at the ragged couple. Each stood chained, uncomfortable, deprived and forlorn.

As Lizzie turned to escape a blast of cold air from the huge doors, she noted a man with pen and paper standing near her father. He appeared to be making notes. The man smiled at Lizzie and bowed as he introduced himself. He assumed the young woman was a friend of the accused.

'It's a shame. I knew Mistress Godfrey and grew up living nearby, so knew little Mary. She was a shy, pleasant child.'

'I knew Old Isabel, but it seems that her ward has condemned herself.' Lizzie spoke quietly as her father nodded in agreement.

'Who among us is sin free?' a gentleman probed.

'I most certainly hope my kin live without wickedness.' Joseph noted. He stood by Lizzie's side smiling benevolently, as he knew naught of his daughter's part in the arrests.

Lizzie felt light-headed. She smiled forlornly at the man, thinking, 'They are damned and I have done it.'

'Sir, does your daughter wish to sit outside for a moment or two? She looks pale,' the gentleman remarked. Joseph noted that although his attire was from London, his accent was local. He smiled.

'Thank you, sir. We have travelled from Oundle and are both tired.' He shared his name and knowledge of the accused with the gentleman as they fanned themselves to move the fetid air. When the great doors were closed the room was hot from the crowds and when it opened the wintery blast chilled all.

Joseph addressed his daughter, but she did not wish to move, for indeed they were crammed tightly making movement most difficult.

As the day progressed, the pallid, elegantly-dressed man replied, 'I'm glad to make your acquaintance. I am Ralph. Ralph Davis. I am due to send to London my views on this trial.'

The man invited Mister Coles and his pretty daughter for luncheon. This they took in a local inn, before resuming their place in the packed room.

Talk ceased as the thin-haired gaol-keeper made a statement on incidents during the accused's recent gaol residency.   His eyes narrowed as he thrust an accusing finger towards the bound women. With his tone deferential to the judge, he noted, 'Sir, them women hold a rare magic.' The crowd hushed. With a hostile glance at the women, the artful man again nodded in their direction, 'They jinxed us while in gaol.' The crowd murmured in assent.

'The women, Shaw and Phillips, used their wickedness for evil when locked up below … and I witnessed it all.' He licked his lips. 'First, as I didn't agree to release 'em, they made me their sport an' placed a spell on me. They forced me to dance, bare and naked, in the courtyard for a full hour, M'Lord,' he replied shaking his head. Some men whistled and others cat-called, whilst others laughed.

'What a devious man,' thought Mary.   He accused them of bewitchment while they were chained and detained, with words that influenced the mood of the room.

Elinor now threw back her head and hooted loudly at his spite. 'How can you tell such untruths, to the detriment of his own soul?'

'Why'd we do that?' Mary shouted at the judge. 'What'd be the point?   We've harmed none.'   She expected no response.

'I was much embarrassed,' the narrow, balding man spoke back. He glared, with spittle on his lips, '… an' was raw cold … an' tired too!'

Elinor wildly stared around her at the assembly, then brazenly back at the jailor. With a nod, she yelled,

'I'd 'ave made you keep your clothes on if I cared to see you dance - for you have naught I wish to see.'

She glared at the judge. 'The man is full of lies! Curse you all for believing him.'

The clean-shaven judge coughed and looked down to his notes, then earnestly stared at the women in turn. He viewed the crowd, aware that they awaited any pronouncement. Sensing a hesitation, the room reacted with loud shouts demanding 'the witches should be put to death'.

The judge raised his voice to shout above the noise of the crowd. 'Woman, understand, you are seriously accused.' He paused. 'What do you know of the *Malleus Maleficarum* - the Hammer of Witches?' He awaited an answer. When none came he continued. 'Significantly, "When a woman thinks alone, she thinks evil". I see that your brooding has been open to evil.'

'I've done no such thing,' Nell erupted.

'Elinor Shaw, I am here to prevent future sins.' He turned to look at his fellows, then asked of her, 'Are you declaring before this court that you are innocent of witchcraft? I think not!'

His smug face showed haughty arrogance.

Nell had no time for response, as the shrewd man loudly continued, 'You are witches. Do not deny it. You have condemned yourselves with your actions.' He glared at the women. 'Your craft submits to carnal lust. You have insatiably bared your body to all - including our gaol-keeper. You've consorted with demons and have made this is perfectly clear the court.' He allowed the noise of the courtroom to crescendo, whilst cleared his throat with a sip of water from a flask on the table before him, before continuing. 'You are infected with the heretical crime of witchcraft.' His face had begun to redden and he stopped again to wheeze and cough, glaring at Elinor, who stared back brazenly. There were some in the crowd who fought hard to resist a smirk, but by no means was their audience softening. The judge established they'd cast reproach on the sycophantic jailor. No longer seen as 'simple', the women were 'crude, lewd and loose' and 'accomplished in witchcraft'. This was the crux of the matter.

Sam stood and watched from the rear of the room. Elinor had attracted a title of 'Nell the strumpet', but both were accused of employing witchcraft.

Samuel knew that as the trial progressed it grew in repute, beyond acts of criminality - trespass, threat, assault, indecent exposure, defacement of property or theft. The chattering crowds, agitated by the spectacle, saw not one, but two witches to try! Many were fascinated by the destruction of these undesirable, harmful women. That is, as long as it wasn't happening to them or in their close neighbourhood.

Samuel dared not let true emotion show. He was hurting. Things had gone beyond the point where he held any power to help. He'd heard talk of torture. Without sleep his loved one would gladly confess to the sentinels who watched and awaited familiars. Sam had heard of river-ducking where, if by some miracle a 'witch' survived she was deemed guilty - as the Devil saved his own. If a fated soul drowned they were acquitted, buried and sent to heaven. Samuel prayed this could not happen.

'Mary is going through hell already. Is the warder trusted?' He thought for a moment. 'Perhaps I should give him recompense to allow a visit?'

His friend, Thomas, replied, 'Do not offer the gaol-keeper anything, for he is in the pay of the judge. Prisoners are not allowed favours. I think it best not to ask for anything that can be taken as coercion or a bribe.'

Sam thought for a moment. Prison was a punishment. It was meant to be harsh. He knew that even straw was not provided for the prisoners to lie on. They would be completely alone, thinking that even *he* had abandoned them. He asked Thomas, 'What do you suppose will happen now? Is there a chance that one can go free and not the other?'

His friend reflected with all due seriousness for a moment before replying, 'Sam, I'm sorry. I know well they're your friends, but to tell you true, if they're condemned they're normally taken down the Kettering Road to the common-land ... and the gallows.'

A passer-by, overhearing, paused to add to their conversation. 'That's likely - for they've hexed many.'

Samuel cared not to hear. He'd heard of horse contests on the extensive common. The town tried to ban races as many riders were hurt, but races continued!

'If not, they may be taken to Abingdon gallows,' continued the busybody, do-gooder. He had not noted Sam's face, so earnestly continued, 'With a noose around their necks the cart's driven away leaving 'em swinging in slow strangulation. It's violent, but worthy of many for their crimes. It'll be a fine spectacle.' He looked to the silent, solemn, Tom Ashton and blanching Sam Barnes, whose usual sun-kissed, golden brown skin bore a much paler tone. His voice steadily hushed. With nothing more helpful to say he stumbled away.

...ooo000000ooo...

Daily, news from the court spread fast. Spectators, court-men and squealers (sent to record proceedings for *The London Gazette*) acted as one when presented with the new revelations. The women called out in denial, but were drowned in the din. A well-dressed reporter noted, '*they made such a howling and lamentable noise as never was heard before, to the amazement of the whole court.*' He was well-versed and shrewd, knowing how to write an eye-grabbing headline to sell a paper with dramatic quotations of corrupt utterances and brow-raising narrative to surpass the dry, legal, linguistic discourses. The man doodled a rough sketch of the women that gave little clue to their genuine appearances.

After Elinor noted Lizzie standing to the rear of the courtroom she was beset with fury. She cursed all within hearing (and many who were not) in her vexation, while Mary dropped her gaze to the ground. No words emanated from her pale, pursed lips. She wondered if, perhaps, the men of the court could reach a decisive outcome erring on the side of caution.

'Nell, be discreet,' Mary thought to herself as she closed her dark eyes to repress the scene before her. 'Her lips condemn us both.'

Samuel thought the same as he watched. 'I'll need to tell Father and Wilf on my arrival home. I don't relish my explanation if Mary is to be imprisoned for many years, but they'll know I will wait for her.'

'You idiots, you are absolute addle-plots,' Elinor yelled at the top of her voice, pointing as best she could with tied wrists. 'Can't you see we're innocent? You use cramp-words to hide your meaning. Lawyers, phaa ...' she spat, while waving her hands at them like ripened rye in the summer wind. 'The Devil didn't tempt me, it was the gaol-keeper who wanted my body to ease his own needs - and I was having none of it.' She glared at the man. 'My, he has a wicked tongue. He desired to find what lies within me!' she taunted. 'Can you not see? We lay under threat by that guard. See him standing there with his hands on his hips and his eyes shifting about! He threatened to bring in our friends to add to our crimes. He said they'd be imprisoned or die at the hands of a hangman. To protect our friends, what could we do? They've done no wrong.' She wailed in panic.

All who stood and observed agreed that to protect their own loved ones they would do almost anything. The guard had lied with a misleading trick to betray them. Why did none speak up on their behalf?

'The devil is naught but a man gone bad, so hear ye all honest folk, do not gorge on the lies of those so much more evil than I.' Elinor could not be quelled.

Shocked, once again, Lizzie slipped back into the crowd and silently stole away. Her settling of scores had succeeded, but not quite in the way she had intended. She had gone too far and now it was too late. Powerful escalations rolled with ease from the tongues of neighbours.

When Mr Coles turned to his daughter, she had already left the room. He spun around, but could not see her. Joseph heard the mendacities - non-stop, like a runaway cart there was bound to be ruin at its terminus.

As Lizzie passed behind a row of people, some of what they said reached Lizzie's ears. She passed Samuel as she bustled out. He had already noted her and her father standing inconspicuously at the rear of the room, then bitterly watched as she took her leave.

336

'Never again shall I trust a beautiful woman. She is the true demon, not my Mary.' Sam found himself staring after Lizzie. 'There she goes,' he thought. 'A fine-looking apple - riddled with worms.'

Lizzie held less pity for Mary or Elinor than for herself. She caught Sam's glare and read his thoughts. Despite all, Lizzie knew she was at the heart of the trial, the instigator, who knew she could never again hold any affections of Sam's heart. This was her misfortune. This was the fault of the witches.

Lizzie turned on her heels to run as fast as her feet could carry her, away from the vexing voices. She guessed that prisoners were treated terribly during their incarceration. She had heard that they were chained to a post in prison. Chains that were rough and tight that caused painful swellings. She now did not care where she went, she suddenly needed to be as far away from the courtrooms as possible.

Woefully wading through a laughing crowd, young Mistress Coles was taken aback as she heard a spectator comment, 'They deny it, but we all know it to be true.' She moved further. She swallowed hard on hearing busy exchanges.

'Did you hear what the Shaw woman said?'

'Yea. If they did the things I heard they've done, they deserve all that comes to them.'

'Well, they caused humiliation to folk who went to see them.' The man sniggered. 'Did y'hear they magic'd Mistress Laxton's skirts to fly over her head. She's an old bat, so she deserved it, but then they made the warder dance naked in the yard for an hour. I'd have liked to have seen that. That's priceless!'

'Someone said that even his Lordship could not resist a hidden smirk.'

'I heard he was caught with his pants down, that was all. Well, he jigged one way or the other, didn't he? Ha! So who's he going to blame? Who else was there?' He stopped to contemplate the matter, before quickly announcing, '… The lustful witches.'

'Aye, they are lewd,' agreed his colleague. 'I presume you 'eard what 'appened to their neighbours? They were a-feared for their lives.'

'Aye,' replied another, shaking his head in disbelief. 'Their crimes are lay bare before them. Will they duck 'em? It is a fine punishment for the disorderly.'

Several others joined in. 'Let me know if they're to hang. We need vengeance or no soul'll be safe again.'

'What a ruckus they've caused of their malice.'

'They cursed the keeper to dance when 'e threatened 'em with heavier irons.'

'I'll bet the man was weary to the bone by the time he was finished!' mocked another. 'It's cold out!'

'I'll await a punishment to keep good folk safe.'

His friend summed up by condemning them to the fires of hell with his words. 'Well, in my opinion they should be hanged at the crossroads at Nor'ampton Heath. I'd buy tickets fer the stands fer a better view.' They were further condemned by the man's judgement, 'They've openly vowed they're witches, calling on t' Devil to save 'em, 'n' mockin' us Christian men and women.'

'Y' know rats live in prison cellars? Rather than protecting prisoners from 'em, those suspected of the craft are viewed day and night in hope that the Devil'll visit as a rat t' communicate with them.'

'Well, as the gaoler 'ad threatened 'em, they duly punished him!' came a voice in dissent. 'It's hardly the girls fault! I'd do the same in their place.'

'How can you say such in defence of them?'

'I agree. They're cold and cruel,' an opinionated woman stated, whilst crossing herself in the Papist way. 'They deserve to be dead; then we'll all sleep better in our beds for it. Burn the buggers and be done with 'em.'

Lizzie bumped into people as she moved. She did not apologise and cared little that they protested as she collided and lurched from them. Her grumbling guts churned, making an unwanted gravy that she feared could shortly make its appearance. Her path headed in any direction as long as it was away, to the rear of the crowd, then down the nearest alley as fast as her feet could proceed, for fear of association with the two demon-ridden criminals! Back in the room in the inn, Lizzie sought to wash her hands of the guilt she felt. Then convinced herself that the trial had little to do with her.

...oooooooooo...

Late that night, Elinor awoke with a dreadful feeling in her guts, worrying niggles in her mind and a squeeze in her dry throat. They had been fed a thin gruel that both ate hungrily. Now, Nell gazed into the darkness with disturbing thoughts keeping her awake until a slow dawn broke. She was not hungry, but knowing meals would be rarely provided, gave cause for worry. Elinor rested from time to time, but felt a fear in sleeping.

'I'll sleep for long enough when dead, so need to appreciate every day of my life,' she solemnly held.

Bothered by sounds unfamiliar to her ears and in an overtired dreamtime state, Mary also lay awake. She recalled swimming by the shallows of the river; warm in the sunshine - so far away now. Shifting, she recollected dressing, several days since, in her worn grey dress. This clothing was now damp to touch and decidedly dirtier than it had been before her journey. The material of her gown had a habit of sticking to her cold, glistening skin. Smoothing down the ridges and wrinkles of her shift, she calmed. Sensitive to the gentle touch of her own fingers on soft skin. She pressed her face to the frosted window. A pumpkin moon hung suspended in the sky. She could see it through the iron grating, benevolently calming, held by invisible cords strung from the black, star-encrusted mantle of the firmament. Revived, she heard a local church bell toll in the distance.

Mary soothed herself with memories of autumnal trees, glowing vibrant, as phantom pheasants called seasonal greetings. When would she see these again? She recalled the best times, slowly rewinding her mind with the parish church bells to earlier tolling - on a summers eve calling her neighbours to evening mass. She had watched the massive iron clappers being fixed by a local smith and their ropes plaited by the hemp-man. The bells evoked memories of wedding seasons and summer scents long departed. She recalled a shy, young George Addee, when he married five years since. He'd stuttered and stumbled his way through the service, embarrassed at being watched by all the congregation.

She recalled hearing the bells - having to run to arrive in good time to watch friends swear their everlasting loyalty and love to each other in church. Not long thereafter, in the same year, Mary had watched as Ethel Ailsworth, a childhood playmate, said her vows. Mary had picked a scented posy for Ethel on her special day. Each wedding was distinctively different; each beautiful in their own way. The couples were not pillars of society, but had attended services with regularity and piety. Each saw beautiful bindings of their love. She had witnessed their love, weddings and births of their babies. Incarcerated, she was free to smile at her memories.

Mary repeatedly enjoyed seeing each fresh bride decked in her finest dress, bearing sweet-scented floral garlands. Folk celebrated and congratulated as was their want. Mary wondered how her former friends fared and considered who would birth future offspring now that she was restrained and chained. She guessed it was unlikely she would be greeted by these families again, nor have the pleasure of marrying her own love and birthing her own babies. She felt resigned to her fate as a troubled player in a risky game beyond her control. 'Witch trials were always full of neighbourly denouncements,' she thought. 'Hell, we'll never be released alive!' she had whispered. 'They are playing with us just as pint-sized Catchevole torments each small mouse. This is destiny.' Intimidated by court and overwhelmed by powers judge, she had no control. They played on her mind.

'Hold my hands, Mary,' whispered Nell from a dark wall. The moon-pale woman did as she was bid. Her hands were cold. Elinor paused. She leaned forward into the shaft of moonlight to look into Mary's eye. She spoke clearly, 'May the anger in our thoughts and oaths plague Lizzie Coles with lying friends, ill-dreams and ill-health for the remainder of her life. So be it.'

Mary fast pulled her hands free to hold them against the heart beating loudly in her breast. She whispered, 'Nell, you should not say these things.'

'Well, I have - and wish hatred on all who turned against us. Let that be an end to it,' her friend replied with an unemotional air. 'Lizzie's killed us. I watched her face in court today. She is evil.'

It took time before Mary fell asleep. The usual glittering quality of colour changed her dreams until she stumbled into dark musky, mildew. She awoke to realise the smell was that of her cell. It was dank, dark and dirty. She and her friend were much vexed, tried and labelled. Scuttling of invisible creatures in shadowy corners alongside a strong smell of urine much disturbed her. She would sit awake rather than sleep. Voices in her mind and shadows of the room equally condemned her. She was naught but a leaf that fluttered and twirled in the wind, having no choice in where its path took her. Asleep again, she became a mouldering leaf, swept into a pile, waiting to rot away or be swept into an even larger bonfire. This was her fate.

...oooOOOooo...

Chapter 26
Censure and Condemnation

On Wednesday, the seventh day of March, Elinor and Mary were brought from their cell. Along the familiar dark corridor to ascend the shallow stairs into the large, light room where they again stood accused on another day of trial at the Northampton Assizes. Here they heard more condemnation for their witchcraft.

Packed with jostling people wishing to catch the forthcoming spectacle, the room permitted a certain amount of pushing and jockeying for the best positions from which to hear and see both witches and judge. The worst place to stand was by the door that opened and closed with regularity, frequently letting in the bone-chilling draught.

Edward Stratford held all powers of arrest as part of his office. As High-Sheriff of Northampton, he was the foremost law enforcement officer in the county. He held the oldest secular office under the Crown and, besides collecting taxes, one of his many jobs was to oversee trials and executions. Although it was an honour to be chosen as the straight-talking Sheriff, it was not an easy position. Parts of his job were arduous.

He opened the proceedings with the women standing before him. Each had unsatisfactorily pleaded 'not guilty' in Oundle, so required further trials.

Stratford read from a list. 'You are both accused of – firstly, bewitching, tormenting and causing the death of the wife of Robert Wise of Benefield. Secondly, of the killing by witchcraft, a four-year old child, Elizabeth Gorham of Glapthorne. Thirdly, of bewitching Charles Ireland of Southwick to death.' He looked up from reading from the list. The paper had risen and fell in his hand as he spoke.

The first indictment against them was that on behalf of Susannah Wise, with spoken evidence given against them from the gritty widow, Mistress Peak. Elinor sighed. This woman was a neighbour she had known since she had moved in with Mary. Widow Peak remarked that she and two of her friends had watched over the prisoners after they were first apprehended.

'Well, Sirs, it was around midnight on the first night that they were in the Oundle bridewell, when a little white thing appeared in their room. It was the size of a cat. We all thought it was a cat at first,' she noted.

'It wasn't 'er cat. I know 'er cat, Copernicus. He's black as soot,' someone shouted out from the back of the room. He was silenced with a stiff look from the judge.

Elinor sniffed in disgust. It was clear that the orator didn't even know Catchevole's name. She presumed that they neither could select their house-cat from a small clowder - nor tell the truth.

Widow Peak folded her arms below her chest. She was not a woman easily deterred. She continued, 'It came in bold as brass to sit on Mary's lap a while. I heard Elinor Phillips tell the cat that she was the witch and that it should carry a message for her.' She pointed at Elinor as she stridently continued, '... as *she* was not just any old witch, she was the *very* same witch who killed Mrs Wise by roasting wax effigies of her and sticking it with pins.'

The assembly gasped with excitement.

Mary had been forewarned by the rector, 'Keep your eyes lowered and behave in a demure state in the court or things are likely to go badly,' but this was past the point of 'too much' for Nell to comprehend. She could not bear another word from the devious widow. She gaped at the assembly with a shamelessly brazen attitude.   Undaunted, she would not allow the belittlement of her friend. She stared at the judge in his mighty, carved chair as if in a trance. She was livid.

Samuel saw her unforgiving face starkly written with her thoughts - for all who cared to look. With scared fascination he listened to her mad responses. He silently prayed for God's guidance. 'Please, do not say that. Oh, if it please you, Lord, do not let her perjure herself. Stop Nell, or awful things can happen to you and my Mary if you persist. Keep silent. Do not let them sentence you to die.'

Nell sneered. 'Oh, for an honest judge.'

'Speak only when you are addressed, woman,' retorted the abrupt voiced High-Sheriff. 'Speak when you are addressed, not otherwise or you will be returned to the cells.'

However, she would not be told. Before the passing of an hour both prisoners had ascertained that things they said would be appropriated, ignored or hushed. Magistrate, Phillip Ward, a trained barrister familiar with legislation tried without success to briefly explain the ways of the court to them.

Nell's stomach grumbled. It had been long since she had eaten. Her stomach complained for her as she noted a man in the courtroom busily eating a meat pie. He was paying more attention to his pie than the proceedings, but there again, so was Elinor. Her mouth watered, then her stomach growled with exaggerated loudness that echoed around the room with such clarity that the judge stared closely at her, before smirking. Shuffling his papers, he continued with the proceedings.

Mrs Evans was called to speak before the judge as a second witness. 'I was a-coming 'ome on the eve of New Year, when poor Missus Wise was first taken ill,' she started. 'I saw Nell Shaw look from 'er window opposite my house and 'eard her say, "I've done 'er business, so this night I'll send the old Devil a new year's gift".'

Mrs Evans rubbed her hands together, as if drying them before continuing with her story. 'Knowing the woman was said to be a witch by some in the town, she was concerned that we 'ad overheard her. We all went round to see how Mrs Wise was doing. When we arrived at Susannah Wise's house, we found her sore-tormented with pain. Oh, it was bad. She was crying out in pain, which grew to such a degree that at midnight she died.' The woman drooped to look at her hands, which she still rubbed, twisted and chafed together. Elinor could not believe her ears. She knew it was impossible that Mrs Evans could have clearly heard her from over the road, even if she had called out loudly. The woman was near deaf! How could anyone believe a word that woman said?

The furtive Mrs Evans would not look at either 'witch'. Elinor closely observed her. Mrs Evans was a large lady with a red, bulbous nose. She stood, warmly wrapped in a blanket-sized shawl. From time to time, during her account, she mopped at her nose with an unsavoury, grey piece of cloth.

'While those women,' Mrs Evans pointed directly at Elinor, 'were in Mrs Wise's house, they told 'er she was a fool to live such a miserable life and that if she were a-willing, they would send 'er somethin' round for relief - about the time o' midnight.'

She sniffed and continued. 'Mrs Wise, being a bit contrary to 'er name, agreed.' She lowered her voice to almost a whisper, '… So, that very night two small black things, like moles from the field, came into her bed and sucked at her.' The court room quietened. People strained to hear what she said. Her voice lowered so much that it was almost a whisper. 'The Devil 'ad sent 'is imps to Susannah Wise, 'cause of those women. The Shaw woman and 'er friend didn't care. They'd fornicated with the Devil.' With some finality she coughed loudly, huffed with an equally audible breath and stood stock-still with pursed lips. The rotund Mrs Evans held her voice as she checked her wrinkled, wringing hands, studiously avoiding Nell's staring gaze.

Sam had already heard how only women were accused of lewd behaviour or fornication before the magistrate, while men appeared exempt. None stepped forward to ask how Mrs Evans came to know the information she shared, yet assenting mumbles and nods echoed around the room.

'Hang 'em,' shouted a deep, male voice from the rear of the room, while rumbling assents joined in. 'Get on with it an' 'ang 'em.'

Recovering her nerve, Mrs Evans eyed the room. 'Y'know imps came two or three nights until poor Mistress Wise was afeared for 'er life. Then she sent for the good minister to pray for 'er.' Pale-faced she quietly added, 'Afore the imps left my dear friend, Mrs Wise, 'eard 'em say they'd take revenge on 'er for refusing to give buttermilk to the imps. Then she was sore worried.'

'Madam, may I ask, for what reason did the women require buttermilk?' the magistrate asked, with owl-like eyes staring straight at Mrs Evans.

'They fed their imps on buttermilk an' my friend, the virtuous Mrs Wise was 'aving none of their japes. She said she'd give 'em nowt,' she explained. 'So they cursed 'er, then killed 'er,' she said with some finality. She pulled out a large cloth kerchief from her pocket and blew her nose loudly into it, to great effect. After wiping her eyes with the same cloth, she resumed her story. 'When 'e heard, Minister Danks paid 'em a visit. 'E sought to purify 'em witches of their deeds and cleanse o' their souls, but they were 'aving none of it,' she remarked as an aside.

With this Mary and Elinor called out, resulting in their being promptly taken back to the cell to await the afternoon session. With the court cleared, the judges took a well-deserved break for a robust lunch.

Later the same day, they heard more accusations laid against them. The first concerned the unfortunate Charles Ireland. As his parents were indisposed, it fell to Mrs Dora Croft of Southwick to give their evidence. The aged woman described what had befallen the twelve-year old, Charles. She defined, 'Charles, a quiet lad from my village of Suth-ick, was struck by strange fits the Yuletide before last. After twelve days, he steadily got worse an' started to cough-bark, a bit like a dog.' The elderly woman told the court, 'During that winter, the lad had visits from the two witches and blamed them for his adversity.'

Court men nodded acceptance with stern faces, while Mary scowled. To make her point, the grey-haired woman continued, 'The women told Mrs Ireland to cork some of Charles' urine in a stone bottle filled with pins and needles, then bury it beneath her fire.' She spoke harshly, 'His mamma would do anything to make him

348

well. So, with this done, rumour got around and the witches came back and said it was advisable for the bottle to be removed.' She took a few stentorious breaths and leaned heavily on her walking stick.

'Mrs Ireland refused their offer. "No" she'd said. "Why should I?" She could see the evil women were bothered by this.' Dora Croft looked callously at Mary and Elinor. 'Mrs Ireland accused 'em of ill-craft until the two confessed to bewitching the boy in the first place.' The woman glared at the judge. 'They left the Ireland's house with promises not to do it again, but two evenings later, young Charles fell into a sleep and died.' Her tale complete, the distraught woman slumped onto a bench, lowered her head and wept loudly into her shawl. There was a brief hiatus as she was helped from the room by affectionate friends. As she left, she seemed unaware that this damaging testimony was about to be further confirmed.

Charles' small sisters and aunt were allowed to give their testimony, even though they were only five and seven when the lad died. It seemed the biased testimony of children was allowed in cases of witchcraft, yet disallowed in all other instances. Youngsters were vulnerable, easily swayed and open to suggestion. Yet, the judge allowed the frightened children to say how they had seen the witches dancing by the Ireland family's home after dark and bewitching animals and people.

Now, the women were accused of a third wrong-doing. The nature of this crime was reported by a group of villagers from Glapthorne, who began by telling of their fellow villagers' plight.

'Little 'Lizbeth Gorham, the child of my neighbour, died on the tenth day of spring last year, after being bewitched to death.' Again the women had fingers pointed in their direction, accompanied by hidden signs made to ward off evil. Several crossed their fingers behind their backs to beseech the Lord to protect them as the spoken testimonies continued.

'They went around doing all sorts of ill. Amongst other things they killed horses, hogs and sheep belonging to Matthew Gorham, the deceased girl's father.'

The court noted that, as Matthew was unwell, his evidence could be reliably relayed by Constables Boss and Southwel, alongside their own testimonies. Proud they could offer trusted words, each described how the women confessed to them, saying they were witches.

'The women cursed and then confessed of their misdemeanours, my Lord,' Southwel said with an agreed nod from his colleague. 'They made unguents and filled small bottles with noxious poisons,' he added. 'They killed fifty sheep with lightening!'

'They also professed of knowing charmed cures and told us of 'em,' the irascible Mister Boss noted. 'I believe they're dangerous - beyond laws.' He continued, 'The simpletons gave their confessions thinking we would let 'em go free. For liberty, they told us of magic they used on modest townsfolk.'

'A curse on you for your lies! We did no ill,' yelled Elinor in surprise. 'Bring those that we cured to speak for us. Did you not think to speak to them first? Ask them!'

Spectators murmured and laughed at her outburst, while Mary glared around at the people in the room and at the grim looks on the faces of the judge's men. Were there none who wished to support them?

Elinor was warned, 'Hold your tongue or you will be returned to your cell.' She grudgingly quieted, before whispering to Mary, 'Why was it not voiced that while in their custody they'd threatened us with death if we didn't confess? They promised they'd release us if we spoke their words as they wished. They are naught but liars. They should now admit their sins.'

Elinor stood to demand, 'Tell us just one truth and we will be content.'

The judge sighed and looked to the men of the court as if seeking their approval. A hirsute, finely-dressed man stood to view the judge with pretentious seriousness. 'I have brought examples of their trade - wands, with which they performed their magic.' The man produced two wooden knitting needles. Elinor laughed out, 'They are our needles, not wands,' but an already pulsating courtroom din drowned the words she uttered.

The man turned to Mary and spoke as if to a child. 'Woman, the indications have most been heard.' With this he turned away and spoke quietly with the lawyers and clerks who were busily shuffling their notes. Thereafter, the women were returned to the cell, while others appeared to take turns to speak against them.

Many presumed that Mary and Elinor would not have been tried unless guilty.

'Surely, their destiny for these crimes should be death as a condemned witches?' they asked with little understanding of the lives of these women.

If more than one witch was 'captured', trials were usually arraigned on different days and tried by different juries with a new scribe present each time. Mary and Elinor were largely treated as one person as they lived and worked as one. Both held a disquieted feeling of doom, as they rushed forward to a fate that would stop for no man. Each was shocked at the horde of people packed in the court to hear all who would speak against them. The room was rowdy. A carnival attitude prevailed. Their chance to speak was of a limited nature, so Elinor's mind wandered. She stared around at the splendour of the room and wondered why some people are born to build; others to tear down. She listened for a time as accusations were read out before the assembly.

Mary was in a different dream-like world; believing this dreadful delusion could not be real.

The upright, well-dressed lawyer stood, reading from his notes and continued, 'You are accused of bewitching a woman and two children. You tormented them in a sad and lamentable manner until they died.'

The court murmured and hissed in anticipation. Elinor dropped her gaze to look down at her feet on the swept floor as the man continued in a stern voice, 'Others witnessed what you've done and you've confessed to making contact with the Devil.' His voice droned. 'With the Devil, you took revenge on people, causing grief, sickness and death; then bewitched their cattle to die.' His list seemed endless.

'Can there be anyone who cares enough to help us? Lord, I pray that there is,' Mary whispered to herself. She closed her eyes and repeated the words of the Lord's Prayer to herself. On opening them she heard hushed gasps from around the room.

'See!' came the persuasively bitter voice of a Lawyer as he pointed a straightened arm and waved an index finger towards her, 'Do you not all see? Watch the woman. See her as she curses and calls on demons?' His voice rose with eager alarm. 'Take note. See her as she curses us and casts her spell. See her lips moving as she beseeches the Devil.'

Mary was astounded and shocked by their complete misunderstanding. Her thoughts raced. 'Why do they dislike me so? Do they fear me for speaking out or for helping others?' She spoke out, confused, 'I was praying, not summoning the Devil.'

Without break, the lawyer's denunciations continued. 'You are accused of possessing powers for wrong doing. You have exploited these to mark stain on your town.'

Another haughty man stood to address the women. He looked down his long nose to remark, 'Name all your associates in your evil doing or your atonement will be severe.'

'What?' she called aloud. 'There are no others. How can we tell you of them if there were none?'

Mary shook her head. 'We did not perform magic, only medicine,' she thought. She knew that the Oundle people assembled here would not tarnish their reputations or put their families at risk to assist in her.

Elinor gaped, like a fish in brackish water, as she and Mary found herself hurriedly drawn downstairs and unceremoniously bundled back into the cell while the council took time over trivial discussions and a prolonged luncheon.

Below ground, the women were given a bowl of water to drink, which Nell recognised as a great mercy. She asked Mary how she fared, but Mary did not wish to converse, so remained silently huddled in a damp corner.

After a short recess, the trial resumed.

Here they were indicted as witches.

'Not true. You tell lies, Elinor shouted, 'That is not truthful at all.' The courtroom buzzed. By now, the young woman was fully aware that every deed would be challenged and every word 'mistaken' or misinterpreted.

'I reiterate for you, Elinor Shaw and Mary Phillips, as you are tried for bewitching and persecuting the wife of Robert Wise of Benefield until she died; for killing by witchcraft and wicked fascination, one Elizabeth Gorham of Glapthorne, a child of about four years of age.' The judge took in a deep, exasperated breath while staring at the list in his hand. Emitting a slight whistle as he breathed out again, he wondered if the women understood the charges. They appeared simple to him and demonstrated little learning.

'Furthermore,' he continued, 'a rider has brought news that Mister Gorham is sore ill and may die any day now.' As the people of the room vented vociferous opinions, it took a time before the room quietened for the judge to continue without shouting over the uproar. 'Furthermore, thou art on trial for bewitching to death Charles Ireland, of Southwick, a young man around the age of maturity,' he stared at them glassy-eyed as he sucked in air. The women watched as his chest rose and fell – and rose again. He breathed noisily before continuing, 'Also for killing horses, hogs and sheep, the goods of Matthew Gorham.' He looked severely at the cowering women. 'Mister Gorham said that he sought you out to save his child. Instead, you gave her soul to the Devil then killed his beasts. After a little persuasion you confessed to the constables.' At this, both women cried out, hugged and clung to each other, but knew not what to say or do.

'The man lies,' Mary shouted. 'They struck Elinor a resounding blow and said, "Stop whinging woman, can you not see that it'll do no good." Boss shook her, then thrust her into the arms of Constable Southwel.'

Simultaneously, Nell called, 'They threatened they'd harm our friends, so we ...' Shouts rang out, drowning her words. Despite her plaintive calls, the crowd did not see any unfairness towards the women. Tied and tortured, they put up little resistance.

Finally Elinor, deflatedly whispered 'There's little use in prevaricating. For our own safety we should admit to misconduct.' Mary dejectedly agreed as their confession was re-read in the foul-humoured court.

Constable Boss stood as upright as he could. He began by stating how the women lived together when they were contracted by the Devil. 'The two accused have confessed to Constable Southwel and myself that they sold their souls to the Devil to do unlawful mischief when they pleased.' He cleared his throat. 'At night, on Saturday 12th February 1704, about a year ago, as they were taking to bed, they gained six imps from the Devil, who appeared in the shape of a tall dark man. They'd do as women wished, if that they let 'em suck on their flesh. This they agreed to. Then the devil slept with 'em both with intimate knowledge of 'em. They've said it was the same as havin' a man, only not warm as his embraces were unyielding and unpleasant.' He swallowed as a coughed forced him to pause. Boss flicked a glance towards the women, before his gravelly voice continued. 'The next day, the women sent the imps to kill John Webb's horses as he'd damned them by pointing 'em out as witches. Both horses died in his pond the same day.'

Grumbles and mutters could be heard from around the room as Boss paused. 'My Lordship, two days later, they killed four hogs in the same manner. These belonged to Matthew Gorham, as he'd angered the women by saying they looked like witches. Not thinking this revenge sufficient, the next day they sent two imps a'piece to kill his four year old daughter.' Again, protests resonated around the room. 'This was all over in twenty-four hours; notwithstanding all the endeavours of doctors to preserve the child's life.'

'The women've confessed that if their imps were not busy in mischief they fell sick, but when active in evil-they were healthful and well.' Boss was driven to add, 'They said that at night the imps whispered to them in hollow voices that they'd not feel hell's torment, so they kill'd a horse and two cows of the widow Broughton, as she denied 'em some peascods. Not happy with this, the imps then struck her daughter with a terrible lameness that doctors' fear can never be healed.' As he spoke, the crowd were enthralled by their brazen behaviour. Some called out with their preferred verdict and sentencing decisions. Faces in the crowd showed emotion, with shrugs and coughs that spoke more than words alone. Boss and Southwel relished their information on the Devil's pact. Fatal confessions were swiftly transcribed as men hurried from courtroom to printing-press. The words of the witches were hurriedly printed as leaflet keepsakes for sale at a penny each on the 'big day'. The court 'weighed the facts' gave the impression of overwhelming evidence against the women, particularly with two signed confessions under their belts.

...oooO00Oooo...

Chapter 27
Early Mourning

The following day in a nearby inn, an "old acquaintance" of Mary's, named Ralph Davis, was busy scribbling information down on a docket. Sam, while breaking his overnight fast at the same trestle and bench, asked what he wrote. The man explained that he was writing to his friend, William Simons, a London merchant. Mister Simons, who had interests in the matters, would recompense well for his information.

On a dark Friday in mid-March, Mary and Elinor were revisited by Mister Danks. The God-fearing Minister and lead participant of the Church came with a hope that the two women would show degrees of repentance. This was not likely - and did not happen.

The polite, but self-important, Charles Danks explained that their execution was inevitable. He tried to get the two to confess and pray with him. 'I know you are simple women who do not understand the ways of the world,' he began. 'If you confess of your sins to God, your souls will be saved. If not, there'll be no dignity in your end. You'll burn in hell.'

Elinor asked, 'If our souls are saved, can we hope to be set free and allowed to go home?'

The reverend gentleman vanquished any hope with a short, unambiguous, 'No.'

Each woman guessed that the minister was furthering his faith in attending their terrifying plight. 'I've come in the hope of gaining insights into what you have done. Explain your dealings with the Devil to me and I will present it to God and the Justice of the County Courts.'

The women conferred in miserable whispers. Mary wondered exactly what the man hoped to hear, but Elinor chided her, 'Let's give him what he wants. What's it matter now? He cares not to hear a truth in it.'

Elinor was direct. She tilted her head to one side and dejectedly asked, 'Tell me, Reverend Danks, will it matter if a Devil visited us?'

As she looked him in the eye, the man nodded in assent. 'Yes, obviously,' he replied in a pompous air. He looked down his nose at one, then the other, of them.

'Then I say it is true that a Devil appeared to us in human form. He visited our house and cursed our neighbours for us.'

Mary sat in surprise, while Elinor, with some mirth, watched as the Reverend gasped for air with his creased eyelids opened wide. The man choked and gulped as if he had swallowed something unpalatable, while Elinor enjoyed the effect her words had on him. She glanced at Mary, 'A demon came in the guise of a tall dark man and on each occasion presented us with small imps of different colours, varying from red to black, and these infernal imps did nightly play with us.' She laughed to see how her words affected the man.

Danks breathed deeply, but said not a word. He took out a kerchief to wipe his perspiring face. Nell waited for further effect. The minister gravely nodded as if in encouragement. 'So! It is true,' he said to himself. 'Is there more?' he quietly queried.

Elinor implied the worst circumstance she could think of, leaving the Reverend clearly appalled and scandalised. His face flushed as it steadily turned red and fiery, until it met his ears. He felt compelled to listening to Elinor's confession. She progressed to brag about the numbers of people she and Mary had affected through their witchcraft.

'Why,' she said, 'I will tell you as we were betrayed. In less than a year, we easily killed fifteen children, eight men and six women, all of which I can name if you further wish me to?'

Mister Danks considered his familiarity with local deaths and those he'd administered to, preached for and pacified those grieving at during the last months. He knew that although no deaths had been attributed to witchery, he now saw that it was very possible that these women spoke the truth.

Mary continued for her friend, 'If you wish, we also can list for you the forty hogs, a hundred sheep, eighteen horses and thirty cows, which we destroyed with our powers. We are proud that this has resulted in the ruin of more than one family. They look down on us and would spit on us if they could.' She conjured vast numbers to prove how silly her own arguments were, but Danks drank the words in and believed every one.

Within little time, the Reverend had quietly informed the men of the court of his conversation with the witches. Thus, on their re-entry into the courtroom, the women saw that Mister Danks had been very, very busy. The court had back-checked statements relating to recent incidents that occurred whilst Mary and Elinor were imprisoned. Their stockpile of ammunition grew.

The first prison incident brought to the attention of the packed court, concerned Mister Laxton and his overweight wife. It seems that they had visited the prison to view the evil women and, as they stood at street-level peering down through the grating into the

359

narrow yard of the sub-ground gaol-cell, a peculiar incident occurred.

Witnessed agreed that Mrs Laxton was heard to remark, 'The Devil's abandoned his two lackeys,' at which point Elinor had been annoyed.

Mister Laxton noted that 'We saw her muttering words for several minutes. Then she conjured icy winds and a wind-storm from nowhere.' He looked to his wife for reassurance, before continuing with his dialogue.

'Mrs Laxton's hat was torn from her head and blown down the street. I tried to retrieve it while freezing demons tore at her in an attempt to remove her warm clothing.' The witness continued, 'Thereafter, my wife's smock-dress acted in such a strange manner that her skirts flew up over her head, leaving her exposed and highly embarrassed. ... The more she pushed her skirts down, the more they flew up again.' The man haltingly explained, 'I valiantly tried to right my wife's apparel, but to no effect. Nevertheless, after the witch called Elinor had ensured she'd had a good laugh, she stopped her magic for a time.' The man breathed deeply again and looked sideways at the woman in the dock. 'She thought it a fine jest to raise my wife's skirts. She revealed her arse to all who stood around and, although I tried to keep her skirts down, she re-conjured icy winds to send them up again and again. It was not until she called my dearest a "stewed prune" and "liar" that my wife's clothing finally returned to its normal place. Your Worships, we've talked about it and wish this incident to be included in your reports of the case against the two witches.'

The man stopped, coughed and glared in the direction of the women. His wife covered her pink cheeks with her gloved hands and looked away. Too much information had been given - and she was abashed.

'The wind blew.' Nell cackled a laugh. 'It was naught more than a strong winter wind blowing,' Elinor loudly shouted to the man as the courtroom erupted in turmoil once again as shouts of anger and laughter rang in the air. It seemed to all that it was unwise to taunt the women in their presence.

Listening to the statements of the middle-class family, Samuel stood dismayed as he had begun to realise the women were doomed. He looked to the judge and supporting jurymen, then at the angry crowd, as his awareness grew. Those who stood nearest were jeering and making the sign of the horns with their hands.

Sam felt constricted by the dark wood panels that led aloft to beams and ornate plasterwork. The ceiling included carved beautification of a devil façade and angel mask that hung aloft either side of the judge's seat. The women had been told by their mocking gaoler that the plaster devil would clack its tongue if it heard lies or the accused were guilty of crime. Although, certain she was innocent, Nell crossed her fingers in her skirts in the hope that the tongue wouldn't rattle in the ceiling above her. She glanced up to see the rude, playful face, suggesting her sexual provocation. She looked away, at the wooden panelling that lined each of the mighty walls. The power of the court was stronger than hers. No amount of magic could change its supremacy over her.

A thickset man and his tall comrade had remained standing near to Samuel throughout the trial. They had conversed for short periods. Now they shook their heads in disagreement. Each had quietly disputed whether there was any fact in their sorcery. Both held opinions that strongly contrasted with Sam's. Now the man turned to Samuel again.

'How can these women carry such poison?'

'They do not. I know them as artisans. I've always found them decent and kind,' Samuel replied with honesty. 'They cured my brother's crushed leg and he now walks without a stick.' Sam feared to mention that one woman was much closer to him than he dared to reveal. 'There is no reason for you to fear them.'

The man's thin friend looked on as the fleshy chap puffed out his chest and alleged, 'Well, I don't know about that. Magic is magic, just as poison is poison. It's dangerous – and not tolerable by law.' He stopped in his tracks, as if he had said more than he wished. He looked down at his shoes in thought for a moment, then looked sternly at Samuel. 'Lad, you don't seem aware that ridding ourselves of these witches is important to everyone here. A crime is a crime. They are a danger and a threat. We must look to God to not forsake us. These women must have done something wrong or they wouldn't have ended up here. Just look at them. They look guilty, so don't say they don't,' he hissed.

His lean friend, standing nearby, listening, then openly crossed himself in the old way and added, 'They are an evil, a disgusting distemper. We must be rid of them. Their gestures are obscene and their words condemn them.'

Samuel did not answer. The growing lump in his throat prevented him. He saw there was no way for him to convince either orator to the contrary. If only he could locate the person who first accused them, he could perhaps convince them of Mary's innocence and they could tell the magistrate. Yet, deep in his heart, he knew that there was probably no way back for the two women.

Elinor and Mary protested their innocence to anyone who would care to listen, but there were not many takers! Both were appalled by their abject treatment in court and their imprisonment. Chained and tied inside the cell they were frequently threatened by the gaoler with the option of even heavier iron fetters. Their chains were tight enough to cause raw sores and painful swellings. It was a small relief that they were detained together in the small cell. At night, Elinor heard Mary crying softly, unaware that she could be heard. Yet, Nell could offer little respite or comfort.

As filtered daylight from the small window dwindled, rats appeared and squeezed themselves through the cracked door, in from the dark corridor. They came to eat from the bowl on the floor. The guard laughed and, rather than trying to scare the rodents away, he merely surmised that the small creatures were the devil's brood in special guise coming to commune with them.

Elinor shouted curses to the guard. He kept his unkempt face blank, while ignoring her shouted threats.

Over time, since their arrival, Mary grew disgusted by her own appearance. Her hair had begun to matt without the constant upkeep of her horn-bone and bristle hairbrush. She had little clean water. What she had, she drank. From time to time, she would dip a finger into her bowl and rub it along her eyelid and lashes. She was not certain if this cleaned her or if it made the dirt smear more effectively. By now Elinor knew that it really didn't matter how she looked or smelled. If anyone saw her, all they saw was the grime and dirt of a woman beneath them. Even the people who had known her would not treat her the same as before.

Folk who had travelled far distances to watch the trial. They slowly came to recognize that the unfortunate women may have been tortured. As they watched, none spoke out in favour of the women. Now, it was rumoured that magic charms had been removed from their house to be presented in court. Here were woven corn-plaits and 'dollies' thought to have been used for their ill-practice spells.

In recent evenings around the county town, the taverns and hostelries were full of talk about the witches. 'Prayers heal the sick. Incantations, charms and spells may be effective, but are not sanctioned by the Church.'

'Even if they appear successful, they are cursed meddling and beyond God's will.'

'As their feats are achieved with the help of the Devil, their cures are evil. Churchmen can distinguish God's cures from the Devil's. The Lord uses anointed men and trained doctors, rather than simple peasant women.'

'I hope this trial is not an end to their suffering.' Words heard bantered by bystanders: 'foolish', 'naïve', 'innocent' - or 'indeed guilty'.

...oooooOoooo...

Back in a dark, cold corner of the cell, Mary cried. The warder no longer attended her or sought her favour, yet Elinor still hoped for release. She was happy to remove her thin garments for moments without irons to restrain her. She straddled the gaoler disbelieving he was a rogue bearing untrue promises. The man was sly. He would never release her. It was more than his job was worth. When Mary next looked to Nell, the latter was aghast at her dishevelled appearance.

'What has befallen you?' she asked.

'I have had an encounter with a demon!' her friend sourly replied. 'He touched me all over with no conversation,' she glowered at the reeds on the floor. 'He touched me all over and promised me freedom. I now know that he lied.'

Mary looked at her weeping friend. Nell looked back through tears and saw that her soft, peach-skinned ally had picked at the threads in her skirts in her anguish until she had worn a sizeable hole in them. Her hazel-brown eyes were darkly ringed.

'Mary, look at us … my hair! Oh, for a bone comb. Look at us,' gasped Elinor. 'We look like hags.' Aghast, Mary stared at her bedraggled, unkempt friend.

This is how Sam perceived them as he visited to look down at them in the small yard. Sam had waited for some time for the moments when were allowed an hour to take the air. He stepped out from the shadowed wall and called softly down, knowing full well that at any moment others spectators would arrive.

'Mary,' he called softly. She looked up. 'How do you fare?'

'Not well, Sam. I miss you and home,' she sighed. 'How's Catchevole? Are you feeding him?' she queried.

'No, he's sulking and choosing to hide. I presume he'll reappear when he's ready. Don't fret about him. He'll be fine.' He hesitated. 'Your trial can't last *much* longer. When you are free, we'll meet by the swimming place and laugh about this. We can marry and move to another place to put it all behind us.'

'That'll be nice.' Mary cheered somewhat with the thought of this. 'I love you, Sam.'

'I love you too and when you're free I'll wait for you in the barn, down by the river after the Thursday market. Don't be late,' he grinned and winked at her, but his smile did not reach his blue-grey eyes.

'I'll see you there,' she said, with a sad half-smile. 'I'll won't linger at the market or to be late.'

As new visitors arrived, Sam blew a kiss, pulled his collar higher around his neck, his knitted scarf around his face and - he was gone.

…ooo000ooo…

The court had adjourned for the judge to take his time to converse and deliberate.

As the court resumed, there was no time for discourse as the stunned crowd in the large courtroom heard his verdict on the women. Many appeared astonished, however pleased they were to hear the final sentences. He stood with some severity. The powdered periwig of the judge nodded as he spoke to serve each blank-faced woman with his verdict.

He read slowly. 'You Mary Phillips are sentenced to be hanged to near death, then shall be surrounded with faggots, pitch and other combustible matter, which shall be set on fire until your body is consumed to ashes.'

He then turned his steely gaze to Elinor. 'Elinor Shaw, you are, likewise, condemned …' she heard the same words spoken as for Mary. Shocked, she could hardly listen for the buzzing in her ears, threatening her with a loss of consciousness.

The man added, 'Furthermore, this should occur in the presence of the people. May God show you pity.'

Mary's jaw fell open, yet no words came. This was expected, but unexpected, as she was forced to face her worst fears.

'You are found guilty,' a finely-dressed gentleman leaned towards Mary and spoke with firm, calmness. 'There will be no reprieve.' He shook his head, almost in sorrow.

The courtroom silenced. All stood silently as the minister of St. Giles' stood to speak.

'I desire to pray for the souls of these condemned women *and* for those they injured.'

Mary sank to her knees as Elinor glared defiantly at the judge, who avoided her eye. Whispers and gasps spread around the assembled people.

'The accused are to be executed in one week and three days (on the third day after the new moon) at midday on market day: Saturday the seventeenth day of March of this year, 1705.' With a verdict decided to impart as much pain as possible before their final breaths, the date chosen assured large crowds. They quieted to hear that the women's fate would terminate at gallows' corner on the northern edge of Northampton Heath, a common site for executions.

Gasps and whispers of 'No,' passed through the small group standing beside Samuel. He did not move his head to watch, but knew his love and her friend had, most assuredly looked aghast at the cruel verdict placed upon them.

The magistrate coughed and stood to collect his papers, hat and cloak. With this, the assembly were considered dismissed from the proceedings. His Lordship did not look around, but held his haughty head aloft in a self-important gesture as he walked from the room. His assistants did the same. Without glancing at the women they left the room to the remaining people. Mary and Nell were dragged, almost carried, from the room down the central steps. They were once more steered downstairs within the cool building, accompanied by shouts, howls and cries from the crowd upstairs.

...ooo000ooo...

Days crept past. Time passed imperceptibly. The two asked many questions - not many were answered. They had no idea where the heathland was. They were told it was "a short ride away", by their sour-faced, but now much entertained gaoler.

'It's being used as there's plenty of space to assemble crowds an' everyone gets for a good view.' With this, he locked them in for their final night.

That evening, Mary and Nell sat within easy hearing of each other, despite not being able to see clearly for a lack of light. The March winds whistled under the cracks in the door. The women remained cold, for their gaoler had not bothered lighting his brazier.

'We were tasked and we failed.'

'I thought I was changing my life for the better when I moved in with you, Mary,' Elinor remarked with sadness. 'Now I'll share what remains of my life accordingly.'

Mary smiled dejectedly. 'Well, you had a choice, then made the move! None made you come to live with me, Nell. I am sorry that it has ended this way for us.'

Elinor smiled weakly, 'It may be for the better. I sometimes wonder. I could have died in the bitter cold if I had not met you and if you'd not shown kindness.'

'Aye, you were so young then,' she pondered. 'You've been a good friend to me too, Nell. You're skilled and know almost as much as me.' Elinor did not reply, so Mary softly continued, 'What I'd give now for a warming fire, a comfy seat and purring Catchevole on my knees.' She could see in her minds' eye the bright sparks, like tiny wayward sprites, as they caught in the rise of hot air and flew like fays up her chimney into the cool, wintry air above. She felt the comfort and warmth of the small, purring feline. She wondered where he was now. Inclement weather penetrated the frozen rooftops as piercing sleet blasted the walls and severely numbed any who cared to pass-by.

Condemned, they mourned future mornings they would never see. The sun dipped below the clouds in the dark and dismal sky. This day was soured in many ways.

...oooO00Oooo...

Chapter 28
Scorched Cinders and Ashes

On a cold mid-March morning, both Elinor and Mary were wide awake before the first misty sun-light appeared through their meagre window. They knew that they would not to see this sun set again. Their day began with a fledgling priest arriving unannounced in their cell. He was accompanied by their guard. The man explained that he had been sent to hear their confessions.

They explained to the man they were scared, but unrepentant, as they knew they had done no wrong.

'How are we supposed to apologise for what we are accused of? We have not done nothing wrong?' Mary questioned. 'It is our accusers who've performed the greatest wrong!' She continued, 'We've done naught to equal the things we're blamed for.'

The wan churchman did not reply, for he was already convinced of their guilt. In the cold gaol cell, each lifted their heads to the rowdy sounds of people outside. Growing numbers swelled the volume of continued shouts. Mary had heard of incidences of ribaldry, vicious violence and drunkenness during executions. She knew they would likely be followed from the cell to the place where they would die. They heard the sound of a watchman calling the hour.

A harsh day beckoned and raced the hours away.

Mary recalled the day the old woman had met them in the lane. She now saw that the crone had cursed them - with no hope of reprieve. Making the most of her notoriety she turned to shock pedestrians with random scolds and cries. She distressed them with snippets of her life as a witch and had then laughed, 'You fools will believe anything. Our trial was based on false reasoning. You have heard untruths, but cannot reason truth from lies.' She screamed out, 'Surely there must be one amongst you who is conscious of this?'

...ooo000ooo...

Samuel had arisen and dressed with speed in his shared lodgings. As he did so, he tried to determine if Mary had used witchcraft. Her words said so, but her heated courtroom outburst was angry and distraught. Sam discerned she had sworn and cursed through vexation, but had danced and loved with joyous abandon in his safe arms throughout the year now gone. He'd seen no guilt or admissions in her before.

The hour was late. The sun had risen. He left the inn without nourishment. He walked slowly toward to the gaol and, before he reached the corner, could hear a hubbub as the women were brought forth.

Cruel jeers were heard and rotten scraps thrown towards them as they exited the back entrance of the Assize gaol. None attempted to halt the rabble from asserting themselves. At this, Samuel realised that his love had been condemned: 'done for'. He had some ideas on who had done so for her. He guessed where true blame hid. While every crime violates the law, not every violation of the law counts as a crime. He could no longer trust Lizzie or call her a friend. How quickly his trust, love and admiration turned to dust. He looked to the crowd, hearing their shouts with sadness.

Exiting the building, each woman blinked in the powerful, pale sunlight of the late winters' morn. Uninhibited, they looked around. From the back of the gaol building, on the hillside leading southward by Angel

371

Street, Mary could see birds. She knew what they were, for the plumage of the waiting carrion crows stood out black like a coffin-bearer's coat, with a greenly-purple, iridescent sheen.

An individual called out to the women as they were led to the awaiting cart. 'Can you hear your death knell, Nell?'

'Are you Sure or not Shaw?' a gruff male voice in the crowd called out loudly to Elinor, laughing cruelly at their own jest.

'Hang 'em - then they'll be dead, that's for Shaw.'

Another called, 'String 'em up. Watch 'em swing.'

'Ye'll never marry, Mary.'

'Ha, see how they shake!' the townsfolk cat-called as they pointed to each of the women in turn and slapped each other on the back for such jolly puns and quips. In a shouting match of words, the loudest won.

They were rewarded by the guffaws of listeners. 'Giddy-up. Let's hurry to see 'em dance.'

The women were swiftly bundled into the back of the open cart. Elinor, the taller of the two, was able to sit straighter. Her friend hunched uncomfortably with both arms tied at an angle to her slight body. She did not try to protect herself from the momentary lurch as the horses skittered and the dray wheels hit a hidden hole in the road surface. The horses shuffled, then settled themselves.

Elinor lowered her voice to a whisper, but Mary showed no indication of hearing her words. She considered they had been damned by their own neighbours. The wind whipped the branches and people into a frenzy as they awaited the spectacle.

With each of their wrists tied with coarse ropes to the sides of the dray, the women were far too tired and down-trod to struggle. Mary snivelled quietly as Elinor watched her through half-closed eyes. Mary felt a missile hit her shoulder and flinched. It had been lobbed from close proximity. This was the final straw for Nell. Taking a deep breath she stood, still attached by the sturdy rope and glared into the crowd. She ducked as an egg came her way. She raised a finger and pointed it at the woman in the crowd whom she guessed had thrown the projectile.

In fury - and with some difficulty due to her restraints, Nell hitched her skirts before gaoler and crowd, keenly baring her legs and buttocks in an insolent affront, whilst calling, 'I have been assaulted, but at least I've lived - and you, lickspittle, will never enjoy life to the full - but you will always be a daft pillock.'

'Harlot', called a voice. Letting go of her skirts, her fuming tongue turned elsewhere. She threw bawdy remarks to the crowd, who crowed and called in irate response. 'Repent to save your soul,' an ample man called out gruffly.

At the idea of repentance, Mary roused from her silence. She laughed raucously. 'Say I am sorry! Where is my justice?' she called as loudly as possible. She concluded, 'Our friends shunned us, the law lied and our gaoler threatened us with irons. Where's our justice?'

Grumbles and shouts from the assembly, drowned her protests. She continued shouting, 'We were lied to, used and beaten. We're left with naught. What good'll repentance do? You're a simpleton.'

The broad-chested man with a weather-beaten face stared boldly at her. 'Woman, you're shameless. The Devil's has you marked as fiends.'

'Witch!' yelled a girl as a rotten fruit missed her.

Mary responded in shrill voice, 'If you say I'm a witch, then I am indeed.'

Nell joined her. 'Come fairies, demons and beasts of hell, come to me and serve me well,' she intoned. She sneered, whilst onlookers laughed.

'That'll be the demon talking,' noted a cleric. His severe colleague nodded in assent.

Without heeding his words Nell continued, 'May the Devil despoil these pious men - as you have most certainly spoilt me.'

The men shook their heads and crossed themselves as she offered non-stop perplexing words that alarmed them. She saw the men were afraid of curses. The gaol guards were hardened and strong, but like the ministers, each of them motioned in the olden way to protect themselves from her evil.

To draw an end to their words and force them to cease, the two women were pushed back into the cart and forced to sit while their ropes were tied more securely. While Nell took most of the attention, Mary resumed her silent scrutiny.

Without warning, Samuel silently appeared by the side of their waggon. With the sun still low in the sky, he soundlessly sidled towards the shadowed side of the cart, he briefly reached up to take Mary's hand in his. She had little movement as her wrist was tied to a strut. Sam stood of tiptoes and briefly kissed her fingers. He blinked, with his green-grey eyes locked on hers. His lips moved, but she heard not what he said.

The jeering crowd, kept at bay by constables, were deafening. Mary smiled weakly at Sam and leaned forward to hear, hindered by the staves in the cart's side and her uncomfortable bindings. She shivered slightly as she felt the lurch of the cart as it suddenly started to move along the rutted road of mud and cobbles. Sam stepped back and watched it go as the jeers of the onlookers rang out.

Mary's grubby, blue-white fingers held tightly onto the wooden sides of the cart. They slowly turned to ice, hampered and bitten by strong ropes, while she made vain attempts to readjust her cloak for warmth.

They passed the old town hall, between Abington Street and Wood Hill. The town seemed animated in the morning sunlight. As they trundled, the women glimpsed fewer houses as they were carried north-eastward. The Bantam Cock stood outside the town walls. It was the last inn they passed before reaching the common land. It was tradition for carts carrying felons to stop for a final drink at the inn before reaching their place of execution. Mary and Elinor were awarded no such luxury. Their waggon trundled by without stopping.

Sam had paid a coachman for a windswept seat on top of his vehicle. He noted many riders, who rode alongside to the Heath. He was unsure if these were onlookers or had been sent by the court to ensure the women arrived at their destination.

Shouts from the crowds accompanied the progress of the bedraggled women. Their waggon was pulled by a sallow nag and a younger chestnut. Progress was painfully slow with the journey taking just under an hour to reach the open land of the Heath. Today there would be no illegal racing on this ground by the rich who flaunted law and safety to compete for elevated stakes. Here, foliage seemed stark.

Seen from a distance trees looked bare on the open heath. Closer, Mary noticed small green leaf-buds on twigs and branches. The open area held a leaden cold that permeated her thin shift. As they neared the northernmost corner of the heath, they were surprised to see an unusually large crowd by the road side. Its ominous atmosphere caught her in its grip. In the blink of an eye, the cart stopped moving.

Sam noted vendors busily selling food and printed pamphlets of their confessions. He also saw the hangman standing waiting. The man gave the two women no time to speak to the crowd, as was customary in criminal hangings to add a piquancy to the spectacle.

Elinor was unceremoniously, hauled to her feet. She yelled curses, but with stout ropes around her wrists, she could not move very easily.

Raucous calls increased, while eggs and spoiled vegetables flew as missiles. Few met their mark. The local militia did their utmost to hold back the feisty festive crowd, using clubs to prevent the rowdy men from attacking those destined to die. Parents pushed their youngsters forward or fathers held their sons on their shoulders for a better view. Some youngsters clung to the knees of their elders or sat aloft in nearby trees to better see the spectacle.

Traders called out their wares, selling fruit and loaves to the crowd as they passed between waiting families. It appeared to Samuel that some bystanders had already spent too much time in the inns, where they had enjoyed a little too much refreshment. He observed as, without embarrassment, men relieved themselves in ditches or behind trees.

As Mary rose to her feet, a strong wind whipped through her thin clothing. She wished not to be seen trembling, as watchers would assume she was fearful or nervous, rather than blame the forbidding March winds. Elinor stood firm. She remarked, 'Look how many hills and dales we have travelled today from town. We've seen more today than we have in several years.'

Mary did not reply. She could not comprehend how Elinor could find such cold satisfaction in this bleak day. Scared, Mary helplessly looked around at the unfamiliar surroundings - as if to infuse in them before her final journey.

People came from hall and hovel to watch or use their opportunity to jeer the 'evil women' on their way. Nell retaliated and called back threats and abuse as best she could, to no avail. A stout rope was rapidly looped around her neck, as a laughing assistant hauled her like a beast of burden nearer to the trunk of the sturdy tree and rough-built gallows.

Now, their feet were freed to allow them to walk. They tried to hold each other, but were torn apart to stand in an allotted place by their gruff executioner as Elinor whispered, 'We're forsaken - our lives forfeit.'

The dark cloak was torn from Mary's shoulders and dropped onto the ground by the side of the cart.

Mary quietly replied, 'We're leaving our flesh to be with God.' Then, as an afterthought, she added, 'Remember me as a sister,' as tears trickled down dirt-stained cheeks leaving runnels in her grime.

Standing, pale and pinched, Mary finally made a memorable spectacle of her execution. Suddenly, to the surprise of all the assembled, including Sam and Elinor, she shouted a declaration that she was indeed a witch, angrily calling on the Devil to rescue her.

The crowd seemed impatient and rowdy.

'Come on. Get on with it,' they called. 'Let's see 'em dance.' They yelled and waved in disrespect, while their voices carried afar across the open ground.

Mary turned towards her friend. Another tear ran steadily down her cheek and dripped onto her dress. None noticed. Reluctantly, on realisation of her fate she had followed Nell's lead. She guessed there was nothing to be gained from restating her innocence to those who had condemned her. She played to the audience.

Mary was still in her childbearing years, yet seemed frail and much older. She crudely invoked and beseeched the Devil to come to her. Six years younger, Nell writhed and kicked, but was effortlessly dragged like a rag-dolly to be rapidly twisted towards the hanging noose.

As the executioner struggled with her, he muttered, 'I'll make no great profit from these deaths.' He could take the dark cloak that now lay soaking on the ground. He may be able to sell lengths of unburned rope to spectators as morbid tokens, but there was little else to be had. Their thin apparel would burn with them as their sentencing demanded the torture of burning and was not just two straightforward hangings. 'Give me hangings of highway men, any day, so I can keep their property,' he thought grumpily.

This Saturday hanging produced sights worthy of a public holiday. Fixed, at the hanging place, the loose end of the ropes were securely tied to the cart with cumbersome knots. As the horses stamped impatiently, the hangman was torn between presenting an extended spectacle for the crowd and his keenness to get on with the job. He grabbed Mary and hauled her forward.

The journeyman had been busy making rough ropes that quickly clothed their necks. Mary seemed calm. Elinor cried out and struggled. She threatened, tempted and cried out spells and blasphemies inspired by terror, distress and tortured hatred. Before she could swear or blaspheme any further, the executioner hastened his duties, attended closely by a priest.

Elinor offered curses as the cleric asked her to repent. Samuel watched as Elinor spat and snorted as she looked up at the already darkening afternoon sky to summon the Devil. Mary sobbed quietly at their combined fates. As Elinor shouted at the crowd, the hangman gave her a push as the cart lurched forward.

Mary almost threw herself from the back of the cart as she had heard that if her neck broke she would not feel the torment of burning after hanging. Hampered by her bindings she was ineffective. With a flick of a whip the cart jerked as it peeled away from the standing women who were tied by the necks on its boards.

Dangling, Mary choked for air. She could not think or fight. Her lungs cried out for oxygen, but no relief came. The moving waggon had left the two women suspended. Sagging, with feet kicking in vain desperation of finding purchase, they found nothing below them. The women rocked and bucked as the last breath in their lungs was exhausted of oxygen.

As Sam watched in horror, he saw how they fought for life. Unaware, he held his own in response.

'See how they fly!' called a loud, male voice from the crowd. Others responded with laughs and jeers.

Legs dangled and kicked, yet no one dared to pull on them to rapidly ease their suffering or harsh struggle. These women were allowed no easement.

The Rector knew that their death sentences would serve as a warning to others, besides acting as punishment. Seeing this horror left many disturbed - and aware enough to avoid this fate for themselves. Children would grow up remembering. They hid in their mother's skirts. Many of the spectators were convinced the women were witches, after all, they'd had a fair trial. Others whispered that two simple women had been unjustly accused, tried and executed on a whim.

Accompanied by the taunts of the Saturday crowds, the executioner decided the two were near death. Drooping, they were quickly cut down. Immobile and doll-like, they were lifted by hands that grasped them as they were tied to upright posts with the ropes that would burn with them. Dry-wood faggots were hastily placed around their feet. Near expiry they were surrounded by the nickets and brush-faggots that were stacked a-waiting at the base of a nearby tree. Hastily lit torches and bundles of brushwood were cast at the staves beneath their feet by willing hands, wanting to help eliminate the doomed accursed women.

The fire crackled and flared until, united in the end, together they succumbed to the heat, pain and cruelty on the flaming brands. In their half-choked state they drooped unconscious to the pyre, each bound to wooden stakes by neck and waist by their dual-purpose ropes. The fire crackled and burned as it caught the smoky, flaring faggots.

Samuel could not bear to be part of the crowd, but forced himself to stay. He wrapped his muffler around his mouth and took a deep breath. Suddenly, he recalled that Mary had made his scarf and tears stung his ashen eyes. He pulled the wrap around his mouth to cover chattering teeth. It was not the cold that conditioned him, but hurtful knowledge of hatred, condemnation and strong public obloquy. Samuel remained embittered and saddened that friends he had put his trust in or worked with had turned against the woman he loved.

As flames grew, smoke carried, forcing those standing close to blink in the acrid stink. Thick plumes filled the air. Close weather and sky predicted a lightening-filled storm that the women would never see. With little fight left, they gasped through rope-burned throats, as clothing and hair caught alight. They had moaned lightly as their skin became crisp and bloody. Sizzling, blackened crania drooped, while some silently prayed for their quick release.

Samuel had observed in unforgettable horror, as pure, white flesh became mottled and brindled; putrid, black and bubbling. He was ashamed of his fellow men.

'Judges are offenders and rogues. Who are they to speak as the voice of God?' queried an old man as he walked away from their pyre.

Samuel glanced up as he heard another fellow remark, 'Witches! They're like a rotten toothache. If they're not pulled, they infect all the others.' The man had smiled with few teeth of his own, while his equally elderly friend replied, 'Aye, but now we've two less o' the foul women to worry about around here.' The two decayed and edentulous men knew that those standing nearby were listening. None would speak out to contradict their opinion for fear of finger pointing that would suggest pity for the women.

'Well, they lived and now they're gone,' the old man had said.

'Yep,' remarked his sage-like foil, showing what was left of his random yellowed pegs amidst toothless gums.

As Samuel turned from them in disgust he was confronted by a burly man. He had appeared from the throng after starring at Sam for a time. Now he accused Sam of being a devotee of the witches.

'You look familiar? You from Oundle?' Then, as Sam turned from him, 'Hoy mate, I know you. Ain't you a sweetheart of the scraggy witch? You've covered your tracks, but I saw you kiss her hand.'

'Pardon? No, you are in error.' As Sam shook his head in denial, he remained racked with feelings of guilt and duplicity. He mumbled as he hurriedly walked away with a heavy heart, 'I'm a victim of witchcraft.'

By the time the ropes that bound them had scorched through, it was ended. The fire continued to consume their charred mortal remains. Ashes swept by the wind, flew in the air. After the burning, an offensive smell of scorched flesh pervaded the area for days. Many avoided the place or went on their way without venturing near.

The ash remains were left as a warning to others; before they were scattered, swept by the winds to settle into the soft, burnished earth.

...ooo000000oo...

Epilogue: Blackened Souls

Although accused by conversant neighbours and condemned by men of the courtroom, the women had perished on the feast day of Saint Gertrude of Nivelles, the patron saint of cats. Sam thought that Mary would have approved of this, but he remained saddened that Elinor and Mary were destined to hold no grave or marker. Their story was published in biased reports of Fleet Street and in popular penny rags of London, particularly the weekly *Corante*, *London Gazette* and new *Daily Courant*.

In these severe accounts of trial and death, the women were clearly presumed witches. The news men were clever. Two views differed in declaring how the women were suspected of their crimes, for if they had shown anxiety it meant they must feel guilty, while if they acted confidently they were skilled at hiding their guilt. Each view was confirmed by contradictory culminations that led to the same end.

...oooOOOooo...

As Sam had walked from the crowd for the long walk back into town, several of their onlookers paused to glance at the sad young man. A woman viewed him closely with an accusing eye. 'You! You're an acquaintance of the dead witches.'

'No,' he replied, shortly, amazed by a voice so gravelled and vexed. The busybody persisted.

'You've the wrong man. I came to watch - like you. None here knows them.' There was nothing to be gained by telling the truth. It would not bring Mary back.

Sam returned to the inn and wept. Words passed between the ragged groups sitting at tables eating their evening meals. Samuel looked around and saw that he and his friend, Thomas, were figures of interest. He perceived his day echoed the Easter Gospel - with him denying his closest confidant, much as Saint Peter had done in the garden at Gethsemane. He felt a fear that filled his soul with shame and regret.

'What're you looking at?' He growled bitterly at the brusque man on the next table as he pushed the meat from his pie around the platter, 'Let me eat in peace. It's been a long day.' Samuel felt tears of terror prickle his green-grey eyes. He was unnerved, but would not allow his heart to break in public view. He remained appalled by the crowds' expectations. After all, they had seen the hanging as a day out, a day at the fair, a carnival.

With the gruff man's response, he quickly turned on his heels and went to bed. As he went, he brushed past a young child. Glistening tears pricked his pewter eyes as he made his way past her. This wide-eyed girl was aged around five or six. She bore a blank expression, but looked up and stared directly at Samuel. He shivered involuntarily. Sam tried to smile to show empathy, then hurried past.

Thomas, who'd stood-by Sam throughout, completed his meal and washed it down with strong ale. He voiced his fears to any who would listen. 'I know my friend, Samuel. He's a good man.'

Later, Thomas repeated to his friend words he had overheard. 'It's all come about from talk, mob mania and flimsy evidence, along with the public obsession on witchcraft. If Mary and Nell are ... were witches, they'd have bidden magic to release their bonds and fled safely.'

'I know', whispered Sam, distantly. It was all too little, too late. Their healing potions had not warranted persecution and unnecessary death. When Sam sat on the bed with head bowed low, he overheard snippets of conversations from others in the shared room that continued into the night. Eventually, Sam slept. He woke to hear the rain on the roof and the church bells tolling for the Sunday service.

At breakfast, a plump man voiced his opinion - to be heard by all who sat near. 'Damn the overseer of the parish accounts. We had a good day out yesterday, but the area around Saint Giles' is much worse off now.'

'Why?' asked a wheezy voice.

The well-fed man continued unrelentingly, 'Well, would you believe the bloody overseer's put in a request for expenses - for the faggots used in the bonfire!'

'Well I never... Would you credit it?' replied the wheezy man between mouthfuls. 'It'll come from parish funds, not us ... and we're rid of a peril ... God is with us.'

'Friend, we have paid! Someone has to pay for the faggots!' answered the loud, harsh man. 'Where do you think the overseer gets the money? It's from us.'

Sam heard his mean laugh as the man curled his lip and turned away to finish his spread. After a few moments the fellow rose (with difficulty), thrust coins to the landlord and then waddled to the door. In his wake, he was closely followed by a family. A lad staggered down the creaking stairs under the weight of their bags, then hurried to follow after them into the grey torrent. Sam assumed they'd seen the day in town as fine entertainment - with their enjoyment gained from the pain of others. The partisan man with the chesty voice, noting his departure, called out, 'We may be out of pocket, but at least we can sleep safe in our beds now.'

Rapidly, Samuel and Thomas packed, paid and departed from the inn. As he stowed his bag, saline tears dripped down his cheeks in hushed messages of grief. Although he had heard talk of the women and their medicines, Sam knew what he believed. He'd failed to protect the woman he loved. Now, guilt and remorse followed him like angry shades. His life had altered immeasurably - in the blink of an eye. With heavy heart, he and the curious from Oundle collected their bags and returned homeward in the rain.

With the Oundle enchantress' gone, the perils of evil bewitchment were considered wiped from England's dominion – leaving it witch free.

...oooOOOooo...

Catchevole, the patient cat, sat for many days beside the empty house. He was infinitely long-suffering and used to waiting. None had returned to this home for what felt like weeks. He fed himself by scavenging scraps thrown out by neighbours and by catching small rodents and birds that he trapped in barns and hedgerows.

The svelte, hidden feline watched as people, including Lizzie Coles, appeared. Each steadily looted the cottage of goods – with takings of more than a week's worth of pay.

The girl had left with knitted garments, a small oak coffer and a warm cloak. She hesitated on leaving the house, believing she saw a sallow shade in a tattered dress watching from the shadows. Crossing herself, Lizzie believed the fuzzy shape to be Mary, but knew this was impossible, for the apparition dimmed as she blinked, then was no longer there. She deemed the light had deceived her eyes. Nevertheless, Lizzie turned toward home with her arms full of filched goods.

The stealthy cat flattened himself on the cool soil to watch on with rancour as a steady succession of opportunist thieves helped themselves to herbs, pots, pans - even the old mattress and bed cushions. Those pots not required were smashed on the earthen floor. They broke easily.

Silently, Catchevole hid in nearby bushes as he saw men who came in the darkness with flaming torches. They burned the house by setting a light to the thatch. Hot, it blazed throughout the night without any apparent attempt to extinguish the flames. None wanted it. It was tainted by witchcraft. No one would want live there ever again.

Catchevole flexed his retractable claws. This quiet, smart grimalkin held sundry dispositions. He saw that if he waited long enough, some kind body would let him into their home or barn to hook mice from their hiding-holes. He would be fully employed again. Perhaps it could be that nice young man and his family who lived at the farm. As the spring weather improved, Old William had spotted the small, shadowy beast lurking in the budding bushes. He threw a tidbit onto the smallholding rooftop for a several days, but found hungry crows were speedier than a shy cat. William had hoped that the smell of warm bread would eventually coax him in through the open door.

'Come on, puss,' he said gently. 'Come in from this spring shower.'

Catchevole listened – and when the time was right, did just that. Washed sleek, until immaculate, he had strolled through the front door that wafted yeast and fresh baking bread. He had taken a time to look in every nook and cranny, before making himself comfortable. After eating a little cooked fish by the welcoming hearth. William watched as the cat pawed and clawed the old fireside rag-rug in gratification, whilst emitting a continuous blissful noise from his throat.

On the morrow he would repay their kindness by bringing these men a fat rat or two.

Time passed. He would wander past the shell of his old home. He did not abandon hope. Perhaps one day his mistress would return and he could go to be with her – where-ever she chose to live?

Catchevole waited, watched - and survived.

...oooO00Oooo...

End Notes

Appreciative Acknowledgement

I wish to thank all who encouraged and proofed the various stages of this novel. Thanks go to mum, Barbara (whom I love dearly), who advised me to give my 'brain a rest' and stop writing after the publication of *Oundle Memories and Moments*. (You see that I value her advice!)

Infinite thanks go to my sons, Mark and Kit and their respective godmothers, Sharon Cottingham and Suzanne Halliwell, for proof-reading and supporting my story pursuits. Thanks to Kit for his great art work and proofing. (Do feel free to contact me via our publisher or Facebook if you require freelance art work.)

I appreciate Wendy Bollans (my sister), Josephine Black, Sam Marshall, Kevin and Janet Mortimer, who cheered my work; particularly, Edwina Halverson for helping me search Northampton's 'atmosphere' and finding germane articles.

I wish to express gratitude to the Sessions House and T.I.C. staff. Particularly to Roger Coleman, Council Sergeant and Judges' Lodgings Manager, who kindly shared court details whist displaying the Assize rooms, jail and garden. Without his courtesy my data would be all the poorer. Likewise, I appreciate Len Johnson's facts on Oundle Parish Church bells. The Worshipful Company of Grocers, Oundle School Archives and Cripps Library, in particularly Leigh Giurlando (librarian) and Elspeth Langsdale (archivist), yet again provided handy documents and advice. Last, but not least, I wish to thank Samantha Morris and the staff at Upfront Publishing for their kindness and help.

Anna Fernyhough
September 2019

...oooO00Oooo...

Time and Place

This story consists of a small rural community living together in Oundle. Naïve, with little education, the residents find their trust displaced as superstition and suspicions evolve. Events leave little to be done to change the disturbing future.

My tale is strung with interwoven kernels of recorded history and fiction. Artisans living in the late 1600s share scant similarity with mine. I hope I have not been too hagiographic in endowing my central characters few flaws and vices – although they do 'curse' – an issue they were accused of.

Notions of 'magic' initiated when conditions were harshest. Belief in sorcery was nurtured by years that included the 'Great Storm' before Christmas 1703. An overwhelming extratropical cyclone hit France, England and Ireland on 26th November 1703 (7th December by the current Gregorian calendar), when damaging winds affected thousands. It was reported that 2,000 chimney stacks collapsed in London and gales tore down over 4,000 oak trees in the New Forest.

Notions that people controlled their destinies led to fears of magic. Irrational beliefs in 'enchantment' were endorsed through poor knowledge of the causes of illness and fears of death. Folk-medicine, spells and ritual encompassed evil and good. (If a patient recovered, it was good magic.) Witches, mainly women, nurtured or devastated. Beliefs in special powers led to fears that forced some 'witches' to live as convenient outcasts rather than as part of a community with a useful aptitude for dispensing good or bad magic. Healers were easily held responsible, then persecuted when things went awry. They were largely impotent. Without scientific proof, accusations, trials and executions were easy-fare, however cruelly immoral this may seem today.

Witchcraft Acts and Other Information

Elinor Shaw and Mary Phillips were in their twenties by the time of their deaths. They were not 'crones' or 'hags' as some have chosen to describe them. Their deaths are reported to be the last two witch executions in England. Belief in witchery gradually came to an end as suspicion and superstition lessened with interest in technology and science. The Witchcraft Act was repealed by law in 1735 and came into force in 1736.

The "*two notorious witches*" were accused of bewitchment, torment and death. Hearsay bore terrible consequences. Evidence included confessions obtained (under duress) by two constables. It said that '*after some little whining and much hanging about each other's necks they both made a confession*' they were hurried to Northampton gaol. Confronted with their confession in court, both Mary and Elinor denied they made these revelations. Their refrain was thereafter said to have changed. I assume – after intimidation and ill-treatment.

Oundle was a small town, with only 365 houses in 1674. The 1686 and 1811 censuses indicate 2,250 and 1,952 individuals, respectively. Numbers of residents fell in times of sickness. Later, "natural causes" replaced "the Devil" in triggering society's ills.

During the Commonwealth, Peterborough and Oundle supported the Republic (unlike 10 nearby parishes who were Royalist); likely influenced by Cromwell's puritan major-general, William Boteler, building Cobthorne House in Oundle. Royalists and Puritans alike held firm on matters of the supernatural.

Most trials of the time were initiated by the local minister and accomplished by a County Judge responsible for initial instigations of contentious criminal cases and were not often not recorded in detail. Northants magistrate Phillip Ward recorded legal statutes that influenced his decisions (Gray, '*Making Law in Mid-Eighteenth Century England*', pp. 211-233). Importantly, he alleged that only women were tried when accused of "lewd behaviour". Men were largely exempt. Numbers declined as magistrates took a more practical approach towards female sexual behaviour after 1700. Thereafter, accounts indicate that women were sent to a

House of Correction, but not worse. Like Ward, Thomas Thornton retained a jotter of his work as High-Sheriff of Northampton from 1700-1718. It survives today. Thornton may have attended the 1705 witch trial, along with Edward Stratford (replaced by Henry Stratford in the latter half of 1705) as Sheriff (as would the Recorder, the Earl of Northampton). It seems likely they played a part in local trials.

Crimes carrying a death penalty in the early 1700s included: theft of horses or sheep, destroying roads, cutting down trees, stealing from a rabbit warren, pickpocketing goods worth more than a shilling, being out at night in disguise, unmarried woman hiding a stillborn, arson, forgery and murder. Wrongdoing could be as simple as talking to gypsies and vagrants. Yearly, on each cold December solstice, vagabonds and other poor people were allowed to partake in the parish alms-giving custom of accepted begging. This short day was known as Mumping Day. This fell on the feast of (doubting) Saint Thomas.

Within twelve days a Sheriff's duty was to chart notification on 'heretic or witch' or any suspected of practices that caused 'injury to men, cattle, the fruits of the earth or to the loss of King, Queen and Country'. Courts accepted hearsay and people failing to report a witch faced excommunication and punishment. Torture was used to force confessions and enable denunciation. Legally, the accused was stripped, shaved of body hair, interrogated, subjected to thumb-screws, racking, bone-crushing, scalding, beating and starvation. Criminals were publicly whipped or humiliated in a pillory or stocks. Often they were hung in a gibbet. There were no exceptions for the fêted (even Cromwell was gibbetted after death).

The women and their execution was described in Fleet Street broad-sheets: 'hardened in their wickedness' … 'they publicly boasted that their Master (the devil) would not suffer them to be executed, but they found him liar, for on Saturday morning, being the seventeenth instance, they were carried to the gallows on the north side of town, whither *numerous crowds of people went to see them die. And being come to the place of execution, the minister repeated his former pious endeavours, to bring them to a sense of their sins, but to as little purpose as before; for instead of calling on God for mercy, nothing was heard of them, but damning and cursing.'* It went on, *'However, a little before they were tied up at the request of the minister, Elinor Shaw confessed not only the crime for which she died, but openly declared before them all how she first became a witch, as did also Mary Phillips; and being desired to say their prayers, they both set up a very loud laughter, calling for the devil to come and help them in such a blasphemous manner as it is not fit to mention' so that the sheriff, seeing their presumptuous impenitence, caused them to be executed with all the expedition possible, even while they were cursing and raving; and as they lived the devils true factors, so they resolutely died in his service to the terror of all people ... witnesses of their dreadful and amazing exits ... being hanged till they were almost dead, the fire was put to the straw, faggots and other combustible matter, till they were burnt to ashes.'*

Trial conclusions came from the influential via courts. Those accused of witchcraft were often poor, illiterate and powerless. Regrettably, this wisdom is no help in hindsight.

Records, Articles and Extracts

Depending on how long ago we search, trials and executions are not well documented. I chose to spell the names of my protagonists, Elinor (Ellinor) Shaw and Mary Phillips (Philips), in their most commonly used form. Regulation of written English did not begin until 1755 - Samuel Johnson's published dictionaries.

The most likely birth places were Cotterstock (Elinor) and Oundle (Mary). They then resided together in Oundle. The two were described as artisan hose-makers. At execution, they were young by today's standards, Elinor was 18 and Mary aged 25 (25 and 32 according to some genealogical records).

Poor harvests, drought, flood and natural disasters vied with disease and infection to keep the population down. In 1700, if boys survived their first decade they could be expected to live 60+ more. Risk of death for girls was less certain. Mortalities in childbirth somewhat skew life-expectancy records – along with wars and epidemics (i.e., bubonic plague), but once past their reproductive years, women could easily live to 80+ years of age.

With rife superstition, both the sign of the horns and showing the middle finger, date back to ancient Greece. Firstly the finger was meant as an insult, suggesting intercourse but had garnered a superstitious trait of indecency. In Roman literature it represents an act of ill-intent or is an instrument of black magic.

The women were first arrested by constables, William Boss and John Southwel(l) of Oundle. After a short local trial, they were held in Northampton gaol (located in the County House of Correction behind Sessions House). Here, the women were retained in a small (approximately ten-foot square) cell 'below ground'. Some daylight enters the cell from street level through a small window. I was shown the Assizes and how the women's cell has access to a small outdoor 'yard' with a barred, iron-grid over eight-feet above the floor-level. Men were held along the corridor. A 1705 report (later reprinted) tells accounts of visitors (i.e., Mr Laxton and his wife, who spoke with Elinor through the prison grating in Angel Street.)

Shaw and Phillips were executed on open ground at 'the racecourse', formerly Northampton Heath. Death by burning was only used for specific offences (one of such is witchcraft). Seven are recorded in Northants. Allegedly, the final two, Elinor Shaw and Mary Phillips, were hanged then burned on 17th March 1705.

In 1911, American historian and professor of English, Wallace Notestein (1878–1969) wrote "*A History of Witchcraft in England from 1558 to 1718*". Here he declared the 1705 witch accounts were fictional as "no burnings took place". He based his view on similarities between two accounts of witchcraft by one author. He did divulge that St. Giles' Parish Church holds a receipt *"1705 - P'd for wood 5/-"*. He noted that Ralph Davis, the account writer, who *"professed to have known them from their early years, and who was apparently glad to defame them in every possible way, accused them of loose living, but not of adultery"*, as they were unmarried. Notestein opined that the Northampton document was probably recopied in a *"Huntingdonshire pamphlet of 1716"* owing to its similarities. (My opinion is that this does not deem the first tract as any less reliable.)

In 1647, after killing 300 women, Matthew Hopkins retired as Witch-finder General. The same year, he died of supposed tuberculosis, yet his legacy continued with his book 'The Discovery of Witches', which was used as a template for the persecution of witches for a century. James I's Witchcraft Act was repealed in the reign of King George II (1736). The new Act was aimed at frauds pretending to use powers for money. Punishment for witches, fortune-tellers and mediums were slashed to a year in prison and an hour in a pillory.

Inquisitiveness and general interest in the affairs of others bred: In 1722, John Fane, Earl of Westmorland (with his 'country house' at Apethorpe), found cause to complain to the Post Office saying, *'I must protest against the present Post-House Keeper of Oundle who is notorious for opening of letters to the disobliging of all the neighbourhood. There are several persons more fitted for the business than the woman who now has it.'* (Extract from *"John Jones: 1718-1722"* in *"A History of the Oundle Schools"* by [pp. 202-232] William George Walker, 1956). It is diverting to find that gossips and busy-bodies were still extant two decades after the witches lived! Later, executions were held in private at the Sessions gaol, rather than transporting prisoners to open areas for the sport of public viewing.

Individuals

A Mary Philips (*sic*) was born in July 1681 in Benefield. Her father was James Phillips. She grew-up in Oundle. (Note the spelling is not been standardised in the record. It appears with one and two 'L's.) Records indicate that Elinor Shaw was baptised on Wednesday 5th February 1687, when she was a few days old. We know little of her - other than she was known as 'Nell' and grew up in Cotterstock. By end of the 1600s, these two ingénue resided together in Oundle. At the time of their executions in March 1705, Mary was around the age of twenty-four years. Elinor was nineteen. Contrary to interpretation that in the 1700s girls married young, by the end of the century, the average age to marry was 28 years old for men and 26 years for women.

Constable, John Southwel (or Southwell) was born on Wednesday 25th April 1685 in Glapthorn(e). He married in 1701, when in his early twenties. In 1705 the constables were aged 20-25. William Boss lived with his wife Francis. (On some records the letter 'S' is transcribed as 'F', so the name appears as 'Boff'.) Both families lived in Glapthorne. The men were most likely elected to office by businessmen or appointed by the county sheriff to perform peace-keeping, bailiff and civilian enforcement duties. There was no established police force.

I have cited notable persons, who were alive at the time, for story purposes only. Their stories are fictional. The vicar, Thomas Oley, buried on 22nd June 1689 in Oundle, was contemporaneous with Widow Dobbs. Reverend Edward Caldwell died in 1718. For the purpose of the story, I have created several characters by mixing local Christian names and surnames from Oundle in the 1600s.

Rank, rural town and riches (late 1600 - early 1700)

Prime in the pecking-order were land-owners, magistrates, lords and earls who were all designated 'Esquire'. The term 'Gentleman' was used for minor gentry, landlord-victuallers and husbandmen. Doctors, vicars and rectors afford their own learned titles. The title 'Mister' only applied to respected middle-ranks. Labourers were not called 'Mister' by magistrates as the term was only used for yeomen-farmers, masters, wool-merchants, company-businessmen or clerks.

Parish overseers were regarded as officers. The term 'Official' denoted overseers, churchwardens, rate collectors, tax and excise officers, haywards, woodwards, turnpike-keepers, gate-keepers and constables. Inferior were the working artisans and all working their own trades. Stocking-makers, such as Mary and Elinor, were in this category. 'Troops' were analogous to artisans, but untrained, hired militia were 'men'.

'Labourers' comprised of cheaply-hired servants, apprentices, shepherds, plough-men/boys, drovers, rounds-men, linesmen, collier-miners, gravel-pit workers, spinners (out-workers), tinkers (moving from place to place to mend pans/utensils), rag-gatherers, hawkers/higglers (travelling pedlars carrying small saleable goods) and anyone engaged in a seasonal job (i.e., haymaking at harvest). Paupers, beggars and vagrants, were often unemployed, but in need of poor-relief, fell low on the social scale. Lowest of all were those without occupation or domicile. These were classed as 'Indigents'.

The Tabret Inn (Talbot) bore a right-of-passage across neighbouring land belonging to the Dobbs family. It was open *'for guests to come into and from the common fields with carts, horses and cattle'*. The owner of the Talbot at the time was William Whitwell, who functioned alongside Stephen Bramston in local courts. By 1700, respected and wealthy Whitwell was around 38 years of age. A surgeon-barber by trade, he owned the 'Tabret', which he renamed 'Talbot'. I have assumed the locals would take a time to adjust to the name change! On Whitwell's death in 1711 (aged 49), his brood was underage so the inn was run in trust. It appears that fellow-barber-general surgeon, tooth-puller and leech-using blood-letter, John Smith, was a trustee. The Smith family, like the Whitwell's, were well-established Northamptonshire gentry. Smith sold the guest-house inn to himself at a good price so that Whitwell's surviving offspring could divide the proceeds.

The original, old Burystede building stood near the Tabret. Originally an all-purpose hall and adjoining cook-house alongside *"several little garrets under one roof, a tiled stable and malt-house thatched with straw"*. It stood near the High Street, a long road that ran from edge to edge of the tiny town. This is now split (North Street and West Street). The Oundle Improvement Act of 1825 finalised the street development and butter cross demolition.

Currency of the 1700s

Frequent coin shortages made way for the use of tokens and bartering of goods. Two farthings were one halfpenny or "ha'penny". Four farthings were a penny. Half-pennies and pennies were large copper coins. Twelve pennies made one shilling. A "bob" was slang for a shilling and a "quid" was a pound. The plural for pennies was "pence." Five shillings were a crown (hence, two shillings and six pence was a half-crown). There were four crowns to a pound and twenty-one shillings in a guinea. Standard money was silver, but guineas were gold.

Knitted hosiery earned cash or was bartered. Hose were created as two tubes that were laced, suspended from the upper leg; while a stocking was worn on the foot and lower leg. For the purposes of my story 'hose' and 'stocking' are interchangeable as they were usually knitted or woven.

Witchery

The frontispiece image shows '*Three witches riding a hog-like familiar to visit an ill friend*' - taken from "*The Witches of Northamptonshire*", 1612. According to this publication, witches were considered to be the '*vilest of humanity*'. The first witches hanged in Northants came from Guilsborough. Agnes Browne and her married daughter, Joan Vaughan, had offended the lady of the manor by slapping her in rebuke. They were both executed for this crime. Others tried, found guilty and executed for witchcraft include: Arthur Bill of Raunds, Mary Barber of Stanwick, and Helen Jenkinson of Thrapston. Outside Northamptonshire, other 'witches' include the Pendle witches (1612), the Bideford witches (1682) - Temperance

Lloyd, Mary Trembles and Susannah Edwards (who were hung), then Alice Molland was hanged in Exeter in 1685. In 1693, 14 women and 5 men were hanged in Salem, USA. Incidents of reported witchcraft had greatly diminished before Shaw and Phillips were executed. Janet Horne was the last person burned for sorcery in Scotland (1727) and Anna Goldi was last in Europe (1782, Switzerland). Of interest is Scottish medium, Victoria Helen McCrae Duncan (a.k.a. Helen Duncan), was held under the British Witchcraft Act. She was held for nine months. She died of natural causes (years later), at home in Edinburgh in 1956. Her supporters still pursue a posthumous pardon.

Many sentenced signed with a 'mark' were illiterate. The uneducated were controlled by misreported information, which is appropriate today with the carefully crafted 'fake news' spread by the media. It is hard to separate facts from unclear stories and sham truths.

King James I, responsible for the communal version of the Bible in England, also passed an Act against witches. It was abolished in 1736 (111 years after his death). King, gentry and the Church controlled positions of power over those less-privileged. The King James Version of the Bible (Exodus 22:15) states, *Thou shalt not suffer a witch to live*. Recently, British Biblical Professor, Kenneth Kitchen translated the original word 'witch' as "to cut", so believes the archaic Hebrew word refers to cutting herbs (Kitchen, *'Magic and Sorcery'*, p.723), suggesting our interpretation is likely founded on an earlier mix-up.

Execution of miscreants were seen as preventive warnings and spectacles. When street-robber Jack Sheppard was finally hanged in 1724, after four escapes from prison, reports state that "*two-hundred-thousand*" people attended his execution.

A 16-page pamphlet (*Executions in Northampton*) on the trial and execution of the women bears a dénouement based on '*an eyewitness account*'. It states the women: *were hardened in their wickedness that they publicly boasted that their master* (the Devil) *would not suffer them to be executed, but they hound him a liar, for on Saturday morning 17th inst., they were carried to the gallows on the north side of the town, whither numerous crowds of people went to see them die, and being come to the place of execution the minister repeated his former pious endeavours, to bring them to sense of their sins, but to as little purpose as before; for instead of calling upon God for mercy, nothing was heard of them but damning and cursing; however, a little before they tied up, at the request of the minister.* It notes that: *Elinor Shaw confessed not only the crime for which she dyed, but openly declared before them all how she first became a witch, as did also Mary Phillips, and being desired to say their prayers, they both set up a very loud laughter, calling for the Devil to come and help them in such a blasphemous manner as is not fit to mention; so that the Sheriff seeing their presumptuous impotence, caused them to be executed with all the expedition possible, even dyed in his service to the terror of all the people who were eye witnesses to their dreadful and amazing exits.*

Their dénouement is described: ... *hang'd til they were almost dead, the fire was put to the straw, faggots and other combustable matter, till they were burnt to ashes. Thus liv'd and thus dyed, two of the most notoris and presumptious witches that ever were known in this age.* (sic.)

Two '*last post*' letters ('*Licensed according to Order*') from Ralph Davis (Northampton) to William Simons (a London merchant) were printed in 1705 by F. Thorn, near Fleet Street. Davis wrote '*According to my promise in my last [correspondence dated Wednesday 7th March 1705], I have sent you here inclosed a faithful account of the lives and conversations of the two notorious witches, that were executed on the Northside of our town on Saturday the 17th instant, and indeed considering the extraordinary methods, these wicked women used to accomplish their diabolical art; I think it may merit your reception, and the more, since I understand you have a friend near Fleet-street, who being a printer, may make use of it in order to oblige the publick; which take as followeth, viz.'*

Plants and Potions

Country women were well versed in plant usage. Besides their use as food, plants were frequently used in herbal potions and food magic, particularly *Malva Neglecta*, the common mallow. See *plants.ces.ncsu.edu*. Note that many plants are dangerous when misused. Herbs, such as Rosemary were used for scents, cooking and potions.

Some treatments are still used today, with modern refinement. Patient expectation aids therapeutic medicine: convincing and curing (via placebo effects). I have no evidence these women were healers, but it is significant that they were accused of witchcraft, so likely held the lore for symptom relief. It seems likely any traditional healer could be accused of any deaths if things went awry. It is easier to blame any trying to help rather than fault oneself or luck.

Love potions and 'scenting' dough is real and dates to this period, no matter how disgusting this practice may seem today!

...ooo000ooo...

Glossary

Lanthorn - an old pronunciation of lantern.
'Lorks ha' mercy' - derives from 'Lord have mercy'.
A hamlet - smaller than a village and has no church.
Peascods - peas in the pod.

...ooo000ooo...

Libraries, Museums & Web-sites

Abingdon Museum
Ancestry.co.uk
archivist@northamptonshire.gov.uk
news.bbc.co.uk/1/hi/magazine/8334055.stm
     (30/10/2009)
english-heritage.org.uk/7-magic-potions
British Library
Cripps Library & Oundle School Archive
English-heritage.org.uk
freeBMD.org.uk
georgianera.wordpress.com/tag/county-gaol-
     northampton
highsheriffnorthamptonshire.com
historyanswers.co.uk
National Archives
Northampton Archives
Northamptonshire Record Office
Oundle Library (N.C.C.)
Parish Registers (Oundle)
Public Records Office
Sessions House (Northampton)
sharonhoward.org
Tourist Information (T.I.C.), Northampton
vam.ac.uk/articles/the-history-of-hand-knitting

...ooo000ooo...

Bibliography

Ahlers, Cyriacus

   "Some observations concerning the woman of Godlyman in Surrey ... tending to prove her extraordinary deliveries to be a cheat and imposture", 20th November 1726, Royal Collection Trust, RCIN 1090838. (A case of Mary Toft birthing rabbits!).

Bonzol, Judith

   'The Medical Diagnosis of Demonic Possession in an Early Modern English Community', *Parergon* 26:1, 2009, pp. 129–30.

Broad, John

   "Cattle Plague in Eighteenth-Century England", article in *The Agricultural History Review*, pp. 104-115, 1983. bahs.org.uk/AGHR/articles.

Cowley, Richard

   Outrage and Murder: 800 years of criminal homicide and judicial execution in Northamptonshire. Volume 1: 1202-1850.   Peg & Whistle Books (Monkshood Publishing), Barton Seagrave, 2010.

Cox, Nancy, and Dannehl, Karin

   Dictionary of Traded Goods and Commodities, 1550-1820.   See: 'Tan bark - Tawed' (british-history.ac.uk). University of Wolverhampton Dictionary Project, 2007.

Cullen, James

   Practical Plant Identification: Including a key to native & cultivated flowering plant families. Cambridge University Press, 2006.

Darby, Nerys Elizabeth Charlotte

   "The magistrate and the community: summary proceedings in rural England during the long eighteenth

century". Ph.D. thesis (2015), University of Northampton Electronic Collection (N.E.C.). nectar.northampton.ac.uk /9720/1/Darby20159720

Darnton, Robert
    The Great Cat Massacre and Other Episodes in French Cultural History. First published by Basic Books, USA, 1984; Penguin Books, UK, 1985.

Ehrenreich, Barbara, & English, Deirdre
    Witches, Midwives and Nurses: A history of women healers. Glass Mountain pamphlets, 1972. Reprinted by Feminist Press, City University, New York (2nd edition), 2010.

Fernyhough, Anna
    Oundle Memories and Moments, Fast-Print (Upfront) Publishers, Peterborough, 2018.

Fiennes, Celia
    Through England on a Side Saddle: In the time of William and Mary; being the diary of Celia Fiennes, first published 1702. Republished from original manuscript by her relative, Emily W. Griffiths, 1888. Later, *Journeys of Celia Fiennes*, Classic Reprint, 2018.

Gibson, Marion
    Early Modern Witches: witchcraft cases in contemporary writing. Taylor and Francis, 2018.

Gray, Drew
    "*Making Law in Mid-Eighteenth Century England: legal statutes and their application in the justicing notebook of Phillip Ward of Stoke Doyle*". Section in: *The Journal of Legal History*, 34.2 (pp. 211-233), Dr. D. Gray, 2013.

'H.F.' & Levett, John
    A True & Exact Relation of the Severall Informations, Examinations and Confessions of the Late Witches, arraigned

and condemned at the late Sessions, holden at Chelmsford before the Right Honourable Robert, Earle of Warwicke and several of his Majesties Justices of Peace, 29 July 1645. Pamphlet published by Matthew Simmons, Henry Overton & Benjamin Allen, Popes Head Alley, London, 1645. Original signed by 'H.F. an *authoritie*'. Later reprinted by Charles Clark private press, Essex. Reprinted by Messers. Clark, Charles, Longman & Company, London, 1806-1880; F. H. (*Anon*.).

Hopkins, Matthew
    The Discovery of Witches: Contemporary Account, 1647. See CreateSpace Independent Publishing Platform (2017) 24 pages.

Howard, Sharon
    "Gentlemen and personal violence in seventeenth-century Britain". Paper presented at the *British Academy Postdoctoral Fellowship Symposium 2006*, 1, p.407, British Academy, London.
    Also, 'Imagining the Pain and Peril of Seventeenth-Century Childbirth: Travail and Deliverance in the Making of an Early Modern World', *Society for the Social History of Medicine* 16: 3, 2003, p.377.

Inglis, W.F. J.
    "The Last of the Witches", In the *Laxtonian*, Oundle School, Volume 1, Third Series, Number 2 (pp. 102-103), December, 1953.

Johnson, Arthur
    The Witches of Northamptonshire. Thomas Purfoot for Arthur Johnson, London, 1612. [See also British Library documents below.]

Law, William Smalley (Canon)
    Oundle's Story: A History of Town and School. London, 1922. Reprinted by Wentworth Press, 2016.

May, Robert
>The Accomplisht Cook, first published in 1660; later as 'The Accomplisht Cook or the Art and Mystery of Cookery. Wherein the Whole Art Is Revealed in a More Easie and Perfect Method, Then Hath Been Publisht in Any Language. Expert and Ready Wayes for the Dressing of All Sorts of Flesh, Fowl, and Fish', 1665.

McLoughlin, Simon
>"The Folklore and Occult of Oundle". An article in Oundle School Magazine by S. McLoughlin, pp. 14-16, 1983.

National Archives
>'Will of William Whitwell of Oundle, 1711', National Archives, PROB 11.522.
>Also, Public Records Office, P.R.O. Catalogue C-234/27, 23 March 1689.
>Also, National Records Office, (N.R.O.) F-H-2226.
>Also British Library (B.L.), Sloane 972 (f. 7). Papers regarding Northamptonshire witches, 1612: Agnes Browne, Joan Vaughan (her daughter), Jane Lucas, Alce Harrys (sic), Catherine Gardiner, and Alce Abbott (sic).

Northamptonshire Record Office
>Oundle Parish Records of 1545; NRO, ref. 249P.

Notestein, Wallace
>A History of Witchcraft in England from 1558-1718. Published by the American Historical Association (p. 371 & p. 382), 1911.

Oundle School (anon.)
>"Portrait in Miniature" (anonymous extract), in the Laxtonian (Oundle School Magazine), Literary Supplement (pp. 777-778), 1930-31.

Poole, Gary, & Stokes, Karen
    Witches of Northamptonshire, published by the History Press, 2006.

Purkiss, Diane
    'Losing Babies, Losing Stories: Attending to Women's Confessions in Scottish Witch-trials', in *Culture and Change: Attending to Early Modern Women*, edited by Margaret Mikesell & Adele F. Seeff, Newark DE, 2003, pp. 143–60.

Radzinowicz, Leon
    History of English Criminal Law and Its Administration from 1750: The clash between private initiative and public interest in the enforcement of the law. Volume 2, published by Stevens & Sons, London, 1957.

Saunders Watson, J.
    "The High Sheriff of Northamptonshire, 2018-2019". From *The History of the High Sheriff of Northamptonshire*, James Saunders Watson, Esq., D.L., www.highsheriffnorthamptonshire.com/history

Thomas, Alice
    Richard Creed's Journal of the Grand Tour, 1699-1700. Volume I, The Journey to Rome, September 25 to December 23. Tract copied from original volumes in the custody of Mrs Margaret Partridge by Alice Thomas, 1999.

Thomas, Ioan
    "History in our Landscape" (North Northants) pamphlet for Oundle Museum, Inkwell Printing, Barnwell, 2006.

Thorn, F.
    An Account of the Tryals, Examination and Condemnation, of Elinor Shaw, and Mary Philips (Two Notorious Witches), at Northampton Assizes on Wednesday the 7th of March 1705, for Bewitching a Woman, and Two

Children, Tormenting Them in a Sad and Lamentable Manner Till They Dyed. With an Account of Their Strange Confessions, about Their Familiarity with the Devil, and How They Made a Wicked Contract with Him, to be Revenged on Several Persons, by Bewitching Their Cattel to Death, etc., and Several Other Strange and Amazing Particulars. Published by F. Thorn, London, 1705. Reprinted by J. Taylor & Son, Northampton, 1866.

Walker, William George
 A History of the Oundle Schools, published by Oundle School Bookshop. First edition (p. 748), 1956. Also, section by Ralph Davis (p. 211). Reprinted by the Grocer's Company, 1966.

Wright, J. Stafford, and Kitchen, Kenneth A.
 "*Magic and Sorcery*", in *The New Bible Dictionary* (p. 766) edited by J.D. Douglas, published by Inter-Varsity Press, 1962. See also kingjamesbibleonline.org/1611-Bible (KJV 1611).

...ooo000000ooo...

Anna Fernyhough is an art and education graduate of the University of London. She also holds an MA in Anthropology from the University of Illinois, USA. As a qualified teacher, Anna has worked in schools in England, Spain and Ethiopia. She has written and published articles on traditional women in Ethiopia, human osteology and, most recently *Oundle Memories and Moments* (2018).

Cover and other designs, artwork and illustrations by Christopher T. Fernyhough.